To sisters everywhere, and the magic they hold.

All The Wicked

Catelyn Wilson earned her BA in creative writing from Southern New Hampshire University. She lived in three states and four countries before she turned sixteen, and only survived because of her triplet sisters, who she is freakishly close to. Catelyn lives in Texas with her husband and dog. When not writing you can find her obsessing over a new hyperfixation and calling it a hobby.

All The Wicked

CATELYN WILSON

MICHAEL JOSEPH

PENGUIN MICHAEL JOSEPH

UK | USA | Canada | Ireland | Australia
India | New Zealand | South Africa

Penguin Michael Joseph is part of the Penguin Random House group of companies
whose addresses can be found at global.penguinrandomhouse.com

Penguin Random House UK,
One Embassy Gardens, 8 Viaduct Gardens, London sw11 7bw

penguin.co.uk

First published 2025

001

Set in 13.5/16pt Garamond MT
Typeset by Falcon Oast Graphic Art Ltd
Printed and bound in Great Britain by Clays Ltd, Elcograf S.p.A.

The authorized representative in the EEA is Penguin Random House Ireland,
Morrison Chambers, 32 Nassau Street, Dublin D02 YH68

A CIP catalogue record for this book is available from the British Library

HARDBACK ISBN: 978-0-241-68157-2
TRADE PAPERBACK ISBN: 978-0-241-68158-9

MIX
Paper | Supporting
responsible forestry
FSC® C018179

'By the pricking of my thumbs,
Something wicked this way comes.'
William Shakespeare, *Macbeth*, Act IV, Scene i

Prologue

The Underworld

The black river coils into shallow deltas, glistening like snake scales, around a complex of sandstone buildings. Pillars, painted in bright colors, line a walkway studded with palm trees. The fronds glisten strangely, as if the call of rot and decay does not apply to them. The cheery green feels like an ill omen as the god walks down the grand entrance to the largest building.

Spirits, shapeless and nearly without color, line the way. Silent. Watching. The god's skin prickles as he passes them and enters the yawning doors of Osiris' Hall. Braziers line the hall of the Egyptian god of the Underworld, illuminating portions of murals depicting ancient Egypt in fragments.

Crocodiles lurking in the reeds, their eyes hungry.

Peasants laboring in the fields, their backs bent by weight and work.

And the gods, their eyes blank as they watch from above, smiles turning their faces into something cruel.

This hall and the images on its walls are familiar to the god. It was home, once. Long ago. But he is different now. A deity with a taste of mortality on his lips.

Fat birds with golden bodies flutter in the shadowy eaves. The hall is eerily quiet. Only the shuffle of feet sounds as a line of waiting spirits moves forward, one by one, to be judged. The god approaches the bright braziers burning at the end of the hall. A set of golden doors blocks the way.

Two shadows move in the corners of the vast room near the doors. Massive, powerful bodies of men with the heads of jackals. Cynomorpha, the tomb guardians of the Underworld. Their dark red eyes narrow in his direction. Firelight gleams off their bare human chests, contrasting with the sharp white animalistic teeth lining their pointed snouts.

'Welcome back, Lord Anubis,' one murmurs in a rumbling voice. Both step aside to let him pass. 'Osiris is currently overseeing the judgment of a spirit, but he will hear your concerns,'

Anubis steps through the doors. Incense burns somewhere in the shadows, the curls of smoke drifting to his nose. The hall is wide, and lining both sides are rows of seats. A judge occupies each, in traditional dress, their expression blank. They watch the front of the hall, where a throne sits on a dais. It is hewn from sandstone and decorated with carvings of lilies, reeds, funeral barges and scales.

'Lord Anubis,' says a voice from the front of the hall, as smooth as silk. 'It has been centuries since you set foot in my domain.'

As he speaks, the ghostly outline of the man on the throne becomes clear. Green skin, his body wrapped in linen, as if he has been only partly mummified. Black, glittering eyes that see through the visitor.

'I seek a favor,' Anubis says, inclining his head respectfully and allowing his true godly form to flicker over his features in acknowledgment of Osiris' power.

'You are delaying my judgments,' Osiris says from his throne.

Anubis meets the other god's eyes. 'I have noticed a change in the Underworld. A sickness.'

Shadows from the fires shift over Osiris' green skin. He straightens, face a mask. 'You disturb my peace and shirk the duties of a death guide, and now you dare ask me for information?'

Anubis struggles to control his emotions. 'I have been exploring the Underworld since my return from the mortal world. The oldest portions have been reappearing, but the gods that once ruled them are gone.'

Osiris shifts, his dark brows pulled low. 'Our land changes as often as the winds. Humans are fickle creatures with changing allegiances.'

'These are gods that have slept for eons. I searched their lands, but they are quiet. No magic or power rests in their soil. These gods are simply gone.'

Osiris watches Anubis, something unreadable flickering over his features. Finally, he sighs, adjusting the linen robes around his body. 'I hear rumors from spirits new and old to the Underworld. They speak of a resurgence of a society as old as humans themselves. One that seeks our power, not just that of demons, for their rituals. Perhaps they have been feeding on these missing gods.'

Anubis' shoulders stiffen. 'Who are they? What do they want with the gods?'

'The spirits that know of such things are frightened. They whisper of an Order that wishes to take the gods' magic, the very essence of what they are and represent.' Osiris shifts on his throne, clearly uneasy. 'But these are rumors. I have not seen it for myself.'

'I also seek Hecate in my travels. I need her help to heal a mortal above,' Anubis says, his chest fluttering like a human heart. 'Do you know where she is? If she is sleeping, as I once did?'

Osiris' black eyes glint. 'I know why you seek the goddess. For that mortal girl and her sister – the one who caused so much trouble in the land of the dead.'

3

'Please,' Anubis says, though the very act of begging makes his skin crawl. He thinks of Andromeda, her sparkling blue eyes and the sweetness of her lips on his, instead.

The other god sighs. 'Hecate has not been heard of in many centuries. She is sleeping, that is for certain. Some say she is hiding. Protecting herself.'

A breath catches in Anubis' throat. 'Why would a goddess as powerful as her hide? Why sleep when she does not need to conserve energy?'

'Hecate has forced her slumber. So what makes you think the goddess of magic wants to be found?' Osiris asks.

Anubis ignores the impatient line of spirits in the hall, awaiting their judgment. He is uncertain of what they see when they observe Osiris on his throne. Perhaps St Peter at the gates of Heaven, waiting to judge their good deeds.

'If what you speak of this Order is true, could Hecate be slumbering to hide from them?'

Osiris shifts again, his features hardening. 'I fear what they want from us. From her. I am certain they seek Hecate. She would be the grandest prize of all the gods. The power she confers is unlike anything we have held since ancient times.'

'What can this Order do that you fear?' Anubis asks, a chill settling over the judgment hall.

Osiris opens his mouth to speak further, but as he does, a gust of wind rushes through the hall. The flames flare brighter in their braziers, and the golden doors open wide, slamming against the walls. The judges seem to hunch into their seats as the light shifts.

No. They are fading.

Anubis breathes in sharply, his eyes wide. He moves forward, reaching to take Osiris' hand. But he wears an expression of horror. Of pain. The roof of the palace groans. Spirits wail in the hall, shifting and roiling like a mass of storm clouds.

And then the fires dim, sputtering as all the air is pulled from the hall. Osiris crumples on his throne, his green skin turning to ash and his linen wrappings falling to the ground. Empty.

Darkness cloaks the hall, heavy and oppressive. The spirits are gone, as are the judges. Anubis' hand is still outstretched toward the throne, his eyes frozen on the empty spot where the god he once ruled alongside has disappeared.

A silver rectangle rests in the pile of linen. He squints at the carvings, fingertips tingling. The outline of a wolf stands above two human infants. They feed from her swollen teats as her bared teeth seem to threaten and console them all at once.

'It can't be,' Anubis whispers, his eyes wide. 'It's a *katadesmos.*'

A curse tablet. One side bears the symbol of Lupa and the children. The other is etched with Osiris' name in hieroglyphics. Anubis curls his fist around the silver rectangle. The tablet means one thing. Someone sought out Osiris and his powers. Carved his name in the metal and buried it in the earth with a curse.

Anubis knows what the Order is doing with the gods. What it hopes to do with Hecate, the goddess who slumbers and hides from the very thing Osiris fears. The god turns from the ruins of the once grand judgment hall. He must call on his familiar, Wepwawet, the jackal, and send him to the mortal world with a message for Andromeda.

Osiris is dead, and soon Hecate will be too.

I

October

Magic has a peculiar feeling. A weight to it. Like a breath of air shifting pressure, opening a door that was once sealed. It glides along my skin as I stand in the hallway outside Violet's room. My pulse beats against my throat as I hold my breath. Waiting. Listening.

The darkened crack in the door stares back at me. I can only make out the vague shape of Violet sitting up in bed, her side table cluttered with countless pill bottles to combat the nausea and pain from her leukemia treatments. The outline of her skull stands out against the faint moonlight from the window as she dips her head over a large book cradled in her bony, bruised hands. Despite the darkness, I feel what she's doing; the spell she casts calls to the magic in my blood.

I silence it, like a sailor turning away from a siren's song.

I grab the handle before the burning in my throat gets any worse. Violet's pale arm flashes in the moonlight as she shoves a dark object under her pillow and quickly lies down. Something in my chest aches as she pastes a wan smile to her face and pretends to adjust her blanket.

'Hey, Vee.' I gently shut the door behind me and cross to her bedside. 'Your hospice nurse left some notes on the credenza. Looks like you're doing a little better this week.'

'Mom said you'd be babysitting me tonight while she visits Grandma and Grandpa,' she says with a huff, passing a palm over the short black hair growing back on her head.

Her chemo rounds are done for now. She's on a cocktail of radiation and experimental treatments in the meantime, while the doctors wait to see how her frail body responds.

I drag a well-worn armchair closer to her bed and sit down. 'I know you'd prefer Dad, but I fought him off. He can't miss his own mother's birthday, after all.'

She makes a face. 'It's because he's the only one who doesn't insist on watching over me at all hours of the day.'

'Mom is just worried about you,' I say gently, though the bite in her words is like a punch to the stomach.

'I'm at home. Does Mom think I'll smoke between the time the next nurse comes for her night shift?'

I smile, but even though her teasing words remind me of how we used to be, my expression falters a second later. Violet must sense that she's been caught using magic, because she chatters animatedly about the newest gossip she learned in her latest hospital visit. Her eyes dart around the room and her fingers pluck at a thread in the sheets. I let her keep going.

'Dr Kerry, my oncologist, mentioned something about his wife the other day, but I heard from the new intern that he's been divorced for three months and is refusing to accept it, and –' she cuts herself off, finally taking a breath. 'What is it, little star? Why are you looking at me like that?'

'You promised you'd stop.'

'I don't know what you're talking about, Andy.'

My eyes drop to her pillow and she stiffens, arms crossed over her chest like a shield. Before she can even blink, I snake my fingers beneath the pillow and yank a small leather-bound book out into the moonlight. Her sharp intake of breath feels like a blow to my chest.

'Don't lie to me, Vee.' My voice is brittle. Tired. 'Not anymore.'

'It's nothing. Just research.'

'Research?'

Violet huffs, her lips twisted to the side. 'Yes, *research*. And don't look at me like that, Andy. Like I'm some freak.' She reaches out, pale fingers grasping the edge of the leather cover. The tape holding her IV in place catches, and she grimaces, a curse muttered under her breath.

I let her snatch the book back, but not before peeking at the peeling gold foil of the fading title on the spine. *The Book of the Dead.* And below it, what I assume to be the Egyptian name is in equally tarnished hieroglyphics.

'We've talked about this for months.' I lean back in the chair, tired to my very bones. 'The more magic you use, the sicker you get. Your body can't handle it, not after what happened on Duskmoor Island.'

Violet's jaw works and she stares straight ahead. The reminder of her actions last year, the way she tried to bind herself to a demon to keep cancer from ravaging her body, always fires her temper and makes her conscience prickle. 'Magic is the only thing that can save me. You'd know this too, if you bothered to help me find a spell that could work.'

I bite back a snort. Ever since she returned from the Underworld, her body has grown weaker. Frailer. Each time she uses her magic she fades a little more. Magic isn't saving my sister, it's killing her. There's only one thing that can save her. One person. And Hecate is hidden somewhere in the depths of the Underworld.

I shut my eyes for a few breaths. Behind my lids flashes of the demon Ossivorus come into focus. The slit throats of bodies floating lifeless in a cove. I see Richard Greene – the man who founded Tooth and Talon, the secret society that Violet joined at her old school, Ravenswood

Academy – casting spells to appease Ossivorus. I open my eyes before I can see more.

'I will not use magic.' I ball my fists on my knees. 'Ever.'

Violet's eyes soften. She looks nothing like the girl I once knew. Beautiful black hair, bright eyes, and a smile as sharp as a knife. All nothing but a memory now.

She takes a deep breath, the air rattling in her chest. 'I'm sorry. I don't mean to be so . . . angry. But this is something you'll never understand. Magic is part of me, like breathing. And without it, I feel like I'm slipping further and further away. You and Anubis have found nothing in six months –'

'He found the new portion of the Underworld last fall,' I protest, the memory of Anubis, the god who pretended to be a mortal boy as he investigated Tooth and Talon, sharp as it slices my heart. 'Anubis has seen markings of Hecate's name on temple ruins. He's sure if he follows them, we can find her.'

I'd fallen in love with a boy I thought was Jae Han as I searched for Violet at Ravenswood last year. But Anubis had made a vow to the real Jae Han over a decade earlier, promising to wipe out every trace of the secret society that killed his aunt. After everything that happened on Duskmoor Island with the demon Ossivorus, Anubis returned to the Underworld, losing his mortal body as he protected me against Tooth and Talon's magic. He belongs to the Underworld once more. A place I can never be a part of. Not until I'm dead.

He found me at the hospital a few months after Violet returned to the mortal world, with news about a strange new section of the Underworld. He was so hopeful when he found evidence of Hecate, the goddess who blessed Violet's and my lineage with magic. I recall how his dark eyes sparked with purpose as he speculated that Hecate would be the key to saving my sister from her sickness, using the very magic that grants us her power as a cure. But Violet's disappointed expression belies those memories. All I see is betrayal.

A mirthless laugh slips from her chapped lips. 'But he's found no evidence of her since then. It's like she's disappeared.'

'She could be sleeping,' I protest, even though this is the same worry I've pushed aside as Anubis has been searching the Underworld. 'She's out there, Vee, somewhere. And once we find her, she can cure you.'

'How are we going to find her? It's not like you can go down to the Underworld and search with Anubis, without risking demons smelling your magic. And I can't use magic or have it used on me without getting even sicker. Anubis can't come here, and you can't go there. So, we're both stuck here. And all you do is watch me fade away, and help Mom and Dad with bills. We're no closer to anything except my grave.'

That sharp pain in my chest lances deeper.

'Vee,' I protest weakly, a bitter taste coating my tongue as I try to hide my fear, 'don't say that. You aren't going to die. And I'm not asking you to stop looking for answers. I'm only saying you need to stop practicing magic. At least until Anubis and I find Hecate and a cure.'

'I am *dying*, Andy. And if you can't save me, then I'm going to do it myself.' She grips the ancient spell book in her hands, a dark expression stealing over her face. 'Magic is the only thing I have left.'

The skitter of nails across the floor jars me awake. A *click*, *click*, *click* that grows closer, louder. The hairs on the back of my neck stand up, and I breathe in deeply, checking for a hint of sulfur or rot. Signs of a demon coming to call.

Slowly, I edge my feet off Violet's bed and straighten. The moon has sunk, and the only light comes from blinking monitors and the gap in the blinds over the window.

A dark shape slinks along the far wall in the hall, mixing with the deepest shadows. Holding my breath, I glance over to make sure Violet is still asleep before I stand. The chair creaks as my weight shifts. Dust and dirt from ancient graves perfume the air. Slowly, I push the bedroom door completely open and peer into the hallway.

White teeth are bared at me from the far end, sharp and hungry. And then the shape moves, growing larger as it approaches. Pointed ears and dark fur, hackles rising as the creature slinks forward, its golden eyes gleaming in the dark like only a predator's can.

'Hello, Wepwawet,' I murmur to the huge jackal, the messenger of Anubis, as he emerges from the shadows.

Behind him, a shimmering narrow tunnel leads back to the Underworld. The beast lowers his head in greeting, intelligent eyes knowing and ancient. Excitement swirls in my stomach, as does hope. Anubis only sends Wepwawet with news of his search for Hecate. I step closer to the animal as the swirl of smoke spirals in the corner, and the smells of decay grow stronger.

A creak echoes from the stairs, and I stagger back from the shimmering tunnel. 'Mom!'

She stops at the top step, dark circles under her eyes, and her brow furrowed. 'I saw the lamp on when we pulled into the driveway. Did I scare you?'

My heart thuds in my chest and I glance over my shoulder. Wepwawet and the unearthly tunnel are gone. I lean against the wall, my hand on my sternum.

'Is everything alright?' Mom asks. 'Have the nurses said anything?'

'Nothing new,' I reassure her. 'That's good, right? At least she isn't any worse.'

'Right.' Mom sighs and rubs her temple, tries to smile but fails. 'Oh, before I forget. I got a letter from your school counselor. She suggested you send applications to a couple of different local colleges, and some state ones too.'

I blink at her, uncomprehending, for a few moments. And then I laugh, because it seems so ludicrous to talk about college when a god of death has just sent his monstrous jackal familiar with a message from the Underworld.

'I'm not really worried about that right now. Did Violet say something?'

'You need to think about the future, Andy.' Mom toys with her hair, a faraway expression in her eyes as she looks toward my sister's open door. 'Online school was great, but you've already fulfilled all your requirements. Dad and I can handle watching over Violet –'

I hold up my hand. 'Wait. Are you seriously trying to ship me off to a college. Why do you think I did the accelerated diploma? I want to stay with you, help Violet get better, before I even consider the future.'

'Honey, you know what the doctors are saying. You see how she looks.'

My throat is tight as I stare at Mom, at the tension in her expression. The defeat.

'Violet isn't going to die.'

'I didn't say she was. But there's nothing you can do for her.'

My mouth slackens and I rub my brow. 'I'm not going to abandon Violet and run off to college. That was her dream, Mom. I can't take that from her.'

She ascends the final step, moving like she wants to come and touch my hair, soothe me like she did when I missed

Violet when she was away at Ravenswood. But I stiffen and cross my arms, and she stops.

'Don't you think Violet wants to see you happy? To be successful? Just because it's something she always wanted for herself doesn't mean you can't have the same dream.'

I clench my jaw and look down. I blink rapidly, willing myself not to cry. Not to imagine Violet's face, hollow and pale, as I take everything she's ever wanted. Magic. College. *Life*.

'Can we talk about this later?' My voice wobbles.

Mom purses her lips but nods. 'Dad is going to check in with the hospice center tomorrow about bills, and I'll be taking another shift at work. Do you think you can handle Violet and dinner?'

Wordlessly, I nod.

She turns to her and Dad's bedroom, fingers wrapping around the doorknob. Before she can shut the door, she pauses, a flash of her sad, tired eyes peeking through her curls.

'Andy.'

I look back to where Mom stands, already half inside the door. A lamp down the hall illuminates only a tiny sliver of her face just as I sense Wepwawet slinking in the deepest shadows, waiting for me.

'Don't forget that your life matters too.'

Then she disappears into her room, and I'm left with a sour taste in my mouth as the doorway to the Underworld reappears. Wepwawet winds around my legs, dropping a vial onto the floor. Red and a bruising shade of purple swirl together within. A tincture made from the asphodel flowers of the Underworld. A way for Anubis to communicate with me between planes, for brief moments, as I'm suspended between life and death.

The jackal's impossibly black fur brushes my hand as he turns back to the corner of the hall where the dark, narrow mouth of an earthen tunnel awaits. I watch as he slips back inside. The scent of the land of the dead leaves with him, and I bend down to clutch the vial hard in my fist as memories associated with that scent flicker through my mind. Anubis and his lips as he murmured how he loved me. The pain of being pulled apart from him when I returned to the mortal world.

I glance over my shoulder through the crack in the door to Violet, pale and small. Anubis must have news about Hecate. A clue to help us find her, and have the goddess cure my sister. I haven't given up hope yet.

And if Wepwawet is here, neither has Anubis.

I slip into my room and lie down on my bed, preparing for the sensation of my heartbeat slowing to almost nothing so that my spirit can commune with a god of death. Squeezing my eyes shut, I tip the vial of bitter liquid into my mouth and swallow. A sensation of floating steals over my body as my blood stops in my veins and a slow breath slips from my lungs.

Darkness gathers around me until a ghostly image of the Underworld appears before my eyes. Black and white outlines of hills and trees and gray, brittle grass. An oily black river that cuts through the land and separates the east and west banks.

Smoke, bursting across my eyes like ink, outlines everything as the land of the dead comes into focus. I'm neither dead nor completely alive. A shade of myself, briefly touching the other side of the veil. And as I turn, a prickling sensation runs along my ghostly skin, and I see a familiar set of deep brown eyes set against golden skin.

'Hello, Andromeda,' Anubis murmurs, his tall form

cutting across the clearing until he stands directly in front of me, appearing as he did at Ravenswood, wearing the face of Jae Han.

Even though there isn't any blood in this form, heat steals across my skin. I want to reach out and touch his smooth cheek. Feel his lips against mine. But I know it's impossible. His fingers would pass right through me.

'You sent Wepwawet with a message,' I respond, my voice tight as I stare into his eyes. 'Is something wrong? Have you found Hecate yet?'

His expression darkens as he looks out over the endless tomb-dotted landscape of the Underworld. 'It's the gods,' he finally says, his throat working as he meets my gaze again. 'They're dying.'

2

The scent of ash and ancient things perfumes the night. The gray hills of the Underworld stretch endlessly, interrupted only by the velvety darkness of the rivers cleaving apart the landscape. I stare at Anubis, wishing I could do more than simply float before him in a disembodied state.

'Gods can't die,' I finally say.

Anubis' jaw works as he moves closer to me, his fists clenching and unclenching like he wants to reach out and touch my wild curls, even though he can't. 'Back in February, the new section of the Underworld opened up, bearing markers of Hecate's power.'

'And you and I tried to follow it,' I agree, still reeling from his words. 'But there were too many demons who could smell Hecate's powers in my blood, and we decided it would be better if you searched alone.'

'You know I've found nothing but inscriptions of her name on deteriorated temples. Paths to other forgotten sections of the land. But no Hecate. And strangely, no other gods. They should be in their territories. They're ancient and established. No god gives up the treasured patch of their former power.'

His expression is so grave that I wish I could feel my pulse. The floating sensation makes everything feel off-kilter, and as a bone-deep dread settles in my stomach, fear makes the landscape shift around me.

'Is Hecate dead?'

Anubis looks away. 'I don't think so. But all these territories were empty of gods. Only demons and monsters from long ago roam them. At first, I thought these gods could be sleeping, like I was before Jae found me.'

'What makes you think they aren't?' I ask, my voice tight.

Anubis reaches into his pocket, fist closing tight around something as his golden skin turns pale. 'Because I went to visit Osiris. He is one of the few that could know what is happening to the Underworld. He is the oldest death god. All the others have faded in sleep, rendered weak without any worshippers. But Osiris' purpose is to oversee the judgment of the dead. If a soul believes in some sort of judgment before eternal rest, they must cross through his gates before reaching the west bank. He is like Hecate – adapting to every culture and religion. Osiris hears of every new soul, every lost creature in the entire realm, because of his role. He senses these shifts in the land, sections opening, like the ones you and I have searched.'

'Does he know where Hecate is?'

'That's partly why I went to visit him.' Anubis swallows and focuses on a spot behind my shoulder. 'I asked what he knew of the missing gods. After all, I should sense them if they were sleeping. Their territory would become sealed off from the rest of the Underworld, the tunnels that connect them to the rest of the realm blocked, as no spirits need to follow them.'

'How did Jae find you, then?' I ask softly.

At first, I worry Anubis won't answer. He lived as Jae for years, seeking vengeance for the death of his aunt, Min-Jun. And he gave up a chance to experience mortality, and all its pleasures and pain, for me. To protect me from Tooth and Talon as they summoned Ossivorus, on Duskmoor Island, last year.

When he speaks, his voice sounds far away. 'Jae knew that

wandering the Underworld as a human was dangerous, that he would have to find a way to straddle the line between life and death – much like Violet did when she hid herself away in the Underworld to slow the progression of her disease. Jae needed a death guide, not just any god, to ferry his soul safely to Min-Jun's side on the west bank. I always exist somewhere between life and death. I'm not bound to the Underworld the same way as other gods. Sometimes I can reach the mortal realm, during equinoxes or at other liminal times. His belief was strong enough to lead him to my territory. But these other sections I've been searching are not blocked off, they're open and bare. There are no gods sleeping there, conserving energy, defending their old lands, and waiting for a shred of human belief.'

I exhale slowly. 'The gods are older than anything. How could they die? What did Osiris say?'

'He has also sensed the empty sections of the Underworld. The missing gods. He said that Hecate was alive, but hiding somewhere deep in her territory.'

A shiver trails across my skin, icy as the breath of a ghost. 'Hiding? Hiding from what?'

'Something dangerous enough to kill a god.' Anubis finally uncurls his fist.

Sitting in his palm is a rectangle of hammered silver. The face bears an inscription in a strange language of slashing marks below hieroglyphics. Somehow, I know it says Osiris. He flips the tablet over and the stark imprint of a wolf with curled lips, suckling two human babies, glares up at me from the carved surface.

'He said that there is a resurgence of dark, ancient magic in the world above,' Anubis says. 'A group, a society, that does not call on demons to power their spells, but the blood of gods. That they have ancient knowledge from the oldest magic rituals, from a time when gods and man lived together, side by side.'

'And Hecate is so afraid of them that she hides herself away? She's a goddess of death. She's still worshipped today. What does she have to be afraid of?'

Anubis' face is hard. 'That's all he said before he died. His body disintegrated into dust, leaving only this behind.'

A rush of cold fear washes over me as my ghostly form trembles. I want to gasp, but I can't even breathe in my current state. I feel trapped, like a mummy in its wrappings, as Anubis continues to hold out the gleaming rectangle of silver.

'What is it?' I whisper, nodding to his hand.

'A *katadesmos*. A curse tablet.'

The light catches on the deep grooves of the tablet, and my skin tingles as he continues to flip the silver rectangle over and over again, his eyes tracing the pattern like he's reading from a book. Finally, he breathes out slowly.

'One of Jae's memories keeps bothering me,' he begins, eyes glassy and far away. 'He told me how he found Min-Jun, his aunt, dead. Killed by a society in their school in Edinburgh. He remembered how dark it was. How the only lights still on just before dawn were the neon signs of the pub where she'd been drinking with her friends. He'd gone looking for her when she hadn't come back to the common room. And when they rolled her onto her back, after pulling her from the river, he was frozen beside her. He touched her hand. It was so cold. Her eyes were open. Like she was speaking, begging him to help her. And when Jae held her hand tighter, he felt something jab into his palm.'

He extends his hand out to me, and he looks so strange in the gray light, with an undead forest behind him. My lungs constrict as the curse tablet glints dully between us, like the flash of a dagger.

'Min-Jun had a tablet just like this in her fist, Andromeda. I thought I'd followed every society member, everyone who was responsible for her death. That I'd followed the last thread, leading me to Richard Greene and Ravenswood Academy.'

If I weren't suspended between life and death, my breath would have stopped. 'You mean the people who killed Min-Jun are still out there?'

He blinks a few times, his gaze coming back into focus. 'When I possessed Jae's body and vowed to seek revenge on his behalf, it took me to many schools. Many societies. Thirteen years ago, I tracked down those who killed Min-Jun, and those who trained them in magic. It took me to Ravenswood, to Tooth and Talon, and to your sister. Do you know where Richard Greene studied the occult before he founded Ravenswood Academy?'

I think back to last year, and vaguely remember time spent with Jae in the library of Ravenswood, studying its history and clues to its founding. But I was so worried about Violet, how everything seemed connected to her, that the rest is like a distant dream. 'Scotland.'

'The society Osiris mentioned could have trained Richard Greene.' Anubis glares at the markings of the wolf. 'The same place, and the same tablet, with the same symbol. It can't be a coincidence.'

I study the tablet, the symbol etched deep. 'Romulus and Remus being fed by Lupa.' A prickle runs along my skin, telling me the magic from the potion that allows me to speak with Anubis is wearing thin. 'I remember the story. They were abandoned as babies and the she-wolf goddess fed them and kept them safe in her cave. They grew up and founded Rome. But why use this symbol?'

'I don't know. And Osiris died before I could get any more

information.' Anubis curls his other fist, like the memory pains him. 'This society's symbol represents the founding of the most ancient and powerful empire the world has seen. But there is something else. Curse tablets are buried in the earth so that chthonic deities can carry out the curse. Liminal beings. Like me. Like Hecate.'

Another prickle over my ghostly skin tells me the spell is preparing to take me back to the mortal realm. 'Are they trying to find Hecate using these tablets?'

Anubis' face darkens. 'Osiris said she was hiding. Hiding from beings with the knowledge to kill what can't be killed. She must be one of the gods they want. I thought the tablet Jae found on Min-Jun in Edinburgh was just a way to make an offering to the demon tied to the sect at their school.' His lips flatten, and his eyes are stormy. 'But seeing it again, I must have missed something when I hunted those tied to her death. The same symbol, the same tablet, appearing after Osiris died, it can't be a coincidence. Something dark is emerging in Scotland. And if what Osiris says is true, and they want the magic of the gods, none of us, including Hecate, are safe.'

'Another society.' My voice is hollow. 'Whoever put that tablet in Min-Jun's hand is still out there, and now they're killing gods for their power.'

A sick feeling roots in my gut, and it takes everything I have to fight the spell pulling me away from Anubis. The tattoo on my upper thigh burns hot, like the ink is coming alive and eating away at muscle. At bone. The bitter taste of the tincture I swallowed coats my tongue, and the world feels further away. Smoke and shadow.

I blink, and the image of Lupa comes to life behind my eyelids. A goddess in the form of a wolf, rearing the future of a great empire in her cave.

'Yes', he agrees as the Underworld becomes fuzzy, slipping away from me. 'Min-Jun's death, and the society Jae blamed for it, must have been a cover for something darker – a group with ties to ancient rites that has now begun to kill gods.'

'Who are they?' I ask, my tongue feeling heavy, my speech slurred. I reach out, desperate to hang on to him for a moment longer even as the spell wears so thin I can barely see him. 'What do they want with the magic of the gods?'

'I'll send you a message, Andy.' Anubis' voice sounds far away, like my head is under water. He reaches out for me too, and for a moment, as our fingers pass through one another, I think I can feel the heat of his skin and the smoothness of his palm. 'Wait for me at midnight on the harvest moon.'

The scent of loam grows faint, replaced by crisp air, damp pine, and a fresh breeze carried over a lake, stealing in through the open window of my bedroom. But as Anubis' form fades and my body slowly grows solid again, all I can taste is blood.

3

I toss and turn for the rest of the night, my thoughts a muddied swirl of dead gods and Hecate hiding somewhere in the Underworld. When the light outside my window turns gray with the coming dawn, I finally sit up, giving up on any attempts at sleep.

But as I blink, adjusting my glasses on my nose, the light shifts, growing deeper. I swing my legs out of bed and pause as my toes touch dry, brittle grass.

A field, dotted with asphodel flowers that brush against my legs. Burial mounds and mausoleums mark the ground in the distance. I'm in the Underworld. I look down at my hands, searching for the shimmery gray outline of the spell from Anubis' vial. My skin is pale and dotted with freckles, but normal.

An uneasiness works through my veins as I turn in a slow circle at the top of a dusty hill. Ash plumes at my feet. A damp wind rustles in the faraway poplar trees. And my bedroom disappears like a mirage. I twist my head, searching the shadows for signs of Anubis or Wepwawet.

I'm alone.

The silence feels more sinister than before. It bears down on my shoulders, and I shudder. Could my magic have lashed out in my fitful sleep, dragging me down to the land of the dead? Or, for the first time in six months, has a demon finally come to call?

Slowly, the ground beneath my feet changes. Gathers together. The earth sways as a path unwinds like a coil of rope, extending through the hills and stark white flowers. My breath catches as a tingle erupts across my skin. Mist slips over the dark path, winding around humps of earth and blocks of stone that decorate the sides. Gravestones, I note absently. The path cuts through a seemingly endless cemetery.

The sound of my heartbeat grows louder and, inexplicably, I step closer. The magic in my blood that I always try to ignore flares into life. I shudder as the sensation grows stronger, tugs me forward, until I set one foot on the obsidian-colored road.

A statue marks the path, taller than I am. Carved of pure black rock and polished to an incredible shine, three faces stare back at me. A woman in triplicate. Each holds out an arm, gripping a unique object. A torch, a knife, and a key. Like road markers pointing in different directions.

Frost creeps across the stones and crawls up my legs. I pause, but the desire for logic wars with the bone-deep ache, the burning *need* to follow the path, until finally I can't resist any longer. My feet glide over the smooth black stones. Mist curls around my ankles. And something within me shifts as I pass the triple-faced statue, her many eyes flaring a bright, acidic green, matching the flames on the torch.

I'm pulled further down the path by something I can't name.

Time slips by. My thoughts grow fuzzier. There is only the road, and what waits for me at the end. The statue has long since disappeared. I'm alone on an endless lane running into eternity.

Slowly, thick acid-green fog swirls around my legs and washes over the stones. It rises higher, until it envelops me completely. My spine tingles, as if something is watching from within the mist. I stop and listen for the sound of breath or footsteps.

A lupine howl pierces the air, so loud and teeth-rattling that I cry out and slap my palms over my ears. Another howl echoes, followed immediately by a third. Snarling, snapping jaws reverberate from within the thickening mass of fog. The path buckles and shifts and throws me to the side onto dry, dead grass. Something hard pokes at my side. I roll to my knees and smother a scream. A grinning skull, eye sockets and teeth clogged with grave dirt, grins at me. More half-buried bones litter the ground.

The mist flees, and I can see the road curling in dozens of directions. More statues with their glowing green torches and eyes litter the way like breadcrumbs. But one by one, they crumble to ash along with the threading walkway, and I feel a stiff wind that smells of the cloying sweetness of rotting flowers.

'*Find me*,' the statues plead as they crumble.

I push myself to my feet, searching for the path. I scramble onto the dark stones just as heavy paws pad along the slowly disintegrating pathway. A dog? I stand there numbly, my mind unable to comprehend what my eyes are seeing. Because the enormous dog, bigger than a bear, growling and snapping as it comes into view, has three heads.

The three-headed dog turns all six eyes to me. Blood drips from its teeth. The obsidian pavers behind it continue to disintegrate into ash. I fall back a step. The grinning skulls, the endless graveyard, it's a warning. I know I have to run before the path disappears completely, and I am trapped here.

Finally, my feet move, and I turn and run back the way I came. The dog howls again, its breath hot on my back. But I don't turn around. I fly down the road, even as it disappears beneath me, until the glowing green torch and the empty field I first encountered come into focus.

The three faces of the statue seem to contort as I get closer, as if encouraging me. Warning me. With a gasp, I lurch past the carved pillar and stumble onto the familiar ashen grass of the Underworld I know. A howl makes the hairs on my neck stand on end as I whirl around. The massive three-headed dog stops next to the statue, pacing, as if stuck behind an invisible barrier. Slowly, the middle head lowers and drops something onto the ground only a few inches from my bare feet.

Silver gleams from the grass. A rectangular tablet marked with the image of Lupa and the twins, Romulus and Remus. My stomach turns as I reach down with shaking hands and pick up the curse tablet. Slowly, I flip it over to read the name. But all I read are two simple words:

Find me.

And then the sickly-sweet wind turns the statue and the beastly dog into dust.

I wake with a gasp, cold sweat drenching me. Shivering, I reach blindly for my nightstand, fingers scrambling over my glasses. I push them up my nose, heart thundering as I search my room for signs of three-headed dogs and statues.

The scent of magic and the land of the dead is nowhere to be found. A dream, then. It must be. But why such a vivid nightmare after my meeting with Anubis? I rub a hand down my face as weak sunlight filters through my window.

I stand, still feeling the light-headedness of Anubis' tincture, and feel something drop against my toes. Squinting down at the carpet, I reach down and pluck a shiny piece of metal from the floor. My blood runs cold as I see the etching of Lupa. Heart hammering, I flip it over.

Find me.

I look up, staring at my door, to where Violet's room

waits just across the hall, and curl my fingers around the curse tablet from my dream. That path appeared to me for a reason. The statues were of Hecate, I feel it as surely as the ground beneath me. Min-Jun's death led Anubis to Richard Greene. To Tooth and Talon and the halls of Ravenswood. And there is one person I know who has more knowledge than anyone about all of those things.

I cross my room and open the door. My spine straightens as curls of magic whisper to me from the crack below Violet's door.

The curse tablet grows hot in my palm.

I don't bother to be quiet as I march across the narrow hall and barge inside without knocking. Violet jumps, bent over her forearm, cheeks stained pink.

'A-Andy,' she stammers, slapping a palm over her arm. 'Is everything okay? You look like you've seen a ghost.'

My eyes fall to the blood peeking between her fingers. I step forward and pull her hand away, my heart stilling at the sight of a perfect cut on her forearm. Red seeps over the edges, smeared and dark and ugly.

'What are you doing?' I demand.

Her eyes, wide and dark blue, fill with tears. 'I was just testing a theory, I swear. I thought I could do it. A cut, just a small one. It should be so easy to heal.' Her voice breaks and she slumps against the pillows, the fire dying from her expression. 'My magic is failing me.'

I drop her hand, stung. 'Anubis sent me a message last night,' I say without pretense.

She blinks away her tears, her brow creased as she takes in my appearance. 'Did he find a way to cure my cancer? Is it Hecate?'

I open my hand, thrusting the curse tablet below her nose.

'What do you know about the society that uses this symbol?'

'Society?'

I drop the tablet onto her lap. 'I know they have something to do with Jae's aunt's death at their school in Edinburgh. And Anubis told me Richard Greene studied the occult in Scotland before forming Ravenswood and Tooth and Talon. Those two things can't be a coincidence. You know more about magic and that school than anyone.'

Violet brushes the tablet with her fingers. 'Min-Jun? Andy, what's happening?'

My nostrils flare, and heat floods my face. Runs down my chest.

'Tell me what you know, Violet. Because if you don't, Hecate might die before we can find her.'

Violet's room is strewn with books about the Roman Empire. Drawings of Lupa, of Romulus and Remus, dance before my eyes. All of Violet's impressive collection of books, articles and journals about Ravenswood, Rome, and Tooth and Talon are piled around us. My sister sits cross-legged on her bed, bent over a crumbling book that smells like mildew.

'There's a society whose members use that symbol,' she says, rubbing her forehead with one hand, 'but I can't remember where I saw it. All I remember is that Greene wrote a little about it, and it has something to do with a university he visited when he was in Scotland. I wasn't very focused on Greene's life before Ravenswood. I just wanted to understand how he managed to bind Ossivorus to himself to prolong his life.'

I flip a page half-heartedly, feeling empty and cold at the mention of the demon who haunted us last year. 'But they're real. You remember seeing them in his notes.'

'Yes, they're real. But I don't know why they'd frighten Hecate so much that she's hiding herself away.'

'Funny that you can recollect the right grimoire to practice a healing spell but can't remember something this important.'

Violet makes a sound of frustration. 'I get that you are angry right now, but snipping at me while I try to recall something I read two years ago isn't helping anything.'

'Did you forget that Anubis saw a god murdered? And that the one person who could heal you may be next? Or do you keep secrets from me because you enjoy it?' I slap my book closed.

'No, but I'm tired and –'

'You wouldn't be so tired if you stopped using magic for five seconds –'

'Maybe if you weren't being a coward and actually used *yours*, you'd have found Hecate by now!' Violet slams her hand down on the bed. 'But instead, she sends you a dream message and not me? Someone who refuses to even summon a candle?'

I glare at her, my skin pricking with heat. We stare at each other, shoulders heaving, anger sparking between us like embers.

'You betrayed me, Violet,' I say through clenched teeth, every muscle taut with hurt. 'You drew me to Ravenswood, pretended you were *dead*, so that you could use my magic to fuel your binding spell to Ossivorus, to take Greene's place as his anchor. And still after all these months, you won't listen to a word I say. I don't know why Hecate is hiding, or why she sent me that message. But you can do something right now by finding Greene's notes on the Order.'

Slowly, Violet's shoulders drop, and she runs her hand along the bristle on her scalp. Her eyes look a little brighter than last night, like our fight, or even just talking about magic, has revitalized her. And I hate that I feel jealous of something so intangible. That she's willing to get better for *something else* instead of me.

'Andy,' she says softly, her voice choked. She holds out her hand like it's a lifeline. 'I'm sorry.'

I stare at her hand, fingers thin and pale.

My throat stings, and I blink hard. 'What happened to us, Vee? Will we ever be like we were before?'

She flinches, her hand curling inward, untouched. 'I don't know.' Violet gives a wan smile, extending her fingers again. 'But I hope so.'

Slowly, I reach for her. Her palm feels dry against mine, but she curls her fingers and holds me tight, and the knot in my chest loosens a little. She tugs my arm, and I sit next to her on the bed. Violet smooths my messy hair back and tucks my head against her shoulder.

Tears well in my eyes, misting my glasses. We stay like that, neither of us speaking or moving. And I wish, for a terrible moment, that magic wasn't real, even if it could save Violet. Because then, maybe she and I could be sisters again.

But then I see the blood-stained gauze on her forearm, and my fantasy crumbles to ash, just like the mysterious road in the Underworld.

Her shoulders stiffen, jostling my glasses.

'What?' I ask.

She brushes my hair back, humming a thoughtful sound. 'Nothing. I just thought of something about Lupa in Greene's journals. When Mom gets home from work later tonight, we can have her get a few boxes of my things that are still at Grandma and Grandpa Emmerson's place from last year. I'm sure I've seen the symbol before in Greene's writings.'

31

I shut my eyes, inhaling her scent, memorizing her like this. Hints of vanilla and patchouli. Of parchment and ink.

'And you'll stop using magic, Violet? It will kill you before we ever find Hecate.' I lift my head, forcing her to meet my gaze. 'Promise me. You owe me this after everything that's happened.'

She nods once, the movement jerky. 'I promise.'

It's night once more, and my back aches from my shift cleaning the local middle school. Mom did what Violet asked, and now we sit in her room, going through boxes retrieved from our grandparents' house. Squinting at the yellowed parchment, I breathe in the scent of history. Dust and ink. Violet points to the page I'm bent over, her eyes bright with determination.

'In some books Greene brought back from his travels in Europe, I saw the repeated imagery of Lupa suckling Romulus and Remus. All the books come from a school in Scotland that formed around the same time as St Andrews and Oxford. Eidolon University. It's just North of Edinburgh, in a little village called Idyllwood. It's a private foundation that sets its own term dates, issues its own degrees, and handles its own admissions.' She taps the drawing of the scene of the babies and the wolf, identical to the one on the curse tablet. 'I didn't think much of it, because it didn't relate to magic or Tooth and Talon. At least, that's what I thought.'

'That's great! We know where this society is,' I say, jumping to my feet. 'I just need to go to Scotland, get Anubis' help somehow, and stop them from taking more gods.'

'Slow down, little star.' Violet shakes her head, lips pressed together. 'You can't just infiltrate a university like this. This Order *is* the school. You would have to be invited – hand-picked.'

I press my hand to my forehead, excitement deflating in an instant. 'There's no chance I could get into a school like that. There's got to be another way. Anubis remembers what Jae saw when Min-Jun died. He may have connections in the area still.'

'You're not listening to me, Andy. Greene studied the founding myth of Rome because it holds secrets to the way this society operates.'

With a sigh, I sink back into my chair. I flip the page of the book, scrutinizing a lithograph of a fresco found in Pompeii. 'Why would a secret society use this as their symbol?'

'In some stories, Romulus and Remus are the biological sons of King Amulius.'

'And he sent a servant to drown them as babies because he worried they'd support their grandfather and overthrow him.' I recite the familiar story, one I've heard from Violet many times. 'Then the wolf found them and raised them, and they grew up to overthrow their dad and found Rome.'

Violet shakes her head. 'That's one version. In another, the twins are the sons of Mars.'

A tingle starts at the base of my skull.

'They were descended from a god and went on to found one of the greatest empires the world has ever seen. Well . . . one twin did. The gods blessed Romulus. A warrior king and the son of the god of war.'

I shift on my seat next to Violet's bed. 'Why would Greene have cared about that? Even if the stories are true, Romulus and Remus died thousands of years ago. Rome fell.'

'Greene encountered the society Osiris told Anubis about while he was in Europe. Based on his journals I recovered from the library in Ravenswood, it led him to Eidolon University and a society known simply as the "Order" that traces its origins back to Romulus himself – maybe further. This society is ancient, Andy. More powerful than Tooth and Talon could ever have hoped to be.'

'Because the members are like us? Descendants of a god?' I lean away from the book, from the drawings of the twins and the wolf goddess.

Violet moves to tuck her hair behind her ear, her fingers pausing when they encounter only stubble. But for the first time in a long while, she doesn't look devastated at the reminder of her sickness.

'I don't know about that. If they were, why would they be killing gods and stealing their powers instead of using the magic they were blessed with?' She curls her hands into fists on her lap. 'No, I think the Order is trying to bring back the power they had in Rome. Maybe build their own empire using the purest kind of magic there is – the life force of a deity. And another thing. The university, and the Order, rejected Greene, even though he had magic in his blood. That made me realize something that sets this society apart from any other. The Order is meticulous and organized. They pick and choose who they want, based on some sort of criteria that goes beyond what Greene could offer. More than people like Luciano, Regina and the rest of Tooth and Talon possessed.'

'If it isn't having magic or a connection to a god, what is it?'

Violet's pale face looks even whiter. 'I don't know. But this is more dangerous than Ravenswood and even Greene. Whoever these people are, they're powerful.'

I clench my jaw as she studies me, like I'm a breath away from death. 'I'm sure they are. But you know that they're summoning gods to harvest their magic, in the same way that Tooth and Talon used the power of demons to grow their power. They'll come for Hecate soon enough. Osiris thought so, and that's why she's hidden away. She's our only hope of curing you.'

'You can't do this, Andy. They're too strong – and you won't even use your magic.'

My chest feels hollow as she looks at me, her eyes dark with lack of sleep. 'Why tell me this if you think I can't handle it?'

Violet sighs sharply. 'How do you plan on getting to Scotland? And then after that, how will you not only enter an exclusive university, but infiltrate it long enough to locate the Order and stop them?'

'I got to Ravenswood on my own, didn't I?'

'This is different!' she says, tossing the book aside. 'I won't be there for you. I'm stuck here, growing weaker every day. Without me, there's no chance of you blending into a school like that. You have no leads. No idea of where to go or who to search for. And your unused magic will stand out like a sore thumb!'

I clench my fists. 'I've taken care of myself just fine this last year.'

Violet's eyes snap with a familiar fury, a temper that can burn out of control. 'Because of *me*.'

'You? What have you done for me, besides lie here and only make your body waste away faster by using magic it can't handle?'

'You think everything I do is for myself. Even back at Ravenswood, when I kept myself alive by hiding out in the Underworld, you're convinced I was selfish. Stupid.' Violet curls her lip and tears her gaze away, settling her eyes on the piles of books around the room. 'But I have always tried to protect you first. When I awakened my magic and joined Tooth and Talon, I knew it put you at risk. So I taught myself more, I practiced harder. I *understood* magic.'

My nostrils flare and I can't help but snap, 'So you could keep me as an insurance plan to bind Ossivorus to you.'

'I never wanted to hurt you. I kept demons from hunting you at Ravenswood while I was in the Underworld. While I waited for you to come find me.' She breathes out sharply, bringing her dark blue eyes back to me. 'And I don't use magic just to try and heal myself, Andy. I cloak you from demons.'

I shake my head, some of the heat of my anger fading. 'What?'

'Haven't you wondered why you've not encountered a single demon since Ravenswood? Your magic is powerful, lying within you unused, burning like a damn rocket. I keep them away from you. From Mom and Dad. Because you're too afraid to understand and control your magic!'

'Why would you do that?' I sputter, heat crawling over my chest as anger makes my fingers tremble. 'You promised me so many times.'

Violet smiles thinly, her eyes hollow. 'So you would use your magic every day, every night, to hide yourself from demons? All that energy burning through you, you'd tap into it as often as you had to, to protect yourself?'

I open my mouth to answer. Close it again. Memories of last year – that endless parade of fear, bodies and demons – roar through my head. Of Violet standing over me as I slowly died, after she used too much of my magic to fuel her summoning of Ossivorus.

I've seen what magic does to people. What it did to Violet. No, I wouldn't use my magic, not even to protect myself. Not if it means losing who I am to the worst kinds of darkness.

Finally, I shake my head, anger leaking away into a hollow ache.

She nods and settles back into bed. 'So, you see, Andy. Everything I ever do is for you, as well as for me.'

My shoulders slump, and I look away from my sister.

'Maybe you're right.' I swallow the lump in my throat. 'I don't want my magic. And I can't pretend that I'm some brilliant savant who has languages and classical history memorized like it's nothing. You could do this.' I pull my eyes away from the shadows until I meet my sister's pained expression. 'But you're stuck here and Hecate sent me that dream, asking me to find her. If I don't go, we'll lose our chance to find answers.'

Violet breathes out sharply. 'Andy, I'm not trying to be cruel. You could die there. And after what happened last fall, I can't let you put yourself at risk like that again. Not when you can't protect yourself.'

For a moment, I'm back on Duskmoor Island, lying on my back as Violet negotiates with a demon. I'm broken and cold, life slipping from my fingers like the tide. Her expression is the same. I swallow hard, my throat tight as I recall the way she used my magic to fuel hers. The way she doubted me, even after I stopped Greene. It shouldn't still hurt.

'Don't you think that a society older than we can even fathom, one that rejected Greene, must know something about healing your sickness? They could have the answers we need, not just Hecate.'

Violet's spine stiffens. Her eyes widen as her mind turns over the possibilities. 'You . . . you can't go alone.'

'And you can't come with me.'

'No, I meant . . .' She shakes her head, her eyes clearing. 'Take Anubis. He remembers Jae's life. If Min-Jun had a connection to the school, he could find it. And he can protect you.'

I want to laugh at the suggestion. 'He's tied to the Underworld. His human body is gone.'

'Last year,' she begins, her voice tight, 'when I hid myself away in the Underworld, I met the spirit of a priestess of Hecate. I had her bless Ossivorus' devil's trap, and she taught me something else. Another spell.'

'To do what?' My voice is cold.

Violet senses the shift, her eyes darting to the side as she bites down on her chapped bottom lip. She hasn't talked about her time in the Underworld since we returned from Ravenswood. Hasn't breathed a word beyond what I already know.

She hardens her jaw, looking very much like the Violet I remember as she meets my gaze. 'Psychopomps, death guides, don't have to follow the same rules as the other gods or demons. They aren't tied to the Underworld in the same way. Loopholes – ambiguities – in the veils between worlds are open to them. Psychopomps like him need a body. But they don't necessarily have to inhabit a human vessel like he did with Jae.'

I blanch at her words. 'What kind of body are you talking about?'

'I know how to bind a psychopomp to myself.'

All I can do is stare.

'It is not the same thing as binding a demon or exchanging favors,' she says earnestly, eyes wide. 'Hecate is herself a psychopomp. With our blood tied to her, we can bind a death guide to our side for a time. Anubis could remain on our plane, almost mortal, until the spell wears off.'

My breath snags in my lungs. I stare at her, my mouth agape as my fingers tremble. 'You've known about this spell for *months*, and yet you watched me mourn losing him? You knew how it was for me. Being alone like this.'

'You're not alone,' she whispers.

I squeeze my eyes shut for a few breaths. 'Fine. There's a spell. How long does it last?'

'It depends on the celestial anomalies happening around the time you place the enchantment. But usually it's for months – not years.' She hesitates. 'That's why I didn't tell you, Andy. Anubis can't remain here indefinitely. The spell can bind him to you, using your body, your magic, as an anchor of sorts. But it isn't a permanent solution. Why would I get your hopes up for someone who can't stay?'

She's right. Anubis can't stay with me. He knows it too. I've cried for him. Grieved him. Become hollow without someone who fully understands what I've endured. I know he can't be something as mundane as my human boyfriend. And yet, I can't help but feel hurt. She knew of a spell to heal my heartache and didn't share it, while I did everything in my power to cure hers.

Shaking my head to clear it of more disappointments, I glance out the window. 'There is a harvest moon tomorrow.'

Grabbing a notepad, Violet scribbles. Her handwriting is firm and elegant as she draws a star map, laying out stars, planets and galaxies in a flash. The mathematics behind it would make my eyes cross, but Violet seems invigorated, color returning to her cheeks as she makes one last mark with black ink.

'If I'm right –'

'Which I'm sure you are,' I interrupt.

Violet gives a half-smile. 'Since I'm right, then, Anubis should be bound to you until the winter solstice. He can't return to the Underworld in that time, or it will risk negating the spell, closing the loophole that allows someone like him to slip through.'

She rubs her hands together, her teeth pressing into her lips again as she cocks her head to the side. She closes her eyes, lashes fluttering as if she is recalling the exact page of a book in her mind.

'What are you doing?' I reach out and touch her knee, my fingers going ice cold.

'Starting the spell.' Violet cracks her eyes open. 'It'll be better if I do it tomorrow, during the harvest moon. But in the morning, I have that new trial treatment. I won't have enough strength.'

Panic slithers around my spine, like the pain from the needles they use on Violet for bone marrow transplants. For the countless poisons they flood her system with, in the hope it will work. I tighten my fingers on her knee even as I snatch the paper from her lap and let my eyes study the mixture of Latin, ancient Greek, and the constellations of the stars.

'No.' I clutch the paper to my chest. 'I'll do it.'

Violet blinks at me. 'Are you sure? This will require a lot of magic. More than you've used in months.'

I can't tell if she looks proud or disappointed.

With a hard swallow, I try to cover the tremor in my voice. 'I'm not doing this because I want to practice my powers, Vee. I'm doing it because you swore you wouldn't use magic anymore. If you want me to trust you, believe in you, then you need to stand by your word.'

Even if it means I must break the promise I made to myself, and use my magic again.

She looks down at her hands, long fingers laced together. 'I'll walk you through the spell.'

My heart rate slows a little. The hum of untapped magic swells at the base of my skull, and I roll my neck out to stifle the sensation. Carefully smoothing the edges of the paper on my leg, I can't help but feel my tongue ache to form around the words. An instinct so deep in my bones it could guide me home.

Violet's voice is steady as she explains the process. The parameters. The strange rules that accompany a magic so powerful that it defies the ancient finality of death. And as she does, the desire to taste from the well of power hiding in the pit of my soul gets stronger. When she's done, dark circles ring her eyes and she sags back against her pillows, her breath short and her lids heavy.

The light from the hallway lamp slants across the carpet. I stand, folding the paper and shoving it into my pocket. My mind races with everything I have to do to prepare. Anubis mentioned sending me a message at midnight on the harvest moon. But this time, I need to send him word through Wepwawet. And I shudder at the reality that I will have to use my magic not once, but twice in one night, as I summon Anubis between realms like he has done to me before.

I press a kiss to Violet's head before I head for the door. Her pale hand snakes out and catches my wrist. When I turn back to her, she looks paler somehow. As gaunt and hollow as a skull.

'Promise me something, Andy. Like I promised you.' She licks her lips. 'Be careful. Always protect yourself first.'

'With the spell? I'll follow your directions exactly.'

Violet shakes her head, letting out a stuttering breath, and taps her chest. 'With *this*. Your heart. Anubis. Magic. The attention it will call to you. All of it. I can't go with you to find the Order. And I can't step in when you're in danger. It *kills* me, Andy. You have to know that. But I need you to promise me, so I don't go crazy and come after you.' She tries to smile.

'I will.'

Releasing my hand, she closes her eyes and settles into the narrow bed. 'Thank you, little star.'

My breath catches and my eyes mist at the way she says it. So softly. So full of affection. And I want to stay there. With my older sister who gives me advice and warns me about boys and scolds me when I get too cynical. But things are different now. And so am I.

I leave her there, my skin itching with the pull of magic and her voice echoing in my head.

4

Black candles and herbs lie scattered on the ground in a circle around me. The lake near my house laps quietly at the shore, and the buzz of insects on its surface is the only other sign of life. Anubis waits just outside the circle, his form gray and immaterial. The hum of using the spell to bring him here during the liminal night of the harvest moon still buzzes in my skull like a potent drug. Dusting chalk from my hands, I gingerly move to kneel in the center of the circle. I check Violet's drawing to ensure every pattern and symbol is correct. At the base of the casting circle is a crescent moon lying recumbent, just like my tattoo. Attached to it is a solar disk.

Your casting circle will need the sun and the moon, representing an eclipse, Violet had explained. *A time of magic and power, where the rules of the universe no longer seem to apply.*

Lines criss-cross the ring, forming sharp angles and symbols. Each is done carefully, with intent. Constellations, names of power, and enchantments are marked on each dot and curve.

'You're certain this will work? That you're ready for a spell like this?' Anubis asks, his voice strangely echoey.

Wepwawet stalks nearby, pacing in the dense underbrush.

I wipe my forehead, a cold sweat tingling across my skin. 'Violet was. And at the rate the gods are dying, I don't think we have much of a choice.'

Anubis' eyes flash, a curious mix of longing and fear etched across his face. 'But it will only last until the winter solstice. We can't waste any time getting into the university. Pastor Carmichael will help us forge records, and I can ensure our assumed identities are kept separate from our true ones.'

Some of the fearful ache in my chest ebbs at the reminder of Pastor Carmichael, the kindly man who helped me and Anubis to discover the truth behind Greene and Ravenswood, last fall. He's helped Anubis forge records before and has connections with other clergymen who fight demons and societies in their corners throughout Europe.

'We can worry about records once this is done. Are you ready?' I frown at him as I light the candles one by one. His obvious anxiety sets my teeth on edge.

Anubis nods and extends his gray, wavering palm. His long fingers unfurl as he brings a ceremonial black knife to his skin. The dark blade reflects my eyes for a split second before he drags it across his hand. Even hovering somewhere between both worlds, he bleeds onto the ground. A mixture of red and gold.

'As soon as my blood touches you, you'll have to begin the incantation,' he warns. 'You can't hesitate, even for a moment, Andromeda.'

I set my jaw, a bitter taste coating my tongue. Magic practically shimmers in the air. Ignoring my powers for months on end has built up a pressure in my chest until it feels like my ribs will burst open at the mere promise of unleashing a wisp of magic.

Violet's pale skin and sunken cheeks flash into my mind . . . Regina, Luciano, Richard Greene. Magic is poison to people like me. People with something to gain and everything to lose.

'Andromeda?' Anubis' voice pulls me from my thoughts. 'It's only seconds until midnight.'

I glance up. Glittering gold and crimson stains his waver- ing palm. His brow creases with concern. With hesitation.

'I'm ready,' I say, keeping my voice steady. We need Hecate. We need to find the Order and discover what they're doing with the magic of the murdered gods. Even if it means I don't recognize myself by the end.

Before Anubis can say anything else, I reach out and take his hand. His skin is cold, and for a moment I worry that his fingers will pass through mine like smoke. But the force of my unleashed magic hits both of us like a shockwave as midnight strikes and the spell takes shape. Grass flattens, sending plumes of ash up to the sky like wandering ghosts. The flames on the candle wicks blaze impossibly high, bathing Anubis' face in shadows and light as his form flickers between solid and insubstantial.

'Ego te ad latus, O deus mortis, sicut qui vivit, quamquam divina es.'

I chant the words, over and over again. I don't recognize my voice as the unfamiliar sounds echo in the small clearing. Anubis' face shimmers. For a moment, Jae melts away.

Bronze skin, a face too perfect to be human, and deep black eyes stare at me. A fierce wind whips through the clearing, scattering herbs and fanning the flames on the candle wicks into a frenzy. Anubis groans in pain and I dig my hands into the earth, the heat of magic rooting into each bone, until it feels like I am on fire.

The Latin continues to fall from my lips, gaining strength, until the words themselves seem to come alive, making the air around Anubis shiver, distorting him.

I tie you to my side, O god of death, to be like one who lives, though divine you are.

Something cracks, splitting apart. Anubis cries out and crumples to his knees. Sweat sticks to my forehead and neck, and I struggle against the invisible weight bearing me down into the casting circle. The crescent moon and sun disk burn, green fire illuminating the clearing. I try to gasp, to stumble back and free myself from the confines of the circle. But I'm rooted in place as the flames burn at the grass, eating it away until charred embers bite at my fingertips and knees.

I open my mouth to scream, but my voice fails. All that remains is the green fire dancing before my eyes, filling my bones with power. Anubis cries out again as the snapping sounds burrow into my ears. I blink through smoke and heat as he writhes on the ground, his face swimming between two personages.

Anubis. Jae.

Jae, and then the god again.

His limbs bend at unnatural angles. His skin bubbles. Blood coats his teeth, his tongue.

'Andromeda,' he groans, his voice ragged and small, lost in the crackling of flame and the rush of wind. 'Stop! Cut off the spell. Seal off your magic.'

Panic grips me tight, my muscles coiling as I struggle to my knees. The green fire glares at me, as if sensing my desire to smother it. To kill this feeling that threatens to overtake me. I've seen it before, those green flames. Sickly, like a disease. I squeeze my eyes shut, images of a three-bodied woman holding aloft a torch, a key and a dagger spinning through my scattered thoughts.

Andromeda, a voice whispers.

The air stills, the flames sputtering as oxygen leaks away. Numbing cold spreads up my fingertips. My arms. Until I can't draw in a breath. Anubis is still on the ground, his face masked in shadows.

Follow my path, Andromeda, the voice calls again.

With a ragged cry, I slam my fist into the charred grass

and swipe my fingers through the chalk circle, breaking the closed loop of magic. Immediately, I fall to my side, gasping, as sweat soaks through my clothes, only to cool in the low temperature as a wind whips off the lake.

Shivering, I take a few more torn breaths and push myself to my hands and knees. Anubis lies curled on his side, his back to me.

'Anubis?' I whisper, my voice refusing to rise any higher.

A dark tail slashes through the air a few feet away as Wepwawet whines. The jackal lowers his head, and his lips curl back over his teeth. He slinks to Anubis' side and nudges him with his snout. Anubis reaches his hand out, skin golden and smooth, to touch the animal's head. In a flash, the hair along Wepwawet's spine bristles, and a fierce growl echoes deep in his chest.

'Anubis?' I repeat, gingerly reaching out to touch his shoulder. His skin is warm beneath my fingertips. My stomach knots and my mouth goes dry as I look for jagged white bone to split his skin. He rolls onto his back, eyes tight with pain. But he looks whole and unbroken, appearing as he always does in the mortal world, as Jae.

He shuts his eyes briefly. 'I'm fine. Just need to catch my breath.'

Another growl catches my attention. Wepwawet's eyes gleam in the darkness, his fur standing on end and his teeth stark white against his black lips.

'What's wrong with him?' I touch Anubis' arm again. When he doesn't wince, I let myself relax a fraction.

'I'm not sure.' Anubis sits up, peering at our surroundings like his eyes won't clear. 'Your spell –'

'I lost control,' I interrupt, pulling my hands back and getting to my feet on shaky legs. 'I knew this wasn't a good idea. Look at what I did. I hurt you.'

Anubis' fingers brush mine, and instinctively I pull mine back.

'Andromeda.' His eyes are soft and deep brown once more. 'It worked. That's all that matters.'

My breath catches as I realize I just felt his skin on mine. Warm with blood and life. Every nerve ending sparks as I throw my arms around him and squeeze my eyes shut. Savoring the feel of his body against mine after so many months. But then Wepwawet's uneasy growls pull my eyes away. Everywhere in the clearing is the mark of my out-of-control magic. The pulse of power flattened reeds and bushes like a hurricane. The grass is stained with the pattern of my casting circle. And even my teeth still ache with latent power.

'We should leave,' I say, my voice choked as I step back from Anubis' arms. 'Get somewhere safe and figure out where you'll stay before demons come.'

Anubis dusts off his clothes. Despite a few scorch marks, he really does look fine. His eyes shine as he looks down at his hands and flexes them, as if he can't quite believe the spell is real. That he has the body of a mortal once more. The look of awe on his face makes me ache. Because he's only here with me until the winter solstice. After that, I'll lose him to the Underworld once more.

As we kick aside the last of the candles and prepare to leave, he casts another look at his growling jackal. 'It's like he doesn't recognize me anymore,' he murmurs. 'Let's hope the Order won't either.'

Wepwawet's narrowed glowing eyes are the last thing I see before I turn my back on the lake and enter the night with a god at my side.

5

I wake to the sound of blood roaring in my ears. Sitting up, I instinctively look into the darkest corners of Violet's room, searching for signs of Anubis. But there will be no more shadowy portals to the Underworld, or jackals leading me there. Because the spell worked. He's here, in the mortal world, and for the last two weeks he's been only a ten-minute walk away in some seedy motel. We've hardly seen each other as he worked on gathering records and crafting identities. Still, a sense of jubilation thrills through my veins even as I stand from the uncomfortable chair and stretch. Mom and Dad are both slumped over Violet's bed, their hands entwined across her legs.

Rubbing my eyes, I look out at the watery morning light. It was a bad night. Violet couldn't stop throwing up, even after weeks of these injections. I can still see the tendons in her neck straining and the burst blood vessels in her eyes. The doctors are so hopeful that this experimental treatment will help. So are my parents.

But seeing Violet looking exhausted, pale – and, worst of all, *scared* – I can't help but feel a renewed sense of urgency beating in my skull. But now that Anubis is as human as a god can be, I have hope. There are answers in Scotland. Answers to who the Order are, and what they want with the gods. And perhaps, like I told my sister, a society so ancient may have information on curing an illness like Violet's.

A shadow moves across the yard. Ignoring the protests of my stiff muscles, I creep from Violet's room and head down the stairs and toward the back door. Anubis stands in the yard, morning mist curling from his shoulders. My heart thuds in my chest as I open the door and step into the cool air. His eyes bore into mine, and I want to reach out and touch him. To feel his warm almost-human skin beneath my fingertips. But the window to my sister's room is just above us, and I don't want my parents to see.

'How is she?' he asks, startling me from the thrill of seeing him here like this.

'Worse.' My voice catches and I blink until my eyes clear. 'Did Pastor Carmichael send our records to the university yet?'

Anubis' eyes are filled with sympathy as he pulls something from the inside of his jacket. 'Carmichael outdid himself this time. The waiting has been worth it. This came to my motel room last night. International express.'

He hands over a large manila folder stamped and embossed with a school crest. Two snarling wolves face each other on a diamond-shaped shield, golden laurel wreaths framing the top. And below, etched into an intricate scroll, is the school's motto: *Non ducor, duco.*

I am not led; I lead.

I flip the folder over and see my name in neat, sharp cursive. *Andromeda Emmerson.* I still feel strange handing over our real names, but Anubis – *Jae* – and Carmichael insisted. The fewer lies, the more believable our ruse. I undo the twine holding the flap down and reach inside.

A thick cardstock letter with scrolling gold foil on the borders holds the laundry list of lies used to get into Eidolon University. All of the accomplishments are Violet's. The only thing that is mine is my name. My tongue tastes bitter as I scan the gushing acceptance letter to a school so prestigious and exclusive only someone like my sister could have gotten in.

We are pleased to welcome such a bright young scholar into our hallowed halls and our prestigious classics program. Between your excellent grades, impressive internships, and wonderful letters of recommendation from such illustrious mentors, we have no doubt you will join the ranks of the few and revered Eidolon alumni.

I stare for a few more moments at this version of myself. A person who pursued her interests, no matter how much better her sister might have been. Who had the world at her feet and opportunities at her fingertips. An ache starts in my chest as I stuff the letter back inside and pull out the thick packet of papers containing instructions and information about the school.

'I still have access to the bank accounts I used when I was living as Jae. Everything is paid for, plus a few donations, just to cement our story.'

I nod absently as I thumb through the pages. Two days. That's all it took to fabricate this other Andy. A spell or two, a few careful favors, and everything was set. I suppose I understand, at least in part, what appealed to Tooth and Talon. To Violet. Money is hardly a concern when you can bend magic to your will. But something like this, the ability to get what everyone dreams of, and so easily, has an attraction that lingers like an aftershock in my bones.

Anubis holds his own folder in the crook of his arm. The name Jae Han stares back at me. Another lie. That ache of stealing a life that does not belong to me grows stronger behind my ribs, and I look away.

'When do we leave?'

As if sensing my internal agony, his eyes flick to the darkened window of Violet's room. 'The semester starts in five days. We need to get there at least a day before that. Carmichael helped me book tickets for tomorrow night.'

'So soon?'

'Eidolon's term starts later than the public institutions. But we can't wait any longer,' Anubis says.

My throat tightens and I have the insane urge to throw the folder full of pretty lies on the floor and march back to my sister's side. But I squeeze my eyes shut and remember how she looked last night. How everything in this world seems to hurt her. The Order, and the university, are my last hope of finding Hecate.

A warm hand tentatively squeezes mine. I open my eyes, caught in Anubis' familiar gaze. Since he lost his mortal body last year, he has been so careful about touching me. About not promising anything beyond what he could offer as a god bound to a realm I don't belong to. A few moments together, brief and aching. And the loneliness I've been nursing since last fall feels like it could lift now, with him here by my side. With a heartbeat and eyes that see into the deepest parts of me.

I grip his hand; afraid he'll disappear before the winter solstice if I don't keep hold of him. 'Tell me again that this is the right choice.'

His eyes soften, and his gaze travels to my lips. 'It is. Hecate is alive, hidden somewhere in her territory in the Underworld. The Order wants her magic, but you are her descendant, and she wants you to find her. We'll do that before the Order, and she will heal your sister, Andy. I promise.'

My breath is stuck somewhere in my chest. I feel his hand tentatively move to brush a wild curl from my face. Our eyes lock, his a dark brown that swims between human and something more. Like a magnet, I'm drawn to him, to the sweetness on his breath and the spicy scent of his skin. Before his hand can tip my chin up, bring my lips near his, the door behind me opens with a groan. I breathe in sharply and whirl round, my face burning and my mind spinning with explanations.

Mom stands in the doorway, her eyes marked with dark circles. She glances into the yard, bathed in the early dawn light. Words stick in my throat, some brilliant explanation as to what I was doing, almost kissing a boy in our backyard, but my words die in my throat.

The yard is empty. Jae – Anubis – is gone.

'Everything alright?' Mom asks. 'What's that you have?'

I thrust the envelope under her nose, my cheeks still burning. She sees the embossing. The Latin and the crest. Her eyes widen as she stares at the papers inside. A little piece of me feels like it's withering away, buried under the weight of the lies I've created.

'You leave tomorrow?' she asks breathlessly.

'I thought about what you said,' I croak, wincing at the insincerity in my words. 'I want to go to college. For Violet. Eidolon is everything she wants for me. I wasn't sure if I would get in, being so close to the start of the term. But my counselor pulled a few strings. I know it's soon –'

Mom's eyes fill with tears, but she smiles and crushes me to her side in a shockingly powerful hug. Her lips are pressed to the top of my head, rustling the curls around my glasses as she speaks. 'I'm proud of you, Andy. I know this is what Violet wants for you too. And you'll be home for Christmas, and she'll be doing better, and everything will be fine.'

I pull away as she wipes her cheeks, the dark circles under her eyes a little less pronounced as she smiles at me. And for a moment, I feel jealous of this fake Andy that Mom is so proud of. Woodenly, I follow her inside, glancing over my shoulder once to search for Anubis in the morning mist.

6

The train carriage rocks and sways. The cabin lights are dimmed, and deeper patches of darkness are the only things that interrupt the endless night outside the window. I stare as hills rise and fall. Anubis sits across from me in the private compartment, his eyes closed as he leans his head back against the plush velvet-covered seat.

We arrived in London late this afternoon. Following the directions in our joining instructions led us to an exclusive waiting room at King's Cross. A private train operated by a single company, comprising only a few carriages emblazoned with the school crest, arrived at a closed platform half an hour later. An attendant for each carriage welcomed a handful of other students aboard. We made three long stops as we journeyed through the quiet countryside, picking up a few more students along the way. But as we pushed on into Northumberland, night fell. The lights and villages got further and further apart, as sweeping valleys and craggy mountains and hills replaced all signs of civilization.

Despite the long hours of travel, I can't bring myself to sleep. Between the opulent train carriages, with their tinkling crystal chandeliers, and the weight of the envelope on my lap, I feel wired. Like I've had too much coffee on an empty stomach.

An attendant knocks on the polished mahogany door before sliding it open. He wears a crisp white suit and black slacks, the university crest embroidered in gold on his breast pocket. He doesn't ask for our tickets, merely dips his head in acknowledgment.

'We will arrive in Idyllwood in an hour.'

Anubis stirs as the attendant disappears down the hall, his soft knock and carefully neutral voice carrying the message to others. Dragging a hand down his face, Anubis leans forward and peers out the window. No lights mark the tumbling hills. We're taking a different route around Edinburgh, one that skirts the city completely and leads us to the little village where Eidolon resides.

'You remember our story?' Anubis asks, smoothing back his hair.

Even though we've been traveling for the better part of twenty-four hours, he still looks good. Barely rumpled. Meanwhile, I've bitten my nails to the quick and reread my velvet-covered packet of information so many times the thick cardstock stamped in gold foil has become creased and bent.

I nod. 'We met on the train. We don't know each other beyond that.'

He purses his lips, as if my tone isn't convincing. 'You can't call me Anubis. We can't let on about your powers, about being a descendant of Hecate. If we're going to infiltrate this society, we have to use our magic carefully.'

'I know all this,' I sigh. 'Between you and Violet, how could I forget?'

Violet's warnings ring in my head endlessly. Demons and monsters know who I am, and what I can do. Without her protection, and with so much unused magic built up inside of me, I'm a beacon. They will come and search me out, bringing the scent of sulfur and death. And the Order could suspect me in a heartbeat. Using magic isn't something I want to do. But now, as the train pulls closer and closer to Idyllwood and Eidolon, it beats against my chest like another heartbeat.

Anubis' expression is drawn. 'We'll both work together to locate the Order's members. Once we're in the society, spending more time together won't seem so strange. Until then, we'll just be careful.'

'I'll have to try and keep my hands off you, then.'

His cheeks darken a little and he rubs his neck. 'They can't suspect –'

'That we mean anything to each other. Like I said, I know.'

'I'm just worried. Tooth and Talon, Regina and Luciano, they're the lowest rung on the ladder.' He adjusts in his seat, eyes roaming the darkened hillsides. 'I remember Min-Jun talking about the university. About how exclusive it was. How she had to bribe someone in admissions just to get her transcripts looked at, since she didn't have the right connections to powerful people. This place is different from Ravenswood – from any of the schools outside Europe. They've been operating far longer.'

I clear my throat. 'You mean those are Jae's memories.'

He blinks a few times, as if registering my words. 'Right.' He shakes his head, as if clearing cobwebs from his thoughts. 'Sorry. It's odd, coming back here. I'm remembering things from my life, and his.'

We sit in silence after that. As the train begins to slow, and the telltale glow of morning light over a small village beckons in the distance, I study Anubis. His brow is knitted in concentration as he studies his hands, like he doesn't recognize them.

The small village of Idyllwood rests against the backdrop of two large peaks. The cobblestone streets are damp from the morning rain, puddles forming along the gutter and in low-lying depressions. Dark gray stone, mined from the nearby quarries, makes up the quaint village. Ivy clings to walls and neat, manicured gardens line the streets. Bookshops, cafes and pubs look cheery, with painted windows and signs.

The soft light of the morning can't hide the unease burrowing beneath my skin as Anubis and I, along with other students from the train, leave the station and head for a waiting bus idling next to a quaint grocer's.

'Do you smell that?' I murmur under my breath as Anubis walks ahead of me, boarding the bus and astutely avoiding my gaze.

'Sulfur.' His deep brown eyes quickly scan the dozen other students waiting behind us to board. 'Someone summoned a demon.'

I sit behind Anubis on the bus as the rest of the bleary-eyed students pile onboard. The bus pulls away from the curb and rumbles away from the town, heading down a long, narrow road lined by woodland and craggy open fields. The scent of sulfur grows stronger, and my fingers flex involuntarily. A list of spells, a slip of paper Violet insisted on sending with me, flit through my mind. Protective enchantments and their words itch along my skin, begging to be spoken. Anubis looks over his shoulder briefly, his brows pinched with worry.

A large gate looms out of the morning mist. Weak sunlight filters through the low clouds, highlighting two gatehouses made of gray stone. Slowly, the wide, scrolled iron gates open inward. I hunch close to the window as we rumble across the threshold and emerge into the school.

A long road stretches all the way into the distance, lined by neatly trimmed hedges and stone walls. The river I noticed the night before meanders around the clusters of buildings, separating the main section from a large grassy plain at the base of the two peaks, complete with a ruined abbey squat-ting in the distance.

The brakes hiss as the bus stops in front of a semi-circular drive. Framing the shape of the drive is a U-shaped build-ing of white marble, with Doric columns and Greek revival architecture studding the facade. The bus doors open, and I stand automatically, hefting my bag over my shoulder and following Anubis off the vehicle.

The air smells fresh and clean. But as the bus rolls away, the scent of diesel and something much more pungent ruins the idyllic illusion of the university. Two older stu-dents, probably in their early twenties, descend the steps, shadows cast by the columns dappling their skin.

I swallow back nausea as another whiff of sulfur snakes through the group of waiting students. I narrow my eyes, studying the faces of those around me. All look either bored or over-eager, but none look particularly suspicious.

'Welcome to Eidolon University,' says a girl with a subtle German accent. Her eyes are pale brown, her hair straight and unremarkable. But as she tucks a few strands behind her ear, a fake smile pasted to her lips, a flash of curling black ink winks out from the neckline of her sweater. She adjusts her clothes before I can see more clearly, but the tattoo on my leg tingles in response. 'I am Antonia Müller, and this is Rohan Mahajan. We are not just your tour guides today. Both of us lead student societies in political science and law. A mixer will be held for each college tonight and tomorrow, where you can make connections with groups like ours and find others in your field of study.'

Rohan doesn't smile, merely checks his watch and adjusts his satchel, bursting with thick books with yellowed pages, and glances at the group of students. 'Antonia and I will take you to your college and then bring you to orientation.'

With that, the tall boy with dark hair and distracted eyes turns on his heel and marches away from the semi-circular building, toward a cluster of structures hewn from honey-colored stone. Victorian architecture mixes with the cleaner lines of Georgian buildings as we drag our suitcases to a square four-story building with excessive amounts of stone carvings. A bronze plaque announces the name: Alexandria College.

The males and females separate, each heading to a different section of the building. The scent of sulfur fades as I enter my room and re-emerge into the main hall to wait with the others. Anubis descends the main staircase, his hands in his pockets. To anyone watching, it would appear we don't know each other. But as he reaches the hall and leans casually against the banister, his eyes meet mine, and I sense a flare of his magic calling to mine.

A warning. He knows something about the summoned demon.

Our surly guides wait impatiently for the party to rejoin. A young man with light brown skin, thick lashes and startling green eyes descends the stairs last. The scent of sulfur that accompanies him is so strong, I half expect to see a demon latched onto his shoulder. He grins rakishly at Antonia before he comes to a stop a few feet ahead of me. My eyes water and I struggle to breathe through my mouth. No one else seems to notice.

As Antonia and Rohan lead us out of our college and back onto the wide main road, signposted *Appian Way*, I keep a few paces behind the boy who reeks of demons. I only half listen as we pass by quads of manicured lawns, ornamental gardens, and plenty of overly grand architecture. Only when we enter a massive gothic building with an oxidized copper dome in the center of the roof do I first sense something dark and hungry.

Antonia's endless prattle – a recital of facts about the history of the school – barely seeps past the thick fog of evil pressing down on my lungs. 'Morrowood College is one of our largest complexes; the buildings were completed when the school first opened in 1690. While it primarily focuses on economics, you'll also find our performing arts amphitheater inside, large enough to accommodate nearly all the student body. Through here is –'

My heart stutters in my chest as we enter a dark hallway lined with heavy velvet curtains. I've fallen back until I'm at the rear of the pack of students. The boy with the green eyes walks a few paces ahead. As we emerge into the auditorium, his shadow extends along the floor. Horns, a bent spine, and broken wings follow at his heels. Sulfur, loam and ash fill my mouth.

Through the low hum of voices from the gathered first-years, I hear a deep, rattling voice.

'*Child of Hecate . . .*'

My hands curl into fists as we file into a row at the back of the first section of seats. Deans, professors and other faculty line the stage, seated in plush upholstered chairs. Each is dressed in expertly tailored clothing, and they all wear identical pinched expressions of thinly veiled impatience.

A dean stands to address the gathered first-years. A few droning sentences of welcome later, lights dim and a video plays on the screen descending over the stage. I catch sight of a set of shoulders and dark hair disappearing through a narrow hallway blocked by heavy curtains. An entrance to the backstage, by the looks of it.

Anubis is sitting too far away, sandwiched between a bored-looking Rohan and a lanky boy with freckles all over his face. I glance around covertly as the room darkens and a prerecorded history of the university, containing an endless list of accolades, drones over the speakers. Ducking my head, I step over the legs of a girl to my left and slip past the curtain that still sways from the green-eyed boy's touch.

The air is cool as the narrow hall descends, as if it dips below the ground as it loops around the back of the stage. The walls are painted black, and stacks of costumes, storage boxes and props cram every inch of space. I follow the smell of rot and decay deeper into the belly of the back rooms.

That gravelly voice that whispered my name echoes somewhere to my left, where a warped wooden door stands ajar. I peer inside, my fingers curled around the door frame. Cords, pulleys and lights crowd the walls. In the center of the dusty room stands the boy. He holds a bronze disk in his hand, and a swirling cord of pure darkness extends a few feet from the disk like a leash. It lashes around the neck of a crouched demon with leathery dark skin, a set of wicked horns, and twisted wings. The boy looks the same age as me, probably eighteen. But as he converses with the shadowy demon, he looks anything but young and innocent.

'Your time is running out, boy,' the demon hisses between jagged teeth. 'It is only a matter of time before your hold on me weakens and I escape to someone stronger than you.'

The boy laughs. 'The favors you owe my family might be almost up, but I still hold your fate, Ushum. As long as the devil's trap is powered by my ancestor's spell, you belong to me.'

'That little trap cannot hold me for long.' The demon nods at the bronze disk etched with complex symbols and patterns in the boy's palm. 'You may have me bound to you for now with your little tricks, but there are others here that could feed me far better than a spoiled child with only a little magic in his blood.'

The boy's green eyes seem to darken with interest. 'The

rumors are true, then. The Order is located at Eidolon. Tell me, Ushum, how can I be admitted? How can I pass their trials?'

The throaty laugh of Ushum skates down my skin like rubbing velvet the wrong way, and I duck a little further behind the door.

'The Order is not found. It seeks out its members, child.'

'Then tell me how to make sure they find me.'

Ushum rolls out his crooked limbs, teeth flashing in the dark. 'The Order always knows when a magic-wielder enters the gates of Eidolon. Whether you are enough to entice them is another matter. You cannot rely on me to fuel your powers if you wish to enter their ranks.'

'We'll see about that, Ushum. I'll collect the favors owed to my family soon enough.' The boy says something in Arabic and twists the bronze disk in his hand. With a muted roar, Ushum swirls into shapeless darkness before being pulled into the amulet like a genie caught in a lamp. The boy turns toward me, and I jerk away from the door.

My foot tangles in a web of cords and cables. With a sti-fled curse, I yank my leg free and retreat down the hall. My breath is labored as I struggle to keep it quiet. The sounds of the orientation grow louder, but before I can pull back the curtain and breathe air that doesn't reek of demons and dust, a hand clutches my shoulder.

'You're in my college,' says the boy. His other hand is stuffed in his pocket, as if he still holds the devil's trap, waiting to use it. 'Any reason you're wandering dark tunnels beneath the school?'

I lift my chin, keeping my expression neutral. 'I lost my way to the washroom. What's your excuse?'

He smiles and sticks out his hand. 'My name is Masoud. Masoud Anwar.'

I stare at his hand for a moment before briefly clasping his fingers in mine and dropping them unceremoniously. 'We should get back to the orientation, don't you think? Or do you have someone you're meeting back there?'

He makes a flourish with his arm, his grin growing. 'Of course. Lead the way.'

I turn my back to him, acutely aware of his presence behind me. When we rejoin our row of seats, Anubis shoots me a look over the heads of the other students. I keep my face impassive but flick my eyes to the side as Masoud flops down in the chair next to mine and kicks his expensive shoes up on the one in front of him.

By the time the orientation ends, and our group is ushered out of the auditorium, Anubis has worked his way over to me. We stand in a larger quad. The air is cool, and the cloud cover has broken up over the school, dappling the mixture of architecture in sunlight. A tall man with black hair graying at his temples waits for us. He wears a tailored navy suit and a pocket square folded in a complex pattern.

Our group gathers around him, and I press a little closer to Anubis as a few dozen students from other halls crowd together, their tour guides leaving them to stand beneath the arches surrounding the quad.

'Welcome to Eidolon.' The man inclines his head. His voice is tinged with a subtle accent. 'I am Dr Ambrose Giatsou.'

A girl I recognize from the train last night perks up, leaning close to the boy at her side. 'He's the head of the archaeology department! He can get into any country, any dig, with just a flick of his fingers. I even heard he's leading a new expedition to locate Cleopatra's tomb.' They murmur excitedly for a moment before turning their attention back to the dean.

'Our university prides itself on our world-class education. We are pioneers in research and discovery, as well as culture. Your acceptance into Eidolon is no mistake. We expect great things from each one of you. That being said, every student is scheduled to meet with a faculty advisor this week. They will ensure your classes align with your goals and those of the school.' Dr Giatsou smiles as a murmur ripples over the students. 'Over the course of your time here, you will experience everything Eidolon offers. Our history is rooted in greatness – we will accept nothing less. Once you enter these halls, you will forever belong to the school. The connections you make, the fellows and professors you encounter, will help you reach the heights of your chosen fields.'

Antonia, standing aside with the other guides, checks her phone, the corner of her mouth dipping slightly. She motions to Rohan before she slips behind an arch to take a call. The other student guides share a look with each other as the dean continues his speech. Instinctively, I breathe in, searching for sulfur. There is nothing but the scent of damp stone.

Anubis crosses his arms, angling his body slightly toward me as he whispers, 'Where did you go?'

I flick my eyes to Masoud, who stands next to a few girls from our hall, a crooked grin on his face. The dean continues speaking, providing enough distraction that I feel I can step a little closer to Anubis.

'I followed the boy from our college who smelled like sulfur.' I glance once more at Masoud as he turns his attention to studying the other students and grounds with marked interest. 'He has a demon bound to him with a devil's trap and mentioned it owed his family favors. He was asking it about the Order – how to join their ranks.'

'Then we aren't the only ones looking for them. Maybe if we follow him, he could lead us to the Order.'

A gasp rushes over the quad. Horses thunder onto the lawn, their riders clad in frilly dresses and tailcoats. Anubis grabs my arm and yanks me to the side as they cut across the grass. At least a dozen people on horseback, carrying parasols and top hats, gallop into the space. The students from the orientation stare, unsure if the few adults present will control the strange situation.

The riders dismount and spread out blankets. More people stream from the covered walkways, dressed like servants from the late eighteen hundreds. They swirl around us, making for the center of the lawn. More murmurs and gasps ripple over the crowd. Porcelain and silver tea sets appear on the blankets. Platters of desserts and fruit come next.

Horses nicker and snort as the servants disappear back into the halls, only to be replaced by more students dressed in polo attire. They mount the waiting horses, laughing and calling out to each other as they stream around the blankets. Anubis and I press our backs to the stone pillars as students scatter with surprised shouts.

The dean and another woman from a different department push through the crowd, their faces lined with disapproval. A boy, probably twenty-one, doffs his velvet top hat to the crowd, and bows. Surprised laughs echo off the stone walls before the students break out into applause.

'Mr Valerius!' Dean Giatsou calls out over the commotion.

The boy in the center of the display merely smiles, his icy gray eyes glinting with mischief. 'Welcome to Eidolon,' the boy says, mocking the accented tone of Dr Giatsou. 'We merry few are here to announce that the Covenant of Vespers is accepting initiates for this term. Do you have what it takes to join us?'

My blood runs cold and I meet Anubis' eyes. Could this over-the-top display of wealth and influence be the same Order that is stealing the powers of the gods? Or is it nothing but a silly fraternity made up of the bored elite?

The boy smiles before he takes a bottle of champagne and pops the cork. The first-year students nearest to him are quickly bathed in a spray of bubbles as the others dressed in Victorian attire follow suit. Students cheer and shout, pressing closer to the frivolous display. Dean Giatsou yells something over the crowd, pointing to the boy in the top hat.

More professors and faculty enter the quad. The group quickly retake their mounts, whooping and tossing food around. Before anyone can so much as reach for them, they thunder out, leaving behind a mess of blankets, cravats and torn-up grass.

But as the first-years laugh and shout to one another, dizzy and drunk on the extravagant show, something silver catches my eye. While the deans try desperately to maintain order, I spot Antonia, a bonnet still on her head and a sly smile on her face, as she steps from behind the arches. As she and Rohan help to gather the other students from our hall, I cross to the spot where she appeared from.

I kneel and pick up a small silver rectangle. Flipping it over, my heart sticks in my throat. Stamped on the reverse side of the silver coin is the image of a wolf suckling twin children. I glance over my shoulder at Anubis.

It seems we were wrong about one thing. Some of the Order's members *want* to be found.

7

The rest of the day is a long, exhausting procession of orientations, tours, and speeches about the history and accolades of the school. Anubis and I are separated when we're organized by our areas of study. I follow the other first-years to the cluster of buildings dedicated to the Classics School, facing the river and the ruined abbey of St Mary's. Anubis leaves for the Laertes Museum, led by Dr Giatsou, and the prestigious anthropology and archeology courses.

By the time I get back to my dormitory, my eyes are blurry from reading so much information. Setting down another folder of maps, course descriptions and syllabi, I close my eyes.

With a sigh, I check my phone for the first time today. I'm not surprised to see messages from Violet lighting up the screen. She begs for pictures of the campus, information on professors, and even pleads with me to send her a copy of the absurdly detailed course schedules. I can practically taste her excitement, her envy. So even though I feel like a monster sitting in the exact place she's always wanted to be, I comply with her wishes and promptly hurl my phone onto my bed.

I'm not even given the luxury of a few moments of quiet. Feet echo down the hall, voices following suit. The floorboards creak above and beneath me. Music starts somewhere across the closest quad. LED lights in a rainbow of colors light up the other dorm windows. Then a whisper of paper flutters under my door.

I take a step away from the metal frame of my narrow twin bed. The floorboards bow a little as I cross to the thick wooden door and crouch down. A deep ebony envelope made of thick paper with an iridescent shine to it stares up at me. A wax seal, blood red and stark against the black paper, bears the letters 'CV' in swirling script. I pluck the envelope from the floor and slide my fingernail under the seal. Ink stains my fingers as I unfold the handwritten note.

Andromeda Emmerson,

The Covenant of Vespers has seen fit to extend to you an invitation to determine initiates for the new term. Entry to the Vespers is severely limited. Your background could be of great use to us. We are certain your insight could shape the next class of initiates, and in return you will gain access to resources and alliances not available through conventional channels. Join us at ten o'clock this evening at Leonidas Court. Be advised that this is a closed party – no plus ones are allowed into the hall.

I let the thick note flutter onto my lap as I pass a hand over my forehead. The display on the lawn earlier – tea and mock polo matches – doesn't match up with a bloodthirsty sect killing gods for their magic. I check the time, my eyes feeling like sandpaper after the long day.

I have a little under an hour to figure out where Leonidas Court is and find Anubis. If the Vespers turn out to be just another university drinking society, then at least we'll have crossed off someone on the list of suspects for the Order.

By the time I make my way down the narrow staircase, pushing past dozens of students holding bottles to their lips, I've texted Anubis to meet me in the hall's foyer. Someone plugs in a speaker and a low bass rattles my teeth and glasses. Stepping past the plastered walls into the foyer, I catch sight of a familiar figure with dark hair and green eyes ducking out the front door. Masoud glances over his shoulder once, an ebony invitation in his hands.

'You got the same invitation?' Anubis asks, shrugging a coat over his shoulders as he appears by my side.

I nod, my eyes still stuck on the door. 'So did Masoud.'

'Our friend with the devil's trap?' Anubis looks toward the exit. 'Maybe there's something to this society throwing tea parties on the lawn, after all.'

'Maybe,' I agree. 'But would an order as old as the Roman Empire give themselves away like that?'

'We'll have to find out tonight. Come on, we're in the same hall. I think we can get away with walking together.' Anubis gives me a crooked smile, the kind that always makes my heart flip in my chest. I want to reach out and hold his hand, but I match his smile and we step into the damp night.

At every turn, parties fill the air with music. Lights flash in windows. Shouts and laughter drift down the roads. Dark figures walk along the dimly lit pavements and disappear into buildings. I tuck my hands into my coat pockets. The university looks more ominous at night. The spires and rooflines like jagged teeth, dark and broken.

We reach the road where the gatehouses stand guard against the night. We have to cross it to the other side of the campus, where the observatory and the most prestigious halls sit.

'Appian Way,' Anubis muses, breaking the silence between us. 'Like the road the Romans built to conquer the other Italian states.'

I still have the silver curse tablet from my dream of Hecate in my pocket and trace it with one finger. An uneasy feeling builds in my chest as we cross the road and pass beneath a massive stone arch leading into a sprawling park. On the left, near the gatehouses, is Leonidas Court – an exclusive hall that only offers membership and never accepts applications, according to whispers around our dorm.

'Did anything like this happen when you were following the other societies as Jae?' I grab the iridescent invitation from my coat pocket.

His eyes get a faraway look, as if memories are pushing to the surface again. 'The ones connected to Min-Jun were more vicious than the others. They tended to be secretive. Aloof. Like Tooth and Talon. This –' he shakes his head, expression clearing – 'this feels like some kind of joke. And I wish I knew why.'

I square my shoulders as we cross the court, stepping over its intricately laid paving stones. Candlelight glows through the windows, waving hypnotically. The music is different from the blaring bass of every other first-year party. Haunting strings sing mournfully, spilling through the courtyard. The vague outlines of people in suits, walking slowly with silver trays in their hands, move like ghosts through the windows. The party isn't as big as the ones happening all over Eidolon, but it feels more intentional. Like the music, the lights, and even the smells are a siren song designed to lure a sailor within.

The invitation sits heavy in my coat pocket as we climb the stairs. Statues stud the portico, seven of them standing like sentinels before the wide double doors. They're a little larger than life-size and carved of impeccably white marble. I don't recognize who they're meant to represent, but seven grave male faces with beards and robes follow us with their hollow eyes as Anubis reaches out and slams the bronze knocker against the door.

'Wait a few minutes and then come inside. We shouldn't be seen arriving together,' he says.

The doors swing inward with a rush of air as the pressure changes. Instantly, my spine stiffens. Through the typical smell of cologne, alcohol and cigarette smoke is something else. Like the scent after a rainstorm, or the smell of freshly turned earth. A hint of magic. Anubis must notice it too, because as the butler – an actual *butler* – takes our coats and points to the back of the grand foyer, his breath catches.

'Your invitations, please,' the butler says, his face reminiscent of a bulldog. He accepts them before gesturing to a set of double doors where the haunting music plays beyond the round foyer and its glittering crystal chandelier.

I don't speak as I pretend to fuss with my shoes, allowing Anubis to walk ahead over the marble floors, a mosaic of swirling, alternating patterns that make my head spin. I study the mosaic for a few seconds as Anubis pulls open the door leading to the party and disappears inside. Seven rings of smaller tiles shift like a kaleidoscope. I push my glasses up as the butler waits patiently by the main entrance, his eyes trained on nothing at all. Seven statues outside. Seven rings of a mosaic. I want to poke around more, but the music spilling under the door reminds me I have other plans.

Approaching the same doors where Anubis entered, I pull the handle. A grand ballroom appears; more chandeliers hang from the vaulted ceiling and drip crystals that catch the countless flames of candles decorating tables, sconces and walls.

Much like the display on the quad, dozens of students are dressed in Victorian attire. Shining satin gowns and frilly cravats swirl around as they dance to the music of a string band on a small stage. Long tables line either side of the room, laden with food and crystal goblets of wine.

I blink in the low light, frozen at the entrance to the ballroom as the hypnotic display assaults my senses. 'What is going on?' I whisper under my breath. I search the crowd for Anubis, and spot him and other students, dressed in normal clothes, scattered near a low banqueting table. Other initiates, I'd wager.

The grandness of the ballroom, from the sumptuous clothing to the expensive chandeliers, screams wealth and elitism. Other first-years around the room eye everything hungrily.

Slowly, I wander around the edges of the party, scanning the room for Masoud. The demon he has attached to the devil's trap owes him favors, that much I gathered this morning. What I don't understand is how Masoud knows about the Order at Eidolon, and why he wants to enter it so badly.

'Would you care for a drink, madam?' someone asks at my side.

I turn my head to see a waiter in a tailcoat, his hair slicked back and white-gloved hands holding a silver tray bearing goblets with deep purple wine. He looks young, like a student, and I stammer a surprised 'thank you' as I take a glass.

Before the waiter can move away, I clear my throat, catching his attention. 'What is the story here with the dresses and candles?'

The waiter smiles, and for some reason, it sends a strange sensation over my skin, like a cool misting of water. Numbing and enticing. 'The Vespers is the most exclusive society at Eidolon. Why don't you enjoy the food and drink? The show will start soon.'

'The show?' I ask, but he's already gone, weaving through groups of people drinking deeply from their cups.

Suddenly, a hush falls over the ballroom as the music fades away with one last trilling note. The double doors shut, sealing us into the room. The couples dancing break apart, some with flushed cheeks that seem to be more from alcohol than physical exertion. They line up across from each other as the band rests their bows against their instruments, ready to play once more.

'Welcome to Leonidas Court,' says a female voice at the head of the room. It's our tour guide, Antonia, I realize, as the party-goers crowd in around the dancers to get a better look. 'And welcome to the Vespers annual ball. The Covenant of the Vespers is Eidolon's oldest society. We choose only twenty new members per year. So, if you wish to have access to our countless resources, from internships to connections with past alumni, I recommend you ensure we know just how valuable you truly are.' Antonia lifts her glass of wine to the crowd, eyes glinting in the candlelight. 'Enjoy the show.'

Everyone else lifts their goblets and takes a deep drink just as the music begins again. Instead of the haunting, almost eerie strain from before, this one is more lively, encouraging the dancing to begin again, even from those dressed in regular clothes. The music sends thrills down my spine as I duck out of the way. More people dressed in elaborate costumes spill from a door at the head of the ballroom. Some hold gleaming foils in their hands and wear masks over their eyes. The clang of their narrow swords punctuates the notes of the violins and cellos. Others offer the first-years strange fruits, their skins brightly colored and odd.

My head feels fuzzy as the music swells, and I tear my eyes from the swirl of full skirts and laughing faces to realize I've moved over to one of the tables. More purple wine spills from goblets, the scent cloying and sweet. Glancing into the goblet in my hand, I see myself reflected in the liquid, a smile on my face as society members whirl around the room, murmuring in their dance partners' ears, and laughing. The air smells thick with that curious scent from before: turned earth and deep secrets. That scent is important. But I can't remember why as I bring the glass closer to my lips, suddenly desperate to taste the wine.

A shoulder collides with mine, knocking me against the long banqueting table. The wine spills over my hand and I drop the glass, the crystal shattering into thousands of tiny pieces. The sound interrupts the music, and I turn around, ready to demand an apology, when the words stick in my throat.

Masoud slips past me, heading for a thick curtain draped across a far wall. His face is focused as he tucks a bronze disk back into his pocket. The devil's trap. I blink hard and look around for Anubis, unsure of when I lost him in the crowd. I don't even remember walking to the tables. I turn and cross the dance floor, passing other students with purple-stained lips, their pupils massive as they laugh and talk and dance. My heart thuds in my chest as the smell of the wine turns sour, and finally, I spot Anubis near the head of the ballroom, his eyes narrowed as he studies every corner. The trickle of magic I noticed in the courtyard gets a little stronger near the far end of the room. A whisper, like a trail of fog leading somewhere distant. I can't tell what it is, exactly, only that it makes my skin itch and my blood cool.

'Anubis,' I whisper harshly, grabbing his arm.

He glances at the dancers quickly. 'We shouldn't be seen together,' he whispers.

'Something is wrong here. We need to leave.'

A first-year nearby takes a deep drink from his cup and looks at us as the dancing grows more frantic. 'Nothing is wrong,' the boy says, his voice dreamy and far away. 'Why don't you enjoy the show?'

That unsettled feeling of unearthly coldness brushes over

my skin as Anubis and I share a look before backing away from the table laden with wine. A similar feeling washed over me when the waiter spoke and when Antonia lifted her glass. Some of Violet's words echo in the back of my head. How I ignored my magic for too long. How I can't recognize things like she can.

I curl my fists and glance at the curtain Masoud headed for. It flutters a little, revealing a door set into the highly decorated plaster wall, and the thread of magic beyond it calls softly to my powers. The candles flicker as the music swells. 'Through there,' I murmur, tugging on Anubis' sleeve. 'This party is a distraction.'

Anubis trails behind me, glancing over his shoulder to make sure we aren't followed. We slink into the darkened edges of the ballroom and slip behind the curtain. No one notices as I dig my nails into the small gap of the door and step through it. As soon as it shuts behind us, everything falls eerily silent.

Anubis presses a hand to his brow. 'The room is enchanted. So is the wine.'

'The Vespers are trying to distract people,' I agree.

There aren't many lights on in this section of the building, but even in the darkness, white marble reflects light off every surface. The walls are thick, barely any sound from the party leaks through. If I hadn't just crossed through the ballroom, I would think we were now in a museum.

'Maybe it's a test from the Order. The ball and the wine are a distraction, a way to weed out people without enough magic in their blood to sense the spell.' I focus on that tugging sensation against my magic. An urge to follow an invisible thread further into the hall. 'Masoud went through here. He had the devil's trap in his hand.'

Anubis follows my eyes toward a staircase. 'The demon

75

may have granted him a favor, letting him know how to get noticed by the Order.'

I cross the marble floor, heading for the stairs.

Wood paneling, gold leaf and statues are at every turn. I thought our hall was far too nice for a university, but this looks like an aristocrat's manor from the 1800s. Our footsteps reverberate softly as we walk.

'I thought the Order was exclusive. There has to be at least a hundred students living here,' I whisper. Even though we're alone, I don't trust there not to be prying eyes and listening ears hidden behind one of the many portraits or within a suit of armor.

'This can't be their headquarters either,' Anubis agrees, frowning as we pad up the steps and reach the first landing, passing tapestries that are older than some countries. 'It's too open to the rest of the student population.'

I pause, eyeing our surroundings. 'So, it's a front?'

'It could be.' Anubis scrubs at his jaw. 'The Order is probably responsible for every other society I encountered living as Jae. Offshoots, defectors that started their own groups. But the Order must have a system for protecting themselves, one that lets them fly under the radar. I missed them, somehow, even after more than a decade of searching. The Vespers could be how.'

I want to say something comforting, how it's not his fault, how Min-Jun and the real Jae are at rest together on the west bank. But footsteps, muffled by the lush carpet runner, sound as someone descends the stairs. A head of wavy black hair appears around the last banister. I pull Anubis back into the shadows next to an alcove where a statue stands. Shadows dance across the floor, light leaking toward our feet as a flashlight is switched off.

My fingers curl around Anubis' wrist as Masoud stops

76

on the first landing. He's so close I can see something that looks like soot on his fingers as he straightens the lapels on his coat. I hold my breath, pressing back further into the alcove, hoping that the shadows can hide me and Anubis. Masoud glances down at his palm, ignoring the statue we cower behind. He holds the bronze disk, the devil's trap, in his hand. Mixing with the smell of magic is that of rot and death.

'Will the Order accept me if I follow the instructions they gave?' he whispers into the bronze vessel.

A gravelly voice comes from within. 'If you pass their trial. Now that I have helped you locate their test, do we have a deal?'

Masoud's eyes glitter with excitement. 'I won't free you yet, Ushum. Not until I am accepted fully into the Order.'

An outraged growl echoes in the devil's trap as the demon spits angry words, and curses the boy. I breathe in sharply, the sound overly loud in the silence. I slam the heel of my hand over my mouth as Anubis shoots me a desperate look.

Masoud pauses, his eyes passing over our hiding spot. Just when I think he's spotted a flash of our hands or feet, he smiles to himself before tucking the devil's trap into his coat. He hops off the last step, and with a tune whistling from his lips, he opens the door to the back of the ballroom and re-enters the party.

My eyes follow the path Masoud traveled from the top of the staircase. We wait a few seconds before emerging from the alcove, catching our breath.

'The demon is helping him access the Order,' I say, gripping the banister as I climb the stairs. 'Whatever we need to find must be upstairs.'

Anubis follows behind me, his breath rustling the curls at the nape of my neck. 'I can feel something here,' he agrees

We reach the next landing, and I glance back at him. The arched window that takes up the entire wall behind the staircase catches my eye. The top is a stained-glass scene with seven men. They hold scrolls and are flanked by what looks like an ancient Greek amphitheater. They look familiar, like the statues outside.

'What is it?' Anubis asks, following my gaze.

'Nothing. It's just the same pattern again. Seven things repeated. I've noticed it all around Leonidas Court.' I shake my head before gripping the banister. 'Let's check this floor.'

The sensation of magic, the pulse of seductive power we've been following, fades as we pass through the rooms. There is also no sign of a summoned demon to indicate where Masoud has been. No scorch marks or lingering dread. Only scattered belongings and luxuriously appointed rooms.

'Let's check the next floor,' I say urgently. 'Masoud found something, or he wouldn't have summoned that demon.'

Anubis nods, panting as we climb more stairs. 'If what we heard Ushum say is true, Masoud is walking a dangerous line. You said you overhead Masoud mention that the demon owes his family favors. But a devil's trap can grow weak without a regular blessing from a priest, or if it isn't controlled by someone with strong enough magic. I don't sense much within Masoud. He's using the demon to get this far. Ushum could break free soon enough.'

'Great,' I mutter as we reach the last story and step onto a lush Turkish carpet runner that cushions a plain wooden floor. 'Just what we need, a demon on top of missing gods and bloodthirsty ancient societies.'

He chuckles as he stops in front of a large carved door in the center of a plain, white plastered hallway. The hall stretches in either direction, but there are no signs of any other rooms. I step up to the door, peering at it closely. The posts and lintels are carved in a spiraling pattern, like a column, with ivy clinging to each groove. But what catches my eye is the brass doorknob. It's shaped like a wolf's head; jaws open wide as if threatening whoever dares to touch it. I raise my eyebrows at Anubis and he shrugs before twisting the handle. The door opens with a sigh and a rush of the same magic that has called to me all night.

I cough and wave my hand in front of my nose as dust swirls through the air. Everything smells musty and damp. Moisture sticks to a few tiny windows, obscuring what little light filters into what appears to be a massive attic. Sheets cover furniture and bookcases. Sconces, some with stumps of candles still in them, stud one side of the wall. Slatted boards, dust filtering through the cracks, break up the yawning space.

'Andromeda,' Anubis whispers, pointing to the floor. 'There.'

I follow his finger to a spot on the weather-warped boards. A telltale circle is burned into the gray wood. A perfect ring with dozens of symbols swirling around the perimeter. It's an imprint of Ushum's devil's trap. I glance into the darkened corners and stare at the yellowed sheets. But nothing lurks behind piles of junk. No other demons follow the scent of magic. We're alone.

For now.

My pulse races in my throat as I walk through the stacks of furniture and trunks. Nothing stands out in particular. No suspicious footprints in the dust or sheets knocked askew. But something pulls at me, at the far end. I can't quite name it, but it feels like a memory. I shiver as I reach the end of the drafty attic and run my fingers along the slatted boards. The hallway outside was a little longer than the attic appears. The wall must separate where we stand from another room. But with no doors, either in the attic or out in the hallway, how can we get inside?

'There has to be a mechanism,' I murmur to myself.

Anubis crouches next to me, running his fingers along the edges of the slats, feeling for hinges of some kind.

I do the same, decades of dust and grime sticking to the pads of my fingers. I even try to tug on the boards, but they're surprisingly thick and resilient. As I move to the far side of the wall and press my palm to a darker, more aged board, something hisses. Another cloud of dust puffs from the place I touched. I choke on the taste and step back, wiping at my watering eyes.

A wooden wheel now juts from the board.

'It's a dial of some kind.' Anubis leans forward to inspect it. Wood and wire weights and counterweights glare from within the hollow it sprang from. It clearly opens something heavy.

I brush at my itching nose and touch the dial. It's polished wood, almost like a wheel you'd see on an old ship. It's about the size of my hand, with seven short spokes protruding from the center. A silver medallion is pressed into the middle. I'm not surprised to see the imagery of Lupa.

Anubis grabs hold of two of the spokes, and turns. The wheel clicks as a mechanism within turns. He swivels it to the right. Something groans and, with a clatter, the dial snaps back into place as the whole attic shudders. Plaster rains down on our hair and shoulders, and we stare at one another in the darkness, hardly daring to breathe, as we wait for the sound of students rushing from the hall to investigate. No one appears.

After a few heartbeats, he tries again. He turns it to the left, and this time the resistance in the wheel is significantly less.

'Are any of the boards moving?' Anubis grunts, bracing his legs as he continues to turn.

I race along the wall, searching for new indentations or dropped passageways. 'Nothing,' I call back.

He curses and lets go of the wheel, shaking out his hand. The dial spins again, the clicks of the gears growing louder and more chaotic until it returns to its original position.

Voices drift through the poorly sealed attic. I cross to one of the small windows and use my sleeve to wipe at the condensation. Small figures stream from the doors of Leonidas Court and into the night.

'The party is breaking up,' I groan. 'Classes start tomorrow. They'll be clearing out the hall before it gets too late.'

I press my lips together as I peer through the glass to see a few more party-goers leave the hall. Blurry figures stumble down the steps and into the courtyard. Their shadows mix with those of the seven statues. I straighten, pushing away from the cold glass. The statues, the stained glass. Even the columns all have a pattern. I breathe in sharply and cross back to the dial.

'What is it?' Anubis follows, pushing his hair from his forehead.

I grip the spokes and repeat Anubis' movements, turning the dial to the left. 'Didn't you notice all the paintings and statues and rooms downstairs? Seven. Seven of everything. It's a strange number – not exactly the symmetry of classical architecture.'

The gears click a fourth time, and I concentrate on not turning the wheel further than I need to.

'Seven is a divine number. It could mean something.'

Five turns. Another click.

Six.

Seven.

A smooth rolling sound fills the attic. The boards withdraw from the other end of the room, near the windows. They seem to collapse in on themselves, folding like a piece of paper. And then they retreat into the other wall, the dial neatly tucking itself back into the hollow before disappearing.

A new room appears, and this time, we're not alone.

Antonia, the same girl who led our orientation and who opened the party for the Vespers, lounges in a chair next to a massive fireplace. Two bronze statues of Lupa frame each side, complete with Romulus and Remus at her feet. At Antonia's side is a small wooden table with a stack of familiar velvet envelopes.

'Well,' she murmurs, her eyes glittering in the darkness, 'it's not often we have two initiates pull themselves from the spell in the ballroom and arrive at the same time.'

My tongue sticks to the roof of my mouth as panic roars through my system. But before I can say anything, Antonia stands, neatly plucking two envelopes from the pile. Her dress whispers against the floor as she crosses to us.

'Congratulations on following the trail. I'll see you both tomorrow night for your initiation into the Order.'

Anubis and I accept the envelopes without a word as Antonia flicks her hand at us, indicating she wants us to step back. We do, and as she twists a bronze dial next to the fireplace, the walls groan as the secret panel unfurls from its hiding spot and slides back into place, concealing the room like before.

As Anubis and I share an uneasy look in the darkness, surrounded by falling dust, I can't help but feel the thread of magic I followed here tighten like a noose around my neck. For better or worse, the Order has found us now.

8

'Have you had any more dreams about Hecate?' Violet asks, her voice weak and tired as it crackles though my phone.

I juggle my phone and backpack between my hands as I slip under the portico of my lecture hall before setting the speaker at my ear again. 'No. But Eidolon holds the answers to where and why she's hiding. I know it.'

'It sounds so beautiful there,' Violet says dreamily.

'Right,' I snort. 'The bloodthirsty ancient society murdering gods really adds to the Scottish charm of the place.'

Violet sighs, and I can hear her nurse rooting around in a bag, no doubt preparing another round of injections to ease the pain in Violet's exhausted body. 'Andy,' she says, lowering her voice so her nurse won't hear. 'The only way to find out why the Order is killing gods, and what they're doing with the magic they steal, is to infiltrate its ranks. You can't do that if you don't blend in. Besides, I'm sure it can't be all bad. There must be something you like about the place.'

I glance around. Eidolon University is entirely different this morning. Gone are the flashing lights and droning bass. The neat streets and sidewalks are free of cups and bottles. Dozens of students walk by, noses buried in books and hands stuffed into the fur-lined pockets of expensive coats as unseasonably chilly air grips the valley. It looks like the picturesque version of the school they showed at orientation. Academic, rigid, and proper.

'I guess,' I say grudgingly.

But a new invitation burns against the tattoo on my leg

as I tap my fingers against the thick cardstock in my pocket. And nothing feels picturesque in my world. A light drizzle drips onto my curls as I wait outside in the central square where the Classics Department is housed. My first lecture begins in only a few minutes, and I still need to speak with Anubis about the plan for tonight.

'It'll be alright, little star. And I'm here to help you with any schoolwork. Blending in is important, but you also need to focus on the plan.'

'I know.' I shut my eyes and breathe out slowly. 'I just wish I knew what they wanted Hecate for. Why have they waited to take her, if she's so valuable?'

'Ready for your meds, Violet, honey?' the nurse asks, her overly sweet voice cutting through the speaker.

My sister mutters a curse under her breath. 'Just a second!' she calls out brightly before lowering her voice once more. 'Worry about that once you're in the Order. I'll see what I can find out from here. If there are any clues.'

'Alright,' I agree, my heart aching as I imagine her alone in bed, waiting for a rescue as her body slowly shuts down. 'How are you feeling today?'

'Just peachy,' she says sourly.

'Vee.'

Finally, I spy Anubis' broad shoulders moving through a crowd of students entering the square. Shouts and laughter fill the damp air and I bite down on my cheek, fingers gripping the sharp edges of the note in my pocket. Anubis shakes out his jacket, raindrops hitting the ground, as he steps beneath the portico beside me.

'I have to go,' I tell her, my voice catching.

'Listen, I'll be fine.' Violet's voice sounds falsely sunny. 'Nurse Jackie and our parents have everything under control here. I'm holding out hope the stem-cell treatment I

84

had before you left keeps the infections under control. I love you.'

'Love you, too,' I mutter, before hanging up.

The stone of the portico feels colder than before, pressing down like a coffin, as I hang up and slip my phone into my coat. Anubis is quiet as I reach into my pocket, pulling out the dark burgundy envelope. 'What are we going to do about the initiation tonight? Should we show up together since Antonia already saw us last night?'

A muscle in his jaw twitches. 'We have the same invitation. She knows we live in the same college. I don't think there's a way around it.' His eyes soften. 'How's your sister doing?'

I wince and clear my throat to keep my voice steady. 'Fine. She wants us to focus on tonight. On the initiation.'

He nods, and if he's stung by my brush-off, he doesn't show it. 'Something has been bothering me about the invitation. I thought about it all night.' He pulls out an identical card. The sweeping calligraphy bearing his name on the front gleams in the low morning light. He pulls out a single sheet of creamy white paper with the same message as mine scrawled in the center.

'"You have seen through the veil of the Vespers and discovered a token marking you as worthy of ancient knowledge. You are invited to pursue further initiation into the Order,"' Anubis reads, his lips stiff. '"Your tenacity is noted by Romulus, and he is impressed with your talents. If you wish to overcome death, to find a place of belonging, arrive at Athens House an hour after sunset."' His arm drops to the side, and his brow furrows deeply. 'Why would they speak of death and belonging in the same breath as this mysterious Romulus figure?'

I step closer and grab his wrist, pulling his letter up to my

eye level. 'Yours is different to mine. Look, here at the end.'
I unfold my invitation and hold them side by side. Anubis
squints at the identical handwriting, the swooping letters
and the same no-nonsense dismissal and lack of signature.

"'If you wish to overcome death,'" he says under his
breath, eyes scanning my letter. "'To . . . undo the ravages
of illness, arrive at Athens House an hour after sunset.'" He
looks up at me, shaking his head wordlessly.

'They know about us. About Violet. Who you really are.'

'There's no way,' Anubis argues. 'Our records were
scrubbed clean at Ravenswood, and at every other school I
infiltrated. Carmichael helped us with fake transcripts, and
our spells were airtight. They can't know.'

I glance up and notice the thinning crowds of students in
the square. A few stragglers walk toward the doors behind
me. I snatch my invitation back and push it into my coat
pocket.

The strap of my backpack digs into my shoulder as I
adjust it, the heavy books on philosophy and Roman archaeology doubling in weight. 'We can't walk into the initiation
tonight without some kind of plan. If they know about us
and Violet –'

'They don't,' he says firmly. 'The Order could have done
research on our aliases. We tried to construct families and
friends and pasts. They could refer to anything. Just . . . just
trust me for a while longer. We're close to getting deeper
into this society. We can't risk anything.'

I nod, my jaw clamped tight. Anubis checks over his shoulder before he briefly touches my hand and heads for his
lecture hall across the square. I watch him go for a moment,
the morning mist thinning enough that the sunlight filtering
through the gray clouds illuminates his body. And for the
first time, I realize that he doesn't cast a shadow at all.

Turning, I shove open the heavy wooden door, my shoes squeaking on the freshly cleaned tiles. Heavy gray stonework marks a wide staircase. Scalloped crosses stud the intervals between the balusters. Carvings of creatures mark the worn stone newel posts. Tapestries and flying buttresses of musty-smelling wood make the place feel like a medieval castle. As I march up the stairs and prepare to cross a wide foyer brimming with benches and plants, I pause.

On the landing of the next staircase, leading up into the tower of the building, Masoud stands, his forearms on the stone banister. He flips a bronze disk between his fingers casually, but his gaze is a palpable weight on my shoulders. I meet his eyes as I open the door to my classroom, voices filling the cavernous hall. He smiles and tips an invisible hat at me before turning.

And when he disappears up the stairs, a dark red envelope flashes in his hand.

My head aches after a long day of lectures. The three classes I'm taking this term appeared manageable on paper. But I forgot how schools like this operate. Assignments and pages of notes swim behind my eyelids. A tension headache pulses in my temples as I wait for Anubis in the fading light of dusk at the corner of our hall and Appian Way. I text Violet, pretending that everything with my classes was fascinating and not overwhelming. I don't want her to worry that I can't handle this on day one, like she could. A bitterness coats my tongue as I imagine Violet here, diving into studies as she expertly infiltrated an ancient order. A bubble pops up at the bottom of the screen as she types a reply, and before I can see it, I say we are making progress on our 'project' – the code we have for the Order – and put my phone back in my pocket.

87

Anubis emerges into the warm lamplight cast in even intervals down the wide road. His mouth is set in a thin line. 'Masoud hasn't left yet. His room is above mine.'

I bite down on the inside of my cheek as we step off the curb and head toward Blake Quad, the massive, immaculately groomed plaza where Leonidas Court and the mysterious Athens House sit. I tried to research in the sliver of free time I had between hour-long lectures but found little information on the hall we have been invited to tonight. Nothing beyond arbitrary building dates, where the stone was sourced, and inconsequential remodels over the years.

'Any sign that he'd summoned his demon?' I ask.

'Not that I could tell. But if he's invited to the Order, he could get suspicious about us. View us as competition for a spot.'

We reach the wrought-iron gate cutting off the private courtyard of Athens House from the rest of the quad. Ivy clings to the bars, wrapping around the scrolling metal like snakes squeezing the air out of struggling rodents. I hadn't noticed it here last night, half choked by vegetation. But now, as I test the gate and it swings inward, I wonder how I missed it.

If Leonidas Court was ostentatious, then Athens House is downright imperial. A classical rectangular building of ghostly white marble rests in the shade of two large weeping willows. A triangular pediment crowns a row of columns. Within is a frieze of the same bearded and robed men from the statues last night. Seven. And as we approach the door, I count seven steps, seven windows, and seven ornamental pillars.

Anubis lifts the brass knocker. 'When we're inside, sit apart from me, like we're just acquaintances. Whatever they want us to do inside, mirror the other's attitudes.'

Before the brass knocker can fall back against the waiting door, it opens, and a familiar face looks at us from within the dark, cool interior. Antonia steps back, motioning for us to enter.

'Wait here. The others will arrive shortly.' Her dark eyes flick between us briefly before she jerks her chin toward a sitting room to one side of the main entrance. It's open to the foyer and furnished with antiques so costly I cringe as I sit down on a wing-backed chair. Anubis takes the end of a sofa on the other side of the fireplace, nonchalant as he crosses his ankle over his knee.

'Others?' I ask her. 'You mean Romulus?'

Antonia smiles, but it doesn't feel friendly. 'No. The other true initiates. As for Romulus and the other house leaders, you'll meet them if you pass.'

I stare at her for a few seconds as she smirks and returns to the door, once again opening it just before a hand can rap the brass knocker against the wood. A soft murmur of voices comes from the other side. A boy and girl enter, their eyes darting suspiciously around the room. They join us in the sitting area as Antonia reaches to open the door again, but no one makes a move to introduce themselves or even break the silence. Candles flicker around the room, casting strange shadows across faces.

'Ah,' a smooth male voice floats to my ears. 'Familiar faces.' Masoud lifts a dark eyebrow and saunters past Antonia with a dismissive wave of his hand before he drops himself onto the cushion beside Anubis. 'Two of my hallmates. What are the chances?'

'There were plenty from our hall at the party last night,' Anubis says, smiling thinly as he avoids my eyes.

Masoud grins wolfishly, his gaze skating over the four others gathered in the room. 'But hardly any who discovered the hidden summoning room. And the others from our hall didn't receive a pretty red letter like ours.'

'How do you know that?' Anubis asks lightly. His face is expressionless, his body loose and casual. But I can see the way his eyes narrow, how his nostrils flare. After years of hunting down societies, he is experienced in reading people connected to magic and secrets.

Masoud lifts one shoulder. 'The same way you and I discovered the summoning room. A sense of something special. The others who attended the Vespers ball, but didn't find the summoning room, were admitted into the Covenant of Vespers, and were offered rooms in Leonidas Court, for a monthly due, of course. But they will never know what we learn about the Order tonight. They don't have what we do.'

The other girl, lanky and with flawless dark skin and short-cropped curly hair, scowls at him. 'How do you know so much about this?'

Masoud seems thrilled to have an audience. 'Because we are different from the others that spent their night dancing, and drinking enchanted wine. I am the nephew of the King of Jordan. My parents are extremely influential diplomats for my country.' His eyes turn to the other boy. 'You are Marco Pérez, son of Alejandro Pérez, majority owner of Laboratorios Internacional – the largest pharmaceutical company in South America.'

Marco sits forward, a frown on his face. 'How did you know – '

'You, my lovely,' he points to the girl, 'are Amina Al-Fayed, the daughter of Othman Al-Fayed, CEO of the largest banking company in all of Africa.'

I lean forward before Masoud can turn his attention to Anubis or me. 'Congratulations on being able to use the internet. Everyone at Eidolon is connected and wealthy, so what is your point?'

The door creaks and I hear two male voices greeting Antonia. Masoud doesn't seem worried by my tone, or the angry glares Amina and Marco shoot his way. If there's something rich people don't like, it's being compared to other rich people.

'My point,' Masoud says emphatically, his teeth flashing as he smiles at me, 'is that we are all more than simply wealthy or connected. We are *important*. The Vespers need only money. The Order, they need something more.' He sits back against the couch, as if he has said something worthy of the great philosophers of old.

Two more first-year boys cross into the sitting room. Antonia waits until they're both seated in chairs flanking mine before she stands in front of the crackling fire, her eyes sharp as flint.

'Mr Anwar is correct on one point,' Antonia says drily. 'Each and every one of you is different.'

Amina huffs and crosses her long, delicate arms across her chest. 'I am tired of this cloak-and-dagger stuff. Tell me what is going on before I get the board involved.'

'The board,' Antonia says with a sharp smile, 'does not know the Order exists. All they know of us is what we want them to know. That is the Vespers, and things like the party you saw last night.' Antonia's eyes flash as she scrutinizes Amina. 'And if you wish to keep that sharp tongue in your head, you will keep everything you see tonight a secret. The Order cannot operate with endless mundane interferences.'

Amina glares at the other girl but remains silent. As I turn my attention to the others in the room, unease knots my stomach. There are seven of us seated around the fire.

Antonia continues, 'Each of you has been hand-picked to continue the initiation process into the Order. We are selective about who joins our ranks. Only those with strong and potent magic can locate the summoning room in Leonidas Court. The party last night was simply a way to sort through the potential candidates. Many who find their way to Eidolon have some level of magic in their blood. But very few have enough to catch our attention. Observations from myself and other high-ranking members are the only reason you are here today. The Order has two branches. The Vespers, what you witnessed last night and during orientation, provide candidates for us to choose from. They make money for us to fund our research grants and the upkeep of our halls. They organize social events, and they serve as the face of our society . . .' Antonia pauses, letting the weight of her next words fall like a pendulum. 'And the other branch, well, you'll see if you pass your test.'

Amina stands, her eyes flashing with annoyance. 'I travel from my home in Marrakesh, endure two days of endless parties and noise, and receive an invitation that cryptically claims you can help me, and yet you wish to test me, after already knowing I have magic. It is insulting. I am here to succeed, and I have no interest in games.' She storms past me, heading for the heavy door.

'Don't you wish to learn how you can regain control of your inheritance from your dear step-mother?' Antonia asks, her voice saccharine.

Amina spins on her heel, eyes wide and mouth agape. 'How did you –?'

'Each of you has something you desperately want. Something you would kill for. The Order can grant this to you, if you prove your magic's strength and your loyalty. Your magic pledged to our cause, in return for our help.'

Marco shifts in his seat as Amina continues to gape from the foyer. 'How do we know you are telling the truth? From what I've seen, this Order is nothing but a silly club. I've seen more magic from what I've learned in my own studies.'

Antonia's brown eyes darken with something very near to laughter. She lifts her hand, and with one crisp movement snaps her fingers. The room is plunged into darkness. Someone curses as another stands so abruptly their chair tips back and clatters to the hardwood floor. But then, a soft glow emerges from where Antonia stands, highlighting her outline. The light moves to surround Marco, encasing him in a flame-like glow. Another flash and he disappears as if he never existed. Masoud staggers back, tripping over the fallen chair. Before anyone can even gasp, Antonia snaps her fingers again. Marco appears next to the fire, his clothes soaking wet.

Marco wipes water from his eyes, shivering violently as he chokes. 'W-what did you do to me?'

'A little dip in the river Aoife ought to cool your temper, don't you think?' Antonia smiles.

'Shit,' Amina mutters under her breath, her hand braced against the wall to steady herself.

Antonia lifts one eyebrow. 'If you are interested in learning far more than that simple party trick, take a slip of paper from the bowl.'

The atmosphere in the sitting room changes. Gone are the confused looks from before, the narrowed eyes and suspicious glares. Even the water-logged Marco's anger shifts to something else. Hunger. I mechanically take a slip from a silver bowl, my hands numb.

Each of you has something you desperately want. Something you would kill for.

I've already killed for Violet. As I unroll the slip, my fingers clumsy, I wonder if I have it in me to do so again.

My vision swims as I stare at the paper in my hands, the words blurring into a meaningless jumble. I rub my eyes behind my glasses. But nothing changes. A series of letters strung together is all that is printed on the crisp white slip. I look up just as the others do.

'You will have precisely one hour to solve the riddle and locate what it wishes you to find.' Antonia moves away from the fire toward the front door, her lips in a thin smile, as if reveling in the shock she has instilled. 'If you haven't figured it out by then, you'll be escorted from Order property, never to be invited back. The next group of seven will arrive promptly at the time your trial ends. The doors will unlock then.'

'Unlock?' Masoud scoffs, his cocky mask slipping an inch. 'What do you mean un—'

Antonia slips out of the door, and the rattle of a heavy bolt sliding into place is the only answer Masoud gets. A grandfather clock ticks steadily in the foyer as the seven of us sit in silence.

Finally, someone gets up the nerve to speak.

A boy with pale skin and a shock of red hair, says, 'Do you really think she locked us in here? Is this some kind of escape room?'

Masoud laughs. 'Didn't you see what she did with Marco? This isn't a game. This is real.'

'So, what do we do?' The redhead's neighbor asks. 'Do we compare papers? Search the entire house?'

'I don't care what you do,' Masoud sneers, pushing to his feet as he heads directly for the staircase set in the back of the foyer. 'I am going to solve it myself.'

The others murmur as his footsteps echo and then fade.

The red-haired boy shakes his head and stands, before cross-ing to the door. 'I'm going to see if she actually locked us in.'

No one is surprised when it doesn't budge as he shakes the handle. Anubis stands and unrolls his paper again, squinting at the letters. With Masoud gone, in the belly of Athens House, I don't care if anyone suspects us. I reach his side and peer at his slip.

Tig Viaku Arceqeg wecv mbt bxrd aof zlnywma Uyaj Hwojwez

The same jumble of nonsense as mine. I open my mouth to speak, but he shakes his head subtly. Amina and Marco bend their heads together, as do the two boys. While no one besides Masoud will do this on their own, no one is eager to form an entire group, either.

Anubis jerks his chin in the other direction. We leave the sitting room and cross the foyer into a white-paneled room with gold-leaf moldings. He shuts the door with a soft click. A grand piano sits in one corner and a harp in the other. A music room. Nothing looks useful for solving a riddle.

'Do you know what this is?' I ask, shaking the paper in my fist.

He rubs his temple and squints at the letters. 'I tried count-ing every seventh letter and seeing if it solves anything.'

'Like an anagram?' I stare down at the riddle and shrug. 'It's as good a guess as any.'

'K, e, b, o, m, w.' Anubis searches the room for something to write with, finding a stack of sheet music and a stub of a pencil in the piano's bench. 'None of the combinations are words that seem to matter.'

I consider the groupings of letters. The capitals. It seems like it won't need to be unscrambled at the end.

'Violet tried to teach me some ciphers as a kid,' I grum-ble. 'I guess I should have paid more attention.'

Anubis smiles at that. And then something hits me. Some

ciphers are complex; they require keywords or phrases to unlock them. But Violet always said that the simpler a cipher was, the more ingenious. Regular people won't care if they see jumbles of letters somewhere. Those with secrets to keep go for ostentatious ones, as if proving to everyone else how smart they are. I map the letters out in my head, but there are too many possibilities.

I take the pencil from Anubis' hand and flip over a crinkled sheet of music. Kneeling over the piano bench, I draw a vertical and horizontal axis, listing the alphabet on each one before drawing hasty grid lines. Anubis peers over my shoulder, his scent of incense and turned earth washing over me and making my pulse quicken.

'Trithemius?' he asks, a tone of surprise in his voice. 'You think it will work?'

I nod as I quickly fill in the rest of the grid. And then I plug the key into the riddle, my pencil flying. 'It's one of the easiest ones to learn. The horizontal axis meets with a letter in the grid from the vertical axis, revealing a different letter. Violet wanted to write to me in a secret language that no one else knew. Since I'm not a savant, she tried ciphers, until I gave up when she only ever told me what we were having for dinner in code.'

Anubis chuckles, his breath tickling the back of my neck. A shiver skates down my spine. I shake my head, focusing on the task.

Slowly, words assemble below the table. The pencil stains my fingers with graphite, smudging some of my work. But soon, I have the entire phrase rewritten. A pulse of pride beats in my chest as I recall those early days with Violet as she was coming into her talents. Her intelligence. The way she tried to include me until the very moment she left for Ravenswood. When everything changed. Including her.

I lean back on my heels and look up at Anubis.

The Seven Sisters hold thy fate and whisper, 'know thyself'.

He scratches his chin as he thinks. 'The Order certainly has a favorite number. Maybe there are seven statues of females somewhere in the house that lead to the next clue?'

We rush through the lower level of the house, searching for signs. Occasionally we come across a pair of other initiates, some still bending over their slips of paper. It only takes a few minutes to realize that, unlike Leonidas Court, Athens House does not appear to have any statues inside it.

'Know thyself,' Anubis mutters to himself as we reconvene in the music room. 'Thales of Miletus said that.'

My head aches again as I try to recall the ancient philosopher, and I sigh. 'But what are the Seven Sisters? It was capitalized, like they were referring to real people.'

Anubis' eyes brighten. 'The Seven Sisters. They're a constellation.'

'The Pleiades,' I gasp, another memory shooting through me. 'Violet loves a painting called "The Pleiades" by Elihu Vedder. Seven sisters, the daughters of Atlas and Pleione. Orion pursues them across the sky.'

'We need to look for stars,' Anubis agrees.

Emboldened by the fact that Violet's teachings have solved not one, but two of the clues of an ancient order, we head to the second floor. Masoud is nowhere to be seen, but the scent of a demon-summoning lingers near an empty room full of boxes.

We enter a massive library. Floor-to-ceiling shelves of rich cherry wood house endless tomes. A gallery overlooks the lower floor, and a domed ceiling is gently illuminated around the rim by soft lights.

'The ceiling.' I point upwards. The dome is painted in soft hues of purple and blue, a night sky turning over into a sunrise. An entire Milky Way is painted on the ceiling, including the gentle clouds of nebulae and endless golden stars.

Anubis cranes his neck back, searching the imitation of the heavens. 'There it is. Orion's bow points to the Pleiades.'

I follow the line of his finger until I see the cluster of stars. The constellation is too far above us. We wouldn't be able to touch it even if we were leaning over the railing of the gallery above.

Turning in a slow circle, I scan the library. The circular room has few windows, and besides the painted ceiling, there is little by way of decoration. Only a bronze statue in the center of the room on a plinth. My eyes jump back to the statue.

A man on one knee straining below the incredible weight of the world on his back.

'Atlas,' I whisper. 'He was the Pleiades' father.'

I approach the statue, kneeling until I'm at eye level with the Titan Atlas. His face contorts in pain, his eyes cast heavenward, as if cursing Zeus for trapping him there, alone, doomed to watch his daughters flee from the hunter Orion for eternity.

'Andromeda, look,' Anubis says, kneeling beside me, his fingers skating over an inscription on the plinth. 'It's a line from Hesiod's *Works and Days*.'

Etched deep into the bronze it reads:

And if longing seizes you for sailing the stormy seas, when the Pleiades flee mighty Orion and plunge into the misty deep and all the gusty winds are raging, then do not keep your ship on the wine-dark sea but, as I bid you, remember to work the land.

'Is there a ship somewhere?' I shake my head at the inscription. 'What are we supposed to do with this now? We only have ten minutes.'

Anubis' jaw works as he checks his watch again. Another riddle to solve, and not enough time to do it. I press my lips together and bite down. I can't see the connection, and despite the chill in the library, sweat sticks to my spine.

'I'm not sure,' Anubis admits. 'None of the other societies I've encountered had initiations like this.'

I stand up, lacing my fingers behind my head and staring at the painted sky. The cluster of seven stars sits almost near the center of the dome, with Orion's positioned slightly above. I pause and then move to one of the few windows and peer out.

Through the tree branches, I struggle to find the matching constellation. There are a few scattered clouds, but finally, I find Orion's belt, and then his bow, and follow until my eyes nearly meet the horizon.

'The Pleiades on the ceiling don't match how they appear in the night sky, in the autumn.' I turn from the window, my heart thumping with excitement.

'They disappear in the winter. That's what Hesiod was talking about. It's too dangerous to sail when the Pleiades are at this position, and it's the perfect time to plow and reap crops.' Anubis jumps to his feet. 'We need to reposition the stars so they're on the horizon.'

I return to his side. 'How? The ceiling is painted. We can't just climb up there and cut them out.'

He furrows his brow and studies the room like I did before. I can practically hear the sand slipping through the hourglass. If we cannot solve this clue, we'll be kicked out of all property belonging to the Order. Our chance to find answers will be over before it even begins. Anubis is quiet for another minute.

'We have to do something,' I say sharply.

He grabs the globe on bronze Atlas' shoulder, and twists.

99

The ceiling moves, rotating with a groaning sound. I watch, dizzy, as the faux sky adjusts, like watching a time lapse of the Milky Way, until the cluster of the Seven Sisters slides into place along the western wall.

I hold my breath, waiting for something to happen. Slowly, a bookcase on the far side of the library opens inward, a passage to another room. Anubis and I look at one another for a few moments before his face splits into a wide grin. Before I can process what's happening, he has his arms around my waist and pulls me to his chest.

I barely remember to breathe as I return his embrace. When someone emerges from the secret room, Anubis and I break apart, my cheeks burning as Antonia cocks one hip against the door frame and watches us.

'Congratulations,' she says. 'Welcome to the Order of the Seven Sages.'

9

Anubis and I follow Antonia through the door. Stairs descend to the bottom level before an earthen tunnel slopes even deeper, dipping below Athens House. The smell of damp soil and groundwater seeps into my pores. We're silent as Antonia continues to guide us further down. The air grows colder, and soon I can no longer see roots springing through the ceiling.

Up ahead, the tunnel diverges into two forks. We stick to the left, where the hint of firelight gleams. But even as we walk further into the network of underground passageways, I can sense something else nearby. A familiar thrum of magic, a concentration of it lying below the earth. A strangely warm breeze tickles my skin, originating from the right fork.

A convergence is nearby, a hotspot where magic and the Underworld merge more freely with ours. It feels far more powerful than the one below Duskmoor Island, where Tooth and Talon completed their sacrifices and rituals. My teeth ache as I pretend I don't feel it calling to my blood. I clamp my jaw so hard I taste copper on my tongue.

Antonia stops at a wooden door, the frame tilted slightly as if the earth surrounding it has moved. It's warped and waterlogged, but candles glint between the cracks in the boards. She sets her hand on the knob before meeting us with a steely gaze. 'If you cross this threshold, there is no going back. The Order will be a part of you, never to be separated again.'

Neither Anubis nor I say a word.

She opens the door and steps through. My pulse beats in my throat as I glance at Anubis. His shoulders are stiff as he takes a breath and crosses into the room. I think of Violet and join him in a small antechamber. Stalactites drip from the ceiling, and humidity makes my hair frizz into a cloud around my head.

Three candles burn on the ground. Two men stand behind the center and right candle. Antonia moves to stand behind the third. I blink a few times, my eyes adjusting to the darkness. And I recognize both of the young men before us. Rohan stands on the right, his hands clasped behind his back. In the middle is the boy who announced the Order was accepting initiates for the term, after throwing the wild picnic in the quad. He has white-blond hair and slate-gray eyes. He nods to Antonia and crosses his arms over his chest.

'Both of you have proven yourselves worthy of entering the Order.' Antonia extends her palm. Inked into the skin is part of a tattoo. The symbol of the order: Lupa and the twin babes. It glimmers silver, as if mercury is threaded below her skin. 'Magic is as ancient as we are. The Order was founded millennia ago with the first kings of Sumeria. The seven Apkallu, the wise men, who brought magic to humanity to feed the gods.'

My blood chills as Antonia rolls up her sleeve. The rest of the tattoo crawls up her arm, the snarling face of Lupa giving way to words written in cuneiform. Rohan and the young man with the gray eyes remain silent as she continues.

'The Order was lost for a time after the fall of Rome. But then the Enlightenment returned missing knowledge, and magic thrived once more. This new age led the founders to create Eidolon University. They were driven from other places of higher thinking because they did not agree with the tenets of strict Catholicism or other sects of Christianity. They believed in other gods. In demons. And they knew they could use their power for themselves.'

Finally, the boy in the middle speaks. His voice is even and calm. But his eyes flash in a way I can't quite name, like he is seeing inside my head with only a glance. 'My name is Damian Valerius, and I am the Order's Romulus, its leader. My job is to lead our society to a new age, like our ancestors. And we only accept the best, the strongest magic wielders, into our true ranks. I am impressed by the speed with which you solved our riddle. Most never make it past locating the constellation.' His eyes turn to Anubis, studying him with that same heavy aura.

'Anyone with educations like ours could solve it.' Anubis shrugs, appearing nonchalant.

'Perhaps. But only those with potent magic in their blood can cross through the wards and spells etched into the threshold and enter the library to turn the globe.' Damian's eyes turn to me as he uncrosses his arms, and for the first time I notice that his skin is a mess of raised scars. Silvery in the candlelight, they mark his forearms and the backs of his hands before disappearing into his sleeves. The only inter- ruption in the brutal pattern are endless tattoos. Symbols and animals and other languages. My skin itches, like he's peeling back my flesh, reading the secret of my blood. My throat closes as I imagine what he sees. Hecate in my bones.

Anubis stiffens at Damian's words. 'I turned the globe. Andy was helpful in solving riddles, nothing more.'

Damian nods, his eyes moving back to Anubis with renewed interest.

Antonia resumes her speech like she's recited it a thou- sand times. 'Though you have magic, it is raw and untamed.

The Order will help you refine it, control it. And in return, you will not only help us keep our secrets but use your magic to spread our cause across the earth. You will go where we tell you to, take jobs that we want you to, and ensure that the Order's influence and magic are everywhere.' She points to Rohan. 'We are the leaders of the lower levels of the Order. I am called Prometheus, head of the house of Sophos. And I will decide if you show enough promise to advance to the next stage.'

Rohan smiles, his eyes that mix of cold and disinterested, as I recall. 'I serve as Thoth, head of the house of Lector. You are only deemed worthy of advancement if you show enough promise to safeguard the knowledge kept in Lector's halls. Very few ever make it past Sophos.'

'And I,' Damian says, his voice heavy with authority, 'am Romulus, head of the house of Oracle, the highest rank of the Order.'

My head spins as I try to absorb their structure: the levels and their names, and the symbolism I'm certain are hidden within them. Damian watches me for a long moment. I meet his gaze, determined not to look afraid.

'If you call yourself Romulus, I assume you have a second-in-command. A Remus,' I say.

Damian's eyes glint like steel, a spark of pleasure in their depths. 'Of course. But Ramsey is otherwise . . . occupied. You'll meet him, eventually. For now, you must complete the last rite to fully enter the house of Sophos. You must "know thyself".'

Anubis lifts his chin. 'If you mean acknowledge we possess magic, I assure you we already do.'

'You would not get so far in the sanctum of Sophos without such knowledge, nor such strong powers,' Damian agrees. 'No. The Order can give you what you want – what you need – only if you commit yourself, body and soul, to us. Only then can you achieve your potential. Only then can you receive what was promised.'

'And how do I know you can get me what it is you think I want? Your message was vague. I only came out of curiosity.' Anubis manages to not look at me, to appear as if we only used one another to solve the riddle.

Damian's eyes flash with interest as he studies Anubis. Like he senses more beyond my spell binding him to the human realm. 'The two of you caught our eye the moment your names were flagged through our members in the application department. Ravenswood Academy in America and Eidolon share unique bonds across the Atlantic.' He looks at me, and a shiver runs down my spine, before turning back to Anubis. 'Your reference letter from a pastor in Edinburgh with known skill in demon-summoning, Jae Han, let us know you were not to be trifled with. As for what you want, knowledge is power. And power is something the Order has in spades.'

Antonia and Rohan step forward over their individually burning candles. The air grows heady with the scent of herbs, kinds I've smelled before at Ravenswood. Magic is burning through those wicks, preparing for a spell. A rite of passage.

'Hold out your arms,' Antonia commands. 'We will mark you with the sign of Sophos, the constellation of the Pleiades. With this mark, you will be connected to the convergence, the well of magic the school was built upon. You will learn our secrets and, eventually, learn enough to proceed to the next house.'

Needles glint in her and Rohan's hands. Like crude, barbaric tattoo guns. Black ink drips like an oil spill from their wicked tips. It's another layer to their challenge. I'm sure of it. A test to see who runs and who stays. Who will sign away their soul to the devil.

My heart rate speeds up, pushing the blood through my veins faster, until I feel light-headed. The Order is older than Tooth and Talon, than Ravenswood. Hell, it's older than *Rome* itself. But if I don't do this, if I don't let them consume me, I'll lose Violet. I could lose Anubis to whatever dark magic they're using to steal gods. So, I extend my arm and grit my teeth.

Rohan captures my wrist and sets the needle to the sensitive flesh of my forearm, between my wrist and elbow. He moves quickly; the needle injecting thick, dark ink into my pale skin far faster than any normal tattoo. The seven stars of the Pleiades appear one by one on my skin. And when he makes the last stroke, I feel something coil in my bones.

The tattoo flashes silver, and my thigh burns with the memory of how it felt when Violet tapped into my powers through the sigil she designed. Something is tied to me now; I can feel it like a millstone about my neck. As if in response to my thoughts, I swear the convergence hiding beyond the antechamber hums in satisfaction, my blood a delicious offering.

Damian holds out his hands like a benevolent shepherd welcoming his flock. 'Between your magic and your cunning, you both will go far in the Order. I expect you to join the other initiates who pass their test at the first sanctioned meeting of the house of Sophos later this week. And then, your study will truly begin.' He breezes past me, before pausing by the door. 'I look forward to seeing what you can do, Jae Han.'

Anubis and I walk together in the dark, back to our hall. We didn't see any of the other initiates in the grounds of Athens

House except Masoud as he scurried back toward our hall, rubbing the skin of his arm where a tattoo of the Pleiades peeked from his sleeve. I wonder if he called in another favor from his demon. And I worry what will happen when the wards of the devil's trap break down.

We cross onto Appian Way. No one is around, and not a tree or building is near enough for someone to hide behind and eavesdrop. I stop walking in the middle of the wide road. 'Something about this doesn't feel right.'

Anubis swallows, his eyes scanning the dark road and quiet buildings. 'I couldn't sense any of the wards Damian mentioned in the library. Not one.'

'I didn't either,' I say, the worry and frustration on his face making my blood run cold. 'Only the convergence nearby.'

'Convergence?' his head snaps to me. 'I didn't feel that either. Where was it?'

'On the right fork in the tunnel. But it's stronger than the one at Ravenswood, or at Duskmoor. It almost felt like . . .' I shake my head, trying to put it into words. 'Like I was actually in the Underworld.'

'Why can't I feel it?' he mutters to himself.

I put my hand on his arm, the dark ink of his new tattoo nearly touching my fingertips. 'It has to be the binding spell,' I say, even as my heart twists at how strange it must be for a god to be cut off from the magic that makes him who he is. 'You have to appear mortal. That means no godly powers.'

'Don't look at me like that,' he murmurs, his hand covering mine. 'I don't regret giving up those powers to be here with you.' And when he smiles, that same aggravating grin that makes him look so handsome it hurts, I can't help myself. I grab two fistfuls of his shirt and pull him to me.

His lips taste like rain and incense. I kiss him with all the painful loneliness I've felt since he returned to the

Underworld a year ago. With every stolen moment and broken shred of my heart. He wraps his arm around my waist, pulling me closer. His fingers tangle in my hair as he returns my kiss with the same fervor, a need bordering on desperation.

'Anubis,' I whisper against his lips.

He pulls back so suddenly it almost hurts. Gentle mist falls from the sky, dampening my hair and shoulders. He blinks a few times, like he can't see clearly. And then he pulls his hands away from me. I take a single step back, my heart a bruised, tortured thing beating in my throat.

'What's wrong –?'

'Andromeda,' he says, screwing his eyes shut and stepping back from me. 'We can't.'

'Why?' I demand, my voice cracking. 'Because you're worried the Order will see what we are to each other? I don't care about that! We can't ignore one another, and we've both been accepted into the society, so there's no need to pretend.'

Anubis opens his eyes, and they're dark and hard. 'Because in only a few weeks I'll be back in the Underworld as a god. And you'll still be mortal.'

It feels like my chest is caving in. But I keep my jaw firm, my lips pressed together. Partly to keep them from trembling, and partly to keep his taste on my tongue for a moment longer.

'Andy,' he says, voice ragged. 'I'm sorry. I want –'

I hold up my hand, cutting him off. 'I understand. It's not important.' I wipe under my eyes quickly with the heel of my hand, my throat stinging as I ramble. 'What do we do about the Sophos meeting Damian mentioned? Do you think they'll reveal what they're doing with the gods then?'

He hesitates, his eyes still boring into me in a way that

makes my chest constrict. I cross my arms tightly and look anywhere but at him.

Anubis clears his throat. 'I don't know. But it's obvious that Damian and the Order want magic-wielders with immense strength. Binding a god isn't easy, and killing one is even harder. I'm sure the two are connected.'

'Maybe we should go to the Underworld and search for the path of Hecate I dreamed about. There's no sense waiting here for another god to be killed when it could be her,' I say, avoiding his eyes.

'I can't go,' Anubis reminds me, his voice tight. 'Not until the binding ceremony wears off at the winter solstice.'

I pinch my eyes shut for a moment. 'Then I'll go by myself. I can make the *Subitae mortem* tincture and –'

'No,' he says forcefully, his eyes flashing in the dark. 'Not yet. If you're right, and the Order knows about us, or is even suspicious, going to the Underworld could tip them off. You'll have to find a time when they're distracted, and with the Sophos meeting coming up, they'll notice your absence.'

I want to groan in frustration. How can I find Hecate's path in time to help Violet? And after Damian's comments this evening when we passed the rite, I'm sure the Order is watching us. 'We just have to get far enough into the Order to find out how and why they're stealing the power of the gods. Maybe the first house is all we need to infiltrate.'

'We know so little about them, Andy. They have three levels, different heads of houses, and secret sanctums we don't even know about yet.' Anubis' forehead furrows, and he sighs. 'For now, we need to blend in. And you and I need to appear like we don't know each other beyond Eidolon. If Damian suspects you . . .' he trails off, leaving the rest unsaid.

He's right. And I hate that I'm trapped here, waiting for

the next disaster. I turn and begin walking back to our hall, my shoulders stiff and my pride bruised. Burying my hands in my pockets, I try to keep my composure and focus on the dull ache from my new tattoo.

'I'll see you at the meeting, then, whenever that is,' I say over my shoulder as we enter the hall and I grab the railing of the staircase in a white-knuckled fist.

'Andromeda,' Anubis says, so softly I almost miss it. But I don't turn around. Because I can't face him, not as a human boy, and definitely not as a broken god who I will lose again.

10

I spend the next two days avoiding Anubis. Every time I think about that kiss, I throw myself into studying for my ridiculously difficult lectures and digging in the library for any clues relating to the Order. My cheeks burn as the double metal doors to the lecture hall for my class on architecture in Hellenistic Greece and Imperial Rome slam behind me, and my eyes swim with names and architectural drawings.

My footsteps echo off the colonnade of dark gray stone. The air smells of old moss and damp rock, and I take a deep breath. It's early evening, and the sun has broken through the clouds once more, bathing the scenery in soft orange light. The ruined abbey hunches in the distance, separated from the school by the winding river and a grassy plain. The double hills behind the abbey are dark, the sun slipping behind them. If I squint, I can make out some roofs and chimneys of Idyllwood village in the distance.

If it weren't for the new tattoo marking the pale skin of my inner arm, I could almost pretend that this was a normal-enough school. That I'm not Andy Emmerson, descendant of Hecate. Just a girl lost in a world of history and architecture.

My phone vibrates in my pocket. Two messages: one from Anubis and another from Violet. I click on Violet's name and read her text, practically a dissertation on the temple I've been assigned to analyze. A crooked smile tugs at my lips as I read her message, the excitement threaded through the words. I change the fantasy in my head as I put my phone back without reading Anubis' message.

I imagine Violet is at my side, healthy and carefree. We're not magical, and there are no such things as gods and demons. Just sisters, together and happy. I cross through the clusters of buildings, avoiding shoulders and heavy book bags. And as I enter my hall, shoes squeaking on the newly polished floors, my fantasy disintegrates into ash and smoke.

Antonia leans near the cold fireplace. Beside her is Masoud. Their eyes turn to me the moment the door opens, and I stop in my tracks. Antonia grins, though it reminds me more of a sneer than a friendly gesture. She hands me a simple cream envelope.

'Details on the Sophos meeting tonight,' she explains. 'Be on time. You have an hour.'

'Should I call you Prometheus when we're out in the wild?' I raise my eyebrows as I accept the note. Masoud chuckles behind her.

Antonia crosses her arms. 'Believe it or not, initiate, there is a reason the words "secret" and "society" are often put together.' She gives a warning look to Masoud over her shoulder before she saunters to the door. 'Don't be late and don't be stupid enough to tell anyone who shouldn't know about your evening plans.'

After Antonia leaves, Masoud and I are alone. He nods at the paper in my hand and I open it. It reads much the same as the last invitation, curt and to the point:

When you are ready, the House of Thales will open to you.

'Any chance you know where the House of Thales is?' Masoud asks, drawing a carton of cigarettes out of his jacket.

I shrug, studying the note again.

'You know,' Masoud says, a lighter clicking in his hand, 'I'm glad that you and the other boy made it into this order.'

'Oh, really?' I refold the note and put it into my pocket. Even though just the thought of seeing Anubis again makes my stomach clench, I need to text him. Make a plan.

Masoud saunters to my side, setting a cigarette to his lips. He offers me one and I shake my head, the scent turning my gut. 'You and him seem . . . different. Far more attuned to this world than the others we met at Athens House.'

I cross my arms. 'I could say the same about you.'

His eyes darken with interest. 'I'm sure you could. Perhaps we could help one another.'

'Oh, I'm sure you'll need help soon enough,' I scoff. 'But I've got a mysterious sanctum to find.'

'Perhaps I already know where it is,' Masoud says.

'Really? Asked that little devil's trap of yours, did you?'

A wolfish smile crosses his lips. 'Possibly.'

I don't like the way his eyes scan me, like he knows far more about me than he should. Ushum, that demon attached to his side, could feed him information. I still recall the way his voice sounded below the stage during orientation. How he called me Child of Hecate. As far as I'm concerned, the sooner Masoud wears out his favors, the better.

Brushing past him, I head for Anubis' room in the men's wing. I check over my shoulder, making sure Masoud isn't following me. When the coast is clear, I reach the second floor and head for Anubis' door. Finding a mysterious sanctum is not something I plan on doing in the company of a spoiled child of a diplomat with a demon on a crumbling leash.

The door is slightly ajar when I reach it. I push it open, the invitation already unfolded in my hand. But I pause when I enter the room. Anubis leans against his desk, looking at someone sitting on his bed. A girl I don't recognize, with smooth dark skin and a series of complex box braids cascading down her back. A tattoo, a cluster of stars, winks at me from her arm when she pushes herself off his bed.

'Good luck, Jae,' she tells Anubis, brushing by me and out into the hall.

I stand in the doorway, my tongue glued to the roof of my mouth. Anubis stands, grazing his fingertips along his jaw where a shadow of stubble has grown.

'Andy,' he nods at my hand. 'You got the invitation, I gather.'

I nod woodenly. 'Antonia met me in the foyer.'

'Lourdes just delivered mine. We're in the same anthropology lecture.'

I don't respond. Anything that wants to come out of my mouth is petty and jealous. I hate that I feel like that just from seeing a pretty girl in his room.

His cheeks are a little pink as he approaches me. He stops a few paces away, hesitating, like he isn't sure where we stand. I sure as hell don't know.

'She gave me a hint,' Anubis says, clearing his throat.

'What?'

He raises his brows. 'Lourdes. She gave me a hint about the line on the Sophos sanctum, the House of Thales. He was the one who is attributed with saying "know thyself".'

'From the riddle.' I look away, my face curiously hot. 'Did her hint say how to find this mysterious sanctum, then? Or is that all your new friend gave you?'

'Andy,' he sighs. 'It's not like that.'

I give him my sweetest smile. 'I'm sure I have no idea what you mean.'

'That phrase was written on the Temple of Apollo, in Delphi. I think that means the entrance is hidden in the center of the property the school sits on.'

'What makes you think that?' I'm still too busy recalling

the way Lourdes sat on his bed like she was perfectly at home there. Anubis sighs again, drawing my scowl away from his bed and back to his face.

'Delphi was considered the center of the world. The Omphalos Stone, a cylindrical carved rock placed there, represented the navel of the earth.' He raises his eyebrows like I should know this, which only makes me bristle more.

'Perfect,' I say flatly. 'Let's go, then. The meeting starts in less than an hour.'

We walk in silence, the sun slanting low across the sky. It feels wrong to head to a meeting for a secret society while there is still daylight. Perhaps it means that there won't be any dangerous or evil rituals taking place. I doubt it, but a girl can dream.

We reach the end of Appian Way. A park takes up a small section of grass with well-manicured flower beds framed by low stone walls. Beyond it lies the river. Statues of Romulus and Remus flank a stone bridge that crosses the gently churning water. Entering the small park, rose bushes and trees wilt sadly in the slowly cooling air. And just as Anubis said, in the middle of the park is a cylindrical piece of limestone, carved in high relief with a latticework of branches. Immediately, the thrum of magic comes to life in my bones.

I glance at Anubis as we stand in front of the stone. 'Do you feel it? The convergence?'

He shakes his head. 'Nothing.'

For a moment, I feel a thread of pity for him. How strange it must be to lose his connection to his godly powers – he's always had them, even when he was pretending to be Jae for over a decade – and instead only have the same access to magic as a mortal. Turning away from him, I study the stone.

'Do you think it's an "open sesame" kind of thing?'

He chuckles, and the sound sends a shiver of delight down my spine. 'I doubt it. It must be warded, probably enough to divert those without magic away from it.'

I consider the stone, pacing a circle around it. Besides the nearby convergence, nothing appears special about the park. On my third rotation around the rock, I spy a small carving at the base of the omphalos. A tripod of some kind, with curling feet and smoke rising from within, like the stool the Oracle of Delphi sat on. It doesn't look as old as the original carvings. More recent, and less weathered.

Reaching out, I brush the small blemish. A thrill of magic rushes through my arm, concentrating on my new tattoo. With a rattle, the plinth that the omphalos sits on moves backward. Steps appear as stone grinds against stone, and the tattoo on my arm gleams bright silver. With a gasp, I yank my hand back. But my fingers still tingle and light shines through my sleeve. I clamp my hand on it and look up at Anubis.

'I think the note meant that the entrance would know us,' he murmurs, his own tattoo fading back to regular black ink.

Light still creeps through my fingers, and I grit my teeth, trying to control the surge of power in my veins. It calls to the convergence, as if desperate to reach out and meld with it. I take a deep breath and mentally snap the cord between me and it.

'I guarantee whoever is inside this sanctum would have felt that,' Anubis says, the skin around his eyes tight. 'We have to keep your connection to Hecate a secret. The stronger the spell you wield, the more obvious your heritage will be.'

I throw him a glare, rubbing my arm as the silvery glow fades away. 'I can't really help it, you know. It probably has something to do with this university being built right on top of a magic hotspot.'

Anubis takes my hand, and I notice how cold my fingers are, like ice. He shakes his head, a line of worry between his brows. 'They'll want what you have, Andromeda. You can hide what I am, but I doubt we can hide your connection to Hecate.'

My heart hammers in my ribcage. 'If you have any ideas, I'm all ears.'

'Whatever they want us to do down there, let me take control. Your magic is still too volatile, too raw. Use the smallest amount, and I'll take care of whatever the rest of the spell requires.'

His eyes are too deep, too caring to look away from. That ache in my heart, the one that feels like it will never fade, grows deeper. 'If you think it will help,' I mutter, pulling my hand out of his grasp.

'It has to,' he replies.

And together we descend the stairs and into the earth.

While I wasn't entirely sure what to expect in the House of Thales, Sophos' most secret sanctum, it wasn't a crowd of middle-aged people in suits sitting in theater-style boxes above us. Other students, members of Sophos, are already seated in what appears to be a wide underground theater. Red velvet chairs embroidered with gold thread decorate the floor where an orchestra pit would be. And on a slightly raised dais are three thrones facing the audience.

Following the cues of the other members, we file into the rows and sit. The eyes of the older men and women watching from above set my teeth on edge, and my foot taps a rhythm on the lush carpet beneath my shoes. Their boxes are on two balcony levels, and the shadows disguise their faces. I can't tell how many there are, but it seems to be far more than the young students in Sophos. Murmurs ripple through the adults, as if they are commenting on animals at auction. Anubis' eyes meet mine as the lights dim.

Four people emerge from behind the tapestries lining the walls. The tunnel leading into the House of Thales didn't have any offshoots or doors, so I can't tell where the rest of the people in attendance came from. Spotlights kick on, highlighting gentle dust motes in the air before landing on the now occupied seats on the dais.

A boy I don't recognize stands in the shadows behind the thrones. A bodyguard of some kind? Damian Valerius occupies the middle with the authority of a king. He can't be over twenty-two or twenty-three, but he has an aura about him that takes up the entire room. I see it in the way Antonia and Rohan perch in their seats on either side of him, almost unconsciously wary of the power exuding from their leader. Even the adults, the strangers watching us like vultures, seem to adjust uncomfortably, Damian's steel-gray eyes scanning them with slow, determined purpose.

Finally, he nods, the movement barely perceptible. Antonia stands and moves to the front of the dais, the soft spotlight following her and shrouding Damian and Rohan in darkness.

'Welcome to the first meeting of the term for the house of Sophos,' Antonia says. She scans the boxes, and I realize she's addressing them instead of us. 'We have welcomed six new initiates into our ranks. Six of the best and most promising to take our order forward. Romulus has declared that this year will mark the beginning of a new age. For us.' She looks back over her shoulder at Damian. 'For the world.'

Damian moves to stand at the front of the dais. His eyes lift to what must be alumni gathered in the boxes, acknowledging them.

'The Order of the Seven Sages has gone through radical

change since my father died three years ago, and I won the right to become Romulus. But those who have remained loyal have benefitted.' His eyes fall to the students in the orchestra pit. 'This is your future. The tattoos you received bind you to a magic within the convergence that is far more powerful than you could wield on your own. We will train you. Guide you. You will help us achieve our goals, and in return, you will be taken care of well into your future. Sophos is the first house in the Order. If you show promise, you may be invited to initiate into Lector, where knowledge unlike anything you can imagine waits.'

Someone shifts in the shadows behind the chair. The boy I thought was a bodyguard. He has neat auburn hair and pale skin, his face twisted in a murderous scowl that anyone would be hard pressed to miss. But what makes my spine tingle with awareness are the scars and tattoos on his arms. They remind me of Damian. Except this boy wears a grisly scar across his face. It looks deliberate. Painful. It's dark purple, as if it has healed badly. As Damian speaks, the boy's expression grows more and more bitter. Hateful.

This must be Ramsey. The Order's Remus.

'Prometheus will guide you new initiates into our ways. Sophos has an important role in keeping our Order safe from prying eyes, within the school and without. Your duties are to use your strengthened powers to cloak our activities from the outside world. To hide our summoning and protect our interests. Whenever Prometheus calls, you will answer. You will obey. She will guide you, hone your magic. And you will reap the rewards when we see fit.' Damian's eyes glitter in the spotlight. 'Remember what we promised each of you. Your deepest desires, your most lofty ambitions. I will give them to you, as long as you stay loyal.'

I shiver, shrinking back into my seat as the air drops in

temperature. At first, I think I imagine it, the way my fingers go numb and my lips feel heavy. But then my breath frosts before my face and ice cracks across the floor, snaking over the carpet and walls like a tomb.

From the wings of the stage comes a small group of people. A man I estimate to be in his fifties, his face black and blue, brow split and bleeding, is forced to his knees before Damian, at the lip of the dais. Anubis' fingers find mine, and I don't pull away. The ice continues to crawl across the room, radiating from Damian himself.

Two other men hold the beaten victim by the arms, forcing his swollen eyes up to Romulus' face. Damian pulls a bronze dagger from within his jacket. It's curved and heavy, the handle adorned with carvings I can't see from my position. But the kneeling man's eyes widen and through a mess of broken teeth, he mutters something pleadingly.

Damian trails his finger down the blade as he stands over the man. 'The first-born son in each succeeding generation of the four founding families is given to the Order from birth. We are trained in the magic that flows beneath our feet and in our veins. And when it is time for a new Romulus to be chosen, we fight for our title.' He sets the tip of the blade under the man's chin, forcing his neck to be exposed. 'This is Jan Arskell, the former Remus who served my father for three decades. He took part in this very rite himself all those years ago. He understands the sacred duty we have to forge the strongest Romulus we can. The man with the most power. And still he betrayed the Order. He and a group of traitors tried to summon demons to kill me, to steal and bargain. All so his family, *his* son, could take the mantle of leader.'

'Because you are mad!' Jan cries. 'Your plan will doom us all!'

Damian shoves his knee into Jan's stomach, and the older man bends over, gasping. The people in the boxes boo and hiss, hatred so visceral I can feel it as strongly as the ice in the room. I hold on to Anubis' hand even tighter. Ramsey stands, stiff and unmoving, behind Damian's throne. His eyes are black with fury. But he doesn't move, even as I realize this beaten man, Jan, is his father.

'Remember, initiates, the Order is your family now. For the rest of your life, you will benefit from our coffers, our companies. You will become untouchable. But the price for betrayal is death.'

I shut my eyes just as Damian lifts the blade and his face contorts into something inhuman and ugly. I expect a gasp of terror to take over the crowd as a heavy thud signals that Jan Arskell has slumped over, stabbed with the knife and put to death. Instead, a cheer comes from the boxes. My throat is tight as I slowly open my eyes, keeping them trained on the seats in front of me. Even Marco, another brand-new member of this dark world sitting on Anubis' other side, looks drunk on the magic flowing in the air.

The two men drag Jan's dead body off the stage, leaving behind a dark red streak. Damian re-sheaths the bloody knife. Warm air stings my fingers and toes. But I can't stop shivering as I stare at the dark-red blood and the face of Ramsey Arskell as he simmers with rage behind the seats. Damian nods to the boxes, and I hear dozens of feet retreating into the tunnels below the school. The alumni saw what he wanted them to.

A threat. A promise.

When all that remains in the cavern are the new members of Sophos, Antonia stands. Her cheeks are flushed. The power radiating from Damian, from his magic as he plunged the knife ruthlessly into Jan Arskell, is as intoxicating as wine. The dark, heavy press of the spell pushes down on my shoulders. I want to flee this place, run as far as I can. But the tattoo on my arm aches like a phantom pain. And I know I'm trapped.

'Welcome to Sophos,' Antonia murmurs, a smile spreading across her face as she steps into the puddle of blood on the floor without remorse. 'And most of all, welcome to our family.'

11

A few days after my initiation into the Order, I sit in a wide lecture hall, the seats arranged in a U shape, while my philosophy professor stands at the front. It reminds me of an amphitheater in ancient Greece. The inside of the building is cool stone, the floor white marble. The seats pitch sharply downward, and the voice of Dr Kane rings clearly over the sea of students, even though he's a mouse of a man with a tiny voice to match.

'I trust you all enjoyed your Plato reading last night and his thoughts in *Protagoras*,' he says, dimming the lights as the projector overhead rattles to life. 'But now we shift our focus to those who came before Plato, our cornerstone of philosophy. The Seven Sages.'

I fight the urge to clear my throat and readjust in my seat. The tiny folding desk suddenly feels too constricting as seven marble statues grace the screen. The names below the busts aren't as familiar as Plato or Diogenes. But my skin still prickles as I look covertly around the darkened auditorium, searching for faces that show more interest than others. Others that know the importance of those words like I do.

'The lists of the seven change, depending on authorship, but the heart of these wise men, these lawgivers, and their defining work that shifted the very foundations of the western world, remain.' Dr Kane's voice seems to deepen as he speaks, and his thinning hair and wispy mustache look like a disguise as his eyes brighten with something akin to hunger. 'Does anyone know why this group of philosophers is so important?'

Seats creak, and I lean forward. The Order of the Seven Sages takes its name from this group of men. What could they have found so compelling that their society was named after philosophers who died thousands of years ago?

A rustle to my right indicates that someone has raised their hand. Dr Kane nods in their direction, the light from the projector casting long shadows below his cheekbones and eyes.

'The sages are the reason philosophy exists today,' a male student says. 'Their law reforms paved the way for our political systems.'

Dr Kane offers a thin-lipped smile. 'Indeed. But why are these men immortalized in mosaics, in friezes, and preserved in precious literature? Is it simple politics?'

The door at the top of the amphitheater opens, allowing a slant of daylight to cut across the faces of the class.

'If I may, Professor?' Damian asks from the entrance.

Dr Kane's squint changes to a wide-eyed stare. 'Mr Valerius, to what do we owe the honor?'

My fingers curl around the edge of my desk as Damian descends the staircase. Most of the students simply look between the professor and the newcomer, unsure why a student his age is in a foundation philosophy class.

'I have some business with Dr Giatsou in this building, but thought I'd stop by to check on my favorite professor,' Damian says with a slow grin. He reaches the bottom step of the lecture hall and strides easily over to the podium next to Dr Kane.

The older man's cheeks are flushed, and a fine sheen of sweat reflects off his forehead and neck as the light from the projector wavers in the air. 'Of course, of course. Perhaps you can shed some light on this topic for our young first-years.'

Damian waits for Kane to step aside and then leans one elbow on the podium. His sleeves are rolled up halfway, and even from a distance I can make out the dark tattoos, the ancient symbols marking the spaces between his brutal scars. His eyes scan the lecture hall until I swear they land directly on me.

'Seven is a sacred number. An ancient one. Seven days of creation, deadly sins, heavens, chakras, days and seas. And there are the Seven Sages of Greece.' Damian counts them off on his hand, and as he does, I think about the Pleiades, the seven sisters. The seven hills of Rome. What does it all mean?

He continues, 'My family is one of four that broke off from other universities such as St Andrews and Oxford. They were too stifling, too draconian. They left and formed Eidolon, a haven for higher thinking and learning, free of the constraints of the Church. You've all heard the speech at orientation. Think. When did this exodus take place?'

Other students look at each other, unsure.

A girl slowly raises her hand. 'It was at the beginning of the Enlightenment,' she says, looking to our professor for reassurance. 'Europe was . . . awakening. New ideas, political and social, were taking root across the Continent. People wanted freedom from the fear cultivated by the Church.'

'Exactly. The sages were much the same in their day. They fought for social and political change that would benefit many. Myths were no longer convincing enough for the Greeks. The sages provided logic, wisdom and a rational worldview. They offered freedom from oppression, from a wound deep within humanity's bones. The oppression of gods.' Damian's eyes flash in the light, and my chest tightens as his voice takes on a sharp, fervent tone. 'They began the golden age of the classical world, paved the way for

Hellenistic Greece and ultimately Rome. These men fought against the darkness of ignorance, of control, and yet they themselves are semi-mythical, just like their numerology.'

Ignorance and control. Is that what the Order thinks it is doing? Using its knowledge, its skills, to free the world from a second dark age? Damian said that the Order was recently turned on its head after his father, the former Romulus, died and Jan Arskell attempted some sort of coup. What is his plan – one that caused a former Remus to attempt murder – for the school and its students? For the world beyond? The empty eyes of the Seven Sages stare at me from the screen. Waiting for something.

Dr Kane clears his throat in a wet cough, breaking the hold Damian has over the class. I take a deep breath, my lungs finally expanding enough to allow in air. Damian steps back from the podium and reaches out his hand for Kane. He grabs the man's hand and shakes it firmly, leaning in and saying a few words in his ear, too quiet to be picked up by the microphone. Dr Kane's face pales and, impossibly, he looks even more sweaty as Damian pulls away and offers a smile to the class. And then he leaves through the door beside the chalkboard.

'Very good,' Dr Kane says, mopping at his forehead with a handkerchief, his face twisted. 'Let us move on to some excerpts from Herodotus on the subject of the sages.'

Even as Kane tries to move back into the rhythm of his lecture, the very air seems off. Thick and poisoned with promise. And when he reaches out his hand to write on the chalkboard, the same hand Damian shook, a flash of dark ink shows in his palm. A tattoo, like a brand, the skin around it red and angry. It's a dagger, the tip dripping blood as it pierces a heart.

The mark of treachery.

12

The smell of paper and ink is everywhere as I shut my massive textbook on Roman archaeology. Out of my three courses, I find this one the most enjoyable. It's one that I don't need Violet's endless help with. Something I'm good at, for once. Though I wonder if learning about sites like Pompeii and Jerash are worth it as the rest of my assigned group packs up their bags, wearing the same bleary-eyed expression as me.

'We'll meet one more time before the presentation next week,' says Daniella, our group of four's de facto leader. She's from Edinburgh, as local as any Eidolon student can be, and is outspoken and intelligent in a way that reminds me of how Violet was before Ravenswood. 'Tanvir and Nour, you two make sure we cover Pax Romana and how individual conquered territories displayed their culture despite the empire's expansion, especially in Timgad.'

Our two classmates nod dutifully as they stand and prepare to leave the study room.

Daniella slings her backpack over her shoulder as Tanvir and Nour slip out the door. 'Andy, did you manage to finish the section on the Third Punic War and Rome's control of Africa?'

I close my laptop, more than ready to finish this project and disappear to my dormitory. 'I uploaded it last night.'

'Perfect!' She holds the door open, and we both file out, passing a long stretch of other study rooms, their whiteboards covered in scribbles and charts.

Daniella looks at her phone as we step outside into the chilly night. The university is quiet, the narrow sidewalks empty. But a lamp burns in almost every dormitory window, outlining hunched shoulders and glowing laptops.

'You know, I'm heading into Idyllwood to meet some friends at the pub.' She tucks her phone into her back pocket and looks at me. 'Why don't you come?'

I blink a few times. 'It's getting late. I should probably go to bed.' The truth is, I can't imagine going to a pub with my peers, pretending like I didn't witness a murder only a few nights ago in a cavern below the school.

'Come on, it'll be fun! You're always working so hard. I never see you around town.'

'I don't know anyone,' I protest, my fingers tightening around my bag.

Daniella laughs. 'You'll know me. And besides, another boy from our class will be there. It's good to get out. Studies aren't everything, even at Eidolon.'

She watches me expectantly, still smiling. I hesitate, glancing once down the cobblestone road that leads back to my college. It would be so simple to return and check for messages from the Order. To worry about what Antonia and Sophos will have me do. What Anubis is doing and who he's with. But Daniella is nice. Over the last week working on our project, she has reminded me that I always enjoyed history. That I haven't had a friend since Munia at Ravenswood.

Finally, her smile and expectant eyes win out, and I find myself saying, 'Sure. One beer can't hurt.'

'Exactly,' she says, turning toward the front gates and the small road that leads directly to Idyllwood. 'You're in Scotland now. Need to take advantage of being an eighteen-year-old American who can legally drink!'

We laugh and chat about school and classes. The university

itself and the gossip in our individual colleges. By the time we reach the sleepy town and the low lamplight surrounding the pub, I feel almost like a normal student. Like this is an average night for me, exploring a picturesque town.

Inside the pub the air is stuffy from too many bodies and the endless puffing of vape pens. Daniella jostles at the bar, grabbing two drinks for us before she rejoins me by the door.

'My friends are at the table by the window.' She points and I follow behind her, weaving through other students who are laughing and shouting over each other to be heard.

A round table by a window facing the back gardens is jammed full of people. I follow Daniella as she sets our drinks down and squeezes into a chair with me beside her.

'Everyone, this is Andy. She's in my Roman architecture class. Andy, these are some girls from my college.' She rattles off names I'm sure I'll forget immediately and then turns to a boy half-hidden by shoulders and empty glasses. 'This is Ramsey Arskell. He's in the same class as us. How's your project going, by the way?'

The careful smile I've had on my face slips as soon as I make eye contact with the boy. Beyond the dark auburn hair and brown eyes is a long scar along his jaw. Blood roars in my ears as he answers Daniella's question, his eyes slipping over me, clearly not recognizing me.

Why would he? I was sitting in a darkened auditorium as Damian Valerius stabbed his father through the heart. I can smell blood as clearly as I did that night, while the others at the table talk and smile. Ramsey joins in, responding when asked a question, but otherwise seems quiet and reserved. Anytime he smiles it doesn't reach his eyes.

I can't grasp any of the conversation, can't taste the beer on my tongue as I force myself to drink and act naturally.

But my skin prickles whenever Ramsey says something. Whenever he looks at me.

'You were at the Vespers party last week, weren't you?' a girl on my other side asks.

'Oh,' I stammer, half choking on my next swallow of beer. 'I was. Sorry, I don't remember seeing you there.'

She shrugs. 'It was pretty packed in there. Did you get in? I never got the invitation to live at Leonidas Court or make a donation. It kind of sucks, though. I always wanted to be part of those secret but not-so-secret clubs.'

'The Vespers? What do you know about them, Marcella?' Ramsey asks, his eyes finally focusing on me. There's a spark there as he leans his elbows on the table.

Marcella, the girl at my side, raises an eyebrow at him flirtatiously. 'Come on, you graduate in the spring, Ramsey. Your family founded Eidolon. You really mean to tell me you haven't heard about the school's most famous secret society?'

He tips his head back, taking a long swallow of his drink. I notice for the first time that the tips of three of his fingers are missing. 'Not a very secret society if everyone knows about them, including first-years.'

'A girl in our college got in,' Daniella says. 'She moved out after the party last week and into Leonidas Court. She says she already has a full list of former Vesper alumni contacts for internships.'

'Why don't you tell us about them?' Marcella asks Ramsey. 'You know everything about this place. I've heard all kinds of rumors about the Vespers. How much of it is true?'

Daniella rolls her eyes. 'There is no way they actually do blood sacrifices on the full moon.'

'How would you know?' Marcella challenges. 'You weren't even invited to the party.'

'I think we'd hear about sacrifices in a place as small as Idyllwood,' Daniella answers. 'And besides, I think it's more likely that the Vespers just get away with their crazy parties because they donate more to the school than anyone else. It's just a privilege thing.'

My skin prickles as they continue to bicker back and forth. Ramsey's eyes remain on me the whole time, and I clutch my empty glass with ice-cold hands.

'Well?' Marcella faces me. 'How much of it is true?'

'W-what?' I stammer.

'The rumors. You got into the Vespers, didn't you?'

Ramsey leans back in his chair. 'What's it like then, Andy? These secret societies embedded in the school?'

His smile makes my pulse pound hard in my neck. Is this a test of some kind? A way to see if I'll remain loyal to the Order? My Pleiades tattoo doesn't burn or itch, but I harden my jaw anyway. If he can act calm and collected after witnessing his father murdered right in front of him, I don't want anything to do with Ramsey Arskell.

'I wouldn't know. I didn't get into the Vespers.'

As the conversation steers away from the clandestine activities of the Vespers, I feel Ramsey's eyes on me. As if he can see the tattoo marking me as one of them. Property of the Order. Another soul signed over to the devil.

It's Sunday night, three weeks since I entered Eidolon. Between my classes and endless papers, I haven't seen Anubis in days. After the first meeting for our house, we parted ways, the only two initiates who seemed horrified by the grisly murder performed on a former leader. Everyone else was hungry to prove themselves. They murmured together afterwards, eager to show that they could ascend through the ranks. And I wonder what the Order has promised them all in return. What slogging through Sophos grunt work will gain them in the end.

Since I've been initiated into Sophos, I've been run ragged by Antonia. Anytime a spell in the upper houses goes wrong, or someone in Idyllwood becomes suspicious of strange purchases of rare herbs and parts of dead animals for spells, or reports students meeting in town late at night, Antonia summons us. At all hours of the day or night, we are expected to answer her call. Often, we work in pairs, using spells Antonia taught us. Sometimes we must banish a rogue demon escaping from a summoning circle. Perhaps orchestrate a scapegoat from the Vespers to take the blame for property damage resulting from a spell gone wrong. It is Sophos' job to clean up the messes that get too big, and to grease the hands of local officials when things get too rowdy.

Basically, we're the janitors of the Order.

In the last few days, I've wiped the memories of three different pub owners to distract them from pressing charges against the school for extensive damages. I've hexed local cops to get rich and influential Order members out of the drunk tank, and made more good-luck talismans that I can count. The payroll of the Order is extensive, and it seems everyone in town has their hand out for favors, money, or small magical tokens in exchange for silence.

Rain pelts down on my shoulders, and I tug my hood over my hair. Antonia's message was brief and crisp. I was to meet her at the Horse and Dagger pub in Idyllwood to clean up a mess left by a foolish, newly initiated Lector before the cops come. No other details. So, it's midnight, and I walk alone in the dark to the village as rain drips down my hair and I lose out on another night of sleep.

The street lamps of Idyllwood grow stronger. It's the

same pub I went to with Daniella and her friends. Eidolon students pour out the door, leaning against walls and smoking cigarettes. Others nurse their drinks on the covered patio as music thuds inside. Antonia's rigid posture stands out against the stumbling drunks around her. I weave through the crowds and stand under the pub's sign.

'You're late,' she says.

I scowl, flicking water from my glasses. 'You texted me when I was about to go to sleep.'

'You can sleep when you've proven your loyalty to Sophos.' Antonia jerks her chin to the overgrown garden at the back of the pub. 'You and another initiate are to clean up the mess back there. I'll return the Lector member to Ibis Park to meet with Thoth for his punishment.'

'Can't you just say Rohan? What's the point in using these titles when we know each other's names?' I rub my brow, an endless headache beating at my temples.

Antonia scowls. 'Because titles are important in the Order. If I speak to Damian, I call him Romulus. It denotes respect, and deference to his power and control.'

Instead of answering, I roll my eyes, my head aching too much to comment.

I follow Antonia behind the pub. A small wooden gate, the iron hinges rusted almost beyond recognition, groans as we enter the garden. Thick ivy coats the wall, and overgrown hedges stick out in all directions. The grass is lumpy and uneven, and every rosebush is wilted and sad. As far as gardens go, it's pathetic at best.

'What are we cleaning up, exactly?' I ask, hunching my shoulders as the rain comes down harder.

'A Lector member tried out a spell for augury, summoning a demon with a bit of blood harvested from an innocent girl.' She guides me around the corner, into a dark, weed-choked

133

tunnel of greenery. The rain doesn't slip through the thick branches, so I push my hood back and clean my glasses. A figure crouches next to a bundle of what I assume to be garbage heaped next to the arbor.

'Turns out he has no idea how to control a demon and the spell went sideways, killing the girl. So now, you and Masoud,' Antonia says, her tone sharp as she scolds me silently, 'are to take care of *that*.'

I follow her finger to the bundle and Masoud kneeling next to it. For once, he doesn't throw a cocky grin my way. He looks somber, which is not an emotion I ever thought I'd see from him. The hairs on the back of my neck stand up. Masoud flicks a black tarp aside and my vision swims, blurring the outline of a dead body. I stagger back a step, my stomach churning.

A pale hand lies against the grass, blood and dirt caked under the painted nails. My blood runs cold, and I nearly fall over as I look higher at the dead girl's face.

It's Daniella.

'What is this?' I demand, turning to Antonia.

She raises one brow, her eyes narrowed. 'A complication.'

'The girl is dead,' Masoud says, his voice flat. 'What do you want us to do about it?'

Antonia's eyes snap. 'I want you to get rid of the body. Throw her in a lake, a river, a ravine. I don't care. Just use the spells I taught you to scrub all the evidence from her body.'

'This Lector member murdered a girl,' I say, my breath sharp as my hands shake at my side. 'And you're just going to take them back to campus like *nothing* happened? I know her. She goes to Eidolon. How can you do this? The school will find out!'

Antonia steps closer, nearly pinning me against the sharp branches of the overgrown arbor. Her eyes are dark, unfeeling, as she looms over me. Slowly, my throat closes, like an invisible hand is pressing against the tender flesh. My magic rears on instinct, and it takes every ounce of will-power I have not to let it free and send her hurling into the night sky.

'I usually find your little comments amusing, Andy,' she says, the grip of her spell on my neck growing firmer. 'But it's time you learn your place in this society. You show prom-ise, I can't deny that. But I am your Prometheus. I guide you in the art of low magic. And as your Prometheus, I am tell-ing you to get rid of the body. Thoth and I will take care of the board and any suspicions in the school.'

I clench my jaw, the lack of air making Antonia's face blur. Hatred burns in my gut as she finally lets her control snap, and I fall to my knees, gasping for air.

'Don't let your feelings over this girl cloud your judgment, Andy. Or you may regret the consequences.' She smiles her regular cold, empty grin that sends a jolt of nausea through me. 'I'll see you both later. And if you do well with this task, perhaps I can put a good word in with Thoth while I am there.' Antonia spins on her heel and walks toward the pub, no doubt looking for the murderer so she can ensure they return safely to the school and walk away from any justice. I watch her go, my eyes narrowed with hatred. Her figure disappears inside, and as she slips around a corner, I catch sight of a familiar face trailing her.

Ramsey, his eyes shadowed by the hood of a raincoat, hugs the outside wall of the pub and disappears into the crowd on the patio, following Antonia as she goes.

I tear my gaze away when he disappears, and get to my feet with shaking fingers. Masoud looks down at the tarp, an expression of contemplation on his face. I can barely control my ragged breathing as I stand beside the body of

Daniella, my lips trembling as I push Antonia and Ramsey out of my mind.

'I was in the pub when it happened,' he says, head tilted to the side as he considers the pale hand lying there. 'House Lector summons powerful, ancient demons. Did you know that? They're far more frightening than the imps we deal with in Sophos. Apparently, Paulo was eager and curious to try his hand in an unsanctioned summoning to try and read the future. The only way to reach a demon with that power is to sacrifice unwilling human blood. A young female, preferably.'

My tongue tastes bitter as I snarl at him, 'Don't you have any shame? I know her.'

He shrugs, head cocked to the side as he studies the tarp. 'She was in the wrong place at the wrong time. And you heard Antonia, she and Thoth will deal with the board. A murdered Eidolon student is a complication, but she doesn't have magic, and she isn't connected to the Order or the Vespers. I already visited the local constable earlier this week. He owes me a favor. Antonia will appreciate it if I call it in, I'm sure.'

'Fine.' I shut my eyes, still struggling to breathe. 'Now how do you suppose we take care of this in the most respectful way we can, considering she was murdered for a damn *curiosity*?'

Masoud looks away from the body for the first time. 'Aren't you at all interested about the other houses? What they're capable of?'

I look down at the body, forcing my eyes to climb higher until I see her face. The earth beneath my feet trembles as anger roars through me like high tide. The leaves on each branch shiver, shedding raindrops onto our skin. A thread of my power slips through the careful armor I've built around myself, and before I can tamp it down, the vines around the arbor snap free, lashing the air. Masoud curses and dives aside as I squeeze my eyes shut and struggle to control myself. But my magic feeds on the anger, the despair I feel at being trapped in this Order, forced to cover up drunken accidents and now the murder of a girl I know. One who was kind to me. Wanted to be my friend. I open my eyes and they land on the pale, blood-crusted hand. To think, that night at the pub with her, I felt normal for a moment.

The arbor lies in splinters around me, the vines sheared into pieces and littering the ground. A perfect circle sits around me and the body of Daniella. Masoud mutters a string of angry words at me in Arabic as he picks himself up from the tattered remains of the arbor and comes to my side.

There is no such thing as normal for me, no matter how badly I want it. Because everyone around me is at the mercy of the Order until I can find a way to tear it apart.

'Now we have to get rid of the body *and* this mess,' he hisses. I shoot him a warning glare as he spreads his hands, ready to summon power from the convergence to wipe away all shreds of evidence. But he pauses, looking sideways at me. 'How did you do that?'

I get to my feet and keep my expression hard. 'I don't know what you're talking about,' I lie, ignoring the pointed, disbelieving look he fires my way. 'What are you waiting for? Aren't you in a hurry to impress Prometheus?'

He narrows his eyes but murmurs an incantation in Latin, one of the many Antonia has drilled into our heads over the last weeks of endless training and clean-up duties. The leaves melt into the grass as the splintered wood trellises turn into dust, the rain washing them away. I'm sure under the tarp that any fingerprints or traces of DNA have vanished into nothing as well.

Guilt sits in my chest like a boulder.

Masoud drops his hands and looks at the bundled body. 'You heard Antonia. Let's go to the river and drop her off the bridge.'

My fingers curl into fists, threatening to unleash another wave of pure power. 'No. We're going to take her back to the school grounds and bury her behind the abbey. Don't you have any respect for the dead?'

Masoud sighs, crouching to wrap the plastic around the body so that she's completely covered. 'I think you are too soft for a society like this if you cannot handle a single body from a mistaken spell.'

'Murdering girls for no reason is something any decent person would oppose,' I say through clenched teeth, and stoop down to carefully pick up her legs as Masoud hefts the front of her body. We head out of the garden, through the back gate, my hands shaking from the cold and the feel of a still-warm body wrapped in plastic beneath my fingers.

The uneven cobblestones threaten to trip us up with every step as we struggle through the darkened streets of Idyllwood, keeping to narrow, abandoned alleys to avoid anyone seeing us. We leave the town and head for the grassy field where St Mary's Abbey squats. We're silent for so long, our shoes slipping on wet grass and our fingers losing their grip on the slick plastic, that I almost forget what I said. But then the half-sunk graveyard at the back of the abbey appears and Masoud's voice interrupts the unending patter of rain.

'You are no stranger to magic,' he grunts as we set down the body of Daniella. 'Neither am I. We both chose to attend Eidolon because we are ambitious. I want more power within my family in Jordan. I'm a distant nephew of the king, and without much magic, I'll be relegated to a tiny pension or serving in the army. The Order is the only thing that can set me apart, grant me power in a world like this. They've promised me an ambassadorship between Jordan and the UK if I prove myself. So, you call it murder. Perhaps they call it a necessary sacrifice.'

Listing headstones, half consumed by earth and lichen, stand out like broken teeth in the forgotten churchyard. The shell of the abbey, its glassless windows like gaping eyes, looms over us, and the rotten wooden chapel from a more recent century creaks in the wind. A rusted shovel leans against a warped section of iron fencing, and I mutter a quick spell, a little unnerved at how quickly the spade obeys my command and begins digging in the soft earth.

'The powerful only say a sacrifice is necessary if they are not the ones bleeding,' I say, my voice breaking a little at the end.

Masoud is silent as the shovel continues its work and the rain grows heavier. When the grave is deep enough, I grab the shovel from midair and prop it against the twisted metal fencepost again.

'The storm is getting stronger,' Masoud warns, glancing up at the sky. 'Let's finish this and report back to Antonia. I don't want any blemishes on my record if I'm going to impress Rohan and reach Lector before my second year.'

My teeth grind together as I try not to set the entire school on fire with a single spell. Masoud, Antonia and the other initiates remind me of Tooth and Talon. Young, sheltered people with their first taste of life-altering power. They're cutting their teeth on animal sacrifice and charms, but the moment their hand stops another human's heart, they're irrevocably changed. Twisted into something cruel. I can't get revenge for every girl that the Order has undoubtedly killed, at least not yet. But I can show Masoud the true cost of what he thinks he wants.

I taste rain on my tongue and dirt in my teeth as I grab the corner of the tarp and yank it backward. The pale, life-less body of Daniella stands out starkly against the trampled grass and empty graveyard.

Masoud flinches, his face draining of color as he takes a step back, fingers pressed to his lips. 'My God! Her – her stomach!'

The smell of copper stings my nostrils as I continue to stare at Masoud. But from the corner of my eye, I can see the poor girl's pale limbs. Her blood-stained dress. The gash across her abdomen and the gore threatening to spill free.

I reach into my pocket and withdraw a coin. It's just a simple ten-pence piece, no magic or spells interwoven with the metal, but it will do the trick. Allow her to cross the river. To rest. Ignoring the way my fingers tremble, I carefully open her lips and set the coin on her tongue.

Masoud makes a retching sound. 'What are you doing?'

Slowly, I stand, rain rolling down my cheeks, mixing with the heat of tears. I don't even have to focus. I simply watch as my magic cradles the girl's body, gently wrapping her in the tarp once more and setting her in the bottom of the lonely grave.

'Call *this* a sacrifice if it soothes your conscious –' I motion to the graveyard, the blood – 'but we are going to bury her with respect.'

He makes no further complaint as I hand him the shovel. Magic doesn't seem to be the right thing as I stare down at the lonely grave. There are no flowers. No mourners. No solemn words. But at the very least, Daniella, this girl whose life was stolen, will get the dignity of a burial in a church-yard. Even if I can't get her true justice yet. The sound of the damp earth hitting the tarp as Masoud gets to work feels like a blow to my ribs each time. But I watch. Because someone has to.

By the time Masoud heaps the last bit of grave dirt in

place, the rain has lessened to a drizzle, and mist has risen around the river, spilling over the hills and surrounding the abbey. He drops the shovel and doubles over, hands on his knees as he gags and spits into the grass.

'Ready to go?' I ask coolly, my jaw tight as I watch him.

He wipes his mouth with the back of one hand. 'Can't you smell that?'

'She's buried,' I hiss. 'Maybe you're smelling a guilty conscience.'

Masoud groans again, his face twisted in disgust. 'No, it's worse than that. Can't you smell it?'

The anger knotting in my belly turns to ice. My breath comes in shallow gasps as the scent, one I am all too familiar with, grows. Death and rotten flesh. Curdling blood and ash. My eyes are pulled against my will to the abbey. The fog is so thick it obscures almost every fallen stone, every arch. But something more tangible than the mist stands in an open window. Wings, twisting horns, and a crooked spine.

'What have you done?' I whisper. I grab Masoud's arm, wrenching him to my side.

'What are you talking about?' he hisses, pushing me away.

I nearly fall to my knees and throw up what little remains in my stomach as the smell becomes so pungent my eyes water. 'You summoned your demon earlier tonight when we were in Idyllwood, didn't you? The wards on your devil's trap have broken, he's free!'

Masoud coughs, covering his nose with his sleeve. 'How – how did you know about him?'

My skin chills, like a fever is coursing through my system. The temperature drops, the mist growing thicker. I curse under my breath, grabbing at Masoud again. The smell is overwhelming, reminding me of Ossivorus. A powerful demon without a tether.

'Stop it!' he insists, batting my hand away so he can take out the bronze disk. 'He is bound to me. I control him!'

But Masoud's voice quakes, because the bronze devil's trap that once bound a powerful demon to Masoud is cracked and broken. The ancient wards etched into the surface have finally fallen. His magic is too weak to keep someone as powerful as Ushum in check.

A deep laugh, like clashing rocks, rumbles from the depths of the earth beyond the graveyard. My stomach knots as the cold in my body seeps into every pore, every cell. I haven't felt fear like this in a year, not since I stared down Ossivorus. But I feel it now. The way my teeth chatter involuntarily, my muscles so coiled and tense I can't open my fists.

'Your blood, little mortal,' the demon calls. 'It smells so sweet.'

The mist grows thicker, reaching toward us like hands. My mind races as I try to come up with a plan, a spell. But it's too late. The fog, a telltale sign I should have recognized as an omen, wraps around a winged humanoid figure walking from the depths of the abbey.

Masoud makes a strangled sound in his throat, his feet slipping on the wet grass as he tries to move behind me. 'Th-that's Ushum.'

The scent of the Underworld wafts from the mist, spilling from the abbey. A liminal space, the endless empty arches in a place marking life and death.

'You smell of sacrifice, little ones,' Ushum purrs, his voice echoing off the hills and trees. 'Tell me, girl, have you brought my mortal captor for me to feast upon? An atonement for my centuries of torment? Let us strike a deal so that I can kill the boy and grant you endless riches as a reward.' Ushum draws nearer, moving leisurely, like he has all the time in the world to tear us apart and pick our bones from his teeth.

I lurch back, struggling to pull myself from the web of terror the demon casts. Even though my fingertips are so cold I can barely move them, I grab Masoud by the shoulders, shaking him hard.

'We have to run,' I say, my voice ragged, like I've already raced a marathon. 'Get to the school, to the sanctum.'

'How?' Masoud trembles like a leaf, his eyes so wide the whites reflect the small amount of light shining down on the graveyard. 'He could kill us as soon as we turn our backs!'

I grit my teeth, wishing Anubis was here. But I'm alone with nothing but my magic, the very thing that paints a target on my back for demons wanting deals from my blood. 'Just get to the school grounds. We should be safe from him there, and we can call for help from Antonia.'

If Eidolon is anything like Ravenswood, the convergence below its foundations should ward off demons that have not been summoned. Charms and protections are built into every stone, every brick. But we aren't on school grounds yet. And the river separates us from our only chance of survival.

'Andy,' Masoud whimpers, his knees buckling.

I curse, trying to counter his weight as the soft, wet grass threatens to topple me next. Tearing my eyes from our escape route, the bridge over the river, I feel like crumpling to the grass too. Slowly, agonizingly, the mist releases the demon.

He looks much taller without the tether binding him to the devil's trap. His body is twisted, reminding me of an ancient tree trunk, matching the bent wings on his back. His horns form spikes around his leathery skin like a grisly crown. Each finger is tipped with a long, wicked talon.

He stops a few hundred feet from the graveyard, the

peaks of the ruined abbey piercing the mist behind him. His gaze, eyes as red as blood, falls on us. 'I thought I smelled your magic from within my trap, daughter of Hecate,' he croons, licking his lips with a long, forked tongue. 'Ah, but to experience your powers without a barrier. This whelp and his family have bound me for centuries – forcing me to grant them favors in return for mere drops of blood to sustain me. Feed him to me, and I will bind myself to you. Think of all the things I could show you about the goddess that created your blood. All I could give to you. Power over death. Over the ones that hold the god's fate in their hands.'

Masoud makes another strangled, choking sound as he all but clings to my side.

'Sorry,' I say, my lips numb from cold and fear. 'I'm not interested in deals.'

We have to run. But the graveyard is at least a quarter of a mile away from the bridge. We'll have to cross the river on foot. It's our only chance. I try to remember things Anubis has said, Violet too. And a plan cobbles itself together in the back of my mind.

'Do not be so hasty in declining my offer, little one.' The demon grins, and another wave of nauseating fear washes over me. 'They call me Ushum, bringer of pestilence. Of turmoil and fear. For thousands of years, I have never found a mortal worthy of my knowledge. But I can smell the magic on you and finally broke free of the spell on my prison, and followed your powers here, where the veil is so thin I could pierce it with a claw.'

'We don't need a demon.' Without bothering to ask, I reach over and grab the devil's trap from Masoud's trembling fist. 'I advise you to return to the Underworld willingly, before you force me to rebind you in your prison for a thousand years.'

I move back a step, dragging Masoud with me. A warped iron gate juts into my hip, and I fumble with the rusted hinges until we're free of the cemetery. Ushum narrows his crimson eyes, his twisted body tensing, as if to pounce. My heart flies to my throat as he lowers his head, baring long fangs, like a lion, as he curls his lips back.

'You threaten me, child?' He lowers his horns, long, distorted limbs bending. 'Your blood, even unwillingly spilled, will grant me more power than you can imagine. And I will ensure Masoud and his entire family suffers painfully for what they have done.'

Just as the demon tenses, ready to fling himself down the hill, I grab Masoud and turn him toward the river.

'Run,' I yell, shoving him as hard as I can. 'Get to the center of the river.'

His face, even paler than before, blanches. 'W-what?'

I don't have time to explain. With another shove, I send him tumbling down the steep incline. Ushum's roar rattles my bones, my teeth. The demon hunches on all fours and hurls himself down the hill. I take a gasp of air and lift my hands, letting myself sink into the magic thrumming in the convergence. I wind my power within its branches, letting it swell painfully in my bones. And with a cry, I release a torrent of my magic at Ushum.

An ear-piercing scream shatters the night as he stumbles, his limbs bending inward like a dying spider. He crashes into the metal remnants of the cemetery's fence. Black blood drips from multiple wounds on his body. Parts of his skin are charred, as though my magic burned him. He groans in pain, joints bending the wrong way as he tries to gather himself to his full height.

I don't wait to see the full extent of the damage. I spin on my heel and run, eyes trained on Masoud's staggering form and the bend of the river ahead. Ushum's screams mix with the thud of his limbs tearing into the grassy hill. I focus on the way my powers are coiled like a snake, ready to strike. The warmth rushing through my limbs, better than an adrenaline high as I reach Masoud's side. I feel strong. Unstoppable.

'He's going to kill us!' Masoud moans as we stumble onto the slick stones at the water's edge.

The heat of my spell, one torn from somewhere deep within me, cools instantly. Masoud's fear, the devil's trap in my hand, it reminds me of fighting Ossivorus with Violet. The way her magic was like a drug, a cure to all her earthly troubles, even as it stole bits and pieces of her very being. I glance over my shoulder, the dark body of Ushum dripping black blood as he vaults over the cemetery gate.

'We're not going to die,' I assure Masoud, jumping down onto the shore with a jarring leap. The riverbanks drop sharply to the swirling dark water, tall grasses bent over the sides like rib bones. 'Hurry, we need to swim to the middle of the river.'

'W-why?' he stammers, teeth chattering from the cold even as he obeys and follows me into the frigid water.

I gasp instinctively as the water closes over my chest and shoulders, kicking hard against the current as it tries to drag us the other way, back toward Idyllwood. My clothes feel heavy as we struggle to the middle of the rushing river. Masoud gasps and flails next to me, reaching for my shoulders to anchor himself against the flow.

'Let go,' I demand, my numb fingers scrabbling over the devil's trap as I bring it to my face. My chin barely clears the surface, and the toe of my shoe, wedged between two rocks, hardly keeps me in place.

'Hey!' he cries, his fear momentarily forgotten as he sees the bronze disk. 'What are you doing with that?'

The trap grows hot in my hands, but I ignore the sting-ing as the metal turns orange in the center, shedding sparks that fizzle as they hit the water. Ushum hisses, spittle flying from his sharp teeth as he crawls to the edge of the river. Masoud makes a squawking sound of fear, jerking backward like he's going to head for the opposite bank. With a curse, I use my free hand and grab his ankle, pulling him back with all my strength.

'Demons can't cross moving water,' I shout, even as Ushum tests the limits of his powers. One long arm and its many joints reach out like feelers. A talon touches the dark water and he roars in pain, withdrawing sharply.

Masoud splutters, flopping like a fish as his clothes drag him down. 'Then let's get to the other bank!'

With another heave, I pull Masoud back to the safety of the current buffeting around us. He looks like a wet dog, his hair plastered to his head, his lips pale as he struggles to keep his head above water.

'Little human,' Ushum calls from the bank across from us, his horns blocking the moonlight as he stretches to his full height. 'You cannot stay there all night.'

'What are you doing, Andy?' Masoud whimpers, his eyes falling to the devil's trap in my hand, growing redder and brighter. The symbols glow white as the spells woven into them unwind one by one.

'Rewriting the curse to trap Ushum in this vessel forever.' I'll have to find a priest of some kind to bless it, but it should hold him until then. I grit my teeth as the devil's trap explodes into sparks, a tether of dark smoke rising high into the air. Ushum cries out in rage as my spell continues to form, new symbols etching into the burning hot disk in my hand. Water splashes over my nose and mouth as the demon curses, reaching his inhumanly long arm out over the river, ignoring the way his skin blisters and smokes. Masoud screams in fear, his body slipping from my grasp.

'No!' Ushum screams, the sound unearthly in the night. 'I will not have you thwart my revenge, daughter of Hecate!'

I pull my foot free of the gap in the rocks, the devil's trap tucked in one hand, and pump my arms hard, desperate to reach Masoud. But fighting the current makes my arms and legs weak and cold. Numbness spreads to my fingers, and I clutch hard at the devil's trap. Masoud dives under the water as Ushum reaches out his claws again.

He's going to drown. And so am I, if I can't complete my spell over the devil's trap.

Water closes over my head and I thrash for the surface. I see blurred images of Masoud struggling as the water carries him closer to the bank where Ushum stalks. Surfacing again, I paddle hard, coughing as something catches my attention. A human figure, a lanky boy standing near the gates of the cemetery. Ramsey.

Another splash of water mists my face, but I swear I feel warmth in my bones. Like a spell is chasing away the frigid threat of hypothermia. Something smells hot, like burning charcoal.

Ushum howls in pain, cradling an arm to his chest. I finally reach Masoud, my hand closing around his shirt. I yank him back against me as another spell whips through the air. Smoke curls from Ushum as his skin sizzles. But it isn't Masoud or me causing the pain. It's Ramsey.

He meets my eyes as he hurls another spell at the demon. It collides with his back, sending him closer to the damp bank. Again, a hot bolt of magic pushes the demon closer. I kick against the current as I realize what Ramsey must be doing.

'Ushum!' I cry as he turns around to see who is attacking. 'You want Masoud? Come and get him!'

My arms and legs are tired from fighting the current to keep myself and Masoud afloat. But as Ushum turns toward me, I shove Masoud away.

'Andy!' Masoud screams as the river carries him away from me. Ushum's eyes turn hungry as he reaches for Masoud's head. But just as he does, Ramsey hits him with a final bolt of magic, shoving the demon close to the water and sending him off balance. Before Ushum can grasp Masoud as the current carries him by, I grab the demon's leathery leg and use all my weight to drag him into the water. With a howl of pain, Ushum drops into the river.

Bubbles stream from my nose and mouth as Ushum's claws dig into my skin. We tumble, head over heels, as the river sweeps us away. My lungs burn, and I use my elbow to dig into Ushum's flesh. He releases me and I struggle to the surface, gasping a mix of air and water.

Pain lances through my shoulder, and I jerk backward as Ushum yanks his talon free from my arm. Despite the water burning my throat and the pain growing stronger in my shoulder, I reach out wildly, until my fingers brush grass. With a cry, I grab a fistful and wind it around my fingers until my body jerks to a stop. Ushum flails, his taloned hands grasping my ankles wildly.

'Return the devil's trap, mortal!' Ushum cries, his body twisting in agony as he hangs onto me, his only hope of freeing himself from his new prison: the river. If he lets go, he runs the risk of being torn to pieces. But if he uses me to reach the bank, he could pursue Masoud while I drown. The blood oozing from the wound in my shoulder catches my attention. And I meet the demon's eyes.

I tilt my chin up to keep water from flowing into my nose and mouth. 'I will grant you a portion of my blood to feed you, willingly and without a binding ceremony, if you remain in the Underworld forever, never to harm or contact Masoud or his family again! You can have your devil's trap if you agree to these terms.'

Ushum's body contorts again, silver light radiating out from his body and shining in the water like a torch. I grit my teeth. The pain in my shoulder from the wound, and the scream of my muscles fighting against an entire river with a demon clinging to my leg, grows unbearable. But I clench my jaw and breathe hard, desperate to last just a moment longer. A figure moving along the riverbank, back toward Idyllwood, catches my attention. Ramsey.

I kick at Ushum, ready to decide for him. But then, through a gurgling mess of blood and water, the demon howls, 'I accept your deal, daughter of Hecate!'

With a cry of pain, I let go of the grass with my right hand, my pulse pounding in my injured shoulder. I reach out and grasp Ushum's bony hand in mine. Blood defies all physics as it gathers in the water, trailing down my arm and fingers until it touches the demon's skin. The effect of the deal is instantaneous. With a shockwave of magic, his body is hurled from the river onto the bank.

The sound of the demon's flesh sizzling fills the air as Ushum writhes from his time in the water. But with my blood in Ushum's veins, his wounds heal quickly. The reek of death and rot fills my nostrils as flames, gray as ash, erupt in an intricate circle around Ushum. His blood-red eyes meet mine, and I throw the devil's trap as hard as I can. He catches it, crushing it into his fist with hatred burning in his gaze. And then he's gone, leaving nothing but thick black blood and a scorch mark on the earth.

13

Water drips from my clothes. I shiver, arms wrapped around my middle. Sodden grass squelches beneath my feet as I struggle over the riverbank. The sky is brightening to the east, and the clouds from the storm have fled. I find Masoud at the crook of the river across from the cemetery. He lies on the bank, mud streaking his skin, coughing and shivering. When he hears my footsteps, his eyes fly open, and he rolls onto his side.

'It's you,' he croaks. 'What happened to Ushum?'

'He's gone.'

He pushes himself to his feet, a look of disgust warping his mouth as he wipes mud from his hands onto his pants. 'How did you know what to do?'

'Like you said,' I say, turning toward Eidolon in the near distance, 'I'm no stranger to magic.'

Even as I say that, I scan the horizon for Ramsey. He followed us from the pub, and I don't know if it was because Antonia told him to or not. Maybe he worried about Daniella's body. Perhaps he suspects who I am and wanted to end me. But he helped me attack Ushum so I could drag the demon into the water. I shake my head, water dripping from my curls.

Masoud's footsteps echo mine as Appian Way comes into view, the gardens housing the secret entrance to Sophos' sanctum a few blessed minutes away. Already my mind spins with an explanation to satisfy Antonia and somehow protect my identity.

Masoud catches up to me, his green eyes bloodshot. 'What did you do to Ushum?' His voice wavers, like he's afraid of the answer.

I shoot him a glare. 'I used your devil's trap as leverage to banish him to the Underworld. He would have killed you tonight if he had the chance.'

'Th-thank you,' he stammers through his chattering teeth. 'For saving me.'

'Do you realize how stupid it was to keep forcing a powerful demon to do your bidding when you know you don't have enough magic to control him?' I hiss, anger flooding my veins and momentarily chasing away the cold. 'You don't understand demons, magic – anything, Masoud.'

He shivers, his teeth chattering as he rubs a hand through his mud-streaked hair. 'My family had that devil's trap in our vaults for centuries. I just wanted a leg-up when I came here. A way to make sure I could get into the Order. To matter. I didn't think anything like this would happen.'

'It did happen. You could have become just like that girl we buried tonight. Another body, another inconvenience to brush aside.'

'Ushum called you something. Daughter of Hecate. He wanted your blood maybe more than he wanted to kill me. I should have realized sooner,' he says, any sign of fear and trauma from our night slipping away. 'Ushum could sense you as soon as we reached Eidolon. Every time I summoned him, he would say there was someone here with strong enough magic to sustain him for eons. At first, I thought it was an Order member. Maybe Rohan or Damian. But Ushum wanted *you*. Why? What is it about you that demons want so badly?'

My nostrils flare, and I lean forward, my fists aching to pummel his snide face. 'If you have any sense in your thick skull, you will keep your mouth shut and never breathe a word of what happened – to Antonia, Rohan, or Damian.'

'So, there *is* something to what Ushum said. What does it mean to be a daughter of Hecate?' Masoud's eyes glitter.

'Get out of my way,' I snarl.

Masoud doesn't budge, just blocks my way. He's tall, with broad shoulders. I don't doubt he could physically overpower me, drag my battered, exhausted body to Antonia's feet and reveal my secret. Tell her what Ushum called me. I can see the scheming in his eyes, like he's a bloodhound on a scent trail.

'Help me,' he says, leaning forward, green eyes alight with excitement. 'Teach me what you know. I'm connected to the convergence now; my magic is amplified.'

I snort, my hands balling into fists. 'What makes you think I owe you anything?'

'You don't. You saved my life, Andy.' Masoud hesitates. 'But, if you want what Ushum called you to remain a secret, maybe you'll teach me how to control demons.'

For a moment, it feels like Eidolon melts away around us, replaced by the angry Pacific on a windswept night. The night Violet almost killed me when she tried to bind herself to Ossivorus. I've relived this moment countless times since last fall. But this time it's different. I'm not the one lying on the ground watching my sister fall down a dark path.

This time, I'm Violet. Making deals with beings that will bring nothing but ruin.

I take a deep breath, my gaze hard as I stare at Masoud and his hopeful expression. 'You've seen what the Order is capable of. That girl tonight, her stomach slashed open, and her body dumped in a nameless grave like she never existed. What makes you think you're safe from that fate? What makes you think I can't whisper the right words to the right person?'

His skin blanches, looking sickly as the first rays of the sun break over the horizon. 'Y-you wouldn't. I can tell you're not like the others.'

'If you get in my way,' I threaten, 'then I will have to be so much worse than them.'

'I don't want to get in your way. I think we could help each other.'

I shove him aside, stalking toward the House of Thales with fury bubbling in my stomach.

As I touch the omphalos stone and the staircase appears, a strangely pensive Masoud gently brushes my uninjured arm. 'Andy, wait.'

I pause, my foot on the first stair. I wait for him to ask me more about Hecate. About what I'm doing at Eidolon. But to my surprise, his usually cocky expression is entirely absent. He flicks water from his sleeve and combs back his hair.

'You should take care of your shoulder. I'll meet with Antonia and say we got lost after finding a place to get rid of the girl.'

I press my lips into a thin line, my shoulder burning at the reminder of the puncture through the muscle. But I narrow my eyes, self-preservation overriding pain. 'Why would you do that?'

'Because you saved my life,' he says sincerely. 'And because I'm certain I won't get past Sophos without your help. I need you, Andy. And you need me.'

I pause, considering his words. The moment Antonia or any other house leaders catch wind of Ushum's words, they'll know who I am. Masoud is desperate enough that I don't doubt he would tell them what Ushum said, even if it shows them he isn't worthy of being in the Order. That he used a demon to cheat his way past their tests.

'Fine.' The word tastes like ash on my tongue. 'I'll help you. But if you breathe a word about Ushum, or what he said about me, you'll regret it. And not just because they'll kick you out of the Order.'

My threat must hit home, because the elation I see in Masoud's eyes dies a little. But he nods and moves toward the staircase that will take him into the sanctum. 'Thank you. I promise I'll make it worth your while. And I'll tell Antonia you did exactly as she asked. I'm sure she'll be pleased.'

I say nothing as I clutch my injured shoulder and watch Masoud disappear down the staircase. As the stone slides back into place with a groan, I feel a wave of nausea. Though I avoided making a deal with Ushum tonight, I worry that I've signed my soul away to a different kind of devil.

Pain radiates up my arm as I turn from the garden. It's quiet as I stagger across campus and to my hall. The foyer is empty when I enter, and I grab the handrail, my body slumping over it. Exhaustion sweeps through me, threatening to buckle my legs at any moment. I turn away from the women's wing and pound my fist on Anubis' door. Blood and thick dirt streak across the wood as it swings inward.

'Andromeda,' he breathes, his hair tousled from sleep and his torso bare.

As soon as his fingers touch my skin, I finally give in to the terror of the night. My shoulder aches and burns, and the stench of demons makes my stomach churn. Anubis' arms wrap around me and he lays me down gently on his bed. This is the only place I want to be. Anubis is the only one who can make me feel safe. And as the pain in my shoulder spreads through my bloodstream, turning my vision black, the last thing I see is the face of the god I love hovering above me, dark eyes as black as the Underworld.

*

The smell of incense and something darker, sweeter, fills my nostrils. I blink, my eyes blurry. Soft blankets are wrapped around me, the source of the smell. Slowly, I sit up, pressing a hand to my aching forehead. Warm fingers gently clasp my knee.

'Anubis?' I ask, my throat stinging and dry.

'I'm here.' He hands me a bottle of water and my glasses. 'I have some dry clothes for you.' Anubis sets the T-shirt and sweatpants on the edge of the bed and turns to let me get changed. 'What happened to you, Andromeda? Your wound was poisoned. If it weren't for the immunity you already have to plants in the Underworld, you'd be dead.'

I roll my shoulder as I pull off my wet clothes. Gauze has been carefully placed over the puncture mark. Dark blood sticks to the bandage, but the wound looks small and clean. 'Masoud's demon broke free from its trap and found us while we were doing Sophos business. Ushum stabbed me with a talon. Must have coated it in some Underworld poison.'

Anubis stiffens, carefully turning around once he's sure I'm dressed. He sits on the foot of the bed and his hand finds my knee again. 'Does Masoud know about you?'

'He knows enough.' I take a sip of water and lean back against the headboard, my back stiff and my muscles aching. 'But he won't say anything. At least, not anytime soon.'

'How do you know he'll stay quiet?' Anubis shakes his head, forehead creased with worry.

I wince and adjust my aching body on his bed. 'We made a deal. I'll teach him some of what I know, and he'll keep his mouth shut about Ushum calling me a daughter of Hecate.'

'A deal?' Anubis asks incredulously. 'How could you do something like that? Masoud will do anything to get ahead!'

His tone makes my stomach knot with guilt. With shame.

But I lift my chin and say, 'I told you I have it under control. And besides, it's not like I have a choice.'

Before Anubis can say anything else, a sharp knock rattles his door.

The person on the other side doesn't wait for an answer before they swing the door open and stroll inside. I stiffen, my fingers curling in the blankets as Antonia and Lourdes, the girl from Sophos who often works with Anubis, walk inside. Both of the girls study the scene: me in Anubis' bed, my wet clothes on the floor, and his hand on my leg. Anubis jerks back, but it's too late.

Antonia offers a wicked smile and crosses her arms. 'Well, I see why neither of you bothered to answer my calls for the last hour.'

Anubis stands so quickly the mattress nearly flings me into the wall. 'Andy was feeling sick after being in the rain. I wanted to make sure she was okay.'

'It's cute that you think you have to explain your conquests to me,' Antonia croons. 'I'm your Prometheus, not your mother. I don't care who you sleep with, as long as you do what I tell you to.'

'We're not – th-that's not what's going on,' he stammers, clearing his throat. He doesn't even look back at me. 'And I finished my duties at the party at Leonidas Court before sunrise. Andy finished her task too.'

Lourdes, the beautiful girl with the impeccable box braids, eyes Anubis with interest. 'Antonia knows all about our activities last night at Leonidas Court, Jae.' She winks, and even though he isn't facing me, I swear I can see his skin flush darker. 'This is about something else, not your little first-year fling.'

I try to look as dignified as possible, my cheeks burning as I pull the blankets further up my body, Anubis' clothes drowning my limbs. Lourdes looks over at me, her light brown eyes scanning my rumpled appearance with one dismissive look. I can't tell if it's jealousy or a challenge in her gaze. Either way, it makes the sinking feeling in my stomach grow stronger.

'It seems Rohan has taken an interest in the two of you,' Antonia says, inspecting her nails.

I shift uncomfortably on the bed, a cold sweat prickling down my spine. There is no way Masoud could be so stupid that he'd spill everything that happened last night, the moment he got to the sanctum. Or would he?

'After only a few weeks?' I ask, keeping my voice neutral despite what Anubis just said.

Antonia nods at Lourdes, who produces two creamy white envelopes. I recognize them immediately as Order invitations. I hold my breath as Lourdes hands them both to Anubis. He doesn't meet my eyes as he gives me my letter.

'The two of you have mastered Sophos skills faster than expected,' Antonia says, her expression curiously hard. 'Damian thinks your talents are . . . wasted on the lowest house. After conferring with Thoth and Prometheus, he has deemed you worthy of advancement into House Lector. Your initiation trials will take place next weekend.'

Lourdes smiles at Anubis. 'It's a tremendous honor. The two of you have such promise. Hardly any first-year Sophos members are given the chance to advance, much less so soon into the term.'

Without ceremony, Antonia turns to go, Lourdes at her side. But Antonia pauses, looking back over her shoulder. 'Just remember, Sophos is only the beginning.'

I can't tell if it's a warning or a promise. Before I can so much as blink, the door shuts behind them, and I'm alone with Anubis again.

'So.' I stare at my lap. 'You've been working with Lourdes for the last few days?'

Anubis breathes out, dropping into the chair at his desk. 'Andy, you know Antonia assigns Sophos members in pairs for tasks. And with the way they've been running us ragged, I haven't been able to see you, much less explain who I've been with.'

'No need to explain,' I say coldly, swinging my legs out of his bed, my bare feet flexing on the cold hardwood. 'We came to Eidolon to figure out what's going on with the gods. It's hard to do that, when I haven't seen you for ages.'

'You've been screening my calls!'

I shoot him a glare as I kick my wet clothes into a pile by the door and bend down to grab my boots. 'And you've told me countless times we can't be seen together.'

He shakes his head, setting a hand to his temple. 'Well, it looks like that might not really matter anymore, considering the position they found us in.'

'Pardon me for coming to you after getting impaled by a demon,' I snarl, my throat tightening. 'I wasn't aware that when you broke up with me, you also decided not to help me when I'm in mortal danger. Sorry for getting your signals confused.'

'Andromeda,' he says, his expression softening at the edges. 'Working with Lourdes, with others, is another way I can keep attention away from you and your connection to Hecate. You know why it's better if we don't . . . don't make things harder than they are. We both know how this ends.'

My spine stiffens and I turn away, blindly reaching for the door. 'You'll be dragged back to the Underworld in a few weeks, and you'll lose your body, your chance at humanity, all over again. How can I blame you for wanting to experience everything you can before it's too late, even if it's not with me?'

He steps in front of me, moving so fast I don't have time to turn away. I clench my teeth tightly together, desperate to keep the tightness in my chest from spreading into something that feels alarmingly like a sob.

'Don't do that,' he murmurs, one hand carefully trailing my jaw.

'What?' I ask, tipping my head up. I try to keep my gaze hard, but the burn of tears threatens to overwhelm my resolve.

'Don't assume the worst about me, just because you're hurting.' I watch as his throat works, his eyes so dark they threaten to swallow me whole. 'And don't think for a moment that there is *anyone* I want more than you.'

I breathe in sharply as his hands come back to my face, his long fingers gently cupping my jaw. And even though it hurts when he looks at my lips and hesitates, I find that I don't care. I'd rather have him now, for as long as I can, than lose what little time we have.

'Anubis,' I murmur as he blinks, threatening to pull away. Before he can let me go, I tug at his shirt with my fingers, pulling him close. 'Stop being *noble*. You know how much I hate that.'

At first, I think he'll finally stop fighting and kiss me. That he'll realize that any time together is better than nothing and he doesn't need to protect me from a pain I've already endured once before. But his dark brown eyes grow guarded again, and he steps away.

'I'll . . . I'll see you later,' he says.

'I see,' I say, my voice shaking as he reaches around me to open the door.

'Andy,' he says. 'I'm still here to help you. Please, let me.'

I leave his room before he can see the tears misting my glasses.

14

Books slam shut and desks fold into the armrests with a clatter, pulling me from the turmoil of my thoughts. I look up at the emptying room after my Roman archaeology class, unsure of when the lecture started, much less ended. My thoughts are too full of last night. Of demons and blood and scars. Of Daniella's body buried in a forgotten churchyard.

Slowly, I gather my unopened textbook and slip it into my bag. Voices fade as students leave, and I watch as my mousy professor, Dr Catalina Rosetti, gathers her things at the podium and heads for the exit door at the bottom of the hall. As she opens it, a familiar face peers inside. Dr Kane. The doctor's eyes are wide, the whites showing with fear, as his gaze flicks over my shoulder. His hand flexes, the same one with the mark I saw when Damian spoke during the lecture. Rosetti slips past him, and I swear Kane looks like he's seen a ghost as he continues to stare through me. The heavy double doors slam, sealing Dr Kane and his clenched fist away.

For a moment I sit still, unable to will myself to leave the hall and its semi-circular rows of seats. Scribbled notes on the whiteboard and posters of Bronze Age pottery stare back at me, along with graffiti of the Vespers. The semblance of normality I feel at being in a classroom is suddenly so impossible to reach, knowing that in less than a week's time, I will descend deeper into the Order.

'Are you planning on staying here all day?'

I jump in my seat, nearly spilling the contents of my bag

across the narrow aisle. Twisting, I finally notice Ramsey perched at the top of the hall, one shoulder leaning against the exit. His arms are crossed, displaying his scars and missing fingertips to my gaze.

I clear my throat and sling my bag over my shoulder, wincing as soon as the strap digs into the wound from Ushum's claw. Ramsey's face twists with sympathy and he pushes off from the doors, descending a few stairs until he's close enough that I can see every detail of the purple slash on his jaw.

He nods toward my shoulder. 'You got that taken care of?'

'I did.' I shift on my feet, considering for a moment. 'Thank you. For helping me last night, I mean.'

His dark eyes are serious. 'You've been invited to Lector, I gather.' He looks nothing like the quiet, easy-going person he was when we went to the pub in Idyllwood only a few days ago. Back when I could still pretend that everything was normal. That I wasn't hunting god-killers and losing pieces of myself to the Order.

'Antonia delivered the invitation herself.'

'I can't imagine she was pleasant about it. She and Rohan aren't exactly fond of sharing Damian's attentions.'

I want to understand him – the Remus of the Order. A man forced to watch his father killed for treachery but who did nothing about it.

'Well.' I clear my throat again, my nerves still too raw from my last conversation with Anubis to dig much into anything. 'I should go study.'

He glances at his hands, flexing his fingers before he looks up. 'Do you know what happened to my fingers? To my face?'

I tuck my chin, taken aback. But I shake my head, watching

Ramsey as his expression hardens and his eyes get a far-away look.

'You know about Sparta, about their rigorous military training of young men?' When I nod, he continues. 'The Order models the rearing of the first-born sons of founding families like the Spartan Agoge. We're raised strictly. Brutally. Taught magic from the time we can walk, and have loyalty to the Order instilled in us through rigorous training, sleep deprivation and beatings.'

'That's horrible,' I offer when he turns his eyes back to mine.

'I'm not telling you this for pity. Damian excelled as we grew up. Always the strongest, the most resilient. When other boys grew sick from endless exposure, he seemed to thrive. To enjoy it, even. And all of us were expected to use violence toward one another. No friendships. No relationships.' Ramsey touches his jaw, as if remembering the moment he got his scar. 'This is the way the Order gains the strongest Romulus. When the old one dies, an Agoge is prepared to select the next. Three years ago, when Damian's father died, he and I and the rest of the first-born sons of the founding families were placed in an arena designed to test our bodies, minds and magic to the utmost degree.'

A chill slips down my spine. I can't bring myself to speak, or even to look away as Ramsey leans a little closer, something like desperation in his eyes.

'We were locked within a specially designed arena inside Oculus – the sanctum for Oracle – and could not leave until a Romulus was chosen. One by one Damian killed the others with his knife. The same one passed down from his father, his grandfather before him, all the way back to the first Valerius in Rome. He was efficient. Ruthless. I thought I knew cruelty at the hands of my family, of the other boys, but nothing, *nothing*, could have prepared me for the Agoge.'

'I know Damian is dangerous,' I murmur, the thrill of fear radiating across my body growing stronger. I can clearly see his prized bronze knife in my head, murdering Jan Arskell with calculating precision.

Ramsey smiles, the expression mirthless. 'And that's why I'm telling you this, Andy. We were the last two left. I survived by hiding behind rocks, jamming myself into hollows. Anything to get away from the blood. But when he found me, he didn't kill me like each Romulus usually does to his Remus, early in his reign. Instead, he declared that I would live as a reminder to the Order that I was weak, that my house was weak. And that the Valerius line would never fall.'

I can't keep my eyes from slipping to his jaw. To the scar that is still purple against his pale skin. He touches it again, purposefully showing the missing fingertips as he does.

'Damian carved this with his knife so that I could never forget how spineless I was in the Agoge. So that every time my father and the rest of my family saw my face, they would be ashamed. Ridiculed. And then he snapped off the tips of my fingers just for the fun of it. Maybe a way to ensure that my family would never rise against him. Clearly, that didn't work.' His lips twist, and I know he's thinking about his father. 'But Damian always thought that I would be too afraid, like I was when I hid in those rocks and watched eight boys I'd known since infancy die in horrific ways.'

I imagine Ramsey a little younger. Lankier. With freckles more prominent and an unscarred face. A nineteen-year-old boy sent to the slaughter by his family for something as useless as honor.

Slowly, I open my mouth to speak. 'And did it work? Are you loyal to the Order. To your Romulus?'

His eyes seem to sparkle, like I've finally landed on the right question. 'It depends on how well you remember *why*

Romulus killed Remus. And exactly why Damian should have followed in the myth's footsteps.'

Ramsey smiles again, and this time he seems normal, unburdened by his past and the blood it is drenched in. He turns and heads for the doors, hands in his pockets and scars hidden from the world once more. As he uses his shoulder to push the doors open, he pauses, not turning when he says, 'During your initiation into Lector, remember what Damian is capable of. And *never* let him see your weaknesses. Sometimes it's better to hide among the rocks so you can live to see things change. That's why I helped you last night, Andy. Because I can see you're like me.'

And then he leaves, and I'm alone in a cavernous hall, my heart beating in my throat as I imagine Damian as a wolf, gorging on the bodies of his enemies.

Ibis Park, the sanctum of the house of Lector, is at the end of the road where my hall sits. The semi-circular colonnade of white and gray marble houses not only the school's largest library, but the upper floors also contain endless vaults of secret texts, objects, and other knowledge invaluable to the Order – a place only those in Lector or Oracle can enter.

Anubis and I stand side by side in a room on the second floor of the sanctum, awaiting our initiation ritual. It's empty of any furnishings except for a large painting of some kind of low barge cutting through reeds. Candles mark a circle around us and Rohan, with old wax from previous ceremonies crusting the ground. He wears long white robes emblazoned with an eye of Horus across his chest. On his head is a grotesquely detailed mask of an ibis. He fully embodies his title of Thoth, the god of knowledge.

Damian and Antonia flank him. Ramsey stands far back from the others. His face is half hidden in the shadows of the candles, but even from this distance I can see the scars decorating his cheek and arms. He meets my eyes, and part of me wonders if I imagined our conversation last week in the lecture hall. The leaders of the Order's houses don't acknowledge him as the ceremony begins. He's like an insignificant moon in the orbit of a much larger planet.

'The Order of the Seven Sages is an ancient group,' Rohan begins, his voice amplified by the beak of his gilded mask. 'The four founding families can trace their lineage beyond the rulers of Rome. Beyond Greece and Egypt. And you, new initiates into our cult, are some of the few permitted to witness the secrets the house of Lector guards. The power we wield. Only Oracle, the highest house, can accomplish more than us.'

Rohan extends his fingers and the flames on the candle wicks grow taller, brighter. Heat licks at my skin as our circle constricts, forcing Anubis and me to step closer together, our arms brushing. Damian's gray eyes reflect the fire as he watches us and approaches the ring of flame and hands a bronze ceremonial knife to Rohan. The same knife Damian used to murder the other first-born sons of the founders.

I think of Dr Kane, the mark on his hand that Damian left during his lecture. Nausea curdles my stomach, but I ignore it as Rohan extends the knife, hand raised above his head.

'Lector embodies the knowledge of the great sorcerers of ancient Egypt. Their mark on this world, on the civilizations that followed them, is deeper than you can fathom. If you pass your rites, you will be welcomed into our libraries, our halls and our secrets with open arms. And you will see through the eyes of Thoth. You will see a truth made especially for you.'

Rohan flicks the blade across his body, slashing through the air. At first, nothing happens. But slowly, like a scroll unfurling, the air in front of him shimmers. A familiar wash of ash fills my nose.

The Underworld appears, like looking through the surface of a shivering lake. But it's not what I'm used to seeing. The endless barren plains that take the space between the rivers, the wasteland where spirits languish, these are nowhere to be seen. Instead, images of the west bank flutter across this mirror.

I gasp, one foot jerking forward before I can stop myself. It's beautiful. Mansions of marble dot the cliff sides, overlooking the winding river. It's as if I'm trapped in this vision as everything shifts and moves further away from the edge of the bank. A winding path of deep obsidian. Pale gray mountains, wild and rough, are dotted with ancient poplar trees. They shimmer, half ghostly, like everything in the land of the dead. My eyes are pulled to the three-bodied statues studding the path, and the brightly burning green torches.

It calls me deeper, urging me to look. The smell of sulfur, of the deepest parts of the earth, wafts from within the abyss. This call feels different. Out of my control. Whatever lurks within this place is waiting for me.

I look deeper, stepping closer to Rohan's vision. Smoke rises from the path.

'Enough.' Damian's voice shatters the illusion. He approaches the edge of the circle, eyes narrowed. 'What did you see, initiate?'

Anubis shoots me a curious look, a line appearing between his brows. My mouth is dry as I struggle to form words, still blinking away the image of the path and the Hekation statues. I know I can't reveal what I've seen. And if Anubis' confusion tells me anything, it's that the vision appears different to all who see it. Like a looking glass gazing into the knowledge that you most need.

'The Underworld,' I admit, careful to keep from revealing more, my gaze flicking over to Ramsey, his words playing over and over in my head. 'I saw the Underworld.'

Damian's gray eyes are glued to me as I gape at the now empty air. The flames die down, but his gaze burns hotter than before. Curiosity mixed with a familiar calculation. 'What do you desire from the Underworld?'

I swallow. 'Knowledge of what happens after we die – how to control my fate.'

It's not necessarily a lie, but it most certainly isn't what I wonder about. I know what will happen to me, just as surely as I know fate can't be ignored. But Damian seems satisfied with the answer, one any other initiate in the Order would have given. His gaze loses the curiosity from before and he looks to Rohan.

Conscious of how close I've come to Rohan, I step back until I'm next to Anubis in the center of the circle of candles once more.

'And what did you see, Jae Han?' Damian turns to Anubis.

'Me?' he says, jaw flexing as if the words are painful. 'I saw myself in complete control of my mortality.'

My fingers are ice cold as I ball them into fists. Magic curls through the air, winds around my limbs and through my hair. The candles on the ground glow briefly, showing a complex sigil marked with more Egyptian symbols than I can read before they are extinguished again.

Rohan nods to Damian, the ibis beak bobbing. 'They're both ready for the rite.'

'Ibis Park holds centuries of the Order's knowledge. It will be yours if you follow Thoth's orders.' Damian flicks his fingers impatiently at Ramsey whose face is blank but whose eyes are full of the same simmering emotion I saw in them when we spoke after my lecture. 'Remus, fetch Kane.'

Ramsey ducks out of the room briefly before he returns with Dr Kane, my philosophy professor, behind him. Kane blinks in the low light of the room as Ramsey shuts the door and moves to stand in front of it. Guarding it.

'Romulus,' Kane mumbles, bowing clumsily at the waist. 'I am pleased you called on me. I wish to call the entire Order together to argue my innocence. If you grant me your support, I would be eternally grateful.'

It feels odd to see a man in his fifties cower to a boy barely out of his teenage years, but then Damian smiles. The cold smile he wears so well, sharp as a blade. It sends another jolt of ice through my veins. 'You know the price of treachery in my Order, Kane.'

Dr Kane's face goes white, and his eyes dart around the room, taking in the candles. The house leaders. And Rohan's grotesque mask. 'B-but your father, Cadmus, never allowed such outdated punishments! And Jan, Jan, would never have stood for this!'

'Jan Arskell is dead because he and his family are weak.' Damian curls his lips as he looks once at Ramsey. 'My father is no longer in charge. Or do you forget how I conquered and proved myself in the Agoge after his death? I am Romulus. I *am* the Order.'

'You can't!' Kane retreats a step, even as Ramsey blocks the doors with his body. 'I have been loyal to this society my entire life! What is one indiscretion in the face of all my years of service?'

A thrill of electricity runs along my skin as Damian advances, taking the knife from Rohan. He skirts the ceremonial circle, eyes trained on his prey. Dr Kane scurries to the side, gazing around the room wildly.

'You disobeyed me. I told you to stop demanding another Agoge for the last year. To stop spreading rumors and lies about my victory, and consorting with Jan Arskell to oust me from my position,' Damian hisses, the cool exterior he wears crumbling to something that reminds me of a panther. The eyes of a predator and the feral grace of a trained killer.

Kane shakes his head violently. 'I had nothing to do with those rumors! We all witnessed your victory against the other first-born sons of the founders.'

'And yet you've proven that your loyalty is to the Arskells, not the Order, when you met with the conspirators who have been thwarting my plans since I came to power. My spies saw you meet with Jan and the other elder Arskells last month.'

'Jan forced me to join his cult of followers! I swear I believe in your plan for the Order's future, Romulus. I had no choice but to join him. He would have taken my job, my position within Lector!' Kane blubbers.

Damian laughs, the sound chilling. 'Jan Arskell was the Remus under my father – and his son serves me now. I could have given Ramsey an honorable death in the Agoge, brought pride to his family name. But I let him live so that all see that I *cannot* be disobeyed, even by my greatest ene-mies. Every one of those who conspired to install Jan as Romulus is dead. All except you.'

Dr Kane backs straight into the far wall. His eyes are wide with fear, the whites showing against the red of his face.

Some sort of conspiracy to overthrow Damian has taken place, a tumult that has shaken this society to its core. The Sophos meeting with the alumni in the gallery was a warn-ing. Not just a show of power, but making them witness Damian murdering Ramsey's father. He was rooting out the last of the conspirators that have been trying to oust him since the Agoge. Ramsey warned me. He wanted me to know, to understand before tonight. Not everyone in the Order is pleased with the secrets Damian is keeping. The murders of the gods. A sick feeling knots in my belly as Damian advances leisurely, even as he holds the ornate knife. He's going to kill Dr Kane right here. And he's going to make me and Anubis watch.

'Your blood will feed the spell needed to initiate these two into the house of Lector.' Damian lifts the blade, preparing to strike. 'And you will die knowing your plan has failed.'

Kane collapses to his knees, his breath ragged as he attempts to crawl to Ramsey's feet. The doctor grabs his ankles, his entire body trembling with terror. 'Remus, help me! Do not let him kill me for using my right to challenge the results of the Agoge. Your father knew Romulus would destroy the Order with his insane plan! You must do something! You must take his place!'

Ramsey's face is drawn as he stands in front of the doors, Dr Kane's only exit. His jaw is tight, eyes averted. He no longer looks angry, like he did when his father was murdered on stage for all of Sophos to see. Now, he looks stricken. Trapped.

Ramsey's jaw works as he mutters, 'Romulus has decided your fate.' He looks at Damian. Knows it's useless, that he's lost. With his nostrils flared, he steps away from Kane and crosses his arms. 'You know what happens when you lose a challenge in the Order, Doctor. The consequences cannot be avoided. Always remember that I am proof of that.'

The mark of a traitor on one of Dr Kane's raised hands blinks as he cowers at the feet of Damian, a boy who decided his fate without a glimmer of regret.

I twist my body so I'm facing the painting of the barge once more. A grotesque, wet tearing sound rips through the air. Kane gurgles as the knife pierces his chest before a hollow thudding punctuates the air as he falls over. I open my eyes once the gurgling stops. Rohan stands stoically before us in his robe and mask as the scent of blood fills the air. Kane didn't even get the chance to scream. Damian's footsteps echo wetly against the tile as he returns to his spot next to Rohan and Antonia.

'Next time,' he says, only slightly out of breath as he wipes the blood from the knife on a handkerchief, 'you will need to kill someone to charge the magic needed for such ceremonies.'

Anubis nods, and I force myself to do the same.

Rohan takes that as his cue to begin. He leaves the circle, taking the knife from Damian, and moves to Kane's limp body, and crouches down. Dipping the blade into the deep crimson spreading slowly along the white tile, he brings the blade against the floor. Metal screeches against the marble as he draws two empty summoning circles, leaving the symbols out. Finally, he returns, eyes hidden by the mask as he stops before me.

'You will use this sacred blade and the spilled blood of an enemy to summon a demon.' He thrusts the blade out and I take it, barely keeping my hand from shaking. 'Prometheus has taught you the base knowledge of all magic. You must now use what you have learned to complete your trap and summon your chosen creature. Once they are summoned, you will ask them a question. One that will grant the Order more knowledge – a way to secure your position in the libraries of Lector.'

Anubis' shoulders grow stiff beside me, and even though I keep my eyes trained on the bloody circle on the floor, I can feel his gaze. The panic winding through him as he realizes the magic I'll wield as I do this. What the demon will say when he smells who I am.

I walk to the circle and stare at the empty rings. What kind of being should I call? If I summon one too weak, I could fail this rite. If I accidentally intrigue one like Ushum, then any hope of infiltrating the Order and saving my sister and Hecate is gone. I wish I could look back at Anubis. That I could see in his eyes what I should do.

But I can't stall any longer.

Fighting down my gag reflex, I lean over Kane's body, careful not to see anything beyond his slumped shoulders, and dip the bronze blade into his pooling blood. My mind races, and I think of Violet as I scratch symbols into the trap. One by one, I dip the blade and draw until the ring is complete. The room is silent as I step back, careful not to break the lines, and hold one palm out.

I think of what Violet would do if she were standing here. And I whisper a spell as I stare at the series of djeds, scarabs and the cartouche of a specific name inked in blood. I pray no one reads it. A tiny wisp of answering magic settles over my shoulders. It's Anubis, his magic carefully reaching out to protect me. Hide me. Relief slams into me even as the blood in the circle gathers into a column, slowly forming over a set of strong shoulders and pointed ears.

I only hope the Cynomorpha I just summoned doesn't ruin it all.

The blood melts away from smooth dark skin, revealing a man in an ancient Egyptian kilt. A low growl pierces the air, and I let my eyes travel up the familiar face of a jackal. Dark fur, pointed ears and wickedly sharp teeth. Amenemopet, the surly tomb guardian who aided me last fall to find Violet's hiding place in the Underworld, glowers down at me. He reaches out as if to pick me up and move me bodily out of his way. When his hand glances off the invisible wall of the summoning circle, his ears flatten and another rumbling growl fills his chest.

'What is the meaning –?'

'Demon,' I say, my voice overloud and authoritative as I stare at the jackal-headed man who once guided me through the Underworld. 'I have called you here and will feed you the blood of my enemy, for a price.'

A low murmur from Rohan and Antonia makes my spine straighten. Did I make a mistake in summoning a Cynomorpha, the tomb guardians of the land of the dead? Amenemopet looks as indignant as any man with a canine snout can manage. But he looks over my shoulder and sees Anubis, the circle of candles, and the other powerful magic-wielders in the room.

His shoulders remain tight, but he dips his head. 'What do you require of me, master?'

If I weren't being watched by Damian and the others, I might have laughed. Amenemopet is proud and arrogant, but bound by honor. Hopefully, seeing Anubis, a god he would have served both in the human world and the Underworld, keeps his tongue from slipping.

I glance back at Rohan for confirmation.

'Do what Horus did in the ancient myths of Egypt,' he answers. 'Ask for knowledge.'

Stomach churning, I turn back to Amenemopet and meet his eyes. The Cynomorpha seems to raise an eyebrow, as if curious to see where this is going. I can't ask for something about Violet or Hecate, not without showing Damian my cards. But I must bring some kind of knowledge to the house of Lector that is useful enough to earn my place in its ranks. After a few agonizing moments of silence, I square my jaw.

'Tell me how to find a way to the Underworld without using magic.'

He cocks his head to the side, as if measuring his words. 'Walk.'

The urge to scowl at his familiar, dry advice is almost too strong to ignore, but I rein it in, pretending to be the ruthless, desperate person the Order wants me to be. 'I have summoned you, demon, and you are at my mercy. Now you will answer my question.'

I can almost feel the wave of approval from Rohan and Damian at my back.

Amenemopet's lips twitch. 'To locate an entrance without calling upon powerful magic and attracting hungry demons, you must follow a convergence. Each point of magic is like a heartbeat, an echo of the world above. The Underworld shifts and changes as humans do, but not the convergences.'

'You may have your offering,' I say. Excitement flutters in my chest, but I stomp it down.

Amenemopet crouches down and stares at the symbols for a moment. He swipes his fingers through the symbols of the cartouche bearing his name and brings his fingers to his lips. His tongue darts out and he tastes the blood of my professor. His lips curl back over his teeth before he bows his head.

'A pleasure to serve you, master.'

Not wanting to risk anyone seeing the familiarity between me and a demon, I raise my hand and mumble a banishing spell. Amenemopet melts away, disappearing with the blood. All that remains is a circle of ash where he stood.

Rohan comes to my side and takes the knife. 'Welcome to the house of Lector, Andromeda. Accept the mark of our house, Apep the serpent god, and you will taste knowledge unlike anything you've ever known.'

I'm not surprised when he pulls a needle from his robes. Another tattoo. Another mark that grants a connection to the magic concentrated below the school. I grit my teeth as he instructs me to bare my shoulder so he can ink the symbol of the house onto it. I watch as an ouroboros materializes – a snake biting its own tail.

Rohan wipes away the last of the stray ink as the connection to the convergence below my feet grows stronger. A wave of magic crawls along my skin, and I fight the desire to revel in it, to let it course through my body freely. Pleased, Rohan steps back to Anubis and hands him the knife.

'Your turn, initiate.'

I stand beside the circle of candles, watching numbly as Anubis creates his own trap and summons a demon, his magic flaring brightly in the room. I don't recognize the creature, but I can feel its power. Almost as ancient and cruel as Ossivorus.

'Tell me how a magic-wielder can absorb the power of another into their blood.'

I can feel Damian lean closer, his entire body prickling with anticipation as the creature spits a spell in ancient Egyptian in response and is finally allowed to taste Kane's blood. Anubis knows almost every creature in the Underworld. He knows just who to summon and what to ask to make the Order hungry for more.

My pulse pounds in my neck as Anubis is marked with his own ouroboros tattoo. His magic is palpable, like a strong wind, as he works to cover my own. Sweat breaks over his skin as he stands back, covering his newly tattooed shoulder. Damian murmurs something to Antonia, who nods. My nerves prickle with awareness, with the extra power in the room, radiating from us like a strobe light.

The flames of the candles extinguish, and the three heads of the Order stand in a line before us. Damian takes the knife back, a curious reverence to his movements as he replaces it in a scabbard at his side. His silvery eyes scan Anubis, a hunger written within their depths.

'Welcome to Lector,' Damian murmurs to him, his voice soft. 'What a strange type of magic you wield, Mr Han.'

'Am I free to go, Romulus?' Ramsey's voice rumbles from the doors.

I look over my shoulder at his pale face, carefully averted from the blood on the ground and the dead body at his feet. Curious, I think, that someone so embroiled in the politics of the Order should look sick when faced with its thirst for blood.

'Not yet,' Damian murmurs, his gray eyes gleaming in the low light, still searching Anubis. 'Prometheus and I have discussed Jae and Andy's progress in the Order. They are promising initiates, with magic that will grow our strength. And you know how I like to keep such potential Oracle members close. We have decided that you will guide them in the ways of our society they have not learned. Teach them what they must know for the ceremony next week.'

Ramsey's brows pinch together. 'That is not the duty of a Remus. That is something a second- or third-year Lector member should do.'

'Perhaps,' Damian agrees, his lip curling back over his teeth as he speaks. 'But it is *your* duty as the son of a traitor to atone for his actions. You are being watched, Ramsey. And if you do not do what I ask, perhaps I will finish what I started in the Agoge.' His eyes flash to the scar on Ramsey's face, still dark against the rest of the pale skin.

Ramsey swallows hard, a fine sheen of sweat beading on his forehead. He says nothing, but as Rohan prepares to show us the secret chambers of texts we now have access to, all I can feel are the eyes of Ramsey Arskell, son of a dead traitor, boring into me.

15

The cavernous two-story library at Ibis Park is eerily quiet as Anubis, Ramsey and I sit there a few days after the initiation into the house of Lector. Through the windows that span the far wall, I can see the pillars of the colonnade and the school beyond. It's Thursday, and almost six weeks since I entered Eidolon.

Each evening since the initiation, Anubis and I have met Ramsey in the main library of Lector's sanctum. Between our quick ascension through Sophos, and the duties of Lector members we must learn, we've spent hours studying the spells and wards that protect and contain the knowledge found in Ibis Park.

'Try the spell again,' Ramsey orders me. 'If you don't contain an artifact from a summoned demon, the magic can lash out. They must be stored correctly, and you must be able to pass through a protection charm without damaging anything.'

'Why does Lector gather and store magic from demons?' I ask, looking up from the faded scroll he has spread out on a long table studded with softly glowing lamps. 'You and Rohan keep telling us that the demons summoned in this sanctum and the deals made with them are to gather and store magic, but you haven't told us why.'

Anubis glances at me from across the table, a look of warning on his face. But I ignore it, as I always do.

Ramsey sighs. 'Damian ordered me to teach you the ways of Lector in time for your first weekly ceremony. That is tomorrow.' His hands flex on the tabletop, and I can't help but look at the tips of his three missing fingers.

'Speaking of –' I lean back in my chair, piles of home-work and essays that need to be written stacked on the seat next to me – 'what is this ceremony? We tried to get Rohan to tell us yesterday, but he said to ask you.'

Ramsey rolls his eyes. 'Thoth thinks he's too important to explain the machinations of his own house. But if the cere-mony goes wrong because neither of you can pass through a protection ward on an artifact without damaging the magic inside, it's not my neck on the line, it's his. Now, are you going to show me you're ready for the ceremony? Or are you sending Thoth to an early grave?'

Leaning forward again, I reach out for the faded scroll. It's written in ancient Greek, a copy of the magical papyri of Egypt, and provides instructions on reading augurs of the future. Before my fingertips can even graze the dry, delicate paper, the sizzle of a protection charm singes my skin. My powers rise automatically, eager to neutralize it, to bend it to my will. As natural as breathing, a tendril of Anubis' magic covers my own, gently urging the protection charm to allow me entry. I glance at him and shoot him a small, grateful smile as we finally master the tricky spell. Without him here during Ramsey's training sessions, I doubt I would have kept my magic, and who it comes from, a secret.

My fingers finally break through the invisible wall of the protection wards. I pick up the scroll and carefully show it to Ramsey. There isn't a scorch mark or sign of damage on the delicate paper.

He grunts something under his breath but nods. 'About time. You'll need to be able to pass a ward just like this to reach the ceremonial chamber tomorrow night.'

'I'm sure Andy and I can handle it,' Anubis says. 'Will you tell us now what the ceremony is?'

Ramsey leans forward, his eyes full of meaning. 'Don't you know what you've gotten yourself into with the Order? You saw what happened to Dr Kane, and you summoned your own demons. Lector is all about knowledge. Storing it, mastering it.' His voice is surprisingly rough, and it feels like it did when he spoke to me in the lecture hall. Like he has a warning crafted specifically for me. 'But since Damian came to power, he's been channeling the magic Lector gathers to himself.'

Anubis wrinkles his nose. 'Why? And why didn't we hear about this in Sophos?'

Ramsey laughs once. 'Because Damian doesn't want anyone in the lesser house to know that magic is fading. Not just from this convergence, but from the world. It would hardly encourage the participation required to keep the Order running.'

'What are you talking about?' I ask, dread settling over my shoulders. It feels like the chill of someone watching in the darkness.

'Each year there are fewer and fewer magic-wielders. Less power to draw on, as gods and their old ways fade. Damian wants to stop that process. Hoarding magic from favors made with demons, from ancient artifacts, makes up for the lack. Each week the extra gathered magic is stored during the Lector ceremony. Damian later channels it to himself so he can find more blades.' Ramsey shifts, curling his fists so his mutilated fingers are hidden. 'He's looking for power-ful people to join the Order to flood it with more magic. People like you two.'

'Blades?' I perk up. 'Like the one Damian uses?'

Ramsey glances at Anubis, his brown eyes narrowed

slightly. 'The knives are ancient. Forged by half-gods when humanity first came into being. They are immensely powerful, and having all seven together is exactly what Damian needs to cement magic in Eidolon forever.'

So, magic is fading slowly from the world somehow. Maybe that is why Damian wants to kill the gods. 'Is that why Kane was killed? He didn't agree with Romulus hoarding magic for himself?'

Ramsey's expression turns sour, and he looks from me to Anubis once more. 'Something like that.'

Anubis leans forward, his eyes narrowed as well. 'How do you know about all this? Your father was killed for treachery. Perhaps you're trying to get revenge through us.'

I want to glare at Anubis. We're finally getting some answers, a hint as to what Damian is up to, and how it might connect to the gods. But Ramsey just smiles, and the movement pulls at the scar on his cheek.

'I'm just your lowly Remus, here to do Damian's bidding without question.'

'But there has to be a reason why –' I begin, but Anubis clears his throat, and I remember where we are.

A clock chimes somewhere deep in the stacks of the library. Ramsey glances at his watch, his face tired and lined once more. He stands up, carefully rolling the scroll and placing it back into its protective container. 'It's late, and I'm sure you have plenty of work to do for your classes before tomorrow night. And I have a Vespers party to plan, to cover up any suspicions over Lector's weekly ceremony.'

Anubis stands as well, shouldering his backpack. 'I need to head to the anthropology labs before they lock up. I'll see you tomorrow night, Andy.'

I watch him weave through the study tables and

bookshelves until he disappears out the doors. Ramsey grips the scroll in his other hand, absently rubbing at his cheek, and the dark purple scar still healing there. A reminder of the competition that took place to become the leader of the Order. A competition he lost.

'You leaving too?' he asks, looking less tense now that Anubis is gone.

'There's still an essay due for Kane's class, even though he's . . . been replaced.' I pull out my laptop. 'I never told you that I was sorry about what happened. To you, and your dad, I mean.'

'Don't say that.' Ramsey's face darkens at the reminder. 'You know about the Agoge and Damian. My father made mistakes and trusted the wrong people. But I'm not like him.' He leans forward, hands braced on the table. 'I think I've found the exact person to trust.'

I meet his gaze, my eyes slitted as I study him, but I can't quell the thrill of excitement in my chest. 'I remember what you said after class the other week, about Remus in the myths. Romulus killed him because he thought the sign he'd received from the gods, indicating where to build his city, was stronger than his brother's. Killing Remus allowed Romulus to build Rome where he saw fit, without challenge. You said it would have been better for Damian to follow in the footsteps of the myth. But Remus' death represented Rome's habit of fighting each other for power.'

'And despite not killing me he still showed that the Order tends to follow Rome's pattern. Look at what happened to my father. To Kane.'

My heartbeat thuds faster, and I lean closer, certain that I'm right. That Ramsey is someone I can trust too. 'You told us about magic fading and Damian's plans to gather it for himself for a reason, didn't you? You've warned me about Damian, mentioned blades and his hunger for magic, because you want the Order stopped as much as me.'

He puts a finger to his lips, glancing around the library. But he smiles, and I swear he looks relieved. 'Good luck tomorrow, Andy.'

An hour later, the automatic lights in Ibis Park shut off, and I rub at my temples as I scan the article on my laptop, trying to finish an essay. Without Violet, I'm certain I would have failed each of my classes already. Between my duties to the Order and my investigation into the missing gods, my schoolwork feels pretty low on my list of priorities.

It's a little past midnight, and most everyone is back in their halls or in Idyllwood. Rubbing at my eyes under my glasses, I struggle to type a sentence.

The battery icon on my laptop turns red, and I send off my lackluster essay for Violet to edit. Before I shut my screen, I see her reply on a banner across my screen.

You're misspelling Diogenes on purpose now, aren't you? XO Violet

I smile at that before slipping my laptop into my bag. Stretching my arms over my head, I take a deep breath. The air smells of paper and ink, and it relaxes the knot of worry constantly in my chest. Despite it being a sanctum, I like Ibis Park. It's quiet, and full to the brim with books and manuscripts and antique furniture in every nook and cranny. Maybe, if it weren't home to a bloodthirsty, ancient society, I would come to a university like Eidolon for its academic excellence.

Shaking my head, I grab my backpack and gather up the loose papers on the desk in front of me. Thinking like that doesn't get me anywhere. Mom called me this morning to let me know Violet is still weak from the experimental treatment she's been undergoing. Every day she sleeps a little more and eats a little less. Letting myself get caught up in useless dreams of a regular life is nothing but a betrayal of my sister. Of myself.

I stand and as I turn again to pick up my things, a flicker of white catches my eye.

It's too dark to see clearly as I weave through a few stacks, my footsteps swallowed by the tall shelves. The flicker of white disappears around a stack further back, leading to the last bookcase against the far wall. I hesitate, the constant scratchy tiredness behind my eyelids growing stronger. Maybe I'm imagining things now. I prepare to turn back to the main doors.

'Find her.' A soft feminine voice echoes off the marble floors; a flash of a white dress blinks in the direction of her voice. She sounds frightened, like she's running from something.

My stomach churns as I think about Tooth and Talon's ceremonies, the white shifts they made their sacrifices wear. And before I can think clearly, or even text Anubis, I'm running through the shelves.

The glimmer of white slips behind the last bookcase in the darkest corner. My breath comes in gasps, and my backpack bangs against my spine as I come to a stop. I blink a few times in the dark, staring at the bookshelves. How did she disappear? There isn't a space behind the wood – it backs up directly to the wall itself. Next to it is a small nook in the wall, maybe a meter wide, where a statue with an outstretched hand juts from a pedestal and a small oil painting of a long boat cuts along a green river.

Something cold slides along my skin. I jerk away instinctively, stumbling until my back collides with a shelf. A few books tumble to the ground. But nothing is there.

Blood roars in my ears as I slowly turn in a circle, my

breath rattling in my chest. Another book topples. But this time, it's from the shelf across from me.

Slowly, something white and vaporous melts from the bookshelf next to the statue and the painting. My skin goes ice cold. It's a person – a ghost. A girl with long white hair and baleful eyes wears a dress of smoke and beckons me closer. A wicked slash mars her throat, and her front is stained with dried blood. Despite her appearance, I'm not scared. I lean forward, my breath frosting the air before me and fogging my glasses.

'She waits for you,' the girl whispers, voice jagged and whistling, like even in death her wounds pain her.

'Who?' I ask, my lips too cold to properly form the word.

Slowly, the ghost sinks back into the shelves next to the statue. She points at it, her eyes wide and dark. She's afraid. I feel her emotions like an echo around me.

'What happened to you? What do you want?' I step closer as she threatens to disappear through the wall once more.

The ghost's wide eyes reflect my face, pale and stark in the darkness. 'You must stop him before he finds her.'

'Hecate?' My stomach hollows out.

The ghost nods. 'The blood of the sacrificed soaks the earth, Andromeda. And if you do not stop them from taking her, the gods and the Underworld are at risk.'

'Wait!' I reach out for her arm and my fingers pass right through a mist of ice. 'How do I find her? What does Damian want?'

The ghost shimmers, her form so tenuous I can barely see her features. 'I cannot stay here – none of Hecate's hand-maidens and familiars can, or he risks uncovering her hiding place. I offer a message: seal with a handshake.'

She flickers again, like the flame on a candle wick being blown out. I lunge for her, a messenger from Hecate herself.

I'm desperate for more answers, for hints on how to find the goddess responsible for the magic in my blood. But she disappears, and my hands slam against the bookshelf she was standing in front of a moment ago.

More books tumble to the floor, and I hold my breath, listening. No one is coming. For now, I'm safe.

The white marble juts from its plinth at chest level. The fingers are long and slightly curled, as if waiting for a handshake. I lean forward, peering at the plinth. One word is carved into the space where the statue is secured in place.

Syndexoi.

To seal or unite with a handshake.

I reach my hand out and clasp the sculpted hand without another thought. The cool stone beneath my fingertips remains nothing more than a carving. I'm about to let go, to let myself wonder if I imagined the ghost, when searing pain radiates down my fingers and wrist.

The statue clamps down on my hand, holding so tightly the bones ache. I gasp, falling to my knees as I try to get enough leverage to slip my fingers free. Dust fills the air as the wall behind the statue shudders. It slides backward, revealing a roughly hewn limestone cave. The painting of the barge disappears with the wall. But even in the darkness, I can see a new painting directly on the stone of the cave.

Another flatboat, this time decorated in a style familiar to me: tomb paintings from burial chambers in Egypt. A sun flanked by two outstretched wings hovers above the barge floating down the green river. The painting continues, the river descending deep into the cavern where no more light reaches.

Finally, I jerk my arm free with a popping sound and clutch my hand to my chest.

I get to my feet, dusting off my pants with my uninjured

hand. The cave remains open, cool air leaking into the library. This is where the ghost went. She wants me to know about this place, perhaps even to descend into the cave. Follow the river. That thought makes my spine stiffen.

Follow the river.

Amenemopet told me to follow convergences to find an entrance to the Underworld. The Underworld's landscape twists and changes with humanity's beliefs, but the river never does. And convergences gather at weak points at the veils between worlds. This must be another convergence – one Damian didn't mention during the initiations. And based on the dust and cobwebs, no one has visited in a long time. Years. Maybe even decades.

This is how I'm going to reach the Underworld undetected and without my magic. This is how I'm going to find Hecate and discover how to save Violet. Gritting my teeth, I gingerly grab the statue again. Just as I suspected, the wall slides back into place.

I can't go to the Underworld yet. Not until there's a distraction taking up the entire Order's attention. Until then, I have to tell Anubis what I've found. Hoisting my backpack onto my shoulder, I glance around to ensure I'm still alone. And then, with determination driving my feet, I head into the night of Eidolon.

16

Overly starched robes scratch at the skin of my arms and neck as Anubis and I stand at the back of a line of similarly dressed Lector members. The ceremony, the one all Lector members must participate in each week to store magic gathered from deals with demons, is about to begin. At the head of the line is a set of carved wooden doors. The handles are bound with a complex rope – like the seals on the tombs of Egyptian Pharaohs.

Anubis' breath fans across my icy cheeks as he turns his head to look back at me. 'There?'

I nod subtly as we pass above the hidden alcove the ghost showed me, barely visible through the detailed iron spindles of the gallery. As the newest members of the house of Lector, we're at the back of the procession for the weekly ceremony. Still, I glance around, waiting to see a flash of eyes or a hooded face watching from the shadows.

'I just need a good time to slip into the hidden chamber.' I shuffle forward as the line moves another step, somber and quiet except for a few hushed whispers.

Anubis' lips flatten, and he faces forward again, voice so soft I can barely hear it. 'We don't know when that could be. At the winter solstice, I'll be gone.'

The wooden doors get closer. A flash of sickly purple momentarily bathes the darkened hall of the gallery each time a member touches the rope seal. The doors open a sliver, allowing one person to pass at a time.

'Damian likes you. He couldn't take his eyes off you during the Lector initiation,' I whisper, my throat tight.

Anubis' shoulders stiffen and I glimpse his profile as he looks back at me. 'He senses *your* magic, Andromeda. And if he finds out who I am –'

'He won't,' I say firmly.

'Just don't do anything until we can both agree on a plan.' He shakes his head. 'And I wouldn't put too much faith in Ramsey. How do we know he doesn't want Damian's position for himself?'

I press my lips together. 'I don't think he's like that.'

Anubis huffs, the sound somewhere between a laugh and a sigh. 'Look at where we are, Andy. Everyone in the Order is like that.'

I fall silent, my thoughts in turmoil as another flash of purple illuminates the hall. Anubis steps up to the seal and glances at the two Lector members flanking the door. Their faces are covered with gold masks, the features eerily blank. Dark black robes, like ours, hide their bodies, and a blood-red sash bisects their middles.

Anubis touches the rope without hesitation. The sizzle of a protection charm working to fight back rings in my ears. But just as quickly, the fibers fall away, unraveling like a snake. He slips through the gap in the door and it shuts firmly behind him before I can glimpse what lies beyond. I'm alone now, with only the silent masked sentinels left. My mouth is dry as I step forward, tripping a little on the hem of my robes. My fingertips tingle as I stretch out my hand.

A spark of energy, whipping like plasma, arcs from the seal to my hand. A surge of warmth radiates up my bones, winding around my arm until it curls into the ouroboros tattoo on my shoulder. I grit my teeth as the rope slithers away, scales replacing the winding flax fibers. The eyes of

189

a cobra flash at me as it shifts into a living thing, unwrapping its tail until the door eases open. I want to snatch my hand away, but the cobra watches, forked tongue flicking and tasting the air as if searching for hesitation. For fear. Humid air fogs my glasses and sticks to my skin as I enter a darkened chamber.

Feet shuffle on pebbles. Murmurs echo against walls I can't perceive. The smell of wet stone and earth washes over me. A soft bluish-green glow is emitted from the back of the chamber, casting ripples of light on an uneven ceiling. Water. A river.

I stumble forward, cold sweat sticking to my back as I search for Anubis in the darkness. A sea of black robes and red sashes stands before me, the members inching closer and closer to the water. A match sparks, illuminating Rohan's face. With a rushing sound, a series of torches along the wall ignites. Rohan stands on a platform before the underground river and a hush falls over the crowd. Only the sound of dripping water echoing against the cavern walls remains.

'Welcome,' Rohan murmurs as he dons his grotesque Thoth mask, 'to our augmentation ceremony.'

The rest of the house members murmur a reply before donning masks of their own. The same gold featureless ones, eerie and cold. Someone taps my shoulder and I jump. One guard by the doors thrusts a mask in my hands and I take it, fumbling with the string on the back as I secure it into place.

I can't see Anubis, and my glasses are smashed uncomfortably against my cheekbones behind the mask. My breath is trapped behind the plaster, making the humid air even worse. Rohan raises his hands, and the crowd splits in two, like a conductor preparing for a symphony. I jerk to one side before I can be caught out, stranded in the middle.

'Many of you have attended this ceremony every week for years. For our newest members, I'll review the importance, the vitality, of this rite for the Order.' Rohan motions to the river behind him. 'The rivers of the Underworld flow in spaces that sometimes touch our world. These convergences are spots of power, fuel for us to burn. Damian initiated this rite when he ascended to the role of Romulus three years ago, a way for us to grant the Order more power. More knowledge. The magic you have gathered this week from bargains struck with demons must be purged through your blood into the river. Our Romulus will drink from the waters later tonight, gathering his strength to lead the Order, and receive wisdom from ancient rites.'

He steps down, brushing his robes aside as he moves to a small outcropping of limestone rock, worn smooth by the flow of the river. I can feel the thrum of magic beneath my feet, smell the hint of death where the river dives back into the stone and disappears from sight. Rohan kneels, and an attendant hands him an ornate goblet. He lowers it carefully into the rushing waters before holding the full cup aloft.

'The branches of this river are rare, but Eidolon was built on three such tributaries. One has faded, and another crosses beneath the sacred Sanctum of Oculus. The convergence flows beneath our feet at each sanctum and feeds our magic. This branch, the last branch, is also unique, unlike any other convergence in the world.' Rohan tips his head back, golden beak rising in the air as he swallows a mouthful. A trickle of water courses down his throat as he opens his eyes. 'The river Styx supplies Lector with a peculiar magic, one full of knowledge, one that makes our spells more powerful. But the waters are hungry, and our house is tasked with feeding them, sating them. In return, the convergence ensures that vows made over these waters are unbreakable.'

My skin prickles with awareness as the same attendant takes the goblet from Rohan. Unbreakable promises? What is Damian planning, as the new head of the Order, that requires vows fed by the Underworld itself? I stare at the water in the tunnel below the earth. It feels . . . alive. As if it breathes and listens, tasting the air and waiting for something.

'Each member of the house must spill their blood into the waters of the Styx. Your essence, your magic, and what you have gathered this week, will ensure this branch does not fade from this spot. Sometimes, on the rarest of occasions, the river will taste pleasing blood and bless us with a rare gift: a prophecy for the good of the Order. This reward is never given lightly, and we pray the river will grant us such knowledge once more tonight.'

With that, the first member in each line steps up to the lip of the stone bank. The water surges, swelling as it rushes by. A potent mineral taste floods my tongue, and flecks of cold water pepper my skin. Two attendants flank Rohan as he observes the procession, watching as each member of the house of Lector bares their arm, the same one inked with the ouroboros, and is cut with a familiar ornate bronze dagger.

My teeth clench painfully as I shiver, stepping forward as the lines move quickly. The smell of blood grows stronger as I approach the water's edge. Where is Anubis? The green waters darken with blood as the few people ahead of me bare their arms and allow the attendants to cut them. Deep red offerings drip into the river, and I swear I can feel it groan in satisfaction.

'Initiate,' a stern voice barks, pulling my eyes from the living river. 'Your arm.'

I swallow down the nausea building in my gut and shakily

pull my sleeve back. I search the other line for Anubis, but the masks make it impossible to tell anyone apart. I hiss as the knife cuts into my flesh, leaving a long angry mark. Crimson sticks to the curved blade as the attendant turns my arm over and squeezes. Blood falls in a sickening stream into the mouth of the river.

A humid wind rustles my curls. I can taste my breath, the stale air of the cavern. The attendant drops my arm and I cradle it to my chest, staggering out of the way. Murmurs ripple over the members as the river churns. My eyes are trapped, my gaze frozen as the current seems to reverse, defying all the laws of physics. White foam gathers as the waters swirl and a deep booming moan echoes from within the tunnel.

Rohan staggers to the front of the lines, his eyes bright behind his mask. 'Impossible.' He kneels at the water's edge, his eyes wide. 'The river has not yet drunk from everyone.'

My stomach plummets to my toes. The moaning sound grows stronger, higher pitched. I wince, wanting to cover my ears. I search madly for Anubis, my muscles tensed and ready to flee. This was a mistake to come here. To join Lector. My blood feeds immortals, grants them power. Could the river Styx have a form like a god? What will she do when she finds me?

A hand grips my shoulder and my gasp is swallowed by a crash as the river surges and breaks over the lip of the bank. My shoes slide on the stone and the person behind me drags me back a step.

'Andromeda.' Anubis' voice comes from within the gold mask and his fingers sink further into my shoulders. 'Just breathe. I need to hide you before your blood attracts more attention from the Underworld.'

I nod mutely, sucking in air as my ears pop. The pressure

changes, sending another dank wind over the cavern. The water gathers in the center of the chamber, leaving nothing but a tiny stream in the deeply gouged river bed. Rohan holds his hands aloft in supplication as the form of a woman takes shape.

My heart stops beating as the woman made of water opens her eyes. Her hair flows behind her, wetting the ground as she steps forward. Her eyes are the same color of mineral green. But she looks alive, powerful. Styx gazes at the mass of Order members without interest until her eyes land on me.

'Hello, little mortal,' she whispers, voice smooth as the rocks beneath our feet. 'How good your blood tastes on my tongue.'

17

'Styx,' Rohan murmurs, bowing so low his beak glances off the stone. 'Your presence honors us, and we await eagerly the knowledge you see fit to give.'

The river goddess looks down her nose at him, her swirling hair sending rivulets of water down her skin. 'Do you? How curious, considering what your Romulus has done to those like me.'

A few members look at one another in confusion. Rohan stammers as she walks by him dismissively, her hungry eyes still glued to where I stand. Anubis has gone rigid behind me, his fingers almost painful as they anchor me in place. I can't tell if he's trying to keep me from running or is paralyzed by the same fear turning my blood to ice.

'The offerings of these mortals have kept me from slipping into a deep slumber,' Styx purrs as she advances toward me. 'Sometimes I taste a particularly sweet sacrifice and must reward those who grant me a morsel of deeper power. And you, little one, taste sweeter than any wine.'

She stops before us, towering at least a foot above Anubis. Her eyes and hair swirl and shift as she watches me and licks her lips, like she wants another taste. I can't lash out with a surge of magic, not here. The Order will stop me from threatening such a powerful benefactor. All I can do is stand and hold my breath as the goddess circles us.

'Styx, what prophecy do you have for our Order?' Rohan has stumbled his way over the slick stones to the goddess's side.

She casts him a dismissive look. 'I will share it only with the one I wish, Thoth. You know this.'

Rohan steps back, bumbling over his apology. 'Of course, my lady.'

The goddess turns back to us, eyes on the golden masks. I wait for her to whisper who I am. What I can do for someone like her. Her hand reaches out, ice cold. I brace myself for her touch, for the end of everything I've sacrificed so much to accomplish. But her hand skates over my humidity-swollen curls and wraps around the base of Anubis' mask

Part of me wants to collapse to my knees with relief. Anubis' spell worked. He's hidden me again, protected me. But then I see the unmasked hunger in Styx's eyes. The curiosity there. She tips his chin up and sweat breaks out across his golden skin.

'Such a handsome face, mortal,' she murmurs, eyes narrowed. 'And the most decadent of blood. If you weren't tied to this little order, I would have you for myself. Ah, the things we could accomplish if you and I bound ourselves together.'

'My lady,' Rohan protests, but Styx cuts him off with a raised hand.

'I know how this arrangement works, Thoth. I can only form because of your weekly sacrifices to strengthen your convergence and Romulus, and for that I must not interfere with the Order.' She casts Anubis a longing look before she drops her hands. 'This one is powerful. He will grant the Order a new future. The one Romulus dreams of.'

Rohan seems to burst with anticipation but holds his tongue as Styx leans closer to Anubis. Her lips brush his ear, and she whispers something. Magic gathers around me like a cloak as she speaks in another language, one as old as the earth. She's speaking the tongue of the gods. Does she know Anubis can understand it because he is like her?

Even as Styx steps back, her eyes bright with new power, my heart refuses to resume its normal beat. Anubis' face is stoic as she returns to the river bed, her hair growing longer, snaking around our ankles as she smiles at Rohan.

'Until next time, Thoth.'

And then she collapses in on herself as the rush of the river fills the cavern and thunders past stone and earth, disappearing into the depths of the Underworld.

The upper rooms of Ibis Park are eerily quiet as the members of the house of Lector sit and wait. Rohan and Damian's voices slip underneath the doors leading to the staircase, but their words are muffled. Anubis sits next to me, clutching his golden mask in his fists, head bowed and shoulders hunched. He spent only ten minutes on the other side of the door, sharing Styx's message with Damian.

The thirty members of the house stare at Anubis from seats scattered among rolling stacks and glass display cases housing ancient artifacts. A clock chimes softly from the floor below, and each time it tolls Anubis' muscles grow tighter.

'What did she say?' I whisper, fingers damp as they curl at the lip of my golden mask. 'What did you tell them?'

He shakes his head, looking at the water droplets still clinging to his shoes and the hem of his robe. 'She said, "The final blade is in my possession."'

'Styx has a blade? Like the one Damian has? Ramsey said there were seven.' I worry the inside of my cheek with my teeth, eyes darting around the room. The shadows of Rohan and Damian slowly drift back and forth beneath the door. Like they're pacing.

Anubis nods, his face pale.

'What do you think happens when Damian has them all?'

'I have no idea,' he murmurs, knuckles white. 'The message wasn't for me. It was for Damian. And he wants the blade desperately. Something about its power to kill what can't be killed.'

I sit back, eyes slipping to the door once more. 'If Styx has it, this blade will be in the Underworld. Another reason for me to go.'

'Andy,' he whispers harshly. His hand curls around my wrist to anchor me in place, as if he's afraid I'll attempt to slip into the hidden tunnel this instant. 'Damian will do anything to get that blade. And now he's suspicious of who or what I am.'

Anubis drops my wrist and leans away, his face impassive and cool as Damian strides inside, Rohan and Antonia in tow. I draw my brows low at the sight of the Order's Prometheus brought to Ibis Park. She and Sophos don't deal in the deeper, darker magic of Lector. Sweat makes my curls stick to the nape of my neck as the house leaders assemble before the tired, damp members of Lector.

Damian crosses his arms over his chest, the pale scars seeming to glow, to shift beneath his skin. 'Our Order has been blessed this night by Styx, goddess of old.' His icy gray eyes settle on Anubis, but it feels as though they've seared through my chest. 'Thoth regaled me with the feats of our newest initiate, Jae Han.'

Anubis doesn't move beside me. His fists are curled tight, resting on his knees as he stares at the three house leaders, expressionless. I hold my breath, gently sending out a pulse of magic, searching for our connection. The spell keeping him in the mortal realm remains tightly in place. So why does a sense of foreboding claw at my stomach?

'Magic is fading from our world more quickly than we can hold on to it,' Damian continues, striding across the rug, long fingers skimming the top of a glass case housing a weathered human skull. 'Lector has performed admirably, strengthening the convergence's hold to Eidolon with your sacrifices of blood. But now and then, our Order is instilled with fresh power. A member with more than a mere aptitude for what the convergences can provide, but with something living in their blood.'

Anubis swallows, but manages not to glance my way. Not to betray a hint of emotion. Me? I feel the blood drain from my face, my fingers.

Damian comes to stand before Anubis, his eyes almost silver in the dim light. 'For the first time in two decades, we invite someone not born of the founding families to initiate into the house of Oracle. You will be my apprentice, Jae Han, the right hand to Romulus.' Damian waits as gasps rip from open mouths as every member of Lector leans forward in unison. 'We are the new Order, and our dawn is near.'

Rohan's lips press into a thin line, jealousy making his shoulders stiff, but he manages a weak smile in Anubis' direction. I sit, stunned, as Damian offers a hand to Anubis, the scars playing across his forearm so prominent I can make out their shapes.

An ankh. A djed. Cuneiform phrases mixed with Aramaic and Pictish symbols.

The tattoo on my leg aches as Anubis slowly stands, grasping Damian's hand in a handshake. Blood roars past my ears as Damian congratulates him and promises him glory and greatness at his side. The tattoo my sister crafted sears down to my bone as Order members surround Anubis, congratulating him and staring with unhidden envy.

All I can feel is Damian's magic, inked into his very skin by blood and pain, curling around Anubis, hiding him from me.

18

Anubis

Anubis follows the scarred figure of Damian back into the large chambers of Thoth. Rohan and Antonia dismiss the gathered Lector members in the waiting room. Anubis stands in the center of the large chamber crammed with books and scrolls and hides his worry behind a blank expression as Andromeda leaves with the rest. Damian sits at Thoth's large desk, gray eyes devouring him like a wolf with prey in his jaws.

'Your official initiation will take place after the council has conferred and agreed upon a day,' Damian says. 'Prometheus and Thoth are gathering the grand council now. They will meet us here soon.'

'Thank you,' Anubis replies automatically, his mouth dry. 'It is an honor to be considered to join the highest rank of the Order.'

Damian's eyes and sharp features look like marble as he studies his new apprentice. 'Once you enter, you are Oracle's forever. The Order will be your family, your friends and your future, the moment your blood kisses this blade. As Romulus, I am your fate.' Damian waits, and flashes of bright blue eyes and wild curls fill Anubis' head.

'I understand.'

Damian stands and draws the blade from his belt. Anubis makes no outward movement, but every muscle in his body tenses. Magic pours from the knife and radiates down his spine. It calls to the godly side of him. A warning.

'The council will surely have many arguments against me picking someone like you to join Oracle, but it is not their opinions that matter.' Damian brandishes the knife in one hand and sticks out the other, waiting. 'It is mine.'

Anubis thinks of Andy, about what is going through her mind as she is ushered from the grounds of Ibis Park. He can't feel her familiar magic gathered around him, like a fingerprint only he knows how to read. Whatever magic Damian wields with the blade has torn them apart. It stings like a deep wound.

Despite that, Anubis holds out his hand. Damian's teeth are sharp as he smiles and digs the tip of the knife into Anubis' finger. Bright red blood, red as any human's, wells up against his skin. Damian swipes his fingers through the blood and makes a mark on the inside of his arm. A symbol of a winged sun disk on his scarred forearm. The symbol of rebirth.

The crimson blood sinks into Damian's skin, and a rumble echoes below the ground.

'The convergence below has accepted your blood. The council may argue and fight amongst themselves, but you will be permitted to attempt the rite to initiate into Oracle.' Damian returns to the desk and sits like a king on a throne, setting the blade on the smooth wooden surface. 'With the blessing Styx granted us after tasting your blood, the last blade will be ours before the year's end.'

Anubis hesitates, eyes flicking to the exit as he considers what entering the final house means. 'What is it you want me to do for you, Romulus?'

'Magic is fading, Jae,' Damian says simply. 'If we do not do something about it, people like us will lose our power. Gods are meddlesome things, but when joined with man, they are nearly unstoppable. There is only one way to keep magic rooted in our world.'

'How's that?'

Damian smiles again, and Anubis' stomach twists at the sight. 'The blades Styx mentioned. And they can only be recovered under . . . *unique* circumstances.'

'What circumstances?'

Once more he imagines Andy. Her sister. Their blood blessed by Hecate.

Damian touches the knife on the desk lovingly. 'The blades I have been gathering are touched by ancient gods who did not trust my ancestors and the power they wielded. Because of this, the knives have been cursed to only be recovered by those not of the founding families. And you, with your magic stronger than even most Oracle members, are just what I need. Once you become part of Oracle, once I have trained you, prepared you to bear the weight of the spells hiding the blade, you will retrieve it for me.'

'What are the blades for?'

Damian touches the hilt of the one at his belt. 'Gods are not easy creatures to kill. Nor is their magic easy to control.'

Blood roars in Anubis' ears. This is the answer to so many questions. And yet, he cannot stop now. Not until he is buried beneath the weight of the Order.

'Why would you kill a god?'

'They embody magic, elements and belief. When they are killed, their magic is absorbed into one of the blades. When I learn to harness them, when I am strong enough to control such power, their magic will keep the Order alive, even as magic fades from the world, one generation at a time.'

Voices gather outside the doors. Council members answering Romulus' call. Before the doors can open, Damian leans over the desk, catching Anubis' hand, the one he took the blood from. 'Can I trust you, Jae Han? Can I trust the intriguing magic in your blood? Remember, once you enter the sanctum, you will live amongst us. Work with me. Become central to the Order.'

'Of course.'

Damian nods, something lurking behind his eyes. 'When you complete the ritual to enter Oracle, I will bring you to the place where Styx has hidden the blade. In return, I will grant you what was promised in your first invitation from the Order.'

Anubis' heart thunders in his chest, such a mortal reaction. But even so, he cannot deny the dark part inside of him that desperately wants what was promised him. A way to stay. A way to belong here. To *her*.

The doors creak open and Rohan peers inside. Damian nods once, permitting the council to enter. As voices grow, a dozen people spilling into the chamber, Anubis catches Damian whisper softly, 'And when I have the last blade, it will taste the flesh of the goddess.'

19

Lightning flashes outside the window. Rain lashes the glass in angry sheets and my breath clouds before my face. I sit up, skin prickling with awareness. The night is deep, endless. All the lights of Eidolon have been extinguished, and the radiator below the window is silent. No power. The storm must have knocked it out.

I rub my eyes, holding the scratchy wool blankets on Anubis' bed beneath my chin. I can't tell what time it is, or when I fell asleep. It's been a week since Anubis left with Damian to join the Oculus compound. I know he must live there now as an Oracle member, but I've spent night after night with no sleep, hoping that he's alright, waiting for him to come back for his things. For answers. I must have finally drifted off, exhausted.

Something creaks, the sound swallowed by a clap of thunder. The temperature dips again, almost painful. A flicker of green flame flits in the corner of my eye. I swallow, my throat dry as I scramble, fingers searching the bedspread for my glasses.

'Andromeda,' a voice whispers, so softly I think I might still be dreaming.

I swing my legs out of bed, still fully dressed. Lightning strikes so close that my teeth ache and spots dance across my eyes. The same movement as before. I hold my breath, icy fingers digging into the bed as I contemplate using my magic.

I can't take a full breath as I whip my head around, shoving my glasses up my nose.

Solidifying from thick, vaporous green mist gathering in the darkest corner of the room stands one of the three-bodied statues. Shining black obsidian glints as one arm holds aloft a torch, another a dagger, and the third a key.

'Is this real?' I ask, my throat tight and my voice so quiet I can't tell if I've spoken aloud.

The statue moves, the three bodies crawling like spiders as they pull themselves off the plinth. The timbers of the floor creak and groan as their weight thuds against them. My head swims, like I've had too much to drink. The green mist grows thicker, wrapping itself around me like a shroud.

'The wolf feeds now on the body of the sixth god,' one statue says, though her hard, carved lips do not move. She holds out her hand.

My eyes struggle to focus on the silver tablet gleaming against her fingers. The image of Lupa snarls up at me. 'Hecate?' I all but whimper.

The statue drops the tablet in my palm. With clumsy fingers, numb and almost without feeling, I flip the curse tablet over. The name is in ancient Greek, and my stomach knots. But then I make out the symbols. Vulcan. The god of fire. It isn't Hecate.

The second circles around me, her torch dripping green flame that sizzles on the floor.

'Dead bodies of the gods line the oldest river,' she murmurs, her blank eyes boring into mine. 'They feed the six blades, granting Romulus power. The seventh is near. The last. And he wants her power to charge it.'

I sway on my feet, my eyes heavy as the three statues continue their strange dance around me. Their voices pierce my head, and the sickly-sweet smell of the mist floods my body, making it as light as air.

'Hecate,' I say, my tongue thick as it struggles to form words. 'What does Damian want with her?'

The final statue, the one with the key, stops in front of me. Though her expression does not change, I swear she looks afraid. 'Death is never permanent under Hecate's hand.'

My blood thrills at that, pushing away some of the otherworldly lethargy threatening to pull me down.

'Does he know where she is?' I plead, stepping toward the statue even though my feet feel like lead.

More green fog seeps through the floorboards, whispering over them, shifting and changing until the planks melt away, replaced by smooth obsidian stones. Hecate's path. The one I dreamed about.

One of the statues reaches out for me, grasping my chin, holding me in place. All three statues speak as one, voices echoing in my head, speaking over one another in a painful cacophony. 'The final blade will fall into his hands,' they spit. 'And if it does, it will taste Hecate's blood. Find her. Awaken her with her keys. She awaits you.'

My stomach drops just as the mist and the path beneath my feet dissolve. Sharp stone fingernails catch against my cheek as I fall. The last thing I see as I tumble into an infinite darkness is three sets of black eyes watching from above, like mourners peering into a casket.

I blink up at the ceiling, confused, as a sliver of weak sunlight filters through the room. It smells damp, like rain, the too-sweet scent of green mist gone.

'Andromeda,' a tired voice says.

I struggle to banish the grainy feeling behind my eyelids. Something warm touches my shoulder, shaking it. Instantly, my muscles tense, and I push myself up to sit. My arms buckle as I flail, trying to get my bearings. Watery morning light streams through the window, haloing a figure kneeling by the bed. I blink, realizing my glasses are folded neatly beside the pillow I was just resting on.

'Anubis?' My voice shakes as I disentangle my limbs from the blankets. 'What happened to you?'

He gives me a weak smile as I sit up, swinging my legs over the side of the bed. 'Damian had me meet with the council and the rest of Oracle. The interview process was rather . . . prolonged. They released me only this morning to move my things to the Oculus Sanctum.'

There are dark circles beneath his eyes, and his face looks pale and slightly haggard. My nostrils flare as I smell something familiar: deep earth and the mineral tang of river water.

Shaking my head to clear the dream away, I say, 'Do they suspect who you are?'

'Your spell still holds.' He smiles again, but it fades quickly.

My thoughts still feel sluggish, as if I'm struggling out of anesthesia. I stare at Anubis, uncertain if he's real or a waking dream. Dreams. The Hekation. 'Hecate is going to die next,' I whisper, still feeling adrift, like I've been on a rocking boat for weeks and have just stepped on to dry land. 'The seventh blade is for her.'

His brows draw low. 'How did you know that?'

'A dream.'

'A dream?' he repeats, eyes dropping to my mouth. My skin flushes as he reaches for my chin again, tilting it. 'What happened here?'

My breath sticks in my throat as I try to think with him so close, smelling like the river and looking at me in a way I can't name. 'What?'

'There are cuts on your chin and cheeks.'

His words are like a splash of cold water. I stand and cross to the mirror hanging on the wall. Against the pale cast of my skin are five red marks, spreading from one cheek, under my chin, and to the other side of my face. Perfect little crescents. The imprints of nails.

'It was real,' I murmur.

Anubis twists to face me, his clothes rumpled. 'What happened last night?'

'I saw Hecate, I think.' I swallow and turn from my reflection. 'Or at least, some version of her speaking to me through a Hekation.'

'What did she say?'

With a deep breath, I try to banish the after-effects of the Hekation's visit. 'Damian is using the blades to kill the gods. He used the sixth last night to kill Vulcan. And Hecate will be next. She is the final one he needs – something about her death magic.' I press my fingers to my aching forehead.

The hunted look returns to Anubis' face, and for the briefest of moments his form flickers between human and god. 'Until I'm inducted into the house, I can't witness Damian's rituals. He must have summoned and killed Vulcan last night once the council was finally finished deliberating. He told me the blades kill gods, but not why he is doing it. Why does he want Hecate's death magic?'

'He didn't tell you?'

'He won't.' Anubis rubs his jaw before sitting heavily on the edge of the bed. 'Not until I pass the rites to enter Oracle. And based on what I saw, they won't be pleasant. I could smell blood throughout the compound, could taste dark magic in every hall. All I know is that he needs Hecate. She is one of the few gods who has never been forgotten. Her power is immeasurable.'

'If it isn't because he knows you are a god, what does Damian need you for?' I ask, nervousness making my palms sweaty.

'To retrieve the blade that Styx knows of. The final one. He said only someone not born of the founding families can retrieve them, like a fail-safe.'

I hesitate, eyeing his exhausted features. The determined but grim expression on his face. 'Maybe we should act now. You're already tied to Oracle, but if you pass the tests and join, who knows what will happen? Damian has enemies. Ramsey must know what's going on. And we both know he's no friend of Damian. He could help us.'

'No,' he says, grasping my hand hard. 'We can't trust Ramsey. He's still the Remus, still part of the Order. And who's to say he won't turn you over to Damian if he finds out about your connection to Hecate?'

I press my lips together and sit next to him on the bed. 'He's been tortured by Damian. If we could get his help, someone on the inside, maybe we can stop Damian from retrieving the last blade. Keep you from Oracle.'

'It's too late, Andy.' His voice is hollow. 'The rest of Oracle is readying my trials.'

'Then let's go to Ibis Park,' I say, scooting closer, 'to the library and the tunnel the ghost showed me. Hecate needs me to find her before Damian has the blade. That's why I've seen the path.'

'My trials are tonight. I came back to find you, to warn you.' He stands and grasps my hands. 'Damian wants the power he senses in me. *Your* power. And if I give him even a moment to suspect what I am, or how you've bound me to you, he will use you as a way to get to Hecate. He's ruthless, Andy. You've seen only a fraction of what he's capable of. Human sacrifices are child's play to him.'

'All the more reason to leave now,' I argue, but something in his dark eyes feels as impenetrable as stone. My heart races and dread pools in my stomach.

'Andromeda,' he says firmly, 'my initiation *is* happening tonight. And you know I can't leave the mortal plane until the winter solstice. That's in one week. Damian wants your power desperately, and I won't know why until I join Oracle. I won't know what he's doing with the gods' magic or these knives until I've earned his trust. You have to go to the Underworld alone.'

I stare up at him, forgetting about ghosts and secret tunnels and talking statues. 'I can't abandon you here. If Damian is as dangerous as you say, then you need someone watching your back.'

He counters, 'What about Violet? She needs you to find Hecate. She's the only one who can cure your sister.'

I grit my teeth at the reminder. But to abandon Anubis? To leave him at the mercy of a bloodthirsty young man with a plan we don't even know. It's unthinkable.

But I can't deny the urge, the insistent pull in my bones that Violet is running out of time. I've felt it for weeks. Sand slipping through our fingers.

'Anubis,' I whisper.

He gives me a heartbreaking smile, the one that makes him look so human I can't catch my breath. Carefully, he tucks a wild curl behind my ear, thumb ghosting over the tiny cuts on my face to brush my bottom lip. 'Tonight, every high-ranking member of Lector and Oracle will gather at the Oculus compound to watch my trials. They'll be distracted enough that you can slip into the Underworld unnoticed. Find Hecate, wake her as fast as you can. I'll do what I can to delay Damian's plans until you're back. Whatever they are.'

Kane, and those loyal to Jan Arskell, didn't want Damian to kill the gods and take their magic. Anubis looks troubled at that. The mystery of Damian's goals, the reason behind the deep dissension sown between the members of the

Order. I know he's thinking of Min-Jun. Of his time spent hunting societies, snuffing them out, one by one. This is his chance, a way to redeem himself.

'Why does it sound like you're saying goodbye?' I try to smile, to sound like I'm not falling into a panic at being completely alone once more. No Anubis. No Violet. Just me and the Underworld again.

'They need me back at the compound.' He brushes my lip again. 'If they find out what I am ... if they –'

I cut him off with a sharp shake of the head. 'Don't. Don't say if you die, you'll find me in the Underworld. We've already done that once. I'm not losing you again, winter solstice or not.'

He looks like he wants to argue, that tormented look in his dark eyes again. But I'm tired of worrying about what happens when the spell breaks. When he's back in the Underworld as a god once more. So, instead of having the same argument, I pull his lips down to mine. He makes a surprised sound that quickly fades into a low groan as he wraps his arms around my waist, lips parting against mine.

For a few moments, nothing exists outside of this. Just two normal people lost in a kiss. He threads his fingers through my hair, deepening the kiss until I can't feel anything but him. Just as my breath hitches and my fingers ache to pull him even closer, a shrill ring breaks through the silent dormitory.

He pulls back, lips pink and swollen. 'Your phone,' he murmurs, voice thick.

I fumble for it in my pocket, as a picture flashes across my screen. It's Violet, when her hair was long and her smile wide. I glance up at Anubis, my mouth still tingling from the force of his kiss.

'I have to go,' he says, eyes soft as he brushes my hair back again. 'Damian needs me to prepare to take on the power of the convergence below Oculus tonight. But I know your spell will hold.'

'You'll be careful?' I ask as the phone rings again.

He gives me a wry smile as he grabs a backpack from his desk and slings it over his shoulder. 'As careful as you'll be.'

I answer the phone, lifting it to my ear. 'Hang on a minute, Violet.' I mute myself.

Anubis digs into a pocket and withdraws something. A statuette of a jackal made of onyx. The eyes are rubies, and delicate gold leaf adorns the ears and neck. He folds my fingers around it. 'A way to contact me. Wepwawet will find you when you break it.'

I open my mouth to say something, but my phone buzzes. The call-waiting screen flashes over with multiple text messages from Violet. With a sound of frustration, I look up at Anubis helplessly.

'You can do this, Andy. Hecate has waited for you to awaken her. I can distract the Order, give you a few days before they know you're gone. Just be back by the winter solstice. That's when Damian is planning on using the blade, that much I know.' He doesn't say goodbye. Only kisses me again, feather soft.

Anubis leaves the dormitory as quietly as he came, a bag of hastily packed things on his shoulder. I watch him go for a few heartbeats, my throat tight and stinging. I blink hard, brushing under my eyes before I unmute the phone and set it to my ear. Violet doesn't even give me time to snap at her for ruining my moment when her voice, shaky and desperate, crackles through the speaker.

'I had a dream last night. A Hekation spoke to me and warned me about Hecate, and a seventh blade. Damian doesn't want just any god's blood for the last blade. He needs *hers*.'

I suck in a breath at the fear in her voice, unconsciously touching the marks on my face. 'Vee, what's going on?'

'If he gets it, the knife, and it tastes any form of Hecate's blood, he will absorb her magic, Andy. Her power over death! Do you understand what this means?' A soft groan of pain cuts through the speaker. She struggles to speak again, her tongue tripping and slurring the words like she's in too much pain to think clearly.

'Violet!'

'Sick,' she pants, like she's about to pass out. 'Too sick.'

A thudding sound, like a body hitting the floor. A door slams and footsteps sound against the carpet. My heart thunders as voices and rustling come from the other end of the line. Mom and Dad. A nurse.

'Violet!' I scream again, my throat tearing with the effort. No one answers from her side. And then there's a muffled thud, like the phone has been knocked aside.

The line goes dead.

20

Sweat sticks to my skin as I sneak through the stacks of books at Ibis Park. It's cold outside, the wind fierce and angry. My skin is covered in goosebumps by the time I reach the small alcove housing the hand statue. I reach without hesitation for the marble. I don't wince as the fingers clamp tight around my own, hard enough to bruise. Nor do I shudder as the false wall slips away, revealing the dark, yawning tunnel to the Underworld.

Mom called me later in the afternoon to update me on Violet. She's been slipping in and out of consciousness for days. Last night she fainted and hasn't woken up since. A coma, the doctors are calling it. Except I know better.

Something has happened to Violet. Hecate sent the same message to Violet as she did to me. My sister had a warning to give me about Damian. It can't be a coincidence that she suddenly fell into a deep slumber right before she could explain. Violet is dying, slipping away from the mortal world like she's being dragged by an unseen force.

Hecate is our only chance, and she's wrapped in her own subconscious, asleep somewhere in the Underworld, the last victim Damian needs for his collection of blades.

I step from the marble tiles onto soft earth. The wall slides back into place behind me forcefully. My hair flies around my face and I take a step forward, boot sinking a little into the damp ground.

Steadying myself with one hand against the intricately painted wall, I wait for my eyes to adjust. Low light shivers up ahead, with telltale ripples dancing on the walls that speak of the river waiting beyond. A convergence that will lead straight to the land of the dead without extracting an iota of my magic.

I follow the painting on the limestone ceiling.

Finally, my feet drop a few inches as the tunnel becomes steeper. It feels different to the cave used by Lector for their ritual with Styx. This river seems calmer, deeper. It's a brilliant bottle green as it emerges gently from a crack in the bedrock. It slips along a smooth bed before gently ducking back into the belly of the earth.

Magic crawls over my skin. Not unpleasant. A pure convergence, I realize. One that has not been marred and twisted to fit the needs of the Order. A natural occurrence of magic. Of life and death. It's the lost branch of the river rooted beneath the school. The one that Rohan claimed faded away. But here it is, hidden.

I approach the edge of the water, the toes of my boots brushing the lip of the bank. On the other wall across from me is a simple carving. A sun disk flanked by two outstretched wings.

The mark of Ra. Of rebirth.

Without even holding my breath, I step off the ledge and into the river.

Despite the calm movement of the water above, the current is strong, pulling me quickly into its depths. Like being wrapped in a protective embrace, the river cradles me, pulling me deep into the earth until everything is black. Magic rushes by my ears, twines through my hair and dances along my fingertips.

The magic here is pure and clean. Unlike what I've felt at the forced convergence at Ravenswood, the blood-tainted ones at Eidolon, this feels right. Like the sun melting snow at the beginning of spring. Natural and good.

Slowly, like waking from a dream, the warmth fades to biting cold. The sunny feeling crumbles to ash, and the images of a fruitful delta are wiped away like a slate. My lungs burn and I snap my eyes open, kicking for the surface, fighting through water that is now oily and black.

I blink water away, amazed that my glasses remain in place. The mighty twisting river of the Underworld gently eases me toward the bank, where the gray shades of damned and forgotten mortals wander. Sloshing through thigh-deep water, I shake out my clothes, patting my pocket to ensure I still have the statuette from Anubis.

The air is still as I walk across the damp bank and climb a hill to get my bearings.

Nervously, I trace the outline of the jackal statuette in my jacket pocket, wishing Anubis was here. I think of him in the bowels of the Oculus compound, sworn by an unbreakable oath to serve the Order's dark purpose.

Feeling a familiar pull of magic, ancient as the dust of the earth, my eyes land on a soft hint of glowing green in the distance. A torch marking the entrance to the path that appears through gaps in the dead forest. Eyes set on my goal, I descend the hill.

Dried branches brush my hair and skin as I fight through the undergrowth and toward the torches. A clearing appears, dotted with asphodel flowers, their waxy white petals and sickly purple centers oddly comforting. At the far end of the meadow waits a Hekation statue. The visage of Hecate in triplicate. One hand grips a key, the other a dagger, and the last holds aloft the glowing green torch.

A whisper of power shudders through the trees. Branches snap and wood groans as the trees part, their roots emerging from the ground to rearrange themselves. I watch, transfixed, as the path to Hecate unfurls through the darkness and into eternity. The only hint of what lies beyond is another trace of a glowing green torch in the distance.

With magic buzzing at my fingertips, I walk forward, determined to meet my fate.

I walk until my feet ache. Until each step forward is agony. I want to stop, to rest, but the compulsion within me to keep going wins out against my will. Stopping is not an option. Whatever lies at the end of this road is tired of waiting.

I'm so exhausted that I don't even notice the shift in the air. The way everything plunges into an icy mist. My feet slow until I finally come to a stop.

A clacking sound interrupts the quiet. The trees above ripple and shift as the road rearranges itself at my feet. I stagger back as it undulates, black stones shuffling into place. A Hekation emerges from the mist, the goddesses' eyes boring into me. Instead of the torch extending out to light the path, the Hecate bearing the key faces me.

Dozens of forks appear before me. Narrow offshoots crawling through the forest, through the odd mounds that decorate the dead grass on the sides of the road. My stomach sinks as my eyes scour the new trails. A trick? I glance at the Hekation, at the key hewn from black marble, and the empty eyes of the goddess responsible for my existence.

Her mouth seems to twist in a wry smile.

Each new trail disappears into the mist, so that I can't tell which one leads back to the main road and up the jagged hill. Unease ripples over my skin as I glance once more at the Hekation before I approach one of the many new forks on the path.

Cool air licks at my neck as I gingerly set one foot on a worn-looking dirt trail. The ground beneath my shoe seems to vibrate, sending a shockwave through my body. I drag my other foot forward, gritting my teeth against the sensation.

Cracks echo behind me. Dry bark crumpling and twisting. My heart sticks in my throat as a branch dips to wrap around my waist and black vines crawl across the dirt to twine about my ankles. I spread my fingers, panic making a spark of magic flow through my body before I can think to quell it. A black vine, thick and undulating, retreats from its pursuit up my leg. But only for a moment.

With a thunderous crack, the vine hurls me off the trail and onto the path next to the Hekation statue. I gasp and rub dirt from my eyes, struggling to catch my breath as the vines recede, slithering like poisonous vipers back into the living trees.

The Hekation's onyx eyes look down at me with disappointment. A shiver courses through me as I sit up, coughing and spitting the dry, acrid dirt from my mouth. The key in her hand catches my eye. Long and slender, with two sharp teeth at the end. Ignoring the unfamiliar aches and pains across my limbs as I drag myself to my feet, I approach the statue.

Engraved into the black marble of the key is a circle. Within it is a maze of sorts, paths winding and curling around a central star. Eight spokes jut out from the perimeter. A *strophalos*, I realize, my breath catching. The wheel of Hecate. A symbol of her aspect as a goddess of life's crossroads. The statue's eyes almost appear to move, watching me. Tracking my thoughts.

Hecate is a triple goddess. Her aspects, the maiden, the mother, and the crone, show her different responsibilities. Her powers. And the very reason she was never forgotten in the world above.

The key, and this aspect, must be representing her dominion over liminal spaces. Crossroads. Doors to new worlds. The dream of the Hekation reverberates through my mind.

The triple statues told me to awaken the goddess with her keys. Plural. My eyes snap to the blank ones of the statue. If I am to awaken her, maybe I need each of her symbols. All three to unlock the door to the goddess.

Fingertips like ice, I reach for the stone key. Another snap of power, like a lightning bolt, shudders through my body as my skin touches the teeth. Power, unlike anything I've ever felt, ripples through my body. A breeze rustles my hair. It smells like freshly turned earth.

The paths spreading up the hill and through the eerie forest unwind like thread on a spinning wheel. I sway on my feet, my head floating. I feel like I'm being gently drawn away. Like Eurydice and Orpheus being guided from the land of death.

I jerk back as the statue's fingers open with the sound of grinding stone. The Hekation releases the key, her black and fathomless eyes boring into mine as she bends slightly, head cocked to the side. Unblinking.

Though she doesn't speak, her carved lips completely still, words blast through my skull as clearly as if she shouted them.

Two more roads wait for you, daughter of Hecate. This is only the beginning.

The statue straightens, freezing into place, hand clasped around empty air. And then, with a shimmer of darkness, the Hekation disappears, leaving only myself, alone with a stone key, and a single road, stretching on and on up the black hills of the Underworld.

The key sits like an anvil in my pocket as I trudge up the hill. The air is bitterly cold and yet sweat sticks to my skin endlessly. Time feels fluid around me, my thoughts coming in and out of focus. Who knows how long it's been in the mortal world? Time moves differently between planes. Will a week above be enough to do my work here? The thought of Violet, cold and lifeless because I was too slow to save her, spurs me on, even as my muscles burn with fatigue.

Though no sun burns in the land of the dead, darkness descends on the forest. Shadows grow long as my steps grow weaker. I struggle, like Sisyphus pushing his boulder in endless punishment, until it's so dark I stumble over a wandering root.

I blink, trying to make sense of my surroundings. Not even the smooth stones of the path show in the impossible darkness. Reaching out my hands, I feel for obstacles. My fingers brush nothing but thick fog. My breath shudders in my chest – the only sound. Even the trees have gone still, no longer touching my hair or skin with curious limbs.

Something thick and cordlike sweeps past my leg. I ball my fists at my side, eyes wide, even though all I'm met with is the endless, suffocating darkness. Another brush at my ankle, winding upwards like the vines from before. I reach down, ready to tear them free, already tired of the tricks the path is playing, when my fingers freeze against something smooth and muscular.

Scales.

Despite every instinct in my body screaming at me to panic, to fling the snakes from my body, I keep myself still. My heart races painfully against my ribcage, and my breath becomes shallow. The serpents feel incredibly large, their bodies powerful as they climb further, until they wind around my shoulders. My neck.

A tongue flicks against my cheek. Tasting my fear. I squeeze my eyes shut, sweat slicking my palms. The endless mist feels like a coffin, trapping me here alone, robbed of my senses. I'm reminded of the snake binding the doors at Ibis Park that led to the Styx. Its beady black eyes and sharp fangs. The way my magic tamed it into something as harmless as a rope.

I breathe in sharply, eyes flashing open. Though the fog is as thick as ever, a hint of soft green light blooms down the path. Black scales shimmer as the snakes twine themselves along my arms. Their fangs bare as they look at me, preparing to strike. That same sense of completeness I felt jumping into the river below the library comes back with the force of a hurricane.

The surge of magic building in my chest doesn't feel dirty or polluted. It feels as natural as the instincts of these serpents. Tension eases from my muscles as I turn my palms upward. A green glow, like the torch of the Hekation, blooms between my fingers before gently cascading over my whole body.

In a sudden burst, the mist flies backward, ripples of my magic making the thick vapor swell like a floating sea. The snakes hiss, though this time I swear it's with approval. Power hums in my skull, in my teeth and bones. I feel lighter as the fog rolls back like a curtain. A burden of some kind lifted away.

I'm at the top of the dark hill now. The mist must have moved me here, spiriting me to the highest point in this strange land owned by Hecate. A forest of poplar and olive trees tumble down dark stone cliffs until they meet an impenetrable wall of fog. Burial mounds, gravestones and tombs litter every spare patch of grass. Streams and springs gather dark water in a vast network of spiderwebs, a delta of the rivers confined solely to Hecate's domain. The scene steals my breath, almost as beautiful and haunting as the west bank of the Underworld.

Though this world feels muted, like the cover of a book faded by sunlight, I can sense the power rippling through every branch. Every stream. Hecate's magic is unlike anything I've felt before, like a dormant volcano waiting to erupt.

The thought sours my awe, turning it instead to cold dread. Damian wants Hecate's power, her control over death, and her free movement between the realms of the living and the dead. But why? And what will happen if he does have it?

Another hiss pulls me from the dark train of thought. The two snakes, their black scales gleaming in the green torchlight, slither off my legs and head further up the road next to another Hekation. Despite the shiver that steals over my skin as they coil and bend around each other, I approach the marble effigy of Hecate.

The three bodies attached to the column remain the same. But one hand is empty, no longer holding a key. The one in my pocket grows cold enough to burn my skin through the fabric of my jacket.

The fathomless eyes of the Hekation stare down at me, looking powerful and fearsome, wearing a crown of live snakes. The magical fire of the torch calls to me, tugging at that urge to call forth my magic deep within my soul. My fingers shimmer, a similar color, as I reach for the torch. Instead of emitting warmth, the flames feel burning cold. When my fingers touch the handle, a flash of ice steals through my blood.

The final path awaits you, daughter. The torch will guide you to my side.

The same voice as before rumbles through my mind, the Hekation who once held the torch speaking directly to me.

With a shudder, I focus on the road ahead, no longer

climbing steeply up a hill. Instead, sharp cliffs rise on either side as the road twists into the craggy canyon. A pulse of energy seems to ripple from that direction. Like a heartbeat. Tucking my arm against the key in my pocket and tightening my grip on the torch, I let the canyon swallow me whole.

My footsteps echo off the immense stone walls of the canyon. The road is smooth and unblemished, but erosion pockmarks the rough rock surrounding me on all sides, and caves and holes of all sizes stud the face. They feel like eyes watching me as I hold the torch in my fist.

The eerie green glow banishes the worst of the shadows, and even sends a thrill of magic through my hand each time my foot collides with the path. But the caves and hollows in the rock create a feeling of foreboding. Like prisons meant to harbor dark beings.

Though I sense the end of the path nearing, there must be one last roadblock between me and Hecate's resting place. The key, connecting to the goddess's aspect of liminal spaces, used my ability to cross boundaries. The torch, and its supernatural guidance, continues to tug me down the road, beating back mist and the growls of beasts waiting in the shadows.

The dagger waits for me ahead. I'm not entirely sure what aspect of the goddess it fits with. The tattoo borne by Dr Kane was the stain of a traitor, a brand marking him for death. Though Hecate is a goddess of death, I can't imagine her dagger being used merely to stab her enemies. Each of her symbols has a deeper meaning, a connection to the magic simmering in my blood. A way to awaken a powerful goddess who has forced herself to fade away.

Rocky outcroppings grow steeper as I plod along. The pale and dark gray mottling on the stones darkens as the sound of rushing water grows steadily. The air smells like minerals and something else. Something . . . like sulfur.

My hackles rise as I come to a stop, like a bird striking a glass window. My lips grow numb at the same time as my fingertips do. I clutch the torch hard enough that the marble handle pinches the skin, drawing tiny drops of blood.

I brace for a demon to come lumbering from its lair in the endless crevasses, hungering for my blood to feed it for decades. Instead, a subtle white glow blinks at the corner of my vision. I spin around, trying to track the movement. The dark rocks highlight a wisp of a creature flitting through the outcroppings. A ghost, like the one that showed me the convergence in Ibis Park. It moves like a sprite, in fast darts and agile movements too quick for me to chase.

Dropping my shoulders, I turn in a circle, searching for that flickering form. I'm alone once more, though my skin still crawls with unease. Turning back to the path, I try to walk forward, only to strike an invisible barrier. My shoulder jams against it, hurling me back with a jarring thud.

I glare at the new roadblock, gritting my teeth as I pick up the dropped torch in my hand and move to push myself upright. My palms encounter cold water. I look down, dumbstruck, as the mineral scent of an Underworld river grows stronger. My jeans are soaked through as I pull myself upright, using the stone wall to support myself.

I hesitate, my throat closing as I lean closer to the canyon wall. A line ripples along the stone, a clear demarcation of higher waterlines. The stone all around me in the narrow neck of the canyon is damp. The rush of water no longer feels familiar but foreboding as a funeral dirge.

I kick my feet, icy dread spooling in my stomach as I realize the water has already climbed to my ankles. It's not a canyon after all. It's a river bed. The flame on the torch sputters as water drips from the walls, seeping like tears. I step back, craning my head to search for footholds and a path up the canyon wall.

A rumble shivers through the water ascending my legs. Ripples collide against stone as the vibrations intensify, rattling my teeth. My hair flies around my face as a groaning wind pushes through the narrow crevasse, carrying the tang of sulfur with it. The water, already at my thighs, stings with cold. I grit my teeth to keep them from chattering and grab the torch, tucking it between my ear and shoulder.

I've already drowned one too many times.

Hooking my foot into one of the many holes and ledges carved by the water, I hoist myself up a few feet. Water drips from my clothes as I ignore the cramp in my neck from holding the torch in place, and reach for a higher hold. Vertigo makes my vision swim as I claw my way up the wall. My shoes slip on smooth rock, and my palms burn, welts and cuts rising on the skin from craggy ridges.

Risking a glance down, I see the water chasing after me, eager to drink me down. It's only a few feet below now, even as the rim of the canyon awaits me, tantalizingly close. I dig my nails into a larger crevice, ignoring the way they tear on the ragged edge, and brace myself against the wall, gasping for breath.

I adjust the torch, moving it to the other shoulder, muscles burning from the effort to hold myself in place. The bend of the river bed comes into view as I resume the climb. The water differs from the other rivers in the Underworld. This one has a silvery quality to it, like liquid moonlight. It would be beautiful if it weren't actively trying to drown me.

Sweat drips down my forehead as I grasp the edge of the canyon with one hand. The torch wobbles precariously under my chin, and I risk using my free hand to right it. I slip a few inches, my stomach somersaulting into my throat. But, by some miracle, I keep the torch in place and heave myself over the side, flopping onto my back to catch my breath.

Blood roars in my ears as the water below froths and boils, colliding against its stone cage as if angry to be denied my blood. Slowly, I open my eyes and stare up at the dark sky above. A chill slithers along my skin, and I grab the endlessly burning torch, sitting up as the feeling intensifies. I glance around for the telltale glow of a Hekation, marking the end of this roadblock.

Getting to my feet, I squint in the low light. A Hekation shines through the dense fog in the distance. I move to take a step forward. My stomach lurches as I encounter only air. My balance is thrown off and I crash back onto the lip of the canyon, nearly dropping the torch into the river. With knees as weak as a fawn, I roll over and crawl to peer over the edge where my foot slipped. Nothing but a steep drop into swirling mist looks back. I shuffle to the middle of the ridge, rocks skittering off both sides in my haste. The ledge is so narrow that vertigo makes my vision swim again.

How am I meant to reach the last statue if there is nowhere to walk?

Vibrations from the swirling water rattle the small stones at my side. I sit back, sweat making my hair stick to my neck and cheeks. The angry river below is no longer an option. If I'm to follow the path the Hekation marked, then I need to come up with something else.

Heart beating in my throat, I stand once more, carefully positioning my feet so they don't brush the edges of the ridge. My mouth goes dry as I take a tentative step forward, half crouched. Rocks tumble and slide from the edges, disturbed by my shifting weight. The torch in my hand sputters as mist from the other side of the chasm rises, cool and damp.

My dream comes roaring back. I remember three sets of eyes looking down on me as I tumbled into an endless abyss.

I take a steadying breath and straighten, holding the torch aloft. It burns brightly, the green flames as vivid as an emerald.

The river swirls a few feet below to my left, and the mist clings to my right, like ghostly versions of one another. Cold sweat sticks to my skin, but I know what I must do. Eyes trained on the faint green glow of the final Hekation in the distance, I step off the ledge and fall into the darkness.

21

Anubis

'Welcome,' Damian says, his voice resounding against the dome of the Oculus, giving it an almost inhuman volume. 'Today we offer a seat amongst the highest levels of the Order to an initiate that shows great promise. Jae Han, a new student this year, has already proven himself to be deeply connected to magic.'

Anubis, the god who walks the mortal world, has never felt this kind of powerlessness before. He stands in the central room of the Oculus, the connection of power at Eidolon, and the most sacred location for the Order of the Seven Sages. Dozens of robed figures sit around a circular dais directly below the opening in the dome, moonlight washing over them, highlighting scars, hands and features. The message is clear: despite the masks, the robes, you cannot hide from the Romulus.

Damian Valerius stands proudly at the crest of the dais. He has been preparing Anubis for this moment for days. Training him to tap into the extra power provided by the convergence below Oculus. How to bend it to his will, to let it flow through his veins like fine wine.

The tattoos marking Anubis' skin feel strange. The newest one burns on his chest, an eagle perched on a legionary standard, its wings outstretched, and its sharp beak parted in a silent cry. The symbol of the Order's reach across the world. And the power it now has over him. Sometimes, the markings itch and ache, as they would on any human's skin. At other times, they seem to disappear, fading, as if his accelerated-healing and not-quite-mortal body is returning in strength as the winter solstice approaches. He thinks of Andy, how he saw her only this morning as they parted. It feels like a lifetime ago as Damian's sharp eyes scan the crowd.

As Damian turns in a circle, silence falls on the gathered members of the ancient order. The moonlight spilling over the bloodstained dais washes out Damian's already pale eyes. He opens his crimson robe, tossing aside the purple sash. He bares the skin of his torso, exposing his chest.

Rippling scars, some pale and flat, others dark and raised, criss-cross Damian's body. Almost no skin is untouched. Decorating the sections not mottled by severe scarring are dark tattoos. He bears the Pleiades on one forearm, the ouroboros on his shoulder, and the eagle across his chest, like all high-ranking Order members. But dozens more symbols litter his arms and torso. An ankh, evil eye, pentacle, and even the eye of providence. No one else bears as many marks as the Romulus. Nor so many scars.

The Order members hush as the ceremony begins. Rohan and Antonia flank either side of the dais, their masks fixed in place. Only Anubis and Damian have bare faces.

'It has been twenty years, long before my tenure as Romulus, that an Order member ascended to Oracle without being born into the founding families of Eidolon.' Damian looks at Anubis, but he speaks to the gathered crowd. The dozens upon dozens of people of money and status that must bend to the whims of the scarred young man with the cold gray eyes. 'Our Order is dying, slowly, as magic fades. Our convergences power us, keep us connected to the influence of the old gods. But there must be more if we are to survive. If we are to shape the world, rather than be consumed by it. My father served the Order with that as his creed. And I carry the legacy as your Romulus.'

Eyes glint in the dark, looking at Anubis. Considering. Judging. Perhaps some are already plotting his death once he serves the whims of the young Romulus. They think Damian eccentric, desperate to show his strength as the new head of the Order. They will indulge him in his pet project of Jae Han, see where it leads. For a time. Until the moment he becomes more powerful than them.

Anubis keeps his head high and expression blank. The last week has not ingratiated him with the rest of the Order. The odd favoritism Damian shows irks the others who have licked his boots, and those of his family, for years. Anubis can still hear the whispers that have followed him since he entered the gates of the compound.

Interloper, they murmur, hatred etched into their faces. *What does he know about the Order? Less than a full semester at Eidolon and already entering Oracle?*

A particular set of eyes feels heavy on his shoulders. Anubis scans the crowd, searching for the person, studying faces despite masks. Off to the side, leaning against an empty chair, is Ramsey Arskell. Anubis fights back the urge to bare his teeth at the boy – another son of the founding families of Eidolon.

Jealousy, an emotion he never experienced as a god, rears its head. Anubis stamps it down. He doesn't trust Ramsey. The quiet way he slinks around the fringes of the Order, as if searching for something. The way he watches Andy, like she's his salvation. Now Ramsey stands near the crowd, awaiting the ceremony with something like fear in his eyes. Tearing his gaze from the other boy, Anubis' skin tingles as he turns his attention to Damian. To the waiting crowd.

'Under the full moon, you are presented to Oracle for initiation. The power created when a new member is sealed to the house of Oracle is a lifeline to our magic. But because it is so rare, it is also deadly. If you succeed, you will join our ranks and learn the deepest secrets of magic and the gods.' Damian's gaze sharpens as he gestures for Ramsey to join him on the dais. 'If you fail, your blood will decorate these stones like others who have gone before.'

Anubis lets his robe fall, exposing his chest for the ritual that will grant him access to the highest echelons of the Order. Absently, he brushes his fingers over the aching tattoos. The Pleiades, the ouroboros, and the newest one emblazoned on his chest like a brand.

Ramsey takes the robe and steps back off the dais. The crowd murmurs in hushed tones, necks craned back to look through the hole in the dome. Silver light grows brighter as the moon hovers perfectly within the hollow of the Oculus. Anubis' tattoos itch again, a warning that the winter solstice is a week away, and that same moon will call him back to the Underworld.

Rohan steps forward, a silver tray in his hands, contrasting with the golden ibis mask perched on his face. He inclines his head to Damian before offering the dagger. Anubis recognizes the blade, has seen it before when Damian killed the traitorous professor, and when he and Andy crafted their devil's traps. It is the reason Anubis is here tonight. To enter Oracle so he can retrieve the seventh and final knife for Damian.

The curved blade and intricate hilt gleam as Damian hefts it and motions for Anubis to kneel. 'Do you pledge your life, your magic, and your soul to the Order?' Damian asks, his voice quiet but firm. It stings like ice against Anubis' skin.

He swallows, breathing hard through his nose as he stares at the knife in front of Damian's bare, scarred chest. 'I do.'

'You understand that this Order, blessed by the seven ancient kings, is your only family?'

A pair of snapping blue eyes crosses Anubis' mind. Wild curls and soft lips that he can coax into a smile reserved only for him. His throat is tight, his voice threatening to crack. He inhales sharply again, forcing down any emotion.

'I do.'

Damian inclines his chin, finger stroking the sharp edge of the blade as he nods to Antonia and Rohan. A door opens at the far end of the meeting chamber, allowing warm incandescent light to spill onto the floor. Anubis keeps his head forward, refuses to look behind him as the doors shut and a pair of feet shuffle into the room.

Anubis has dreaded this part of the ceremony since he learned of it days earlier. He wanted to tell Andy when he found her in his room, lying in his bed with her hair spilled over the pillow. Wanted to reveal every dark secret of the Order, every sacrifice he'd have to make to ensure Hecate and, by extension, Andy and Violet were safe. But he knew she'd protest. Try to protect him in her stubborn, hard-headed way.

So, he swallows his horror as a boy is escorted onto the dais, positioned by Antonia, Rohan and Ramsey into the points of a triangle, with Anubis and Damian at the center. He recognizes the face of the boy. The desperation to claw his way higher up the ladder of the Order. Green eyes drunk on promises of magic unlike anything he's seen before. Power over the will of others. Wealth and influence.

But it's a lie. One told to lure him to this spot. A lamb before hungry lions. Anubis feels the uncomfortable prickle of sweat again as he lifts his gaze, watching with a clenched jaw as Damian steps back, knife poised over his palm.

Masoud stands to Anubis' right, Rohan's grip keeping

him in place. He wears a stark white robe embroidered with silver thread. Crescent moons and Greek incantations line the sleeves, neckline and hem.

'When do I get to phone my father and tell him I have the internship with the ambassador to Jordan?' Masoud demands. 'I was told that I would have the job and then be initiated into Oracle.'

'You are here willingly?' Damian asks, ignoring Masoud's question from before.

'Yes, of course. What is the meaning of this ceremony? You told me I was chosen to join Oracle because of the influence I could bring you across the Middle East,' he says, though his eyes narrow with distrust.

'All in due time,' Rohan says, his grip tightening.

Masoud, ever used to being the one asking the questions, shifts on his feet, attempting to shrug Rohan's hands from his shoulders. 'My Father donated a massive sum to this university when I told him it would help me join Oracle. I'd hate for him to have to withdraw it.'

There's a chuckle from someone in the crowd. Damian's lips draw back into a smile, but it's sharp and dangerous. Like a Roman legionary casually inspecting the well-used edge of his gladius sword.

'We wouldn't want that,' Damian murmurs.

Masoud flinches at the sight of the rippling scars on Damian's skin, but puffs out his chest, nodding to himself. 'My father is a key figure to receive a favor from. Once I am installed with the ambassador, you'll see what I can offer.'

'Is that so?' Damian asks, his voice still carrying that casually cool tone. 'We wouldn't want to keep such an important young man waiting to greet his destiny. Shall we begin?'

A hush falls over the chamber, so heavy it presses on Anubis' lungs. He's frozen in place, jaw clenched so hard his ears ring, and the floor bruising his knees. *It's not your fault he was chosen to die,* he murmurs silently. *You're protecting Andy by killing Masoud. Ensuring the Order does not suspect you. He is a dangerous person to keep alive.*

The same justifications he's been repeating to himself over and over in quiet moments. A way to ease the guilt. But he imagines Andy's horrified eyes as she watches the scene unfolding around him in slow motion. She'd scream, the sharp tang of her magic rearing to the surface, filling his nose. The smell of ancient herbs, of the Underworld. Of home.

Damian tilts his head back, letting the moonlight wash over him. His scars appear to glow against his pale skin. His tattoos shimmer as they connect to the convergence, to the dark rituals he's already done in order to become the strongest member of the Order. When he opens his eyes, they aren't gray any longer, but bright, painful silver. As silver as the curse tablets testifying to his might over the gods.

'What –' Masoud begins, but Rohan reaches around him to slam the flat of his hand over his mouth, cutting off any protest. Any words that will break the spell. Masoud's eyes go wide.

'From the blood of the willing, we offer a soul to our cause,' Damian says, his voice reverberating against the dome of the chamber.

'From the blood of the willing,' murmur the gathered voices of the Order members.

Damian hefts the heavy dagger and turns in a slow circle, showing it to the crowd. 'From the blood of the willing, we take the magic given by the Apkallu, the seven kings, and reclaim it for those strong enough to bear it.'

'From the blood of the willing,' the Order repeats, louder this time.

Damian's teeth bare in a ferocious snarl as he turns to Anubis, eyes wild and bright. 'From the blood of the willing, we offer a path to one worthy of our might.'

Anubis' breathing is labored as he clenches his fists and struggles to swallow back a surge of vomit burning his tongue. He wants to scream for this to stop. But he can only kneel and tremble.

The crowd shouts this time; the refrain stabbing Anubis straight to the core. 'From the blood of the willing!'

'From the blood of the willing, we call forth Jae Han to join our ranks, for his blood to mingle with those of kings, to transcend his low birth and join the true Order.'

Damian turns to Masoud, who has gone pale and quivers. His eyes search the crowd, the dais, and the telltale stains of blood across its smooth surface. He waits for an explanation, some sort of logic he can grasp on to. How could anyone betray him? His whole life he has been catered to. Fawned over. Respected.

Damian pulls Anubis to his feet and hands him the dagger. Masoud struggles in Rohan's arms, desperation threading thorough his movements as he thrashes in earnest. Rohan tightens his grip on the boy as Anubis accepts the blade and takes a step forward. But Masoud must realize what's to come. He brings his heel down sharply on Rohan's foot. Rohan grunts in pain, his hold loosening enough that Masoud breaks free. He screams, running for the doors. But the chamber is full of Order members deaf to his pleas.

Some stand, ready to intercept him. He cries out, skidding to a halt. Then he turns to Anubis. Masoud runs, ducking under the outstretched hands of Antonia and Rohan. He slips on the hem of his robe, sliding to a stop at the edge of the dais.

'Help me!' he pleads, voice breaking with the effort. 'Don't let them do this.'

Anubis opens his mouth to respond, but his tongue is dry. Damian intercepts the chaos, his eyes silver as he grabs Masoud by the scruff of the neck and hauls him onto the dais, flat on his back.

'Wait!' Masoud screams, eyes so wide he looks like a cornered animal. 'Please don't –'

The moment Damian's hand touches the bare skin of Masoud's throat, the other boy's cries of protest die. He lies still, lips together, as if in a trance.

'Are you here by choice, initiate?' Damian demands, breathing hard. Masoud nods at Damian, as if completely at ease. A smile stretches his lips as he looks at something above Damian's shoulder. Anubis' stomach heaves as Damian jerks his chin, gesturing at the prostrate Masoud, his patience gone.

'Jae,' Damian demands, his voice a cold splash of water that jerks Anubis back to the present. 'Now.' Looking away from the boy's face, Anubis plunges the knife into Masoud's chest, cracking through the sternum to pierce his heart.

Blood splatters across his bare chest, pouring from Masoud's open wound to trickle along the lines etched into the dais. The thick red liquid races through the carvings, until the last bit of gray stone disappears. Carved into the platform is an eagle, its wings outstretched like the tattoo all Oracle members bear. Unlike the rest, its talons do not hold a legionary standard. Instead, clutched tightly in its claws, is a still-beating heart.

Damian gets to his feet, taking the knife from Anubis' shaking hand, and wipes the sticky blade against his pants. He glares at the gathered Order members as they hurry to retake their seats.

'From the blood of the willing,' they murmur, completing the spell.

'Lie down,' Damian snarls, his cold silver eyes heavy as the Order falls silent, fear evident in their faces.

Anubis ignores the sickness spreading through his stomach like ice as he lies flat on his back in the center of the eagle carving. Warm blood sticks to his skin, his arms and legs outstretched, while Antonia and Rohan kneel at his side to hold him down. Anubis is not afraid of pain. But as Damian turns from the crowd, his eyes wolf-like, he feels a pang of bitter fear.

Damian resumes his calm demeanor, wearing his invisible mask of Romulus. The entire chamber is deadly quiet, simmering with unease.

Damian kneels at Anubis' side and hefts the bronze blade aloft. Sweat mixes with the blood beneath Anubis' back, and he grits his teeth to keep another wave of sickness at bay. The knife carves into the flesh of his chest, painfully slow, as Damian crafts an incantation directly onto his skin. Words in ancient Sumerian, so old they seem to come from the dust of the earth. Silver moonlight bleeds from the wounds instead of blood, dripping over his sides and ribs.

As Damian finishes the incantation, marking Anubis as belonging to the Order for all time, he feels that thread of fear blaze ever hotter. He stands, accepting the help of Antonia and Rohan. His head swims and he touches his chest delicately. The skin is already healed, the silver light fading away as a surge beneath Anubis' feet threatens to topple him. The convergence hums in his ears, a chorus of words and songs and prayers, mixing with the magic in his bones.

Fear needles at the base of his neck as he thinks of Andy's eyes settling on his chest. On the eagle tattoo that burns like hellfire. Of the way her face will crumple when she sees the line of scarred words forever marring the patch of skin across his breastbone. She will read them and finally see him as the sinner he is. A god of death, one that belongs in hell.

With my blood, I pledge my life.

Everyone waits with bated breath. They wait to see if the magic stolen from the dead boy on the ground will take root and strengthen the rite. If the convergence below will ignore the fact that Anubis was not born from the families that bound it in place in ancient times. If he will soon join Masoud in death.

The convergence rumbles again, but this time it is content, like a pleased purr from a panther. The silver light dims as the moon moves from its position over the dome. Damian grins in the growing darkness as the rest of the members gathered in the chamber cheer and pound their feet. Magic wells in the air, so thick and cloying Anubis thinks he might choke on it.

'Welcome to the house of Oracle, Jae Han,' Damian says, his eyes glinting eagerly. And as he grabs Anubis' hand, hoisting it into the air like a conquering gladiator, all he can think of is Andy, and how she will never forgive him for this night.

22

I fall through frigid air, cool mist kissing my skin, for only a split second. My legs buckle as I fall hard onto solid ground. Opening my eyes slowly, I trace the steep edges of the ridge just a few feet above my shoulders, and the thick mist that barred my sight flees away, revealing the solid path. I sigh with relief that I didn't just plunge to my doom, that instead it was the world's most intense trust fall.

A final Hekation marks the path's last stretch. The triplicate of Hecate stands proudly, eyes bright green instead of cold black marble. Two of the bodies hold empty air, and I pat my jacket pocket. The key and the torch are mine now, two symbols of the goddess conquered. A key to pass between the realms of life and death. A torch that guides me and my magic, like Hecate guided Demeter through the Underworld.

The last symbol is clutched in the hand of the Hekation's third body. A dagger, long and black and wickedly sharp, hangs above my head. The softly glowing eyes of the statue look into mine as I lift my hand to touch the hilt of the blade.

Silently, the statue's fingers open and it drops the knife into my waiting hand without even a tug from me. I look into the statue's face, waiting for a final message. But the Hekation's six eyes suddenly turn as black as the marble it was hewn from, as if dead.

One hand bearing the torch and the other the knife, I press forward on the path, eyes trained on the bend and the promise of what awaits me beyond. An end to this search. Answers for my sister. Hope.

Heart beating in my throat and magic gently curling beneath the surface of my skin, I round a bend in the black stone path and stop, my feet rooted in place. The path is arrow straight as it climbs up a final hill. A burial mound waits at the top, surrounded by black marble columns and an intricate garden blooming with thousands of deadly plants.

The ancient, crumbling Greek tomb is not what chills my blood. It is what stands between me and the end of my journey. That familiar soft white glow I followed in the river bed blinks at me. A ghost, the spirit of a young girl, hovers a few feet ahead. The same one that showed me the secret convergence in the library of Ibis Park.

She smiles at me, her skeleton visible beneath her gossamer skin. The spirit doesn't speak, only watches me as I stare in horror at the scene ahead. Silent voices hum in the ground and in my ears. Wide, baleful eyes turn to me. In my hand, the dagger grows even colder.

Standing between me and the tomb of Hecate is an endless sea of ghosts.

Hundreds of broken tombstones surround burial mounds coated in dry, creeping grass. My breath puffs in a cloud. The clearing is unnaturally silent, though everywhere I look, a spirit glares back.

The silence of the scene makes my ears ring, my brain desperate for sound. Warily eyeing the army of gray beings, I focus on the bright white of the spirit from the library. Her long hair and wide eyes appear innocent, kind even. The ghostly imprint of blood on her throat and the gaping wounds in her chest ruin that notion immediately.

Focusing on the steady flickering of the torch, and the equally steady magic curled within me, I meet the spirit's gaze, swallowing back fear to say, 'You're the attendant of Hecate. The one who showed me the way to the convergence.'

Her lips curl into a smile, and I grimace at the way phantom blood pours from her neck wound as she opens her mouth to speak. 'You found your way along the path. Hecate will be pleased.'

'Did Hecate send you?'

She nods her head, long hair spilling over her shoulders. It, too, is crusted in dried blood. 'I became a handmaiden of the goddess after my death. And I serve her with my entire being.'

Unease tightens into a knot in my stomach, and my palm slips a little over the hilt of the dagger. 'Who are you?' I gesture to the field of waiting ghosts, some almost without form, others flickering and weak. 'What do they want?'

She smiles again, floating closer to me. 'What we all want. Rest.'

'I can't help you with that.' I shake my head, ignoring how the surrounding air becomes almost unbearably cold as she approaches. 'You need a psychopomp like Anubis. Or Hecate.'

Her eyes fall to the dagger, an expression of longing stealing over her ethereal features. 'You forget who gave you your gifts, Andromeda. And you underestimate the value of them.'

A shiver ripples over the other ghosts, momentarily drawing my attention away from the blood and gore on the spirit's front. The road that twines delicately through the burial mounds and headstones shudders.

The dark, magnificent tomb of Hecate shivers on its hill. Dust rains from the stones supporting the columns, and a soft green light ripples over the walls. Every few moments, power spreads through the stones, pulsing like a heartbeat pumping blood through a massive body. The tremble of power travels down the path and to the tomb. Electricity seems to build in the air. Tension and anticipation.

The gathered ghosts hiss and press closer, gray bodies like smoke as their voices interrupt the unearthly silence. I wince, gritting my teeth as I hold the back of one hand to my forehead. 'What are they doing?' I ask, my voice rising in pitch as the torch flares and magic curls in my palms.

'They're restless,' she replies. 'They sense the Order's plan to kill the goddess. The final blade will be retrieved soon, and these spirits need Hecate to guide them to freedom.'

I study the spirit quizzically, noting that the dress she wears reminds me of something from the early 1900s. A white lace blouse with loose sleeves and a long gray buttoned skirt, cinched at the waist. Her voice is lightly accented, likely from the East Coast. If it weren't for her wounds and her wild hair, I'd say she looked like a refined, educated young woman.

A sick feeling crowds my stomach as I gaze past her shoulder to the waiting swarm of dead. They're all women. Dresses from all centuries rustle in an almost-wind, and fine-boned features slowly come into focus. Even the more shapeless ghosts seem to take form under my eyes, as if I've gained a new perspective, one that allows me to see the dead properly.

I wet my dry lips, and a bitter taste coats my tongue. 'The Order killed you, didn't they? That's why you were in Ibis Park. Why you've been watching me.'

'They sacrificed me to locate a demon that could help them divine the outcome of the war. Many had invested in all kinds of weaponry and made backdoor deals with high-ranking officials across Europe.' Her lips thin and she absently raises a hand to her ruined throat. I wince, remembering all too well the pain of such an injury. 'Even then, the house of Valerius hungered for knowledge of death. A way to weaponize it.'

'Weaponize death?' My skin prickles, and I tighten my grip on the knife as it continues to heat beneath my fingers.

She nods, mouth set in a thin line. 'Your magic is deep, Andromeda. Rare. The Order will stop at nothing to get it, just as they will stop at nothing to get Hecate. She slumbers in her tomb, awaiting you.'

I glance nervously at the tomb beyond, at the green light beating in time to my heart. 'Why did she put herself to sleep? Why not confront the Order herself and keep all this from happening?'

'Gods cannot act upon the mortal world freely,' she says. 'They have always needed deals. Blood. Offerings. It was safer to hide deep in her territory where the Order could not find her over the years. And Hecate needed a mortal who she could bless with her powers, someone who could face them on her behalf.' The spirit looks over the crowd of waiting ghosts, clustered around Hecate's tomb as if awaiting her to wake and free them. 'We have waited many centuries for you to rise from that blessing. And the time is now. This is your path to walk. Your fate to unlock.'

I automatically brush a hand over the key in my pocket, eyeing the spirit carefully. 'Will Hecate help me when I awaken her?'

The spirit only smiles. 'I will guide you to my mistress's side. The waiting dead will not harm us.'

My feet itch to continue the climb over the road. I hesitate, glancing once more at the poor spirit before me. Her ruined dress and long hair. 'How did Hecate make you a handmaiden if she has slept for centuries?'

The spirit's expression is fathomless as she glides over

243

the smooth black stones, the sea of ghosts parting before us in a wave. My skin tingles as I pass by them, their eyes stirring strange memories I never experienced in my head. Farms and sleepy towns. Ancient empires and bloody wars.

My feet pass over the thudding stones, energy winding through my limbs. The key in my pocket grows as hot as the dagger in my hand. The flame on the torch grows higher, whipping excitedly as we climb the path, closer and closer to the waiting goddess. The crowd of ghosts thins out as we near the base of the hill until the only tombstones that remain are so weather-beaten that they're pockmarked and unreadable. Utterly forgotten.

My breath catches in my throat as I lift my eyes to the great monolith housing Hecate. Lupine shadows dance along the edges. Three-headed dogs, I realize, guarding the tomb against interlopers.

The spirit has been silent for so long that when she speaks again, I almost jump.

'Thousands of women have been sacrificed to gods, demons and men's selfishness since civilization first began. Our supposed purity, our innocence, is something to be stolen and bartered.' Her eyes grow haunted, and the blood on her throat seems darker than before. 'Many of those killed have had magic, some sort of power or blessing latent in their bones. Sometimes, the very gods that blessed their bloodline with magic will take pity on them, provide a way to serve them and regain the power that was stolen.'

I see flashes of bodies lying cold in the sea by Ravenswood. Dozens of girls thrown into fires to feed hungry monsters. And I see Daniella behind the pub, her blood thick and congealed in the darkness. A shudder makes my teeth clench, and I fight to keep the anger boiling beneath the surface in check.

'And that happened to you?' I ask softly, the spirit's form blurring at the edges with the intensity of her emotions as she loses herself in memories.

'Many of the gods have faded, as you know. Hecate is stronger than most. She remembers us just as we remember her. And even as she sleeps, she gathers women like me to her side, protecting them within her territory of the Underworld since she cannot send them to the west bank for rest. Not as she is now.'

I wipe my sweaty palms on my pants as we crest the hill and finally enter the tomb complex. 'Instead of going to the west bank, you came here?'

'I wanted revenge. I was angry to have my life stolen so young, my future ripped from me.' The ghost considers me with her uncanny silver eyes. 'Horatio Valerius plunged the knife into my neck and stole everything from me as I bled out on the floor of the Oculus Sanctum. Hecate's call kept me from becoming a shade trapped on the east bank. She promised me, and thousands of others like me, justice. And then rest.'

Torches, identical to the one in my hand, burn brightly along a black stone wall that serves as the boundary of the temple courtyard. Spindly trees dressed in dry leaves curve over the small courtyard, their limbs heavy with fruit so ripe it almost smells sickly. Hemlock, belladonna and countless poisonous herbs decorate the garden in a display of deadly power disguised by beauty.

I pause at the threshold of the Greek-style tomb. It's tall, with arches and columns lining the exterior. Within the yawning opening, only darkness awaits. The spirit stops, her feet hovering a few inches above the worn stone of the courtyard.

'This is where I leave you, Andromeda.'

Uncertainty pulls on my nerves as I squint into the opening. 'You can't come with me?'

She shakes her head. 'Even as a handmaiden, I merely tend to her garden and answer the calls she sends through her familiars.' She gestures to the shadows of the building where three-headed dogs watch with glinting eyes. 'Only you can follow the last steps on the path to her side.'

My heart feels as though it beats too fast as I step up to the threshold of the tomb. A soft breeze rustles my hair and fogs my glasses. I breathe deeply. Scents of death, earth and fragrant herbs tickle my nose. Hand tight on the dagger, I glance at the ghost.

'Thank you,' I murmur, my voice thick. 'For helping me find my way.'

She smiles, and as she does, I swear the wound in her neck almost fades. 'Awaken Hecate before the Order can retrieve the seventh blade. Finish the cycle.'

In a breath of icy wind, her silvery-white form disappears into smoke.

The doorway calls me forward just as another pulse of green power emanates from within. I feel magic, addictive and warm, flood my veins in response.

Creeping vines and dust choke every surface of the interior. I blink rapidly, trying to adjust my vision to the low light. The walls are as dark black as the outside, and instead of a soaring ceiling, it's low and cramped. A tunnel. The back of my neck prickles as I shuffle forward, the path pitching downward steeply.

Whispers fill the air, falling from unseen lips. The pad of giant paws comes from behind me, though when I turn, I can't make out the shadowy three-headed familiars. Endless carvings adorn the walls. Images of Hecate, her symbols and animals, mark the marble. Some look like Greek and

Roman friezes. Others are far older, bearing the stylized elements of Egypt and Sumeria.

My shoes slip on the steep path, and I reach out, fingers digging into the grooves of the carvings as I do. Squinting into the dim light, I see the path continue downward. I realize that the entire hill the tomb complex is built upon is one large burial mound. The goddess sleeps even now beneath tons of soil, insects and bone.

Anticipation hums in my chest as I trace the wall and descend deeper into the belly of the tomb. Finally, the air shifts. It becomes sweeter, reminding me of the overripe fruit from above. Light sifts in through tiny cracks in a stone wall ahead. A familiar shade of green, like the eyes of serpents.

The wall stretches to either end of the tunnel, both left and right, blocking me completely. And yet, there is nowhere else to go. The cracks in the stone tell me that something is in a walled-off antechamber. But how to get there? My pocket burns and I reach inside, retrieving the key. It settles into my palm easily, almost eager to help.

I set down the dagger and torch. Smoothing my hands along the wall, I feel for a notch, a break in the orderly pattern of stone and mortar.

My nail catches on the lip of a stone, and I pause, examining it. A faux front encases the block, and I pry it away, fitting the teeth of the key into a perfectly sized notch. The key sinks in easily, and with a twist, dust and soft green light float into the tunnel. One by one, the stones fall away, crashing to the floor. I jump back, coughing and covering my nose and mouth with my sleeve.

The room is large and circular, with a dome supporting the roof. Decorating the ceiling is a detailed mosaic depicting the three aspects of Hecate: the maiden, mother and crone. The walls look similar, friezes carved in all styles, depicting Hecate standing at crossroads. I hold my breath. Dogs and snakes litter the ground, some ghostly and made of shadows, and others firm and real. They crowd around a central raised dais, still as death. Perhaps they are slumbering too.

I retrieve the dagger and torch, my skin clammy as I approach the dais. Green braziers burn in a circle, casting shadows on a rectangular altar covered in a black shroud. The fabric is gossamer, and beneath it, I can just make out the form of a person lying unearthly still.

My breath echoes in the silent chamber, my footsteps scraping the ground as I come to stand beside the head of the altar. The dogs and snakes do not move; the dozen or so of them entombed with the goddess lie still as statues. Waiting.

I shift the torch and dagger to one hand and lift the other to touch the soft shroud. It whispers against the goddess's skin as I gently pull it away. Dust plumes in the air, centuries of it gathered. My heartbeat thunders in my ears as I blink the grime away and gaze down at the face of Hecate.

Her flesh is desiccated, patches of papery skin pulled taut across bones. Empty eye sockets stare at the ceiling, and a white jaw hangs slack. I smother a gasp as I stagger back, eyes fixed on the hollow points of Hecate's face. Her clothes are ornate robes, decorated in swirling gold embroidery. But beneath them her flesh is gone. A skeleton.

My knees give out and I collapse to the floor of the tomb, choking on gasps of air. The torch rolls until it hits the foot of the altar, and the dagger clatters next to my knees. Tears blur my vision as I fist my hair in my hands, rocking forward as I struggle to breathe. She's dead. The seven days Anubis had between his initiation and retrieving the knife must have passed while I wandered the Underworld. Hecate is gone. The Order must have killed her. And now, Violet is doomed to die.

Dust and dirt and mud cling to my skin and my heart twists painfully at the sight of every mark. Proof of the journey I've undertaken, the heartache I've faced. Silent sobs shake my shoulders as I slam my fist against the ground, ignoring the bite of pain that rattles up my arm and the drop of blood that rolls down my knuckles and drips onto the knife.

Everything I have done, everything Anubis has sacrificed, has been pointless.

I don't know how long I sit there, alone and surrounded by silent animals. Eventually, a curious sound, almost like uneven footsteps, draws my attention. Tears sting my cheeks and dust clouds my eyes as I shudder for breath, despair stealing any warmth that remains from my body. I look around the dais and the chamber. The door remains open but empty.

Something brushes by my boot. I pause, lifting my head to peer into the darkness of the chamber. Another scrape against my boot. Blindly, I reach out for the dagger, my fingers closing around the hilt. Eyes glitter back at me in the dark, reflective like an animal's. The air turns slowly from frigid cold to a pleasant warmth. My breath stills in my lungs as the green braziers burn tall, casting a circle of bright light across the chamber.

Snakes coil past my legs and feet, ignoring me completely. As do the massive three-headed dogs, their black, muscular bodies slinking forward to surround the dais. The dagger shakes in my hand as I get to my feet. The drop of blood from my split knuckles catches my eye. It glows the same odd green as the torchlight before it sinks into the obsidian, as if consumed.

With a gasp, I turn back to the withered skeleton of Hecate. Her magic thrums all around me. I climb the three steps to her side and hold my hand out, setting the blade against my fingers. My blood holds her magic. I have awakened it. Retrieved her symbols as I confronted aspects of the goddess along the path. Biting back a hiss of pain, I sink the sharp point into the flesh of my thumb. More blood wells across my skin, glowing the same strange green as Hecate's fire.

I set my thumb against the teeth of the skeleton, smearing it across the bone.

The animals make low hissing sounds in their throats. I look over my shoulder, following their movements as they slink around the dais, restless. The rustle of fabric sounds behind me. My body stills, shivers running down my back. A shadow casts its dark form onto the ground as something rises slowly, a pointed crown like thorns arching from its head. Skin tingling with a powerful sensation, I turn.

The altar is empty. Hovering above it is a woman with long black hair, smooth olive skin, and power radiating so strongly it makes my eyes sting. Her body morphs, sometimes a single personage, and other times three women at once.

In my forays in the Underworld, I have crossed paths with multiple gods and demons. Each powerful and dangerous in their own right. But staring up at the goddess rising from her tomb, I am stunned.

Thanatos, Ossivorus, the Cynomorpha, and even Anubis, pale when compared to a deity that man has never forgotten.

Hecate, the goddess of crossroads, necromancy and magic, opens her black, fathomless eyes, and looks down at me. And when she smiles, her teeth are as sharp as a predator's.

23

Since learning of Violet and my relationship to Hecate last year, I have imagined what it might be like to confront the goddess in the flesh. What answers I could pull from her. Part of me even imagined blaming her for all our problems, for giving us the magic that set Violet on her path and pulled me into her orbit. But any questions, any words at all, die in my mouth the moment the goddess looks at me.

Hecate slowly descends, her bare feet gently grazing the edge of the dais. A black crown rests in her midnight hair, with three distinct points crafted from fine silver. Billowing robes flutter in a ghostly breeze, and two snakes lovingly twine up her arms, wrapping around her like sleeves. The goddess is tall, easily over seven feet. Her lips are thin but stained dark, almost like she has bitten into an overripe pomegranate. Her eyes have no whites, only an endless black that reflects a thousand images. Power radiates from her so intently it makes my skin itch and my bones ache.

This is no mere shade of a deity, like the ones I've seen. This is what Hecate must have been like since she was first formed, worshipped for millennia in every culture since man fashioned civilizations. Hecate could crush me with a look, flay me with a flick of her wrist. My knees buckle as her aura fills the chamber, as life crackles into every stone and carving.

'Andromeda,' she murmurs, her voice soft but echoing, like multiple mouths speaking at once.

A tremor ripples over my body, making my jaw clench. I

can't form words, can't even part my lips to make a sound. As Hecate steps off the dais and circles me slowly, black eyes riveted to my face, I have never been more terrified. I can see why mortals never forgot one such as her. And I suddenly understand how devastating, how unpredictable, life would have been for humans when her kind roamed freely.

She smiles again, baring teeth that taper to a razor-sharp point. 'I sense your fear, daughter, but I mean you no harm. Women are always safe at my side.'

Her words do nothing to ease the rock sitting on my chest, but I take a sharp breath. Hecate is alive, and that means Violet still has a chance. With effort, I pry my jaw open and track the goddess as she continues to circle me, trailed by snakes and her loyal three-headed hounds.

'You were dead,' I whisper, my voice a ragged sound in my chest. 'I thought . . . I thought everything had been a lie. That the path led me nowhere.'

Hecate does not stop in her perusal of me, inspecting from every angle as her eyes glitter and the green braziers cast inhuman shapes across her ethereal features. 'What better way to defend my power from the Order of the Seven Sages than by being as close to dead as a god can be?'

I start at that, my brow creasing as she finally comes to a stop directly in front of me. Though I stand on the dais and she on the floor, her height towers over me so that I have to crane my head back to meet her gaze. Skeletons and the deep black river of the Underworld flicker in her gaze, and I blink quickly to banish the images.

'But other gods have slept, faded away while humans forgot them,' I protest, my voice still quiet and shaking. 'Why did you put yourself to sleep? Why did you choose me to awaken you?'

She smiles, the movement disconcerting as the tips of

her teeth flash. 'Other gods have slept because they lacked power and needed to conserve it. Mine was too strong, drawing the attention of those who would seek to steal it. The Valerius line has been planning my death to charge the seven sacred blades of the old Apkallu, the ancient god-kings of Sumeria, for three centuries. Instead of allowing that to happen, I used my power to bind myself in this tomb and sever my connection to the mortal world and await you. Only my descendant could reach me here after connecting to my aspects, bringing me forth from the darkness when the time was right. Only a mortal as unique as you or your sister could act on my behalf in the mortal realm.'

'The Order can take you now,' I say, ice pricking at my skin.

'Do not fret, Andromeda. The last blade has yet to be captured, and I can withstand any attempt the Order makes to summon me – for a time at least. Enough time for you to vanquish Damian.' She scans my face and must read the panic there. 'I chose your line for a reason, willed the magic in you and your sister's blood to come forth stronger than any other descendant I sired before. You are powerful enough to resist the Order.' The snakes on Hecate's arms hiss gently, as if enjoying their mistress's voice. 'I am pleased with the strength you've shown today.'

'Violet,' I croak, suddenly remembering the reason for every brutal step along this path. 'She's sick. Dying. I searched for you so you could heal her. Without you, there's no hope – even her magic is killing her.'

Hecate inclines her head slightly. 'I chose well when I foresaw the pair of you rising from the line I crafted.'

'Why us?' I ask, staring into the face of the goddess who planned my birth, my magic, for centuries.

Hecate tilts her head, eyes unblinking. 'Because you and

Violet are connected in a way that transcends both sides of the veil. Both of you cheated life and death. The Order's hunger is insatiable, more so than when they first formed during the time of the Romans. Now, they wish for something more.'

I feel like I'm floating outside of myself, not quite believing that Hecate has such grand plans for someone like me. Quiet, sullen, and often relying on saving others, so I do not have to worry about saving myself.

'Death,' I murmur. 'Damian wants to use the power he's stolen from other gods, and finally from you, to control his death?'

'It is far worse than that, daughter.' Hecate's teeth bare in a silent hiss. 'Each blade kills a god and absorbs their magic. The seventh is marked for my blood. But it is not simply my magic Damian wishes for, like the other gods he has killed. He needs my ability to transcend planes, to travel freely and manipulate death. He will raise enemies long buried and harvest magic and knowledge endlessly. With the strength of seven gods in his body, he will be greater than even the Apkallu were.'

'But he can't control power like that in a human body. It will burn him to ashes.' Panic makes my ribs so tight I can hardly draw in a breath.

'The house of Valerius is ancient. They know that control and knowledge are the keys to protecting their magic and their hold on the world. When Eidolon formed, the founders wanted the ability to control the future. Fate and death and the balance of all things. The Valerius family knew if they retrieved all seven blades, and the last tasted my blood and stole my powers, the wielder of the knives would never die. Damian will use my ability to cross between planes and bring forth what was once dead to create a new body. He will be a god, a new and more dangerous kind. I could not let that happen. So, I buried myself in this tomb and hid until I knew my descendants were ready to stop the Order.'

'What about Violet?'

'Violet is my descendant as well. I will heal her. Magic is as much a part of her as it is of me, threaded into every vein.' Hecate's smile turns benevolent, her fathomless eyes softening at the corners as she gently brushes her hand across my cheek. Almost in affection. 'I am yet weak from the spells I used to cast myself into sleep. I have many rituals to complete before I can cross boundaries freely again, and must not waste time. Days have passed in the world above, and the winter solstice approaches.'

She makes a move, as if to leave the tomb – and me – behind. 'Wait! Won't you help me stop the Order?'

'I will meet you above, at the cemetery in St Mary's, with news of Violet once you have left the Underworld.'

'But what do I do? How can I stop Damian?' I want to ask more, but every question, every demand that I once rehearsed in my head dies on my tongue.

Hecate stands proudly before the altar where she lay for centuries. The chamber grows dim and dank once more, empty of all her familiars and the almost comforting green fire.

Before the goddess can disappear into her territory to regain her strength, those immortal black eyes fix on me, reflecting endless centuries of life and death. When Hecate speaks, I feel her words in a thrill that pierces my heart.

'Seize the blade of fate for yourself. Carve your own mark upon the gods.'

24

Anubis

The roar of the Order members gathered in the Oculus Sanctum drowns out Anubis' heartbeat. The ceaseless sound of the knife plunging into Masoud's chest replaying in his head. He pretends to bask in the glory of his triumph, in the blood at his feet. But as the crowd descends to the dais, and wine and drinks are brought out to celebrate, he can't stop the swell of nausea curdling his stomach. The Order members tip their heads back and let wine flow down their throats, as red as the blood staining the dais. He shakes hands. Responds to congratulations. But inside he seethes with anger.

'Come with me,' Damian says, leaning in to be heard over the commotion. Anubis catches the cold gray eyes of the other boy as he nods to a small doorway behind the dais, two tapestries partially concealing it. Damian leads him away from the roaring crowd and their decent into a blood-frenzied party, and Anubis follows wordlessly. No one seems to realize when their Romulus leaves, too busy dipping their fingers into Masoud's congealing blood, and using it for their own spells, to care. No one except Ramsey Arskell, who watches with a crease furrowing his brow.

'Where are we going?' Anubis asks as they cross the threshold of the door and emerge into a narrow hallway.

'To meet with the other heads of houses,' Damian replies, his voice flat.

They continue through the winding maze of halls and rooms that make up the oculus compound, all deserted now.

As sweat sticks to his still-bare chest, Anubis wishes he had remained in the blood-soaked chamber. An unsettling nervousness claws at his stomach as they walk, prowling deeper into a portion of the compound he has never been to before. Damian is not a patient man, and he promised Anubis that they would retrieve the seventh blade revealed by Styx as soon as he entered Oracle. There is no way to delay him, Anubis realizes, as Damian stalks through the halls, energy rippling off him in waves.

Anubis only hopes Andy returns before Damian can make him the next murdered god.

They come to a stop at what appears to be the far east wall of the compound. Tall, curved windows let in the moonlight, shining down on the immaculate park and high fence. Beyond that, Eidolon is quiet, holding its breath.

Anubis licks his lips, barely refraining from shifting his weight from foot to foot as Damian studies him in the dim hall. Cold marble floors and equally cold white walls seem to emit a miasma that seeps into Anubis' skin, chilling the sweat on his chest. He holds Damian's gaze, praying that his expression is neutral.

'You know why I brought you here, don't you?' Damian finally asks, his voice rough from shouting his incantations earlier.

'The seventh blade. Styx holds it within her waters.' He is not used to feeling fear for his own welfare. Only Andy's. But, standing alone with Damian and his wolf-like eyes, Anubis has never felt more mortal. Or weaker.

Damian's lips curl in a smile that does nothing to quell the tension charging the air. He turns, facing away from the windows and toward the dead-end wall. A lone painting decorates the crisp white plaster. The frame is ornately carved and gilded, housing a rich oil painting that depicts an all-too-familiar scene.

Anubis recognizes the seven hills of Rome in the background, wild and bare of the civilization that will one day tumble over the landscape. The Lupercal cave stands in the foreground, a ragged slash in the warm-colored stone. Lupa stands, fierce and immense, guarding two small children that reach to feed from her teats. The symbol of the Order stands proudly in this central hall that winds like a twisted spine through the entire compound.

'It's beautiful,' Anubis offers when Damian makes no further move.

'When I was young, before my father died and he still served as Romulus for the Order, he brought me here. Told me the story of Lupa and the founding of Rome. He told me that the Valerius bloodline was older than Rome itself, that I was descended from kings and emperors from the beginning of civilization.'

Anubis doesn't respond. His bare skin needles with the cold emanating from the marble floor and barren walls. Frost touches the windows.

Damian glances at him, crossing his arms over his scarred chest. 'I've told you the mission of the Order. How we have existed in every major empire, pulling strings and guiding choices.' He faces the painting again, his teeth flashing in a hungry smile. 'I won the mantle of Romulus from Ramsey and every other first-born son brutally. Efficiently. Many met their end at the point of my knife or a drop of poison.'

Anubis pretends to study the painting and not the scarred boy at his side. 'It was merciful of you to let Ramsey live,' he offers, even though he recalls the way Andy told the story.

The casual cruelty with which Damian severed his fingertips and carved up his face just because he could.

'Mercy?' Damian exhales a sharp laugh. 'I did what I needed to do, so I could become the leader the Order needs to survive. Just like my father instructed me to.'

Anubis shifts on his feet, unsure where this is going. The night is deep, the halls whisper quietly. The celebration in the central chamber is far away; too far to hear. A nervous tingle ripples down his spine as the dark yellow eyes of Lupa seem to follow him from the canvas.

Damian reaches out and caresses the painting, fingers trailing the sharp teeth of the wolf before he touches his belt, fingers skimming the bronze knife still flecked in blood. Anubis tenses, muscles bunching as he braces for the lightning-quick strike of the blade sinking into his chest, flaying the flesh from bone and stealing the blood and magic from his veins.

It never comes.

Instead, Damian flips the knife over in his hand, hilt out. With a flick of his thumb, a small, decorative panel at the base opens on brass hinges. The outline is familiar to Anubis as it flashes in the dark – a stylized outline of a wolf suckling two children. Identical in shape and size to the stamps on the silver curse tablets littering the graves of gods.

Reaching behind the thick frame of the painting, Damian aims the hilt at a tiny notch. With a single press, hinges groan, and the sharp scent of musty air and old earth fills the abandoned hall. Anubis steps back a fraction as Damian withdraws the knife and covers the keyhole with the panel again. He grabs the frame once more and pulls. A yawning doorway slowly appears as the painting swings away. The artwork is nearly seven feet tall – massive enough to hide the archway of curiously carved stone laden with chips and subtle cracks.

'Father brought me here when I was ten. Old enough to begin my training to become the next Romulus.' Damian touches a deep white scar on his shoulder, as if remembering how he got it. 'Only the Romulus can decide who enters these catacombs. So far, I have let Rohan and Antonia pass through this door. It is sacred ground. Ground my family has been working to hallow for generations. Tonight, I will bring you into a place few have seen.'

Anubis meets Damian's eager gaze, his pulse thrumming wildly in this throat. 'Why bring me here? I have barely entered Oracle. I'm not from the founding families, or the leader of one of the houses.'

Damian motions with one hand to the opening, where the smell of dust and old earth is growing stronger. Anubis clenches his jaw and steps through the arch, acutely aware when Damian follows, closing the hidden door behind him. Darkness washes over them. Anubis should find it comforting. As a god of death, he is no stranger to darkness or underground places. But something in the air feels too thick. Like a sickness waits further ahead.

A hiss sounds and sparks fly. A torch catches and flames illuminate Damian's face as he moves past Anubis to take the lead. Anubis' eyes follow the glint of the knife, back in his belt, not ready to let his guard down. The torch illuminates walls smeared with centuries of dust and dirt. Pillars line sections of earth before they drop into neatly placed stone stairs. Anubis recognizes the style, the way the arches connect, and the smooth cement that mortars everything in place.

'These are Roman ruins,' he murmurs.

'They are. Left over from when the Romans ruled Britain. They had a fort close to here, almost their most northern one. These catacombs hold the skeletons of hundreds of Roman legionaries, and the remains of the first Order members who came from our ancient homelands and established the area that would become Eidolon.'

Anubis brushes aside a layer of dust with his shoe, seeing the telltale signs of a mosaic floor. Pockmarks and gouges interrupt the pattern from time to time, but he swears there is the outline of a river and a repeating figure holding a sharp blade aloft.

'Follow me,' Damian says, voice echoing. 'This path will take us to the center of the catacombs and to the mouth of the convergence.'

As they walk, embers dropping from the torch, Anubis notes how the tunnel opens into a large chamber. Ruins of crude villas, aqueducts and a town square peer through mounds of earth and reaching roots. An entire buried town sitting below the school. A shudder steals down his spine as they reach a large rectangular tomb flanked by statues of Jupiter and Neptune. Intricate carvings of grape vines twine around evenly spaced Corinthian columns. It reminds Anubis of a burial place fit for a king. Or an emperor.

Damian reaches for two richly carved doors that somehow have not rotted away in the damp underground cavern. They creak open, and the distinct scent of magic tinges the air, setting Anubis' blood on fire. His head aches in time to his heartbeat and he curls his fists tightly to keep his composure. Ancient magic filters through the air, calling to his godly nature.

Damian pauses before passing the threshold. 'Through here are the catacombs and the very first convergence. It is far more powerful than any you may have felt before. The same ancient convergence that gave the Euphrates, Nile and Tiber their power in the old days. And now Styx has guided the blade she found to its waters.' Damian lowers the torch, his ceremonial robes still hanging open, shadows length-ening across his heavily scarred torso. 'You have never felt power like this before, Jae Han.'

He turns and disappears into the catacombs. Anubis holds his breath as he follows him, sweat making his palms slick and cold against his sides. He blinks away dust that floats through the air, his skull buzzing at the base as he stumbles over uneven stones. A single altar stands bare in the central chamber, as if waiting to hold a body. Telltale bloodstains mark the stone footing and smooth marble sur-face. Anubis forces himself to walk further inside, to where an empty arch drops below the buried town.

Damian's torch gleams ahead, lowering into the earth as they descend one last, long staircase laid by hands centuries ago. Heat and cold ripple over Anubis' skin as he follows in the darkness. The scent of magic makes his lip curl, half in longing and half in disgust. His tattoos burn. His pulse quickens. He tastes blood on his tongue.

Bright firelight breaks across his vision, and he squints, stumbling a few steps. Bronze braziers flank the archway through which Anubis and Damian enter, illuminating a tall cavern. Roots dangle through the ceiling in places, and groundwater seeps through cracks. They are far into the earth now. Deep nooks are dug out along one side, creating a honeycomb effect in the semi-circular room. Bones litter each niche, some little more than dust and lingering teeth, and others bleached white and far more recent. Anubis pulls his gaze away from yawning eye sockets and empty ribcages.

About a hundred feet directly ahead is a wide, churning river, so black it looks like oil.

Anubis staggers despite himself. The river is wider and rougher than any convergence he has seen before. The scent is pungent, intoxicating, as if he is back in the Underworld.

His skin burns and itches, wanting to separate from his bones. He grits his teeth as Damian glances over his shoulder, his expression curious.

'What is this place?' Anubis asks, unable to hide his labored breathing. 'It's like nothing I've ever seen.'

Damian runs his hand along the curved left wall that soars high over their heads. 'The burial place of the highest-ranking Order members for thousands of years. When my ancestors founded Eidolon, the convergence in the old lands shifted and followed them, settling here. Bringing with it the power the Order had accumulated and harnessed since the time when gods roamed the earth.'

But that isn't what concerns Anubis. Instead, it is the river – the impossibly powerful river that plunges through the cavern, bisecting it in two. A damp and narrow bank waits on the other side, empty. The eerie familiarity of the scene, a miniature imitation of the Underworld, sets his teeth on edge. He meets Damian's probing gaze, notices the emptiness of the catacombs. He wants to step back, to call on the full force of his magic, even if it means risking the temporary human body Andy worked so hard to forge for him. Anything to quell this awful, alien sense of dread.

Damian touches the curved dagger at his belt again, drawing it free. He gazes at the mirror-like finish of the blade. Anubis tenses, fingertips burning and darkening like soot as a swell of magic stings his ribs and throat.

'Come in,' Damian commands, lifting his eyes from the weapon.

Anubis tenses, the skin on his fingers burning with pain as something inside him seems to fray at the seams. But he pauses, biting back the surge of power threatening to tear his temporary body apart. Damian isn't talking to him, but looks past his shoulder, eyes trained on the opposite wall, smooth and barren of skeletons. Anubis twists, fingers turning back to normal, and stifles a surprised sound.

Antonia and Rohan emerge from an antechamber tucked against the back wall in the shadows cast from the braziers. Between them they carry a long and heavily wrapped bundle. He can't tell what it contains.

'Styx told you of a seventh dagger,' Damian says, still lovingly tracing the one in his hands. 'Over the last three centuries, since Eidolon's founding, my family has been collecting them. Gathering them, one by one. They sat here, among their bones, until I became Romulus three years ago, when I reignited the magic they once wielded by killing a god with each one, their blood and power returning them to the weapons they were during the time of the gods. Styx located the last one, and as a favor for feeding her, she ushered it to this convergence.'

Rohan and Antonia adjust the bundle between them, clearly struggling under the weight. 'Everything is ready, Romulus,' Rohan says. 'The moon will set in twenty minutes. We need him to retrieve the blade before it does.'

Damian nods. 'Tonight is special, Jae Han. Much like you. This knife is the last one I need. The final one. And because of the enchantments placed on them, only one such as you, not born into the Order but marked by its signs, can enter this cavern and retrieve a talisman of the Apkallu before the setting of the moon on the night of his initiation. A sort of fail-safe imposed by the gods before they faded away, lest any man think to take their place.' Damian smiles to himself. 'The daggers are blessed with their powers, their knowledge, and their status as demi-gods. And once I have this final knife, and all have killed a god, I will not be able to die.'

Damian walks quickly, his shoulders tight with anticipation, toward the river. Anubis stands, numb, the taste of magic heavy on his tongue. It isn't until Rohan pushes him forward that Anubis realizes he is meant to follow. Swallowing hard, he moves to stand at the edge of the bank with Damian at his side. The black water churns below, reflecting his face back at him, shattered and distorted. His palm itches to touch his face, to see if it changes from the smooth softness of a mortal to the hard, stone-like feeling of a god.

'It's been twenty years since a new member of Oracle was brought to these catacombs.' Damian smooths back his white-blond hair. 'The first time my father tried to kill a god. He failed, not understanding the magic needed to pull off such a thing. Once I became the Romulus, I used all the magic I'd absorbed from killing the other first-born sons to murder the first god with this very knife. The one my tenth great-grandfather wrestled from the grasp of the convergence on a night like this one. I chose you for this, for a reason. You are no stranger to magic, Jae Han. To convergences and the power it can bring to those like you.' Damian crosses his arms, studying the far bank. 'My family has been working toward this very night since Eidolon was founded. I couldn't risk anyone outside of this cavern knowing what I have planned. Not now that we are so close. A mere breath away from glory.'

Anubis doesn't breathe as water flecks his bare chest. 'What must I do to retrieve the blade?'

Rohan appears at Damian's other side, breathing hard and wiping his bloody hands clean on his robe. 'Antonia and I will meet you on the other side,' Rohan says to Damian, his eyes wary as he looks at Anubis, a question unspoken on his lips.

'Go,' Damian agrees, lifting his chin. 'Jae will join us in moments, I am sure.'

A cool wind breathes through the cavern, rustling Anubis' hair against his forehead. That familiar itch deep in his skin grows stronger, and he clenches his fists to resist the call to sink into his old godly form. It has never been so hard to maintain control, not even for the twelve years he spent hunting down Min-Jun's killers.

Damian reaches once more for his prized bronze dagger. Before Anubis can open his lips to ask once more what he must do, Rohan and Antonia disappear. He blinks a few times; sure it is just a trick of the light. Maybe a torch extinguishing from the unearthly breeze. Something winks at the other side of the bank. A flash of gold from a familiar mask with a long curving beak. The mask of Thoth.

Anubis breathes in sharply. Across the bank of the powerful convergence stand Antonia and Rohan, their clothes completely dry and their long wrapped bundle set on the altar.

'You know of the Apkallu, don't you, Jae?' Damian lovingly traces the curve of the blade with his thumb, silver eyes fixed on the black river. 'Of course you do. You attended so many prestigious schools. One near to here, in Edinburgh, from the time you were old enough to hold a pen. And last year you studied at Ravenswood – a most peculiar school. I have never been, but I hear it recently began reviving the ways of the old world, trying to penetrate the veil of the occult.'

Anubis' heart clenches with dread. He never put Ravenswood on the application to Eidolon, only Andy did.

'I saw your application when it arrived. I go over every person who has learned of my school, who wishes to walk the halls. I need to know who will be useful to me. It was at the top of the stack, littered with so many commendations and letters of recommendation from influential people, I couldn't ignore it. And then I saw your history. Quite inter-esting.' Damian turns from the river to face Anubis. 'I knew you would be perfect for this task.'

'If it's my magic you want –'

Damian lifts the hand holding the dagger, cutting off Anubis' weak protest. 'The Apkallu forged these talismans. Seven blades for the Seven Sages of the ancient world. You know the Sumerians believed the gods created man to till the ground, that by humankind's sacrifices they would be fed. The Apkallu came to teach humanity wisdom and knowledge. They were half human, half god themselves. Eventually, they mingled with humans and became the divine ancestors of powerful kings and emperors. Their descend-ants ruled every great empire. But humans are forgetful, and as they grew and expanded, they steadily lost the need for gods. Until we became this.' He gestures to the cavern. 'Hidden in pockets, pulling strings from the shadows. But no more. Under my reign, we will live as the Apkallu did.'

'And what god will you kill with this blade to achieve your plan?' Anubis asks.

'Once the blade is mine, I will tell you.' Damian points to the bottom of the river. Anubis blinks, following the line of his finger until he sees a glimmer of metal through the rushing current. It glows in the darkness, a soft halo in the endless black.

Anubis' skin burns once more. A warning, perhaps? Or something else. The beginning of the end. 'And once I retrieve this dagger?' he asks, his fingertips numb as he ima-gines emerging from the water only to be impaled through the heart.

'This convergence is the oldest and most powerful. It sprang from the ground at the creation of the world, con-necting the realms of life and death. Gods and man. It will ask much of you, Jae Han. It will take much too. But once you emerge, reborn, my family line will never wither into obscurity again. We will have seven days before I have unlocked the enchantments on the blade and can use it to kill a god.' Damian sheaths his blade. 'When you are down there, remember that the only thing you seek is the dagger. Nothing else.'

Another cool wind dries the sweat on Anubis' skin. This time, he isn't surprised when the space on the bank next to him is empty and Damian's shock of pale hair gleams on the other side of the river. The west bank. An imitation of the Underworld that Anubis belongs to. He must enter the water and turn into something more. But what kind of monster can he become now?

'You will not have long,' Damian calls, his voice over-loud and echoing in the rounded chamber. 'Once you enter the water, you have but moments to leave it again before it seeks to steal the magic in your blood and send you to the next world.'

Anubis kicks off his shoes mechanically as he stares into the surface, eyes trained on the dagger. He promised Andy he would enter the depths of the Order, uncover their secrets. Find out what Damian has planned. As he takes a breath, ready to dive into the churning water, he only hopes he recognizes himself when he emerges.

Anubis sails through the air and cuts through the surface of the river. The cold is shocking in its intensity. But he resists the instinct to breathe in sharply and fill his lungs with water. He is not quite human, yes, but drowning will still damage the body Andy helped to create. The current is strong, threatening to drag him down into the depths of the earth and back to the realm he belongs to.

The bronze knife gleams in the darkness, put there by

the goddess Styx, and he kicks hard, fighting the sucking sensation of the water. He grabs a large boulder, using it to pull himself deeper. His tattoos burn again, but this time the pain is so great he cries out, his voice lost in a cascade of bubbles. The ouroboros twines around his arm, the black ink eating away at his skin. The stars on his forearm burn straight to his blood. And the eagle stretches its wings and tears into his fragile chest.

His body pulls itself apart as he flounders under the surface of the convergence. His magic, a deep, nameless color, leeches from his fingertips, torn away into the waiting grasp of the Underworld. Anubis kicks weakly again, fingers slipping over the rough surface of the boulder. The dagger shifts in the current, tantalizingly out of reach.

Black tinges the edge of his vision. His eyes grow heavy and his head lists to the side as the river pulls at him again. He should return home. Back to the Underworld. To the depths of his consciousness, as he is forgotten and fades away. Slowly, Anubis' fingers uncurl from the lip of the rock anchoring him in place.

Good, a dark part of him thinks, even as the tattoos move over his burning, bubbling skin. *You are Anubis, a god of death. You do not belong here. You do not belong to* her.

Andy's face floats before him, so soft and human and warm that he aches at the sight. The flash of her blue eyes when she is angry with him.

Torn in two. That is what he is. Jae or Anubis, man or god. No one can know, not even the river that threatens to tear his form apart. His eyes slide shut as he feels the icy fingers of the Underworld reaching for him, threatening to drag him back to an endless slumber. He'll rest again, perhaps. And soon he'll forget the sound of her laugh and the softness of Andy's lips.

That will be better, Anubis thinks, uncurling his hand completely to let the river take him away. The pain in his chest when he thinks of the mortal girl will finally leave him. He doesn't belong with her or deserve the golden ray of light she's cast over him.

Gold. He opens his eyes as he rolls along the bottom of the river bed. Wasn't he meant to find something gold in these frigid waters? Pain lances back into his body, chasing away the pleasant numbness of before. Anubis digs his fingers into the rocky floor, lungs threatening to burst as he drags himself against the current toward a flicker of gold in the darkness.

The dagger.

With a painful groan stolen from his lips by the swift water, he pushes against a rocky outcrop and closes his hands around the hilt of the last blade of the ancient Seven Sages. Immediately, sensation rushes into his body. A flurry of power and promise, and visions of Andy waiting for him on the other side, a smile on her face. He wants that. Desperately, and more than anything that came before. More than a mortal body.

Blood roars in his ears as he kicks to the surface, the sting of air on his cheeks as he sucks in a desperate breath. His thoughts are a jumbled mess as hands grab his shoulders, slipping over his bare, wet skin. Anubis comes to his senses as he crawls onto a hard, pebbly shore and flops onto his back.

Water trickles from his mouth as he shivers, staring at his flesh. He expects it to be torn clean from the bone. The tattoos misshapen and broken. But his skin is even and gold. No burns or pain, and none of the aches he has grown accustomed to since arriving at Eidolon. Something is different though, as he lies there. He feels it as strongly as the magic smothering him, filling the cavern. Like a rope is tied around his magic, strangling it.

Damian's face comes into focus, lit by new torches along the wall of the west bank. He smiles down at Anubis, his expression one of ecstasy as he grabs Anubis' arm and pulls him to his feet. Antonia and Rohan stand in their robes, blocking his view of the rest of the sheltered cove that makes up the bank. But that scent tickles his nose again, jarring his jumbled thoughts into focus.

'Welcome back, Jae Han,' Damian says, his voice rough. 'You are reborn in this moment, touched by the Apkallu.'

Anubis sways on his feet, still feeling as though he is being tossed by the current of the river. His ears ring and ache from the cold as he stares at his hand wrapped around a blade identical to Damian's. It hums with power, a song pitched low, like his own magic. It's ancient. Older than even he is.

'Quickly,' Rohan hisses, looking at his watch. 'The moon setting approaches.'

'Get the girl,' Damian responds.

'Girl?' Anubis asks, his tongue heavy and slow.

Rohan moves aside. Braziers burn on either side of a low altar. They cast light over a long sheet draped over the stone. The bundled burden Rohan and Antonia carried earlier. Firelight dances off the carvings of four wolves, each facing outward in a cardinal direction, supporting the base of the altar. The dagger in Anubis' hand feels so heavy he wants to collapse to his knees.

'The ritual cannot be completed until a soul is sent to the west bank to pay for the cost of the dagger,' Damian says, urgency written all over his face. 'A blade cannot be taken from this place until it tastes the blood of a woman touched by magic.'

Anubis recoils, his senses rushing back to him in an instant. He staggers, attempting to drop the knife. But his fingers won't cooperate. They're glued to the bronze hilt, fused like stone. 'I can't,' he says thickly, his limbs weak as Damian pushes him to the side of the altar.

The sheet conceals a body. Terror grips Anubis' chest as Rohan moves to tear the sheet away. He envisions Andy or Violet lying prone on the slab. But as the blanket is cast aside, he realizes he does not know the girl. She is young, and as he looks down at her face, his mind is pulled to another time. Another life. One that does not belong to him.

'Now, Jae,' Damian commands. 'You know the cost of magic; you have seen it yourself. Blood is the only answer.'

He recalls a vision from so many years ago, shown to him by a desperate boy wearing the same face he has now. How he found his beloved aunt muddy and cold. The silver curse tablet in her curled hand. The anger that sent him on a mission straight to the chamber of Anubis.

'Min-Jun,' he whispers, his knees weakening. 'You killed Min-Jun.'

The Order, Damian's father. They stood here on a night just like this, years ago, trying desperately to fetch another blade that might kill a god. And a young Damian watched, learning how so he could achieve this very night.

Antonia makes a sound of frustration as the girl on the table stirs. 'The spell is wearing off!'

Damian's expression fills Anubis' vision as he grabs his arm in a surprisingly painful grip. 'I did not sacrifice this much to bring you into Oracle for you to be weak now. A clean stab through the heart and the last blade is mine.'

Anubis shakes his head, yanking his arm back. But the strength he's always had is depleted. The stranglehold on his magic is firm. Damian's fingers hold fast. Anubis' stomach lurches as Damian grabs him by the neck and all but flings him against the hard stone lip of the altar. He groans, desperately trying to pry the dagger from his hand. He can't let go. Can't escape.

'I can't kill an innocent girl. Your dagger is not worth that,' he protests.

'These daggers will save the Order!' Damian cries so loudly that the cords of his neck stand taut. 'Kill the girl. Finish the ritual, or you will regret ever setting foot in Eidolon.'

Anubis struggles as the girl opens her eyes, fear and confusion written on her face. Antonia and Rohan scream words he can't hear over the rush of blood in his ears. The weakness in his limbs as Damian presses his stomach painfully into the lip of the altar, another hand curling around Anubis' wrist, raising his arm.

Min-Jun laid on this piece of stone over twelve years ago. Stabbed through the heart and bleeding out, alone and frightened, in this cavern before she was tossed into the Waters of Leith like garbage. His stomach heaves as he fights with renewed vigor. But it's no use. He is weak with whatever sickness is spreading through his limbs, tightening around his powers, smothering them.

'Now!' Antonia's shrill voice breaks through the sound of Damian and Anubis' desperate fighting. 'Now, or we'll lose it!'

The dagger flickers in Anubis' palm, there one moment and gone the next. The howl of rage Damian lets out shakes the cavern. His knee connects with Anubis' stomach, and he slumps, breath gone. With both hands, Damian wrenches Anubis' arm up, the golden dagger flickering in the brazier's light.

Even as Anubis continues to struggle, desperate to extend this fight until the moonrise passes, he feels the moment the blade pierces skin. Blood touches his fist and he heaves, vomiting river water onto the pebbles digging into his knees. The girl makes a pathetic sound even as Anubis' fingers finally uncurl from the hilt. Damian kicks him aside, eyes blazing, as he finishes the grisly task.

Anubis lies on his back, ribs bruised, his throat torn from his cries of protest. And as his eyes study the cavern above while blood drips onto the ground by his head, he understands why he is so weak. Why he couldn't fight Damian.

There, scratched into the ceiling, is a complex devil's trap bearing sigils and symbols older than time. Numbness spreads through his chest and down to his fingers and toes. They know who he is. And they'll kill him now, before he'll ever get the chance to explain to Andy what he's done.

Damian heaves for breath, his eyes burning with hatred. In his hand is a silver curse tablet. With angry motions, he pushes the girl's body off the altar and rolls it into the black water.

'It's a shame you failed right when I needed you most,' he says, a feral grin splitting his face. 'But now you're in time for the rest of the show.'

Anubis protests weakly as Rohan and Antonia haul him to his feet. Everything hurts, aching like a rotten tooth. A bruise clearly marks the skin of his stomach, scratches bleeding freely. His head swims as they push him to sit against the altar. Ropes, thick and rough, move around his wrists and ankles.

'Is this what you planned when you invited me to join the Order? When you picked my application for your school?' Anubis slurs, vision blurring so violently that everything doubles. The devil's trap is potent – already he feels weightless, without form. 'All this effort just to kill me when you could have done it long ago.'

'Ravenswood is a fascinating place, Jae Han,' Damian murmurs, squatting in front of him. 'I've had my eye on several students there, waiting to see which ones would be the best for what happens next.'

Confusion chases away the pain from the devil's trap long enough for Anubis' vision to clear. 'Who?'

'Oh, don't play coy now, not when you've delivered the last talisman so perfectly. I'm speaking of that pale girl that follows you around campus. The one with the hard eyes and the wild hair.'

'What about her?' There is a dangerous edge to Anubis' words, sharper than the blades.

'Don't you know?' Damian laughs. 'There is only one way for me to wield all seven blades, one way for me to take on the magic of the most powerful goddess of all time. I need the magic of a death god – one in particular. But she is proving very tricky to get hold of. Lucky for me, her blood runs in the veins of two very interesting girls.'

Rohan and Antonia shed their robes as they move around the narrow ledge of the west bank. A bastardized version of Anubis' homeland. They're lighting candles in a particular pattern below the dozen points of the devil's trap. Tallow candles, he notices absently. The smell of burning fat tickles his nose even as he glares into Damian's eyes.

Damian continues, 'Hecate is the most revered and remembered deity of all time. She had a Sumerian counterpart, and then an Egyptian. Then Greek. Then Roman. She's never faded, not even the Apkallu can claim that. And as soon as I learned about the two girls wandering the halls of Ravenswood chasing demons and madmen, I knew my father's plan could be set into motion. Luring Andromeda Emmerson to Eidolon was the insurance I needed in case Hecate continued to evade me.' His smile turns deadly as he straightens to his full height, raising his hands, palms upward, like some sort of biblical savior. 'And your control of such volatile and rare magic made it clear I would finally retrieve the seventh blade.'

'What are you talking about? Andromeda has nothing to do with your blades,' Anubis demands, his voice barely a growl. The bonds dig into his skin, cutting into the flesh that should not be as soft as it is.

'She is a descendant of Hecate. Her sister too, of course. On the winter solstice, in seven days, I'll have readied the last blade and have everything I need to finally bring that goddess beneath my boot. But tonight is not for Hecate. Tonight, I will gather the descendants of that goddess and bind Eidolon so none can leave and enter.'

Anubis jerks against the bonds, straining to stand, but he flops to the side, unable to loosen his ankles. 'You're mad! Andy is just another Order member.'

'How could you have known that the girl at your side is as strong as the Apkallu once were? Demi-gods haven't existed since the Romans, since monotheism took over the entire world. Make no mistake, that girl is not what she appears.'

'She's human!' Anubis protests wildly, even as dirt pushes into his mouth as he struggles to free the bonds from his wrists. 'I met her on the train. She's not what you think.'

Damian flicks his hands at Rohan. 'Bind him securely this time. We'll need him to draw the girl into the sanctum.'

'You won't touch her!' Anubis warns, a thread of black magic winding up from his fingertips, singeing the delicate human skin there to ash. But the devil's trap swells to life, snapping tendrils of magic growing stronger as the candles burn down to stubs. The hairs on his neck rise as Rohan roughly hauls him against the altar again, doubling the number of knots on his bindings before shoving a gag between his teeth.

Anubis can taste familiar magic on the air as Damian raises his hands and face to the ceiling. He speaks Sumerian, then Akkadian. Anubis recognizes the languages now. How they send a thrill of old magic through the air.

Antonia cocks her head to the side. 'You've found her. She'll be pulled through the convergence once we use the tablet to bind her.'

Praying is useless for another deity. But that doesn't stop Anubis from trying as Damian grabs a rectangular silver tablet and sketches with the sharp point of the dagger into the metal. A name. Even in the dim light from the braziers, Anubis can see familiar letters appearing.

The rush of the river stills completely, frozen in time. Air rushes through the cavern, stealing the oxygen from Anubis' lips until they're cold and blue. The last of the candles extinguish, bathing the deep cavern in near darkness. With a thunderous sound, the river reverses its flow, as if dragging something from the depths of the Underworld.

Damian drops his hands, his words fading away. The silver curse tablet winks out of existence, disappearing. Anubis knows it will land where the girl with bright blue eyes once stood.

A surge of blinding light fills the cavern. Rohan and Antonia cringe away, covering their eyes. Damian only smiles as the form of a girl appears, slumped against the far wall. Anubis breathes hard through his teeth, the gag cutting into the flesh of his cheeks.

'Hello, daughter of Hecate,' Damian murmurs. 'Are you ready to offer your blood?'

25

Thunder roars in my ears as I run down the path of Hecate. Except, there are no clouds in the dark Underworld, just a strip of endless black sky. My breath heaves painfully through my lungs as I dodge a fissure in the road. Stones tumble as the mausoleums and tombs littering the hill crumble and fall. The Underworld is collapsing beneath my feet.

The path I traveled so painstakingly before lies in ruins, the stones thrusting jaggedly into the air like broken teeth. Space bends around me, the hill falling and the exit to the rest of the Underworld growing tantalizing close before expanding again, out of sight.

A tremor rocks the ground beneath my feet, and I stagger, falling hard onto my side. Something pokes against my ribs, and I struggle to my knees and claw at the pocket of my jacket. The jackal statue stares at me from my palm.

'Wepwawet,' I murmur as I bring the figurine down hard on a rock. It shatters into pieces, releasing a curl of black smoke that smells of sweet incense. My heart hammers in my chest painfully as I wait, and I dig my fingers into the dry grass as the earth roils beneath me like a living thing.

A minute passes. And then another. But Wepwawet doesn't appear like Anubis promised he would when he said goodbye in his dormitory. I look around at the tumbling landscape. Behind me, Hecate's tomb shudders, dust and stones raining down. An earsplitting roar shatters the air as the pillars holding up the heavy roof crack clean in half. I stagger to my feet as the entire temple lurches to the side before it collapses in a cloud of black dust.

The magic I've felt since stepping onto the path curls around me like a feline, lovingly caressing my skin. I must use a spell I haven't dared touch in over a year. One attached to memories of Anubis and his lips, and the taste of my blood on my tongue.

The words tumble from my tongue, ones that I never learned, but that come from deep inside my bones. The feeling of pure power makes my teeth ache, and I shut my eyes, reveling in it. With a swell of heat, I flee the crumbling path of Hecate and the grasp of the Underworld. The smell of the river overwhelms my senses and then cold, damp grass touches the knees of my jeans and the palms of my hands.

I blink away dust and grime, wiping my eyes with one hand. The sky is brightening to the east, spilling soft light across the hilly earth, acting as a backdrop to a crumbling church. I'm back at Eidolon, with St Mary's Abbey just ahead.

I get to my feet, eagerly searching the darkness for Hecate. Soon, she'll meet me in the cemetery, like she promised. She'll have healed Violet, and maybe even bring my sister here to help stop the Order.

With that thought buoying my spirit, I jog across the wide meadow, the river Aoife at my back. The twisted metal fence comes into view, framing broken headstones. I pick my way through them and pass under one empty arch into the shadowy interior of the church.

The roof collapsed centuries ago, leaving chunks of stone on the uneven ground that used to be the floor. Grass has grown over the stone, creating a carpet that absorbs the sound of my footsteps as I pick my way through the ruins to the knave. The floor is still shaped in a cruciform despite the dilapidation, and I move to stand at the crossing of the church. It's empty except for a fallen pillar, but that doesn't frighten me. Magic is nearby, so close I can taste it. Any moment, Hecate will appear. And everything will be alright.

Standing at the knave, ranks of decaying arches stretching behind me and to either side, something tickles the back of my neck. I turn, my breath clouding in the cool air. Shadows dance as the nearby trees creak in the wind. I bite back a rising sense of irrational fear.

'Violet?' I call, my voice breaking with excitement. With hope.

A figure, distorted by the shadows, emerges from the gloom of the apse, the back of the church where the main altar once stood. Relief saps the strength out of my body, and I sag, reaching out for a column to keep myself upright.

'Violet?' I half sob, staggering forward to meet her. 'I can't believe you're here, that you're –'

My voice dies in my throat, withering to ash. The tall figure that crosses to stand in the knave just ahead is *not* my sister. Auburn hair messily falls over a pale forehead.

I step back, nausea rising in my throat. The magic I sensed earlier? It had nothing to do with Violet or Hecate. I should have known it belonged to an Order member, especially to one of the founding families. The taste, as old as dust but more bitter than dirt, is unmistakable now.

'Ramsey,' I whisper, a stupor quelling the magic I want to call on. 'What are you doing here?'

His smile is a whisper on his face as he hops over one last jagged boulder and comes to stand before me, one hand in the pocket of his tailored coat. Distrust winds through my gut at his expression. Hecate is nowhere to be found – her path has crumbled to ash. And Violet? She doesn't appear behind the boy who helped me access the secrets of Eidolon.

Ramsey's brown eyes look almost apologetic as he meets my gaze. But I can't trust it, not like before. He's one of *them*, after all.

'I'm sorry, Andy,' he murmurs. 'But Violet won't be meeting you.'

26

The air is bitter and damp as it groans through the dilapidated abbey. Somewhere in the nearby forest, an owl hoots, a lonely, plaintive sound. I take a step back but slam against a toppled column. There's nowhere to go.

'How do you know about my sister?'

'Damian knows about you two,' Ramsey says, sitting heavily on a weatherworn bit of stone below the open ceiling. 'And I make it my mission to know everything he does.'

Dread washes over me. 'I don't know what you mean.'

'Sure, you do.' He gives me a pained smile, making the scar on his cheek stretch gruesomely. 'You're descendants of Hecate. I've known since the moment I met you. Damian knew too. Your magic is impossible to hide from someone like him.'

Magic crackles in my palms as my hackles rise. I don't try to smother it. If he's right and the entire Order knows who I am, why hide it? 'Where is Violet?' I demand.

Ramsey doesn't move from his spot on the rock. 'I don't know. Damian has closed off the entirety of Eidolon University. A barrier even you couldn't break. No one can leave the school. Hecate won't risk stepping through it, or she'll be trapped and killed with the blade.'

'Where is Damian now?' I ask. 'Where is An— Jae?' My stomach drops.

'Damian is somewhere in the Oculus Sanctum, preparing to use the final blade to kill Hecate tonight on the winter solstice. His closest allies are keeping the Order running while he prepares. The news has spread fast since Jae's initiation. Everyone in the Order knows Damian is performing an ancient rite. Something no other Romulus has done before.' He shifts uneasily, staring down at his hands. 'As for Jae, he disappeared after his initiation to fetch the blade for Damian. I haven't seen him since. That was six days ago. Rohan and Antonia don't seem too concerned about it either.'

I shut my eyes and take a short breath. Something happened to Anubis. Why else would Wepwawet not answer my call in the Underworld? My palms are clammy with worry, but I grit my teeth and focus on the present.

'Damian has everyone trapped in Eidolon with this spell,' I repeat, and open my eyes. 'You know what he's planning, don't you?'

'I have an idea.'

I exhale sharply, stepping backward. 'Care to share? Or is there some other reason you've been trailing the head of the Order?'

'You know I'd never hurt you, Andy. The Order has nothing I want.' He raises his hands, and my eyes latch on to the scar tissue on his palms. The missing tips of his ring and middle fingers on his left hand. 'The moment they forced me into the Agoge, stripping away any innocence I might have had, I wanted out. And then Damian won and spared me, only to turn and kill my father like it was *nothing* –' He cuts himself off, breathing hard through his nose to control his emotions. 'You already know I've been watching Damian. He's the last Valerius, and they are not known for their kindness or empathy. So yes, I've been following him as best as the ousted failure of a Remus can.'

Shame burns through my belly, and I drop my eyes. I know beneath the lazy smile Ramsey wears, there is hurt and tragedy. Trauma that runs deeper than I will ever know. The glint in his eyes as he's helped me work my way through the ranks of the Order speaks of his hatred. And as he curls his hands, ruined and mutilated, I take a steadying breath, focusing on the tasks ahead.

'I'm sorry,' I offer lamely, my face burning. 'I thought I'd meet Hecate here. Maybe my sister too. But when I left the Underworld, the goddess's path was falling apart, and now the church is empty. I'm worried Damian has found a way to summon Hecate and kill her with the last blade.'

His eyes flash with worry. 'I know how much your sister means to you, Andy. And I'm not surprised you freed Hecate. I only worry that it's exactly what Damian wanted you to do, that everything with you and Jae has led to this.'

'How?' I cock my head to the side. 'Jae is the one who is missing.'

Ramsey's face falls. 'I'm not exactly invited to the house meetings, but I've gleaned a few things from watching and speaking to other Order members. Damian never wanted Jae, Andy. He wanted you. Hecate has been impossible to find. Your blood is enough to charge the blade. Damian wanted you at Eidolon so he could kill you if he couldn't capture Hecate.'

'Me? He doesn't know who I am. He's always wanted Jae . . .' I trail off, my throat too tight to speak. I think of Damian's careful maneuvering through the Order. His plans to acquire power over fate and death. And how Hecate factors perfectly into those schemes.

'When Jae entered Oracle, Damian erected the wall of mist around Eidolon. He's keeping something in, as well as preventing others from entering. I think that something was meant to be you. But you've been in the Underworld. He must be keeping Jae because he knows you won't let him die. Damian is waiting for you.'

284

'Then Jae is still alive?' I ask, my voice barely a whisper.

'He must be. Damian wants the powers of Hecate,' Ramsey says. 'He must be holding Jae and waiting for you to return to the school so he can lure you to the sanctum. He may even use you as bait for Hecate. Tonight is the winter solstice, Andy. The perfect night to finish what he's started when he began killing gods.'

We look at each other in the darkness, identical worry masking our features.

'Then we have to save Jae without risking Damian using me as leverage for Hecate.' I pace across a small patch of grass, my mind turning over possibilities. 'We'll sneak into Oculus during the day, well before moonrise on the winter solstice. We can free Jae and figure out a way to kill Damian before he can take my blood.'

Determination steels my spine as I look back at Eidolon in the slowly spreading light of dawn. The school looks peaceful and sleepy. The spires of buildings, the statues and cobbled roads appear as innocent as a lamb. But blood has been spilled on the stones, and if we don't stop Damian, he'll consume this place until there's nothing left.

I look over my shoulder at Ramsey when he doesn't immediately agree with my half-baked plan – I know it isn't much to go on, but at least I'm offering ideas – and stop short when I see his expression illuminated by the screen of his phone. His usually pale skin has gone chalky, and when he looks up at me, fear tingles in my fingertips.

'What is it?' I stop pacing, heart thundering in my throat.

He shakes his head, voice uncertain as he turns the screen to face me. 'Looks like Damian has broken his silence. He has called all three houses to a meeting tonight. Every member of the Order is to report to the Oculus compound at sundown – even the newest Sophos initiates.'

My eyes blur as I scan the message, written in crisp, unemotional language. But then he taps the screen, opening another app where code runs across my vision in bright flashes.

'I used this to tap into Rohan's phone a few months ago so I could keep up with the heads of the other houses. Everyone is so concerned with magic and spells that they forget modern technology is just as effective at snooping as anything we can do.' Ramsey's jaw is tight as he reads something. 'Damian texted him and Antonia a few minutes ago.'

The strength leaves my body, panic so all-consuming that I choke as it lances through my chest. I read the words in the private conversation, my head swimming even as I want to crumple to the ground in a heap.

I have the daughter of Hecate. Be ready for the sacrifice.

But I'm standing right here, fresh from the Underworld.

I look up at Ramsey, horror turning my mouth to ash as I stagger, bracing one hand against a rough wall. 'What if he has Violet? Damian could be tired of waiting for me to try and rescue Jae!'

'We don't know that he has her. He could easily have sensed your return from the Underworld and thinks he'll be able to trap you when you rescue Jae,' he tries to soothe me, his expression determined. 'This will be much more difficult, I admit. The compound will be swarming with people now. But we can't let Damian get what he wants. We've both seen what he's capable of. If he has the power over death and the magic from the gods he's killed to host Hecate's powers, the Order will become as powerful as the gods used to be.'

A wobbly, hysterical laugh rips through my teeth. 'What can we do? Hecate isn't here. If she's smart, she will be staying far, far away from this place, probably in her territory in the Underworld. The only person with a shred of a chance at helping us is Jae, and he's somewhere in the compound!'

Ramsey presses his lips together. 'Then we free Jae and we'll stop this ritual from happening tonight, one way or another. With the power shared between the three of us, we stand a chance at killing Damian.'

'We don't know where Jae is!' I cry, shutting my eyes as I imagine Violet strapped to an altar, bleeding to death. But I push the thought away. Hecate didn't bring my sister here with the mist barrier trapping everyone inside the school's property. She wouldn't. Violet is safe, still at home.

'You're right,' he says, and then holds his phone aloft, the screen still running with code as it flips through images and conversations. 'But Rohan does. And now we know exactly where to find our Thoth.'

27

Ibis Park looks so different in the daylight that I almost stop in my tracks to admire it. Morning sunlight streams happily through sparse clouds, illuminating ivy-covered walls and reflecting off bubbled glass panes. It feels like years since I set foot in the library, and despite the chilly winter air, sweat sticks to my back as Ramsey and I enter through a narrow side door swollen with time.

'You're sure no one will see us?' I whisper, despite the spell Ramsey recited over me earlier, one meant to disguise my voice and face and keep others from recognizing me. It wouldn't work around someone as powerful as Damian or other Oracle members, but it should last long enough to get us through the sanctum to the head of the house of Lector.

At least, in theory.

Ramsey scoffs, flicking a drop of dew from the lapel of his coat as a narrow hall deposits us into a backroom stuffed with scrolls and dusty tomes. 'My family has spent generations crafting magic and spells, Andy. I think I can manage this for an hour while we find Rohan.'

'I still think I should have done it,' I grumble, coughing as dust gets into my eyes.

'And light a homing beacon that points straight to you? Your magic is strange, Andy. Anyone in the Order could sense it like a bloodhound and sniff you out.'

I make a face at him even as another knot of worry for Anubis winds between my shoulder blades. We duck behind a stack of grimy-looking amulets, the magic in them long ago drained away. 'You're sure Rohan is on the third floor? The room we were in for our initiation into Lector?'

Ramsey glances at his phone before darting to another narrow, mildew-ridden door. 'Positive. He told Antonia he was going to consult the magic papyri and conduct a divination with an ancient spirit to bless the ritual tonight. There is only one place to conduct a spell like that; you must be in a completely dark room marked with intricate spells. Spells that Lector has engraved in Thoth's chambers.'

'Lead the way,' I say.

Ramsey ducks through the stacks until we reach a white-painted service door marked by an emergency exit sign. When we open it, the hall is cramped and dark. Metal stairs lead directly upward in a steep climb. No windows adorn the walls, so we must be sandwiched somewhere in the center of the building. It's like a secret spine running along the length of Ibis Park.

'Second door on the right, top floor,' Ramsey says, already out of breath as we climb. 'The divination room is used only by Thoth. I guarantee Rohan has asked for complete privacy. The last thing he's going to risk is Damian's wrath if anything goes wrong.'

We climb the last treads of the staircase, the scent of old plaster and mildew strong. A few doors mark the catwalk, all of them old and coated in chipped paint. Ramsey heads for the second door and waits for me, hand poised on the rusted handle. I join him, listening for signs of pursuit from below. All is quiet. With a nod, Ramsey eases the door open.

Low candlelight flickers across the floor. I peer inside, squinting as my eyes adjust. Heavy draperies block the windows, and the air is humid and damp. Beyond the small circle of light cast by the candles, I can make out a lone figure kneeling before rolls of papyri and a deep bronze bowl, easily the size of a sink basin.

I wait for the hinges of the door to creak, for Rohan to lift his head and see us. Ramsey and I enter quietly, slinking along the far wall. But he doesn't move. The papyri on the ground before him shimmer like a mirage, the hieroglyphics shuddering and dancing like they refuse to be still.

Rohan's mouth opens in time with the movement of his eyes as they scan the papyri, and I jerk backward, bumping into Ramsey. I fully expect Rohan to call for help, to lift his hands and attack.

'He can't hear us right now. He's communing with a spirit,' Ramsey hisses into my ear.

I swallow back the cry building in my chest, fixated on Rohan's tight, tortured posture. 'We need to bind him so he can't use his magic,' I say as I lift my hands.

'Don't call on your powers.' Ramsey grabs my wrist. 'Not yet. We can't risk them knowing we were here until we have what we need.'

Ramsey moves quickly, circling the utterly still Rohan and his ring of candles and ash, looking for something. The moment Ramsey's eyes narrow, I know he's spotted a weakness in the spell. He doesn't speak aloud, only mouths words in an incantation I can't understand from this distance.

A startled shout punctuates the air as the candles go dark. A scrambling sound skitters to my ears as I reach for the wall to steady myself in the utterly dark room. Something metal clatters to the ground and shoes slip and squeak on the tile. There's the sound of a fist hitting flesh and a grunt of pain.

Gritting my teeth, I ignore Ramsey's warning and summon a small lick of flame, just enough to illuminate the surrounding scene. Two bodies struggle on the ground, feet and fists flying. One of them kicks a ceremonial candle, and it rolls across the room. I dive for it, transferring the flame to the wick.

'Andy!' Ramsey barks, rolling onto his back, his arms secured around Rohan's throat. 'The scrolls – close them before he can read again.'

With a swift kick, I launch the papyri across the room, where they crumple into a heap at the base of a bookcase.

I look over at Ramsey, his face still coated in sweat. Rohan slowly goes limp in his grip, face growing purple, until finally his eyes slide shut. Ramsey groans and shoves the other boy to the side, getting to his feet. The neck of his shirt is torn, and I can't help but notice the angry-looking scars across one shoulder. They look like someone took a carving knife to his skin and flayed the flesh for fun. I know exactly who that 'someone' is.

Ramsey meets my gaze and shrugs the torn shirtsleeve up higher. 'I'll bind his powers. The sooner we get the information we need, the quicker we can get Jae.'

With a few tugs and some maneuvering, we arrange Rohan on his back, arms and legs straight as arrows. When Ramsey whispers a binding spell, a shiver arcs up my spine. I can feel the moment he reaches toward Rohan's magic, locating where it lives in his chest. Slowly, like a potter smoothing clay, Ramsey binds it somewhere far, far away.

'It's done. It would take the entire house of Oracle hours to free his powers.' Ramsey nods at me, nudging Rohan's stiff body with his boot. The other boy groans and cracks his eyes open, and Ramsey squats beside him. 'He's docile as a lamb. We shouldn't have any problems getting him to talk.'

Rohan's eyes open wide, and he stiffens, his muscles straining as he attempts to sit up. 'What have you done to me?' His eyes flick around the room, to the lone candle and the papyri flung far out of his reach. 'Help! Someone –'

Ramsey puts a finger to Rohan's mouth, making a tsking sound in his throat. 'There, there. No one can hear you, Thoth, no matter how loud you scream.'

'You lie,' Rohan spits, the tendons in his neck straining as he tries once again fruitlessly to move. 'Any moment, the rest of Lector will be here! Unbind me, and I'll consider convincing Damian to spare your life.'

Ramsey's smile is chilly as he looks down at the incapacitated leader. 'Soon enough, Lector, like the other houses, will head to the Oculus Sanctum for the ritual. No one will know you're here, much less Damian.'

Rohan curses, still struggling to move. Despite Ramsey's posturing, we don't know when the rest of the houses will head for the grand meeting tonight, and we don't have time to play mind games with someone as far gone as Rohan.

'Where is Jae?' I ask, shouldering past Ramsey so I can meet Rohan's eyeline.

Rohan bares his teeth, and I feel a surge of muted energy as he tries in vain to cast a spell. 'Damian will be here in moments once he doesn't hear from me! And he'll carve you up like he did to all the others who were too weak to lead the Order!'

Ramsey stiffens, a ghostly expression stealing over his features. I know he's remembering his time in the Order's Agoge. The brutal murders and hunger. The endless twisted games that claimed the lives of so many other first-born sons. How he became an animal trying to survive. I put a hand on his forearm, hoping it's enough to keep him from pummeling Rohan into the ground.

'Damian is a little busy at the moment, isn't he?' I say, drawing Rohan's attention away from Ramsey. 'I doubt he'll even consider coming after you, not when he needs this sacrifice to go exactly as planned. We all know how dangerous it is to take on the powers of the gods. One wrong step and he won't make it.' I cross my arms, pretending a confidence I certainly do not feel. 'Damian won't risk anything tonight. Not until the ceremony is complete and Hecate is dead, isn't that right?'

Rohan's jaw clenches as he glances around, the whites of his eyes stark against his brown skin. He doesn't answer, letting the hate and desperation in his eyes speak for him. I take a calming breath. Rohan's reaction tells me we're right about Damian's plan. The only hope we have is in getting Anubis free and keeping Damian from summoning Hecate or killing me.

'You don't have options, Rohan,' I say, tapping his cheek to get his attention. 'No one is going to come looking for you, and you can't get free. Tell me where Jae is and how to get to him.'

'Jae is a traitor,' he spits, eyes hard and black. 'The only reason he isn't dead already is because Damian plans on stealing his magic to strengthen himself for the sacrifice tonight.'

Ramsey glowers down at him. 'Tell us where he is. If you want a chance at living past the next five minutes, you'll do the right thing.'

'The right thing would have been to kill you and the rest of the Arskells, and anyone who opposes Damian!' Rohan says, jerking hard against the tile floor. His body shudders, but his hands and arms remain bound invisibly at his sides. He lets out a howl of frustration, his eyes turning bloodshot from burst vessels as he scans wildly for some sort of escape. 'There is nothing you can do that will convince me to betray him.'

A dark look crosses Ramsey's face, shrouded with memories, and he considers Rohan, lying prostrate before him.

I open my mouth to threaten Rohan, to beg, but Ramsey holds a hand up. His eyes are so hard that I find my jaw snapping shut without protest.

Ramsey whispers a spell, and the hairs on the nape of my neck stand up. His fingers move, pulling the air apart until a silver shimmer spreads between them. Slowly, it solidifies into a wickedly sharp penknife. The blade reflects in the pupils of Rohan's ever-widening eyes.

'You never watched the Agoge and its trials,' Ramsey murmurs, rotating the knife in his hands languidly. 'At the time you were a first-year and barely clawing your way into the house of Sophos. You think you understand what it's like in Oracle, now that you wear the Ibis crown, but you will never be one of us. A son of the founders.'

Ramsey's lips curl back over his teeth, and he lifts one hand to his collar, unbuttoning the first few fastenings of his tattered shirt. Even with the dim light cast by the lone candle, the scars across his body are prominent. They aren't nearly as numerous as Damian's, but Ramsey's are deeper. More cruel. Made by a hand without remorse or feeling.

'But what you will never understand for yourself,' Ramsey continues, dropping one hand as he eyes the blade in the other, 'is the pain that comes from centuries of crushing family expectation. Years of training, beatings, and time spent bathing in the convergence to grow my powers. All in the hope that, one day, I would become the Romulus the Arskells believe they were owed.'

Rohan smirks, but his eyes follow the narrow, gleaming knife uneasily. 'You were weak. The Order always culls the weak.'

Ramsey smiles, but his eyes are haunted. He slowly brings the point of the blade down to Rohan's shoulder, pressing just hard enough to pierce the fabric and prick the skin beneath. 'Perhaps all your training, all your studying in the halls of the library, has taught you what it feels like to crawl through tunnels, stuff yourself into crevices in stifling heat just to get away from the bloodshed. I bet you understand the pain of your fingers being snapped off like twigs by the very person you adore, Rohan. Or the feel of your flesh being carved with a dull knife, your blood smeared on Damian's face and lips as he declares himself Romulus for all time?'

Rohan stifles a groan of pain as Ramsey digs the penknife into the meat of his shoulder. Blood wells over the sleeve, vivid against the dark color. I flare my nostrils at the scent, my heart stuck in my throat as Ramsey leans over the other boy, a wild glint in his eyes. He looks like he must have three years ago, as he struggled to survive a brutal competition in the name of family honor. Desperate and full of rage.

'Of course, your father never entered the Order, Rohan. He is far away, funneling money to you and your little "drinking club", safe within the walls of his mansion in . . . Chelsea, is it?' Ramsey smiles as Rohan's face grows pale, and he drags the blade down the buttons of Rohan's shirt, neatly severing them from the thread until the other boy's torso is bare and heaving with anxious breath.

My breath catches and I reach out. 'Ramsey.'

He shrugs my hand off his shoulder. 'Because you are so sheltered, so *soft*, it is easy to call me weak just because I did not have what it took to kill boys I've known since infancy in horrible, grotesque ways. But after seeing my father's disappointment even as he was killed, and bearing the shame of my entire family, I find I am not so weak in certain things.'

Rohan breathes in sharply, his body seizing as he tries, and fails, to get away. 'Wait! Wait –'

His voice cuts off in a scream that is swallowed by the spell cast in the room. The knife in Ramsey's hand drags cleanly across his stomach, leaving a horizontal line of red. He doesn't press hard, there's no need with the sheer sharpness of the knife, but the cut is clean and precise, and it must sting and burn like salt on a wound.

I grit my teeth, stomach heaving at the sound of Rohan's cries of pain. Ramsey's face breaks out in a sweat, and his eyes are so far away I wonder if he's even aware of his surroundings; of the boy writhing in pain as he makes another mark, and then two more, across the unblemished skin.

'Ramsey,' I say again, my voice harder this time as I dig my fingers into his shoulders and yank him back. 'This isn't the way to do things.'

He laughs, blinking up at me as he holds the dripping blade against Rohan's flesh again. 'Don't you understand, Andy? In the Order, *pain* is the only way.'

Carefully, I reach out, easing my fingers toward the hilt of the knife. Ramsey doesn't move as I gingerly take it, whispering a spell to banish it from existence. As my words fade away, Ramsey shakes his head, falling backward as he sits heavily, staring at the blood on his palms.

'Thank you,' Rohan gasps, tears and sweat streaming down his face as he tosses his head around, teeth gritted against the pain of his open wounds.

My gut churns as I stare down at him, studying the long cuts along his stomach and the blood dripping heavily onto the floor. 'I didn't do this for you, Rohan. I know exactly who you are, and I've seen you murder in cold blood for a scrap of knowledge. Any pity I might have had is long gone.'

He breathes hard, eyes darting to Ramsey sitting a few feet away, still staring at his bloodied hands. 'You'll do worse to me, then, daughter of Hecate? Is that what you're threatening?'

My palms tingle, a cooling sensation stealing over them.

Flashes of keys, torches and three-headed dogs dance behind my eyelids each time I blink. And though I know Hecate's talismans are far away, wherever the goddess is hiding from Damian, it almost feels like they're in my hands right now. Waiting for something.

Instinctively, I extend my fingers over Rohan's prostrate body. That same cool tingle races up my arms, urging me closer to the feeling building in my stomach. Rohan blurs before my eyes as the temperature in the room drops. His arms and legs, bound tightly at his sides, remind me of a body prepared for burial. I hover my hands, palms down, over his chest. A soft green light suffuses the room, fading in and out like a strobe light.

'Your eyes,' Ramsey mutters at my side, the blood dressing his hands forgotten.

His voice seems to come from far away, echoing and without substance. My breath stops, my lungs deflate. The air grows colder, and I blink at Ramsey a few times, the green glow flashing each time I do, matching the movements. Absently, I lift one finger to my face and brush beneath my glasses, as if I can feel a difference in my skin.

My hands jerk forward once more, like someone grabbed my wrists and wrenched them over Rohan's chest. Ramsey says something again, but I don't hear him. I'm fascinated by the way the cool air caresses my skin. How the lines of Rohan's body fade and shift, as if losing their substance. Like he's made of smoke and spirits.

The only light comes from my eyes, a green luminescence that grows in strength. Slowly, everything melts away, until all that remains is me, the tingle in my palms, and Rohan's wide, dark eyes as his body fades into obscurity.

Something bitingly cold presses into one hand, appearing from thin air. Turning over my wrist, I open my palm and stare down at a long black key with an ornate handle carved with a strophalos. It's Hecate's key – her talisman. The one that controls her ability to cross between the realms of life and death. The goddess is sending me a sign, I'm sure of it. Urging me to use the magic in my blood.

And suddenly, I understand what I'm supposed to do.

I narrow my eyes as I stare at the key and then lift my gaze to Rohan, washing his face in green. Gritting my teeth against the numbing sensation in my hands, I hold the key between my fingers. His eyes are wide as I bring the key to his breastbone and push.

Rohan lets out a startled cry through his teeth, but the sound is swallowed by a thickness in the air. Gentle mist rolls over his body, washing away his skin until his flesh is all but transparent, revealing the white bone below.

'Are you ready to talk?' I ask, surprised at the even tone that slips from my tongue. Despite Rohan's atrocities, and how he has certainly been tormenting Anubis for days now, I don't feel fear or apprehension. I feel . . . powerful. In control for perhaps the first time in my life.

Rohan curses at me, teeth bared between incorporeal lips. 'Never! Damian is the Order's future!'

The key in my hand pierces deeper into Rohan's ghostly chest and I turn it slightly, like fitting the teeth into the mechanism of a lock. His skeleton flickers once more. Panic contorts Rohan's face, but I know he doesn't feel pain. Just fear as I control how close he comes to death. Gently, I ease the pressure on the key, the sensation of the Underworld rippling just beneath the surface of the room we occupy.

Rohan seems to understand the control I have over him at this moment. The way my hand literally suspends him between life and death. He attempts to thrash, but he remains as immobile as ever.

'You'll never win against him,' he pants, the shadows of his eye sockets overpowering his face like a grisly mask. 'He is stronger than anyone. Even you.'

I shake my head, feeling the rush of a convergence nearby grow stronger, desperate to reach out and connect with me. To cart Rohan's body away and into the next world. 'Tell me where Jae is. I won't ask again.'

Rohan pants, his eyes glancing around wildly. I know what he must see. The spirits of the Underworld fluttering in the ghostly trees that slowly burst from the ground. The hiss of water spilling over rocks, hungry to have his blood join its flow. He is teetering on a knife's edge between life and death, and I hold the key – literally – to his fate.

Slowly, the tension leaves his body. The blood crusting his ghostly skin seems to darken like tar. His face is almost imperceptible now over his skull. Rohan looks at the key sunk into his chest. Finally, he opens his jaw, voice weak and hoarse as he whispers two words to keep himself from a fate all men fear. Even one as powerful as the Thoth of the Order.

'The catacombs.'

The numbing cold in my fingertips turns painful, like submerging my flesh in ice water for too long. With a swallowed hiss, I pull the key free from Rohan's chest. The dead poplar trees and surging waters of the Underworld fade away. The smell of blood, real and pungent, burns my nose as I stand and move away from Rohan.

I look down at my palm as the obsidian key melts away into the shadows, taking the frigid cold with it. Rohan is utterly silent, his skin ashen and eyes shut. If it weren't for the subtle rise and fall of his chest, I would think he was dead.

Clearing my throat, I look at Ramsey still seated on the

floor, his face haggard. 'You know where these catacombs are?'

'Below Oculus.' He blinks a few times and wipes his hands on his jeans. 'But all the tunnels below Eidolon connect. We can reach it through the passageway below the omphalos stone.'

I nod, pressing my lips together in a hard line as I open the door leading back to the archives. Sweat sticks to my skin and makes the scent of Rohan's blood all the more gut-churning.

'I almost killed him.' Ramsey's voice is so quiet I nearly miss it over the creaking of door hinges. I look over my shoulder as he hesitates, standing over the silent Rohan.

'He would have deserved it,' I say. 'Even if it wasn't the right thing to do.'

Ramsey exhales slowly, lifting his red-rimmed eyes to mine. 'I've always thought I was different from the others. Better. That I wasn't the cold-blooded killer they raised me to be.' He looks down at Rohan again and his mouth twists into an expression I can't quite name. 'But when it comes down to it, I'm just like the rest of the Order.'

'You're not, Ramsey. He was goading you, using your emotions against you to exploit your weak points. It's what people like him do.'

Ramsey laughs once, the sound flat and hard. 'Maybe we're all monsters. Some of us just wear it better than others.'

We're quiet for a few heartbeats – the only sound that of Rohan's soft breaths. Finally, Ramsey shakes his head, wiping his hands again on his pants, and comes to my side at the door. His face is still tight, but he wears his usual devil-may-care smile, the pain buried somewhere beneath.

'Let's go – the binding should keep him hidden for a

while. The catacombs aren't far from here. If we hurry, we can free Jae before the ceremony even starts.'

I let Ramsey lead the way down the stairs. But as I shut the door behind me, sealing Rohan away, I think of the key and how it formed in my hand like it belonged there. And I wonder if maybe Ramsey is right. That somewhere along the way, I might become as much of a monster as the Order.

28

Dangling roots slip through hard-packed earth and layers of limestone. The air in the ancient Roman village, frozen in time and buried beneath the university, feels thick as Ramsey and I make our way through it. Like a sickness has taken hold somewhere deep within. My teeth ache with the feeling as we emerge into the catacombs, an oddly familiar smell tickling my nose.

Magic. The oldest and most dangerous kind.

My stomach clenches with nerves and I charge forward, ready to fight anyone standing between me and Anubis. We've been traveling through the tunnels for what feels like hours. And I'm desperate to lay eyes on him. To know that he is safe.

'Careful,' Ramsey says, holding his arm out as I slip on a slick patch of smooth stone. 'This cavern houses the oldest convergence, the original branch of the Underworld's river in the mortal world. If you slip and fall into it, you might never have the strength to pull yourself free.'

I breathe deeply, noting the scents of magic and the land of the dead tangled together. It smells of spices and incense, of earth and pure water. It reminds me of Anubis.

'Where is Jae?' I ask, scouring the niches in the wall stuffed with bones and decay. It's so dark in the cavern that I can't even see the roaring river nearby, only feel the vibrations through my feet.

Ramsey mutters a spell for light, and torches on the

wall illuminate, their glow overpowering the shadows. 'If Damian used him to retrieve the last dagger of the Apkallu, he'll be trapped on the other side of the bank. He likes to think only the Valerius family has access to this place, but my father made me bathe in the convergence as a boy to grow my powers. I know the catacombs well.'

Ignoring the dark inviting water cutting through the cavern, I edge close to the bank. Water sprinkles my clothes and glasses, frigidly cold. The other bank is a small crescent shape. A lone altar dominates the tiny beach, and I spy congealed blood gathered on the floor. I suck in a breath, one hand clenching at my chest.

'There . . .' I point, my hand trembling. 'He's behind the altar.'

All that's visible of Anubis is his head and shoulders – covered in grit and cuts. His eyes are shut, lips parted, like he is unconscious.

Ramsey squints, jaw set. 'Only Damian and the heads of the other houses know the spell to cross the river. But with your powers, I think we can create a new one.'

I shed my jacket, letting it drop to the damp floor. My thin shirt does nothing against the cold, but I ignore the goosebumps rising along my arms as I yank off one boot and then the other.

'What are you doing?' Ramsey asks, reaching down for one of my discarded boots.

Twisting my wild hair into a knot, I flex my feet against the smooth stone floor. 'I'm swimming across. We don't know if he's hurt, or worse.'

'Andy, this convergence will overpower you. The sons of the founding families are force-fed this water, made to bathe in it, from birth, to grow our powers. One taste made me so ill I couldn't leave my bed for days.'

I regard the velvety black water with more wariness, but crouch down anyway. 'Then I'll keep my mouth shut.'

He shakes his head. 'This isn't just about drinking it. The river is pure magic, stronger than anything you can imagine. No one, no matter how good they are, can resist wanting more and more. Until you're dragged away.'

I cast a look at Anubis. He's so still that I can't tell if he's breathing. Everything inside of me screams to run to him, to swim across this paltry obstacle and make him better. But the river seems to call on the dark seed somewhere in my soul. The part that revels in the taste of magic in the air and the feel of it coursing through my veins.

'How much time will a new spell take?' I ask, my voice high and frayed.

Ramsey visibly relaxes, but he flicks his gaze to the unmoving Anubis. 'I don't know.'

I bite back a curse and take my coat and boots back from Ramsey when he offers them. In the world above, the sun is high as the afternoon wears on to the evening. Nightfall will come soon enough. My skin prickles all over with cold and the unending pulse of magic flowing through the cavern. It makes my hair stand on end and my jaw clench, like rubbing velvet the wrong way.

'Take my hands,' Ramsey says, offering his scarred ones to me. 'We need to cross to the west bank. It mimics the Underworld here, so the only way to reach it is by becoming incorporeal for a moment.'

I nod, my eyes sliding shut the moment I touch Ramsey's fingers. Ignoring the dried blood caked beneath his nails, I latch on to his magic. Once again, I note how different his is to mine. His powers feel like a knot in his chest, frayed and tangled and alive with frantic energy. Each thread is hard won and desperate.

My magic rises to meet his, flowing easily through my blood and bones like it sleeps soundly, just waiting to be used. I feel the moment they meet, winding together like they recognize each other. The river roars louder, the sound of water slapping the banks growing stronger. Cold touches my feet through my boots, and I want to open my eyes to see what the convergence is doing, but I'm too wrapped up in the spell Ramsey and I are creating together.

The moment he told me we needed to become incorporeal, our flesh and blood momentarily turning to spirit, it was as if my magic leaped into action. It spins around us, taking strength from Ramsey's as he offers it to me. A gentle breeze brushes over my skin, my cheeks. My lips tingle and my fingers clamp down hard on Ramsey's.

Suddenly, Ramsey's powers detach from mine, fading away back into his chest like a collapsing star. I open my eyes, surprised when everything looks muted and gray. Ramsey waves at me, and I realize I can't hear him as his lips move. His skin is sickly gray – like the shades that wait on the east bank in the Underworld.

Hurry, he mouths and points to the other side of the cavern.

I nod, feeling light as a cloud, like I'm made of gossamer. Glancing down at my feet, I see that I'm hovering a few inches off the ground. My body has no substance. Vertigo washes over me, and I shake my head hard, focusing on Anubis' slumped body. I move in a lurching motion, suspended over the center of the river. Ramsey follows, floating just as eerily as I do.

As I struggle to move my incorporeal body, I notice that the torches on the wall have burned low. How long did the spell take? A jolt of panic seizes my ribs, and I feel flecks of water brush my face and lips. I lift my head, catching

Ramsey's eyes as he reaches the other side of the bank. His eyes are wide with horror as my body takes shape again too soon.

'Andy!' he cries, turning solid again as he reaches out a hand.

Gravity takes hold once more, yanking me down without mercy. I throw both hands out, my fingers slipping along Ramsey's. Freezing water wraps around me up to my chest until I jerk to a sudden stop, my hip colliding against a half-submerged rock. I gasp, my tongue heavy with the taste of minerals and magic.

Ramsey groans as he braces against the stone floor with one arm and holds onto me with the other. The current is too strong. It yanks at me hard, trying to suck me below the surface. My fingers slip again, and a startled cry breaks from my lips.

'Hold on!' Ramsey yells, his hair damp from the spraying water as it slams angrily against the banks.

The water is rising, swirling over the pebbles of the beach. It won't let me go. Even now it tugs and pulls, desperate to wrench me into the Underworld, deep into the swirling waters where the branches of the river join into a raging waterfall.

'Ramsey!' I scream, the end of his name garbled as my head slips below the surface for a moment. I break through again, gasping and choking. Panic etches across his face as his other hand digs into the shoreline, leaving long divots as the current jerks him forward.

His breath heaves as he tries to pull again and anchor himself to the beach. But the river rises relentlessly, spilling over the banks. My skin is so cold I feel like I'll shatter. Our eyes meet, a desperate sort of understanding passing between us. The river wants me. And it will not be denied.

I hear Ramsey call my name as my head slips below the surface again, the current buffeting me like a rag doll. His hand scrabbles over my knuckles, but I can feel the moment his grip gives way. The brush of the severed parts of his fingers sliding over my thumb. I hold my breath, lungs burning, as the river prepares to carry me away. I squeeze my eyes shut so I don't see the shadows moving in the river, strange images taking shape that speak of monsters and horror.

Pressure pops in my ears and something grabs the collar of my shirt. A rock catching the fabric maybe? But then fresh air breaks over my head and I suck in a breath, my limbs flailing and heavy.

I blink away water as unknown hands grip my shoulders and arms and pull me from the grasp of the convergence.

Pebbles dig into my back as I lie on my side, coughing up dark water that tastes like secrets. My ears pop and I wipe at my eyes and scrape my hair back from my face. Ramsey squats in front of me, his face pale but relieved.

Someone else touches my shoulder as I cough up more river water.

'Andromeda,' Anubis says in the way that makes my breath catch. 'How many times are you going to drown on me?'

29

It takes a few minutes for my teeth to stop chattering and for the shadows in the corners of the cavern to stop hissing, urging me to return to the grasp of the river. Anubis holds me close to his side until the worst of the shivering subsides. He wears a tattered scrap of a robe over his torso, but he seems mostly whole. Uninjured.

'It's alright,' Anubis says softly, rubbing my icy fingers between his palms. 'It takes a while for the chill to go away, but your magic is stronger than the convergence. You'll be fine.'

My hands are numb, but I hold on to Anubis tightly, afraid that if I let go, he'll fade away. And soon, he will. All the waiting and dread has finally come to a head. I was so busy worrying about finding him, I forgot what happens once this night is over.

'The ceremony is tonight?' Anubis asks Ramsey. 'I can't remember the last few days.'

Ramsey nods. 'It's the winter solstice. Damian has been keeping you here as insurance in case he fails to summon Hecate and needs you to lure Andy. And in case he needs your magic to strengthen himself tonight. I'm sure they'll come to bring you to the Oculus Sanctum soon.'

'Damian said he had a daughter of Hecate in his text to Rohan and Antonia,' I say through my chattering teeth. 'Even though I'm probably playing into his plans right now, I couldn't leave you down here. We'll just have to kill Damian before the ceremony even starts.'

Anubis helps me to my feet. 'Damian doesn't need Hecate, only her blood.'

My blood runs colder than it did in the depths of the convergence. 'I know, but Damian has no idea I'm back from the Underworld. Ramsey and I bound Rohan – he won't be able to tell anyone.'

'It's Violet,' Anubis murmurs. 'When I retrieved the blade, Damian used a curse tablet to summon her. I thought it was Hecate, at first. But he has your sister. He's going to use her blood, and he wasn't going to risk missing the solstice.'

Air freezes in my lungs and I sway, my hand reaching out feebly to steady me against the altar. 'Damian has Violet?'

Anubis nods, and it feels like the massive cavern walls are closing in on me. Sealing away air and light and leaving me, nothing but another decaying corpse, in the crypt. I whirl to face Ramsey, my heart frantic in my chest. 'Do you know the way to Oculus from here?'

Anubis answers first. 'Back through the buried village. A tunnel leads right into the compound.'

'But the entire Order will be there tonight. If we want to reach the chamber before the ceremony takes place, we need another plan,' Ramsey says, shrugging off his mostly dry coat and offering it to me. I stare at it, my fingers like ice. Finally, Ramsey sighs and slings it over my shoulder. Anubis tugs me a little closer to his side.

'We've been here for an hour!' I cry, my fingers curling into tight fists as I sag against Anubis. 'The moon will rise soon, and Damian needs it to start the ceremony. We can't just hike out!'

'The tunnels are the quickest way that I know of.' Ramsey crosses his arms.

'It will be alright, Andy,' Anubis says softly, one hand

gently rubbing my arm. 'We will get to Violet before anything can happen.'

He rubs his forehead with his free hand, and I notice how tired he looks. His golden skin is pale and damp with sweat. Dark circles stain the skin below his eyes, and his lips are bloodless and chapped. He's been held captive, left to rot in the catacombs by Damian until he needed his magic to boost his own. But still, even when I rescued him from Tooth and Talon over a year ago, he didn't look this bad. He should have recovered by now. Regenerated.

'What did they do to you?' I murmur, my voice trembling as I try to even out my breaths. I can't help Violet if I'm panicking.

Anubis opens his eyes and they look bloodshot. 'Devil's trap,' he whispers back, nodding up at the ceiling.

There's a wealth of emotion in his eyes, and something tells me the devil's trap is only one of the things he's had to deal with at the hands of Damian.

'They know who you are?' I whisper, a wave of terror gripping my heart. Anubis' powers, as his godly form returns tonight, represent our last shot, the last chance we will have to stop Damian before he can control the seventh blade.

He shakes his head as Ramsey looks at us curiously. 'I don't think Damian and the others suspect what I am – just that my magic isn't what it seems. They figured I'd be too injured to leave the cavern, and abandoned me here. It's just bad luck that it happens to be the same place he's been capturing and killing gods.'

'Can you use your powers to get us out of here? It's the night of the solstice. You might be able to travel between planes, so we can come up inside the chamber instead of walking there.'

'If we can break this trap. And if we can trust *him*.' Anubis nods at Ramsey, who waits patiently as we have our murmured conversation.

I press my lips together and study the markings on the celling. If it works like any other devil's trap, I need to break the intricate circles of interlocking patterns and symbols. But then Ramsey will know who Anubis is.

'He's helped me before,' I say, turning my back to Ramsey so that Anubis has to look me in the eyes. 'All this time Ramsey has watched out for me. And he came here tonight to help you too. After tonight, you'll be gone, and it won't matter that he knows the truth.'

Anubis' jaw clenches as he glances over my shoulder. 'He was there, Andy. The night I was initiated into Oracle. He looked at me like he knew something I didn't. What if he's helping Damian and the others right now?'

I take a deep breath, grasping Anubis' hand in my freezing one as I turn around. 'Violet is up there. I trust Ramsey. He's saved my life twice now. If he wanted to hurt us, he'd have done it by now.'

'I'm glad to hear it.' Ramsey arches a brow. 'But I feel as though I've missed a vital part of the conversation.'

Anubis goes stiff beside me, his fingers tightening around mine. 'If you're sure.' He sounds far from it.

'I am.' I carefully let go of Anubis, stepping halfway between him and Ramsey. 'We have a way to reach the ceremonial chamber far faster than tunnels.'

'Wonderful,' Ramsey says, but he looks at the congealed blood on the altar and at Anubis with something like apprehension. 'What do you need from me?'

'You know about Damian's mission to capture and kill gods. How he's bound them here after stealing them from the Underworld.'

Ramsey nods. 'I may not be a head of one of the houses, but I know what goes on inside Oracle.'

'Then you know this is a devil's trap designed for gods. And if we're going to use Jae's powers to reach my sister before the ceremony begins, then we need to break it.'

'Damian has no use for the trap anymore. He has all seven blades and your sister for Hecate's blood. Why do we need to break it?'

'For him,' I say.

Ramsey squints. 'Who?'

'Me.' Anubis lifts his chin, his dark eyes glittering in the low light of the torches.

I wait, holding my breath as Ramsey's eyes dart between the two of us, his forehead wrinkled as he tries to piece together what we're saying. The only sound in the cavern is of the convergence rushing by, magic hanging in the air and over our skin. Ramsey swallows hard, his throat bobbing as his nostrils flare and his hands tighten into fists at his side.

'You're a god. W-who –?' he stammers, unable to finish the words.

'Anubis,' I offer, glancing up at the markings on the ceiling. 'And I really need to know if you're going to freak out or help get us out of here. We don't have enough time for it.'

Ramsey's face goes so pale that I can make out faded freckles on his cheeks. He takes a few breaths, struggling to form questions. Finally, he lets out a long breath. 'Alright.' His voice is a little strangled. 'What do you need me to do?'

It's strange that a cool rush of dank air smelling of loam and ash should feel so comforting to me now. But as Anubis clamps one hand on my waist and his other on Ramsey's arm, the shadows in the cavern swallow us whole, and I feel a sense of momentary relief. The Underworld, as harrowing and frightening as it can be, still feels a bit like home. The rush of shadows slowly fades away as they slip through the planes of the mortal world and the land of the dead, whisking us along with them. As the cold marble halls of the Oculus Sanctum come into focus and the last bits of Anubis' magic fade, my stomach clenches. Anubis can use his godly powers again. That can only mean one thing. His mortal body will fade away tonight at the height of the solstice.

A featureless hallway of marble and white paint stretches behind us. We're on the second floor in a rarely used passageway that links to a gallery above the ceremonial chamber. Ahead lies a set of great double doors, the handles carved like snakes. Behind them, I sense the pulsing sickness that waited in the catacombs. It's stronger here, like a massive bruise. Magic, a dark and twisted kind, is happening beyond those impenetrable doors.

Anubis releases Ramsey's arm, and the other boy stumbles, overcome with vertigo and nausea from the trip between worlds. He leans forward over his knees and retches, wiping his mouth with the back of the hand missing the tips of three fingers.

'Please tell me we never have to do that again,' he gasps, straightening up just enough to meet Anubis' eyes.

'It's always bad the first time.' I step away from Anubis to give Ramsey a sympathetic pat on the shoulder.

He gives a choked huff that might be a laugh. 'That doesn't make me feel better.'

The small smile on my face melts as the building rattles like an earthquake below our feet. I glance around the empty hall and then at the sealed doors. 'What was that?'

Ramsey looks up at the ceiling nervously as he wipes his

mouth again. 'That was Damian's magic calling on the convergence. The ceremony is starting.'

'Already?' I step toward the doors, ready to tear them open. 'How are we going to stop Damian when everyone will be inside, ready to protect him?'

Anubis places his hand on my arm before I can tear the doors off their hinges. 'We can't just run in there blindly. We need a plan.'

'The entire compound is sealed off now that the ritual has started, for the protection of the Romulus.' Ramsey looks toward the windows at the far end of the hall where the telltale silvery light of the rising moon spills across the marble floors. 'This gallery is for low-ranking Order members. Sophos mostly. We need to sneak in and stop what Damian is doing before it goes any further. I think Anubis is our best bet here.'

Anubis nods stiffly. 'I can use my powers to take Damian somewhere deep in the Underworld. Keep him there until the solstice passes.'

I want to argue that Anubis should stay at my side. That I should keep him for as long as I can. But my tongue sticks to the roof of my mouth as I look at him in his tattered robes. His skin pale and covered in sweat. He is a divine being I've drawn to my side through sheer force of will. But he doesn't belong here. And if I want to keep Hecate and Violet safe from Damian, I have to let him go. Once the solstice passes, I'll be alone once more. Left to face the wrath of a thwarted society older than any civilization.

But I don't say anything about it – about the truth that has hung over us like a pall for the months we've been at Eidolon. The truth that has made Anubis keep himself so apart from me.

'You'll be careful?' I ask.

He leans close, his breath sweet against my face. He must know I'm asking about more than just tonight. He tries to smile, even as the ground rumbles again.

I grab the tattered robe around his shoulders and tug him against me. It's only a breath, a moment so fleeting it almost doesn't feel real. But when he kisses me back, all the questions and anxiety of our time here seem to pass between us. There aren't any answers, but as I taste incense and ancient things on his tongue, I figure I've gotten him back once before. Perhaps I can do it again.

Ramsey clears his throat, and I'm surprised I can hear it above the sound of blood roaring in my ears and the steadily growing tremors rocking the compound. I draw back, my gaze still full of Anubis' smooth golden skin. Ramsey's mouth is pressed in a hard line as his gaze moves between us, but whatever thoughts are racing around his head, he seems to bite them back.

'Ready?' Anubis asks, his fingers squeezing mine.

'You have to take Violet to the Underworld too,' I say to Anubis, my voice desperate as I realize that, in moments, I won't see him again. 'As soon as you take Damian down, come back for Violet. Take her to the cave she hid in last year. She'll be safe there, no one else knows about it.'

Anubis clenches his jaw, like he wants to argue, but he nods.

Ramsey's hands glow an unearthly blue as he weaves a spell to unlock the sealed doors. 'We need to move fast. The entire Order is in there, and they will all be focused on Damian and your sister. No one will expect an attack, with the sanctum sealed. I'll cause an explosion of Greek fire and Jae – I mean Anubis – will head straight for Damian. Andy, you need to free Violet and run as far from the sanctum as you can while everyone is distracted.'

I nod wordlessly, pulling away from Anubis. My hands are shaking as I imagine what horrors are going on beyond these doors, but I blink to keep the tears back.

It's dark inside the chamber, and I follow Ramsey out onto the gallery. It's nearly empty. Only a few robed figures are clustered at the railing that overlooks the circular chamber below.

Ramsey shuts the door softly, and we crouch behind the back row of seats. Rhythmic chanting sounds from below, but it is quickly drowned out by another rumble deep beneath the sanctum. The ground trembles, rocking violently. The three of us pitch forward, falling to the floor as dust rains from the plaster above and tiny hairline cracks appear across the tiles below us.

Startled cries sound from below where most of the Order are assembled around a circular dais. My shoulder slams against the row of seats and I clench my teeth as the earthquake rolls to a stop.

The chamber is immense. Hundreds of robed figures are clustered around a raised dais. The air shimmers with thick magic. I can't make out faces, but I see the waiting crowd, and seven altars, each with a bronze knife gleaming at the head. My breath catches in my throat as I see the final altar. The only one with a body. Violet lies shackled there, the seventh blade at her feet.

My body jerks forward, but Anubis grabs my shirt and hauls me back down. 'Not yet,' he whispers, glancing at Ramsey.

I choke back a sob, my eyes riveted to the dais. I try to focus, to scan the room for possible exits. But my eyes keep being pulled back to Violet, lying still on the cold stone slab. She has to be alive. We can't be too late.

'My beloved Order,' a familiar voice cries, so loud it makes me wince. 'You have been gathered from all corners of the earth to return home tonight on the winter solstice. Many of you have wondered about my rule, my plan for the Order's security. Tonight, you will see what I have been working toward, despite the countless setbacks and betrayals.'

A figure in a golden robe and a blood-red sash becomes clear at the back of chamber. A roar comes from the crowd as Damian lifts his hood and tilts his head back, arms raised as he basks in the glory of his Order.

'For decades, the Valerius line has labored to ensure your safety. Each year we have fewer numbers. Less control over our members as they seek favors for themselves instead of the good of the entire Order.' Boos and hisses come from the crowd, and Damian waits for them to settle. 'But tonight, all the selfishness fades away. Tonight, I will bring you safety and security. From now on, when people speak of our Order, it will be with the same reverence they used for our ancestors, the ancient kings of the first civilizations.'

Damian takes the knife from the seventh altar and holds it aloft. 'I have done what no other Romulus could. I have gathered the legendary blades of the Apkallu and charged their powers with the death of gods. With them in my possession, I will kill the descendant of Hecate. With the goddess's powers as my own, I will never taste death. And those that serve me well will avoid the sting of mortality as well.'

A shocked murmur ripples over the crowd. The energy in the vast chamber of Order members is almost reverential. Perhaps some of those gathered here are afraid of what they see, but others, like so many in positions of power, are hungry for a taste of the future. For control over humankind. Their curiosity pulses tangibly in the chamber.

'Now,' Damian cries, his voice frayed at the edges as he reaches for the blade at Violet's altar, 'we will finally awaken the powers within the last blade of the Apkallu. It will taste the blood of the most powerful goddess in history. Hecate is as crafty as ever, but her daughter's blood will suffice.'

I get to my feet.

Ramsey catches my ankle and puts a finger to his lips. 'Wait for him to finish speaking. When the crowd applauds, we can hide our distraction in the sound.'

Even though it takes everything in me to stay still, I do. My fingers dig into the seat and I watch, horrified, as Damian circles the last altar where my motionless sister lies.

'With the moon watching us through the opening of the Oculus, the gods will finally see that their time has passed. The Order reigns now, and with their magic at my fingertips, the gods will fall away, leaving only us. Tonight,' Damian says, his voice echoing across the chamber, tone dripping with ecstasy, 'you will see a man transcend the gods!'

Applause fills the air. Stomping and clapping, whooping and cheers.

Ramsey leaps to his feet, determination on his face. He points his palms at the chamber and releases a hoarse shout. Smoke fills my nose as screams and cries of surprise and pain break through the air. Fire ignites on every wall, jumping and leaping, swirling into an inferno. I feel flames lick my skin and tug at my hair as I lurch forward, diving into the throng of bodies.

I reach the railing of the gallery and barely have time to register the pure panic below. Fires dot the banners on the walls and burn along the seats. Bodies flail, red flames licking their skin. Screams and chaos. I grab the brass rail and haul myself over it, ready to drop below, ignoring the danger. As I swing my leg into nothingness, I glimpse Ramsey and Anubis, magic flowing from them so forcefully I can see it form an aura of power around them.

Ramsey shouts for me to go. Anubis' mouth is set in a grim line of determination as his powers gather around him. I forget that in moments he will be taken from me.

I drop, falling through the air as flames and fury rage around me, toward my sister.

30

Smoke burns my throat. Mouths and eyes open wide in horror, and pain fills my vision as confusion reigns. My legs ache from the drop onto the main floor, but I ignore it as I push through the throng. That rotten scent of magic, twisted and wrong, grows so strong that I stagger against an Order member. They push me aside, leaping over others who have fallen, to make for the exit as flames grow higher.

Coughing, I cover my nose and mouth with my sleeve. It has been only seconds since Ramsey and Anubis brought hellfire down on Oculus, but all I feel is a damning sense that we are too late.

I spy the altars through a break in the crowd and lurch for the stage. Damian and his band of loyal followers swat at their clothes burning and smoldering against their skin. Other people run across the circular dais, racing for the doors. In the pandemonium, I leap for the seventh altar.

Immediately, the embers and ashes falling from the ceiling no longer touch my body. I glance around and see Ramsey, his face covered in beads of sweat from concentration, murmuring a protection spell, casting a shield around me.

'Go!' he shouts.

I turn back to Violet, pale and still on the long slab of cold stone. Kneeling in the shadows, I feel along her wrists for the shackles that are anchored to the floor. Her knuckles are bruised and covered in cuts. My throat feels thick as I grasp one anchor and yank on the chain. It doesn't move.

With my breath short and gasping, I shut my eyes and

focus a stream of pure magic at the anchor. With a hiss and a sizzle of molten metal, it releases the chain, melting into a puddle. I grasp the chain holding Violet's wrists together. One anchor left. I don't have enough time to focus on removing the shackles completely. Crawling around the altar as more fire rains down, I melt the other anchor.

The chain goes slack. I get to my feet and grasp Violet's shoulders, pulling her upright. 'Violet!' I scream, desperate for her to hear me. 'Wake up! We have to leave.'

Her head lolls to one side and then the other as she struggles to look at me. Embers fill the air along with smoke. But my eyes see only my sister, her sharp blue eyes as they flutter open. She tries to speak, but her lips are cracked and dry and no sound comes out.

'Stand up! We don't have much time. Ramsey can't protect us for long,' I plead, slinging one arm around her shoulders as I try to pull her off the altar.

Violet slurs something as her knees buckle, sending us both crashing to the marble floor of the dais. Panting hard, I hook my arms under hers and pull her up. She wobbles, struggling to her feet. Her weight sags against my side and I breathe hard, ash smearing on my skin as I turn around, searching for the exit.

A scream catches in my throat as I come face to face with Damian Valerius. The skin on one side of his jaw is an angry red, just beginning to bubble with blisters from the flames. His eyes are hard disks of cold gray as he bares his teeth in a snarl and holds out his knife, ready to plunge it into my chest.

The dagger bounces off the invisible wall of Ramsey's shield, only inches away from where Violet and I stand. Damian growls, shouting something I can't hear over the commotion. I search the writhing crowd and the dying flames and see Ramsey, now on the ground level of the chamber, his hands outstretched, and his face contorted with exertion as he continues to protect Violet and me.

Damian follows my eyeline, whirling around in a rush of golden robes. A hoarse shout rips from Damian, his shoulders heaving as he looks at Ramsey and the defiant glint in his eyes. The hairs on my arms and the back of my neck stand up. A rush of electricity crawls along my skin, hanging heavy in the air. I haul Violet closer to me, shielding her out of instinct. A thunderous crack rips through the chamber. A bright flash blinds me and I stumble. Violet and I stagger, colliding with something hard at waist height. Violet's altar.

I blink away white dots, my hands scrambling for purchase, and push myself upright.

'Andy?' a groggy voice calls. 'What's going on?'

Violet kneels a few feet away, the chains dangling from her wrists. Her hair is a tangled nest around her face. From the corner of my eye, I see Ramsey and Damian locked in a vicious battle. Spells roil through the air, each one more desperate and deadly than the last.

'Get down!' I cry to Violet, just as another crack of thunder deafens me.

Lightning arcs from Damian's hands, colliding against Ramsey's chest. A scream catches in my throat, but I swallow it back. Black shadows gather in a column behind Damian, swirling until a solid shape takes form. Anubis appears, flashing a desperate look over his shoulder. My heart stutters in my chest as he lurches forward and throws his arms around Damian before sinking into the earth in an explosion of darkness.

I exhale slowly, staring at the last wisps of black smoke as they sink into the floor. Hopefully, the difference in time between the Underworld and the mortal world isn't too great right now. I need Anubis to come back and hide Violet away from the knives and the Order until the solstice passes. The further away she is from the seventh blade, the safer she will be.

Even though my throat is tight, I grab Violet's clammy hand and haul her toward the back of the chamber. Order members clog the narrow doorway, all of them just as desperate to escape the chaos as we are. I shoulder past them, ducking out into the narrow hall that leads deeper into the maze of the compound. We run together, taking a few turns at random until the smell of smoke and the sounds of screaming fade enough that I can hear myself think.

'Andy?' Violet asks again, panting hard. 'Where are we going?'

I finally face her, my breath coming in painful gasps. 'We're okay. Anubis will be here in just a few seconds, and he'll take you somewhere safe.'

Violet's eyes still look glassy, distant, but she shakes her head hard, her fingers digging into my palm as she holds my hand. 'Without you?'

'I have to stop the Order. If there is a chance of killing Damian, it's tonight.'

Her jaw hardens, and she shakes her head again, eyes clearing. 'You're a descendant of Hecate too. He'll just kill you instead of me. That's what I was trying to tell you when I called! We both have to leave.'

Footsteps echo along the hallway and I hold a finger to my lips, pressing my back against the wall as I inch forward before peering around the corner. Red robes flutter, hurrying away in the other direction, and I slip back once I'm sure no one else is headed our way.

'Damian will find a way out of the Underworld quickly.

The Order is in chaos right now. We need that distraction to kill him, and I can't do that if I'm worrying about you!'

Violet's brows pull together, and she takes my hand in both of hers, eyes desperate. 'I've been apart from you for two months, Andy. And I didn't endure a psychopath kidnapping me at home with a curse tablet just to leave you behind.'

I try to think of something to say, something encouraging, but my smile fades. Because even though my eyes were riveted on my sister during the entire display in the ceremonial chamber, I suddenly notice how different she looks.

'Your hair,' I whisper, my fingers ghosting over the long, straight black locks tumbling down her shoulders.

She smiles a little, eyes softening. 'Hecate came to my room. I thought it was a dream, that I was dying. But she brought me out of the coma, completely healed, and told me about how you found her. I wanted to beg her to bring me to Eidolon to help you, but she disappeared. And then the next thing I knew, I was being pulled through a convergence and appeared in that cavern, with Anubis bloodied and bruised on the ground. I was so surprised, so caught off guard from seeing Hecate, that I didn't have time to react to Damian or his magic. And before I know it, I'm waking up on that altar, with you breaking my shackles.'

I stare in amazement at Violet's face. Her cheeks are no longer hollow, her brow smooth and unlined by pain. Violet is perfect and healthy again. Hecate upheld her end of the bargain, just as she promised. But just as I'm about to ask her questions about the goddess and what she told her, footsteps slam against the tiles.

Violet's eyes go wide, and she nods as I hold up a hand for quiet. Raspy breathing rattles in a chest as feet slap against the floor. My head rushes with spells to defend us, when a head of dark hair careens into view.

'Anubis!' I cry, dropping Violet's hand to steady him as he slips across the floor. 'Where's Ramsey?'

Anubis breathes hard, his face more haggard than I've ever seen. 'I didn't see him. We don't have much time. Damian is strong from the magic of the other six blades, and he'll find a way out of the Underworld in moments. Midnight is close.'

I reach for Violet's hand and pull her to my side. 'Take her to the Underworld – the cave at the delta of the river – and have Wepwawet watch her in case Damian manages to find her somehow.'

Violet yanks her arm away. 'No! You're not taking me anywhere.'

'There isn't time to argue!'

'As soon as midnight comes,' Violet points to Anubis, 'he'll be stuck in the Underworld, unable to take me back to you. It will take me hours, maybe days, to find my way out!'

I share a look with Anubis, my heart pounding in my chest. He searches my gaze, a grimace of pain on his face as a thousand unspoken things cross between us. Once again, I sense magic building, as tangible as the dark night outside. Damian is rallying, and so is the Order. Despite the way my heart aches as I look at his dark eyes, I nod at Anubis.

Before Violet can react, he grabs her shoulder. The smell of the Underworld rises faintly. I fight the urge to shut my eyes and instead force myself to watch as Anubis and my sister slowly fade.

Shouts echo from down the maze of halls. Dozens of voices growing stronger.

'Go!' I urge Anubis as his and Violet's forms flicker like a flame dancing on the end of a wick.

But they don't. Instead of fading away and disappearing into the Underworld, I watch as my sister's outraged expression grows solid once more.

Anubis cries out in pain and collapses to his knees. His skin goes bone white as I reach for him. His body is clammy to the touch as my fingers catch the edge of the tattered remnants of the robe around his shoulders. He lurches away, doubled over in pain. He vomits a horrific black liquid, his entire body seizing.

'What's happening?' I plead.

'Can't . . . reach the Underworld . . .' He tries to answer, but the tendons in his neck strain against his skin and he collapses onto his back, his body stiffening into paroxysms of pain.

I scream as Violet grabs his shoulders, trying to help me hold him still, but it's no use. His eyes roll back, and red-tinted spittle coats his chin as another seizure racks his form.

'This isn't right!' I look at Violet. 'It's not midnight yet. What's wrong with him?'

Violet's face is pale as she tries to cushion Anubis' head while another spasm rocks his body. 'Let me see if I can try something else, a different spell for vessels —'

'No!' I catch her hands before they can press down on his chest. 'You can't use your magic!'

It doesn't matter that her hair is long and black again, or that her skin glows with health. This is my sister, and I've almost lost her to the addiction of power and magic.

'Andy, everything will be alright now. Just trust me. I can help him.'

But before I can answer through my tears, Violet's face fades away as a surge of darkness clouds my vision.

Suddenly, I can't feel Anubis' feverish skin beneath my palms. I can't breathe in, can't feel the hard tiles underneath my knees. One moment I'm stooping next to Anubis as he struggles on the ground, and the next I'm flying until I collide with the opposite wall. The air is squeezed out of my lungs, and something warm and wet slips from my scalp and down my neck.

Violet screams my name.

Through my hazy double vision, a figure walks around Anubis' prone body, head tilted to the side as if considering a curious map. The scent of the Underworld, of the river, is overpowering. Water drips from golden robes as the figure comes into focus.

'How interesting,' Damian croons, stooping over Anubis. He's flanked by at least a dozen Order members, all of them covered in soot and ash and radiating anger and power. 'I should have known he was one of them. A savage god feeding off mortals.'

The glint of the dagger at his side makes my throat close with fear.

'Stop,' I croak, struggling weakly against the spell pressing me relentlessly against the wall. 'Don't touch him.'

'Oh, don't worry. It's his own fault that he's in such pain. After all, he's broken such a sacred vow.' Damian kicks aside the tattered rags of Anubis' robe on the ground.

Violet is frozen in place, the chains around her wrists snapping taut against invisible anchors, so tight that she can't move. She struggles, trying to stand. But she's just as trapped as I am. 'You can't kill him. He's not one of your playthings bound in a devil's trap. You'll waste the seventh dagger by having it absorb his magic instead of mine.'

Damian laughs, a sound that sends a shiver of unease down my spine. 'I don't want his magic. Look at him! What a pity. I planned on summoning him from the catacombs as soon as I was ready to kill you, Violet. His magic was so intriguing that I wanted to use it to strengthen me, even as I lured Andy to the compound. But I'm afraid he is of no use to me like this.'

I want to scream and threaten Damian to leave, to release us, before Anubis' godly form is unleashed at midnight and kills him horribly. But my eyes snag on the smooth golden planes of Anubis' chest. Or at least, what used to be smooth. Emblazoned in dark ink and radiating from his sternum is an eagle with outstretched wings and a Roman legionary's standard in its claws. But it isn't the final tattoo, the last sigil of the Order, that turns my stomach. It's the words in an ancient language carved directly into the flesh of his chest.

With my blood, I pledge my life.

Anubis' eyes open a slit, and they are pure black. His lips are coated in red as he tries to say something to me. All I hear is a gurgle as his fingers pass over the terrible words carved into his flesh. It almost looks like he's trying to say he's sorry.

'No,' I whisper, my voice breaking as my vision finally clears.

The scars glow a sickly silver, pale and unnatural against his skin. An incantation tying Anubis and his life to the well-being of the Order. A vow he broke in the chamber only moments ago when he dragged Damian to hell.

He knew he would die tonight – not just lose his mortal body. That's why he didn't argue with me when I begged him to take Violet somewhere safe. Why he decided to trust Ramsey with my life. Because he broke an unbreakable vow forged in the convergence. And now he has to pay in blood.

'Your little death god will finally taste what he's given mortals for centuries. And he has no one to blame but himself.' Damian looks down his nose at Anubis disdainfully. 'I have no use for him now, trapped and dying in a mortal body. I've come for you, daughter of Hecate –' he crouches before Violet and grasps the chains stringing her wrists together – 'and to finish what I've started.'

Violet pales, but her chin remains high. 'If you touch my sister, I'll kill you.'

Damian laughs as he motions to the Order members behind him. They surround me and Violet, pulling us from our invisible bonds. Hands grasp my shoulders and arms, twisting them painfully behind my back. My mind races and I try to summon the power I've so painstakingly won from my trials with Hecate, but all I feel is a muted rage. Something is smothering me, choking my magic like a flame starved of oxygen.

Damian meets my gaze, a cruel smile on his lips. 'It's too late for all that. Every Order member is working on binding your magic as we speak.' He steps away from my sister, coming to stand before me and breathing deeply. 'The blood in the veins of either one of you will complete my ritual and charge the last blade. The other, however, I'll kill just for the fun of it.'

Violet hisses an incantation under her breath. I don't have time to do anything but suck in a gasp of fear. But Damian doesn't stagger under the weight of her words, the magic spreading from her lips. The power emanating from my sister is snuffed out ruthlessly. Unnaturally. She gasps, as if the sensation of Damian's growing power is physically painful.

'I told you –' Damian clucks his tongue like a disapproving parent – 'it's too late for that now.' He snaps his fingers at the other members holding us in place, and they drag us back toward the central chamber.

I fight and struggle against their grip, twisting and trying to reach Anubis. But he lies still, eyes rolled back in his head, and blood trickling from his nose and mouth. The marks on his chest stand out, ugly and sharp on his pale skin. As we round the corner and he is pulled from my sight, I realize Damian is right. It is too late.

Anubis is dead, and this time, there is no way I can get him back.

31

A sickening sense of déjà vu overwhelms me as I lie spread-eagled, bound and immobile, on an altar surrounded by blood and ash. The chamber is in disarray, soot coating every surface. Bodies lie burned and unrecognizable against the wall, covered by their own robes. But for the most part, the Order is intact and pulling itself together, gathering once more into the central chamber as the moon slides into place over the eye of the oculus.

Those who tried to escape the fire have already been ushered back inside for the grand finale of the ceremony. Or else have realized they are just as trapped in the compound as Violet and I are. Damian does not want anyone to miss his triumph. And now Violet and I are in in his clutches. Our death and blood to charge the final blade. And then he will be immortal. Unstoppable.

Perhaps even greater than any god.

A row of menacing members stands behind me, a dozen strong. Their magic swirls like an impenetrable force field, keeping me docile. Keeping me still. And worst of all, stopping me from saving myself and Violet from the fate that is hurtling toward us so fast I want to scream at the injustice of it all.

Ramsey is nowhere to be seen. This time, there will be no rescue. I wouldn't be surprised if his ash-coated body is one of the many stacked in the corner. I wish I could feel grief for him. But I'm drowning in more of it than I can bear. Even death won't be a comfort if Anubis is gone.

My sister tries to lift her head high enough to look at me. It's a struggle. Her bonds are so tight they keep her pinned against the cold stone. But I glimpse her face as the moonlight grows brighter, washing out her features, so she looks almost like a ghost. Her dark blue eyes, so cunning and sharp, do not brim with tears like mine. She is steady, almost defiant. I choke on a sob I can't let out. Even facing death, she is so brave. So strong.

I try again to summon enough power to throw aside my captors. Instead, all I experience is a twinge of pain along my spine and a rattling through my joints. Violet meets my gaze again and shakes her head before she mouths something to me.

I love you, little star.

More tears spill over my cheeks. I want to murmur it back to her, the smallest of comforts, but even that is robbed from me. Because I can't move my lips. Violet nods to me, as if everything is settled, and lets her head fall back against the stone.

Damian adjusts his robes, brushing at stray soot as his steely gaze sweeps over the rattled crowd. 'Welcome back,' Damian says drily, his voice the only sound in the yawning chamber, 'to the ultimate sacrifice. Despite setbacks, tonight you will be rewarded for your bravery and loyalty.'

Bronze blades gleam as the oculus is completely swallowed in moonlight. Damian wastes no more time on speeches, on flattery or threats. He simply draws the seventh knife and moves forward. His eyes bounce between me and my sister. After a moment, his lips spread into a cruel smile as he meets my gaze. With a snap of his fingers, he indicates Violet. The six other daggers are quickly arranged around her body by Order members. They make a crude sort of devil's trap, the points all facing inward toward my sister's tender flesh.

I want to scream at Damian to kill me instead. But all I can do is glare at him as my lips remain uselessly pressed together.

Once Violet is dead, Damian will be impossible to kill. The power of seven gods coursing through his veins, all so he can wield the power of control over death.

I want to hang my head as Damian murmurs words in ancient Sumerian. But I can't tear my eyes from the horror. Can't stop trying to twist at the ropes binding my arms to my sides. The blood dripping from the gash on my head doesn't bother me. Nor does the painful weight of the dozen Order members' magic, binding me in place.

Everything I've done, everything I've sacrificed and lost over the last year, has come to this. To nothing.

Bleak, corrupt magic bleeds from the cracks in the tile as Damian tips his head back, bathed in moonlight. The air smells of rot and death. Of evil worse than any demon I've encountered.

Damian opens his cold gray eyes and looks down at Violet staring defiantly at him. His lips curl into a smile and he finishes his spell, the daggers arranged so carefully around my sister rattling with the power hanging heavy in the air. Thick green vapor rises, swirling around Damian's clothes. His eyes change from silver to pure, blank white.

His scars are a tapestry of cruelty on his skin as he lets out a wordless shout, his blade aimed squarely at Violet's vulnerable chest and his face a mask of pure elation. A scream catches in my throat and stays there, useless and unborn, as my world crawls to a painful standstill.

The dagger sinks toward Violet even as her body tenses, her head lifting from the slab of stone. Her hands are clenched tight, forming fists, and just before everything turns to crimson and pain, her lips move. I can't hear what she says to Damian. Can't make out the shapes of the words leaving her tongue.

And just as the dagger sinks straight into her heart, a blinding flash of white sears my eyes and explodes outwards from the altar.

Rushing fills my head as I topple off the altar, landing suddenly on my chest, as the ropes around my wrists and ankles snap. Something strikes me on the back and arms. Heavy thuds rattle the ground next to me. Screams fill the air, and I cough as dust fills my mouth. The earth trembles, rocking violently – far worse than anything before. I get to my knees, the binding spell fallen away like cobwebs.

Ringing echoes in my ears, and I stagger. Heavy marble and thick plaster rain down from above and I reel to one side, shoving a piece of debris off my leg. Dust clouds my eyes, and I cough and wipe at my face, struggling to see through the chaos. Screams echo, but the pain of others is my least concern.

'Violet!' I shout, my voice ragged and heartbroken and furious all at once. I stagger away from my spot, half crawling. Blood dots my knuckles and fingers as I get to my feet amongst rubble.

My sister doesn't answer my call.

I press the heels of my hands to my temples, stumbling drunkenly.

I ignore the softly falling plaster. The dull groan of the foundations cracking beneath my feet. Because on the last altar, the slab completely toppled and sitting precariously on its side, is my sister. Her body is limp, her hair hanging over her face. Her arms and legs are pulled at an angle as gravity drags her body to the side.

A sob breaks from my chest, and I flounder, my feet catching on stones and fissures. Another quake sends me to my knees, and I crawl, tears streaming down my face and clearing the dust from my eyes.

I finally reach Violet's side and grasp the hand closest to me. It's still warm but so still it makes my stomach lurch. 'Violet!' I scream her name again and again. 'You're alright. You're alright.'

Something high-pitched and terrible makes my head split painfully. The marble floor is breaking apart as a deep chasm slowly opens across the center of the room.

I scream and scream, calling her name, patting her hair away from her face. Anguish tears at me from the inside out as the blood on her chest stands out in an ugly stain.

'I'll clean you up,' I say brokenly, one hand caressing her cheek and the other swiping at the slowly trickling blood. 'Everything will be okay. We'll go home. We'll get away from all this. I promise, Violet.'

Dimly, I notice the chaos unfolding around me as the chasm continues to grow wider, inching closer. The animal part of my brain screams at me to escape, to save myself. I clutch Violet's hand and lift my eyes.

Marble and concrete rend apart with a mighty heave. Moonlight soaks the scene of terror as a massive abyss tears open straight through the chamber with a roar, cracking the altar clean in two. I'm thrown to the side, my already ringing head cracking against the broken tiles.

'No!' I cry as the unending rolling of the ground tears my hand from Violet's.

Anguish closes my throat as her altar tips, dragged over the edge of the rift. Another wordless scream rips from my chest as her motionless body, bound in chains, falls from view, down into the depths of the catacombs buried beneath the sanctum.

I lie on my stomach, hand reaching out toward the abyss.

The roaring earth heaves again and swallows the Order members without mercy. Something cold touches the skin of my ankle. Cold as the hand of a ghost.

I hope it's a demon, come to drag me down to the Underworld. At least there I can be with Violet again and finally free of all the pain. All the wretchedness it seems only living mortals can create.

'Andy!' someone calls.

The voice hardly penetrates the haze in my mind. I don't turn to find the voice. I don't care if it's Damian and his new powers, primed to kill me for the fun of it.

Let it end, I think.

The breath is knocked from my lungs as someone collapses on top of me. I don't bother fighting, not even struggling, as the person wraps their arms around me and braces as if for a strike. I just shut my eyes and wait for Violet to come and find me on the banks of the river.

The person holding me shakes me, shouting into my ear. I want to scream at him to stop, to leave me here. But he shouts again. Something about water.

'Kick off your boots and take off your jacket, quickly!'

I blink a few times, surprised that a falling chunk of roof hasn't flattened me yet. Ramsey's pale face hovers above me, his brows pulled low, and his face smeared in ash and blood. He repeats his commands and makes a sound of frustration when I make no move to comply.

'She's gone,' I whisper, staring through him. Through the concern and pity written all over his features.

'I know.' Ramsey winces, but then he shakes me again, shoving me onto my side. 'Here, let me get this off you.' The coat he gave me in the catacombs slips from my shoulders as he flings the filthy garment aside. He looks up and curses under his breath before he folds his arms tight around me, resting my head on his shoulder. 'The convergence is almost here. There's no time for your boots. Hold on to me, Andy, whatever you do.'

Ramsey tenses, his arms squeezing my ribs painfully. A breath later, the aching cold that had been brushing my ankle swallows me up to my chest. Water swirls, thick and black, around our bodies, swallowing boulders and the limp forms of Order members before it roars over the side of the chasm, picking up speed.

'Take a breath!' Ramsey cries just as a second wave of frigid water closes over our heads.

The churning current sucks us down into the depths. My shoulder collides with a hidden chunk of concrete, and I cry out, air bubbles slipping past my lips. But Ramsey doesn't let go, only holds tighter, as we are tugged through the ruins of the Oculus compound.

Air rushes into my lungs as we finally break the surface, our limbs flailing numbly as we struggle against the deluge. Ramsey hangs onto the back of my shirt as we are swept away from the building through a gap in the crumbling wall. I twist my head, my hair slapping against my cheeks.

'Wait!' I splutter, swallowing a mouthful of the strangely sweet water as I kick, trying to swim back to the rapidly vanishing compound. 'Violet! I can't leave her there in that place.'

'No, Andy!' He yanks me back with surprising strength, securing his arm across my shoulders. 'Violet's body is gone.' Ramsey coughs and kicks against the current as the eerie black ribbon of water carries us to where the river Aoife waits in the still night, bathed in starlight. The two streams of water collide, mixing and swirling in a hiss of power.

I flail and struggle, clawing at the river as it carries us away, under the bridge and around a bend. Ramsey keeps murmuring comforting words between coughs, hauling me against his chest every time I try to escape. But I don't hear them, or the water slapping against the stones of a small, familiar beach. Even the sound of our dripping clothes fades into the background as we crawl onto the shore, alone, and so close to the ruins of St Mary's Abbey that I can see the headstones from the graveyard.

All I hear is the choking sounds of my own sobs as I cry for my older sister and the girl I was when I still had her in my life.

Frost clings to my skin as Ramsey and I shiver on the lonely beach near the abbey. He's the first to stand as the last sounds of groaning and the screams fade to silence. Eidolon is still as the clock strikes midnight and the winter solstice passes. I lift my head to stare at the blurry carnage in the distance. The grand Oculus Sanctum is a pile of rubble gleaming in the moonlight. Faint green mist rises from the ruins.

Damian survived the chaos. I can feel it as sure as the fading tremors rattling the stones at my fingertips. With the power of Hecate now part of him, he will never taste death.

'I can't believe it. The convergence must have broken free when the ceremony finished,' Ramsey mutters, stamping his bare feet to get the blood flowing. 'It carried us away from the compound, where the laws of the gods and the Underworld were being polluted.'

'When Damian killed Violet, you mean?' I say through my teeth, curling my fingers into the gritty sand beneath my palms.

Ramsey looks down at me, face grim. 'You have no idea how sorry I am, Andy. How hard I fought him. In the end, he was too strong. Without Anubis there to help –'

I slam my fist into the rocks, not caring when they split the skin on my knuckles. 'Damian killed him too! Everyone, everything I've ever loved, he's stolen from me!' My voice breaks, ragged and full of so much anger I hardly recognize it. Hardly recognize the heat and hatred flowing through me like the convergence that carried me away from the body of my sister.

'I understand how you feel, believe me.' Ramsey squats in front of me, his face raw with his own pain. 'But what more can we do? It's just you and me now. And Damian . . . he got what he wanted from your sister. We have to leave. Damian will kill you for interfering with his plans, and even now he's probably gathering those who survived in the remains of the sanctum.'

I push aside Ramsey's outstretched hand and get to my feet, ignoring my boots, waterlogged and swollen, and turn toward the low hill where the abbey sits. Teeth chattering and hair freezing against my collar, I struggle over the grass.

'Where are you going?' Ramsey calls.

I stare at the broken church, the hunched and twisted form of the moss-covered stones. It's the closest thing I can get to a burial tomb on this side of the Underworld. But perhaps with the convergence roaring wild and free from its spot tethered beneath the university, I can break through Damian's spell surrounding Eidolon.

Maybe I can finally do what must be done. What Tooth and Talon would do. What Violet had the strength to face a year ago.

'I'm going to call Hecate,' I say through my clenched teeth, 'and I'm going to make a deal.'

32

My jaw aches from the endless chattering of my teeth as I kneel in the soft, winter-brown grass in the central knave of the abbey. The sweet smell of the water from the convergence sticks to my skin and makes my head swim. I ignore it, and Ramsey's nervous protests, as I dig my hands into the damp earth and craft a crude pot.

'This won't work,' he repeats again, hovering over my shoulder. 'You need a priest or other religious figure to bless it!'

'I know how a devil's trap works,' I snap, pressing the clod of earth in my hands into shape. 'And I don't need a priest as her descendant. But my goal isn't to bind Hecate. I'm going to offer to be her anchor.'

Ramsey splutters, his pacing footsteps going still. 'Why would you ever want to do something like that?'

My thumbs smooth a ridge of clay until I hold a shallow, ugly little dish in my hands. It may not be fit for a goddess, but once I carve her name and symbols into the surface and suffuse it with my magic, it will serve its purpose.

'Because,' I say, digging my thumbnail into the face as I form Hecate's name in ancient Greek, 'no god can resist something like that. The ability to stay in the mortal world, no matter what, is like a drug. If I offer to be her anchor, she will agree to anything I ask.'

'What do you want so badly that only a goddess can give you?' he asks, moving to stand in front of me. 'Power? Control over the Order?'

'Revenge,' I spit out, making the last symbol in the clay. 'What else is there? She promised to help me, and now Violet is dead. We can't kill Damian now that he has all seven blades, but Hecate could bind him in her territory. She gave me this magic in the first place – so it's only fair she makes it right.'

Ramsey shakes his head, that all-too-familiar pitying expression on his face. 'Revenge against Damian won't fix what happened to Violet.'

'I know that,' I say. 'But Hecate can bring her back. She's the goddess of necromancy, after all. I don't care how she does it.'

Horror crosses his face, but I feel numb to it. Numb to the reality that I'm following in Violet's footsteps from just over a year ago, when she offered to be the anchor for Ossivorus. She always knew the gods and monsters that wanted our blood would hurt me. That I would be too weak to thrive in a world of secrets and shadows. She was right.

But now, I'm going to make the very being that gave us our powers atone for everything that has happened.

A low groan echoes off the silent hills. Ramsey and I both stiffen, the little pot forgotten. He narrows his eyes and motions for me to stay put as he slinks through the shadows of the abbey to peer out toward the river. I watch him for a few moments, my heart beating in my throat.

'Is it a demon?' I whisper hoarsely. 'The convergence breaking away from Eidolon could have drawn their attention.'

Ramsey holds his hand up at me, indicating silence. He disappears through a gap in the stone wall, and I set the devil's trap down and dust off the knees of my damp jeans. I listen for signs of a struggle, of the voices of angry Order members come to finish us. Instead, the sound of two shuffling pairs of feet echo in the corpse of the church.

I squint into the night, searching for Ramsey's face. When he looks up at me, his arm around the shoulders of a battered figure, I relax a fraction. He doesn't look worried or frightened. But then I focus on the person limping at his side and my heart stops beating at all.

'Anubis?' I whisper.

He lifts his head, blood staining his temples, and a dozen other deep cuts visible all over his body. But the blood isn't the dark crimson it was in the compound. It shimmers, half red and half golden ichor. When he smiles, a crooked, exhausted thing, I feel like the world has slipped out from beneath my feet.

'I found him on the same beach we were at. The convergence must have washed him ashore too,' Ramsey says. He takes his arm back when Anubis motions that he's fine to stand. 'I thought you said he died.'

'He did. He was dead,' I say, my voice a strangled whisper. I stare at them, not daring to move. To breathe. Maybe I drowned in the convergence and I'm on the west bank, reuniting with those I've lost.

Anubis lifts one shoulder, the skin mottled with painful-looking bruises, and shuffles another step toward me. 'It seems even the river isn't able to take me away from you, Andromeda.'

I can't speak as I throw myself at him, colliding with his bare chest. His skin is oddly warm, and the golden blood dripping from his cuts feels like fire when it brushes my fingers, but I don't care. I bury my face in his neck and breathe in his familiar scent of incense and earth. He's real. Warm and alive. Something is different about him, somehow. Different from either his mortal form or his godly one I've seen in the Underworld. He still wears Jae's face, one he's been partial to for over a decade, but I can't quite put my finger on it. A strange feeling, one I don't recognize.

One large hand gently strokes my hair back from my face as I struggle to contain sobs, my chest aching. Seeing Anubis miraculously resurrected should make my heart feel lighter, but it only reinforces that Violet is mortal. That she won't be coming back without a god's interference.

'I'm so sorry, Andromeda, I tried everything I possibly could to help Violet – to get her out of there,' he says, pulling back just far enough to cup my face in his hands. 'I tried to leave, but I couldn't access the Underworld. My vow –'

I place my hand on his chest, my breath hitching. 'I know about the vow. Damian made sure of it.'

His dark eyes flicker with shadows, reminding me again that Jae, and his mortal form, are no longer there. Whatever happened to Anubis in the river has changed him irrevocably, allowing him to stand next to me without a mortal body.

'I didn't want to take any innocent lives for him,' Anubis says, 'but I had no choice. He brought Masoud, and I thought everything would be over.' He covers my hand with his own even as his eyes snap with desperation. 'If I didn't kill him, Damian would have suspected something. And Masoud would have revealed who you were. He would have said anything to stay alive.'

'I know.' I swallow hard, my throat tight from crying. 'You wouldn't hurt anyone if you could help it. It wasn't your fault.'

'Damian is always three steps ahead,' Ramsey offers, arms crossed over his chest. 'He would have made sure you couldn't betray him one day.'

Anubis grimaces, his hands tightening on my waist. 'He's unlike anyone I've ever encountered before. His lust for power, the control he wields over magic and his Order, it's the most dangerous thing I can imagine. If I had known what he was capable of, and what it would cost you, I wouldn't have let myself join Oracle.'

'I don't blame you,' I tell Anubis, my voice soft. 'There was no way of knowing what would happen. Violet . . . Violet's death is on Damian's hands.'

He shuts his eyes briefly, collecting himself. When he opens them again, he looks as determined as ever. For a moment I'm back with him in Ravenswood, an age ago. 'We can still stop Damian. I can feel his powers. They're twisted and wrong, tearing him apart.'

'He killed Violet,' I say, my throat raw. 'He has all seven blades. Damian is all but immortal.'

Anubis' fingers dig into my side. 'He's not. I don't know if the magic of Hecate in your sister's blood wasn't enough, but he doesn't have the power over life and death. When the convergence pulled me back from the Underworld, I could sense his magic. It's weak and wrong, like a broken bone. Something happened during the ceremony, something that charged the blade, but weakened Damian, leaving it incomplete. But soon he'll realize that the power of seven gods in his body is tearing him apart, driving him mad.'

Ramsey breathes in sharply. 'We can kill him?'

'The enchantments around Eidolon are falling. I guarantee he'll try to summon Hecate and make sure she is dead. Maybe bind her in a new devil's trap and kill her with the blades. Anything to cement the power he's stolen.'

The shock of seeing Anubis alive fades to an ember in my chest at his words. Slowly, I extract myself from his arms and move to pick up the damp clay pot etched with dozens of symbols of Hecate.

Anubis doesn't need an explanation – not when he knows me so well. He takes a step back, his lips parting as his eyes move between me and the devil's trap. 'Andromeda, you can't.'

I grit my teeth to keep back more useless, burning tears. 'Why not? Look around us – every plan we've made, every good intention has come to nothing. We came here to stop the Order and find Hecate so she could help me, and instead, we lost Violet.'

'But becoming her anchor, trading your body so you can have one moment of revenge, is exactly what we've fought against,' Anubis protests. 'Deals and exchanges with gods and demons only bring more retribution. More pain.'

'Is that what you told Jae when you accepted his body?' I snap back, cradling the clay pot to my chest. His face falls, a wounded expression making his eyes glow with power. I step back, chest aching with shame, and set the trap onto a large, moss-covered boulder. 'Violet was right all along. Magic is something you must be strong to possess, to control –'

'Not like this,' Ramsey interrupts, flicking an anxious look toward Anubis, as if begging him to make me see reason.

I glare at him, feeling a hint of betrayal that he would doubt me after all we've been through. 'Hecate created my bloodline. Now she can have it. She *will* give Violet back from the dead, and in return, I'll be her anchor. And after that, all I want is for her to kill Damian or banish him to the darkest parts of the Underworld. Our plans never work, Anubis. My sister died for this, for nothing. The least Hecate can do is make Damian suffer for what he did.'

'And lose yourself in the process?' Anubis sets his jaw and crosses over to me, standing beside the boulder. 'This cycle of favors never ends well. Look at what I've done, who I've hurt because of it. My vow to Jae is the very reason I put myself in that situation with Damian.'

Tears prick my eyes again and I turn around, so I don't

have to face him. 'I don't need you to understand. I just need you to get out of my way.'

Before Anubis or Ramsey can try to convince me to stop, I shut my eyes and hold my hand over the devil's trap. Immediately, heat flows through my freezing limbs and makes my numb fingers burn. I grit my teeth, images of three-headed dogs and torches flying behind my eyelids as I murmur a spell torn straight from the depths of my heart.

I don't need a priest or minister to bless the vessel. Not when Hecate herself has handed me her keys. Helped me master her aspects, understand her magic. Emerald-green light flashes and I open my eyes as the vessel turns as black as obsidian. Slowly, the etchings I made turn gold, one by one, magic threading through the clay.

My eyes are wide as I follow the path of the golden words. Power wells in my chest, threatening to explode. The rage and helplessness turned my heart to ice and my stomach to ash. For once, there is no self-control, no worry over taking one step too far. And I want it. I want it so that I can watch everyone in the Order suffer and fall at my feet. The world can go to hell, because without Violet, mine is empty.

Before the last symbol can change, a hand grips my wrist, wrenching it away from the trap. 'This isn't what Violet would want,' Anubis says, even as his skin blisters as it touches my arm.

I shudder with the spell hanging in the air, swirling around me and begging to be unleashed. To create a trap that will allow me to grant Hecate what every god wants: endless power and control, in both this realm and the Underworld.

I allow my gaze to lift from the rattling pot and look into Anubis' eyes.

In his face I see myself reflected a thousand times, straight into eternity. Different faces, different hurts. Countless magic-wielders who have succumbed to the allure of the power I hold in my palms. I see Violet's face a year ago as she faced a desperate decision to save herself and become Ossivorus' vessel, or else endure a slow and painful death.

Anubis' hand continues to blister and burn as the magic pools in my palms. Golden blood wells where his skin meets mine, mixing with the blood on my knuckles. And I realize what Violet must have felt that night, the pain and confusion and desperation. But I also remember how it felt to be on the other side and watch her slip down that dark path. Make the decision that almost broke us. I remember the pain.

With a jagged exhalation, I drop my head against Anubis' shoulder and let the spell fade back into the earth. He wraps one arm around me as he takes the pot from the boulder, the clay still simmering with heat and light, and throws it against a far wall where it cracks and shatters into dust.

His lips brush my hair as he turns me away from the shattered remains of the trap. 'No more deals, Andromeda.'

My heart feels like it has shattered into countless shards alongside the trap. Little pieces of black stone shredding my chest until there's nothing left but an empty, gaping wound where Violet should be. Because without this, without me serving as Hecate's vessel, I won't see Violet again. Not until I die and find her on the west bank.

'No more deals,' I whisper back against his bare skin, even though it makes the hole in my chest punch deeper than ever.

The abbey is quiet as we stand there, the hum of unfulfilled magic in the air. It pricks at my skin, still coaxing me to use it, to wield it and shape it into what I want. I squeeze my eyes shut and bite the inside of my cheek to stem the urge to give in. To lose who I am forever.

Ramsey takes a few steps toward one of the empty

windows and sticks his head out, grass whispering against his feet. 'Do you feel that?' he asks, breaking the silence.

I lift my head and peer out the window to see the sliver of landscape it captures. The thread of the river Aoife and a section of the collapsed compound. The three of us are still as we listen, ears straining, as we hardly dare to breathe. And then I feel it, a slight vibration that rattles up the bones of my feet. The green haze that has covered the debris of the Oculus Sanctum seems to grow thicker, reaching for the moon with greedy fingers.

Anubis and I share an uneasy look.

'The enchantment sealing off the university from the outside world is falling,' Anubis says. 'Damian will use a curse tablet to bring Hecate to him and steal her immortality as soon as it's down.'

Ramsey puts his hands on the empty windowsill. 'What can we do? Even if the earthquakes and chasms killed every Order member, Damian still has the power of seven gods at his fingertips, madness or not.'

My mind races with possibilities and outcomes. All seem bleak when faced with Damian and his seven enchanted blades. Before I can voice any of my doomed ideas, a low, plaintive howl cuts through the thick night. Ramsey jerks back from the window, stumbling over tangled grasses and hidden stones.

Another howl, this one much louder than the last, pierces my ears.

'What is it?' Anubis asks, letting go of me as he paces toward the yawning holes in the abbey's side, which suddenly seems far too decrepit to offer any sort of protection.

Ramsey stutters, face pale as he gets to his feet. 'W-wolves.'

'There aren't any wild wolves in Britain,' I counter, but my confidence fades as another howl joins the first, followed by a third. My stomach knots as the cries echo off the faces of the two large hills that form the backdrop to Eidolon.

'Maybe it's just wild dogs?' Ramsey asks hopefully.

We instinctively cluster closer together. If there is one thing I've learned from my time at Eidolon, it's that nothing is ever a simple answer.

'Can you access the Underworld now?' I ask Anubis anxiously as the howls come so near, I can feel the hairs on my arms rising in fear. The sound of panting echoes off the stones of the abbey, making my spine tingle with awareness. Hot breath seems to come from the shadows themselves, smelling of blood and flesh. Damian knows where we are. And he's come to finish us off.

Anubis presses his back against mine as we search the darkest recesses of the abbey for signs of the ghostly wolves. He struggles for a moment, sweat and strain visible on his face. 'No,' he says finally, breathing hard. 'I'm not sure what happened to me after trying to break Damian's vow. I don't think I can leave the mortal plane.'

A day ago, that would have made my heart soar with hope. But now, as Ramsey, Anubis and I cower in the lonely ruins of St Mary's, fear makes my throat close. Perhaps Damian has already killed Hecate and is calling on her powers to find me. To snuff out the last of the resistance to his grand plans for domination of the Order and everyone tied to it.

More growls and the horrific click of clamping jaws press closer. The earth rumbles beneath my feet as if angry. Magic snaps in the air as all three of us prepare for a fight. The one that will more than likely be our last.

Massive black paws emerge in the moonlight. Three lowered heads appear, giant black dogs with dripping lips pulled back over pearly white fangs. A kerberos steps into the central nave, followed by a second. The six heads snap absently at each other even as they growl and sniff the air, tasting our fear. They flank a woman in pitch-black robes as she steps gracefully into the moonlight with bare feet.

'The Valerius boy may hold the powers of the gods,' croons the throaty voice of Hecate from the depths of the abbey's skeleton, 'but that does not mean he knows how to wield such a burden.'

'I heard you have an offer for me, Andromeda.' Hecate's fathomless black eyes peer down as snakes twine around her arms like jewelry. Here in the ruins of the cathedral, with silver light from the moon and stars bathing her, she looks like the goddess of ancient times. Powerful and hungry and unstoppable. But I don't feel fear when I see her, only desperate hope.

Anubis steps forward, his body changing in a flash from the form of Jae to a tall being with deep brown skin and a headdress in the shape of a jackal. 'She changed her mind. Andromeda will not be your anchor.'

Hecate tilts her head to the side, studying the other god. 'Is that so?'

Swallowing back the unexpected shock that seeing the goddess causes, I gently push Anubis aside to face Hecate. 'I've learned from my sister's mistakes.' My chest twinges painfully at the mere mention of Violet, and when I speak again, my voice is strained and breathy. 'I can't sell myself to you, hoping you'll give me justice.'

'I would not accept such a thing anyhow,' she says, her eyes soft. 'Not after I have labored for so long to prevent this night from happening.'

I jerk my head back in surprise. 'You wouldn't want to taste mortality? I thought that is what every god wanted.'

'Gods are singular creatures, but even we are subject to

change.' Hecate's eyes slide to Anubis. 'Isn't that right, my fellow psychopomp?'

Anubis' posture is stiff, but he nods. 'If you're not here to take Andy as your anchor, why have you come?'

My throat closes and I step closer to the goddess despite the snarls of her dogs. 'Is it Violet? Is something wrong with her in the Underworld?'

Visions of her trapped as a gray spirit on the banks of the river make my palms sweat. The goddess shakes her head and suddenly looks very tired. The kerberos prowl around us in uneasy circles as Hecate's form flickers at random. One moment she is a single being, almost seven feet tall and awash with unfathomable strength. The next, she shatters into three different women, eyes a blank green and wavering like a mirage in the desert.

'Do you recall what I told you in the Underworld, Andromeda?'

'You said to seize the blade of fate. To carve my mark on the gods.'

'But what can we do?' Ramsey asks, his face pale and uncertain as he looks at the goddess. 'Damian charged all seven blades. Even if something went wrong during the ceremony, you're here and he can take your powers, ensure his plan happens.'

Hecate ignores him, her gaze squarely on me. 'Your sister made sure you could end the cycle.'

'Violet?' I whisper. 'What did she do?'

A thousand possibilities race through my mind. All of them make my heart ache with fear.

'She did what no other magic-wielder has ever done. She gave up her magic for you.'

Ramsey breathes in so sharply it makes the kerberos to his left growl, its hackles rising.

'How?' I whisper, nearly swaying on my feet. 'How could she do that?'

The goddess shimmers, her entire being dancing out of existence for a fraction of a second before rematerializing, more faded than ever. 'She understands magic in a way that transcends any mortal I have encountered before. Violet knew the risks of such power, and faced them with a determination that bordered on recklessness.' The goddess's eyes fix on a spot over my shoulder, as if lost in centuries past. 'I loved a mortal just like her once. Your ancestor, the one I blessed with a portion of my magic. She was as strong and reckless as your sister, and just as powerful. But, like all mortals touched by magic, she fell victim to the allure of more. The promise of control and power over others. She took and took, until nothing remained but a shadow of the person I once loved. She wanted ultimate control over magic. Over humankind. Just like Damian, she wanted control over life and death.'

The kerberos circle between Hecate's legs, nuzzling her with their many noses. Her face is serene, but barely shrouding a wealth of pain I didn't know deities could feel. 'Mortal lives are such short, fragile things. When she died, I knew that one day others like her would rise. That they would seek me, as they have for countless generations. That the Order would grow in strength and power, as they did in the first days of humankind. So, I hid myself away. I sheltered from mortals and their endless greed, waiting until my bloodline would grant me someone worthy of my powers. Worthy of the gift I gave.'

'But you said Violet gave up her powers,' I say, voice shaking as I speak the words. Violet loved her magic more than anything. 'How is that possible?'

'You know how tempting great power is. Like countless

kings before her, Violet fell prey to the self-consuming call of the darkest magic. But unlike your ancestor, she had someone else she loved more than herself. *More* than magic.' The goddess steps closer to me, her robes whispering against my skin. 'She had you. A bond so strong not even death can sever it. Right before she died, she gave you her powers, using your unique bond cemented with your sigils. Damian's ritual is incomplete. He is weak, injured from the strength of her spell rebounding, and without my magic truly blessing his last knife. Violet gave you the path I foresaw. *She* is your blade.'

My lips part. How could Violet have made such a sacrifice? Why would she give up her magic, the thing she has been prepared to kill for in the past, just so I could stop Damian? My throat tightens and I blink hard, my vision blurring so that Hecate triples before my eyes from unshed tears. I touch my thigh, tracing the tattoo I got on Violet's eighteenth birthday. It feels warm against my fingertips, and Hecate's words hit me like a freight train. The proof that my sister truly did love me more than magic and the power it could give her. My heart aches at the selflessness of it. Haven't I been longing for a sign for the last year that Violet was sorry? That she understood how terrible her actions were at Ravenswood?

I remember the way she smiled at me just before Damian plunged the knife into her chest. She looked relieved. Like she was about to atone for something that weighed on her more painfully than the threat of the Order.

And she did.

I struggle to choke back tears, and share a look with Anubis. His eyes glitter in the dark, mirroring my surprise. Violet gave up her magic, transferred it to me through our bond, our tattoos, and that nameless thread that compelled me to search the depths of the Underworld for her, so I could put a stop to the Order. To the endless killing and cycle of favors.

Hecate smiles at me, as if sensing my inner turmoil. Her sharp canines don't seem menacing as a look of pride etches across her features.

'You can kill Damian,' Hecate says softly, her robes billowing as she fades again before coming back into focus. 'The powers of the seven blades are great, but Damian is not an immortal, thanks to your sister. He will quickly go mad burdened by such magic inside a weak human body. There is hope yet, Andromeda, if you are willing to finally accept the keys I have offered you.' Her dark eyes flick between all of us gathered in the church. 'If you will all do what it takes to end the reign of the Order, once and for all.'

'Your keys?' I ask lamely, my thoughts still full of Violet and the burst of energy she released just before Damian killed her. 'I did your trials in the Underworld. I awakened you. What more are you asking of me?'

The goddess smiles again, a disconcerting thing on a face so unearthly and lovely. 'I am asking you to accept who you are. To no longer fear it. Fear is a dangerous thing. It poisons your ability to choose, to trust yourself and others. And, perhaps worst of all, it makes monsters of even the best of men. It is time to ask yourself, my daughter, if you wish to be ruled by fear forever.'

Swallowing hard, I lift my eyes to hers, staring into their depths and the images of death and life reflected within them. Crossroads and boundaries. Can I face the magic that lives within such liminal spaces?

'How do we kill Damian?' I ask, squaring my shoulders.

Hecate nods, and a breath of wind perfumed by the herbs that grow along the headstones in the Underworld brushes my curls. 'The Order is as ancient as the river of the land of the dead. The convergence that once lay beneath Eidolon is the oldest tributary of this river. It is weakened already, struggling to cling to a land so poisoned by dark magic. To sever its connection to mortals, you must destroy the blades that were forged at the society's inception. As a god, I cannot touch them or interfere. They lie outside my realm, existing in the gap between humanity and godhood.' Her eyes lock onto me. 'Just like you, Andromeda.'

'The blades are the only reason Damian can host the powers of the gods he has killed in his human body, without burning away,' Anubis says. 'If we destroy them, we can kill him.'

'Very good.' Hecate inclines her head at the other god. 'And then your vow to kill all who were responsible for the death of Min-Jun will finally be fulfilled.'

Anubis blanches, his fingers moving to his chest where Damian marked him with a tattoo and the cuneiform vow. 'Is that why I haven't returned to the Underworld?'

'You are at a crossroads,' Hecate answers, her form flickering again, growing fainter than before. 'The river has shown you your choices, but only you can decide which way to take. What you will become.'

I glance at Anubis curiously, but he is lost in thought. A familiar rumble echoes through the valley, rattling the ground at our feet. The convergence shudders as it struggles to remain in the poisoned land of Eidolon. Hecate's form turns ghostly, ethereal as the gossamer of a spiderweb.

'I can't abide here any longer, even with the enchantments fallen. As a goddess of magic, I cannot stay where the rules are twisted and bent. The time has come,' she says, her loyal dogs circling her legs. 'Face your fate, Andromeda.'

'Wait!' I lurch forward even as she becomes so faint, I can

hardly make out her form. 'What about Violet? Was this all a plan for her to die, just so you could take down the Order?'

The goddess meets my eyes, and for a moment all I see is her power. The strength she wields. But then her eyes soften, and I feel a breeze lovingly brush my cheek, as if it were the back of her hand.

'Death is an interesting thing.' Hecate's translucent fingers trail over one head of the kerberos to her right, the snakes around her biceps hissing contentedly. 'Even psychopomps like Anubis and I do not truly control it.'

Anubis watches the goddess, a furrow between his brows, as she fades away, leaving nothing but the scent of herbs and pure magic in her wake. I stare at the spot where she disappeared, my heart in my throat.

'As much as I enjoy being ignored by an ancient immortal,' Ramsey drawls, stepping out from behind Anubis to join our small circle, 'I have to agree with Hecate. Damian is still alive in the Oculus Sanctum and no doubt raising hell with his new powers. Let's put an end to all this. No more Agoge. No more Order.'

'If he's weak like she said, now is our time,' Anubis agrees, a curious lilt to his voice as he studies me. 'It's up to you now, Andromeda. Violet gave you her powers for a reason. She believed that you can end Damian. That you can destroy the blades and bring the Order to its knees.'

I look down at my hands, bloodied and bruised. I don't feel any different, like I have my sister's magic in my veins, mixing with my own. But she gave something of herself to me. An atonement for the wrongs in her past.

Despite Hecate's words, that familiar sense of dread and fear dogs my heels. I look up at Anubis, my pulse fluttering in my neck. 'I don't know if I can do this. Without Violet . . . without having her to fight for, I don't know who I am. What I am.'

His eyes soften, their depths warm and brown once more. He takes my hand and places it over his heart. I feel it beat slowly against my palm. The pulse of a god who has walked both sides of the veil and become something else.

'You are who you have always been,' he murmurs. 'Loyal. Brave in the face of danger. You are good, Andromeda. And that is more than enough.'

Any words catch in my throat as I look up at him, reading his expression. The sincerity there, tinged with something that looks very much like awe. My heart thuds in my chest, desperate and fluttering. But maybe I can be like Violet, fearless and strong, while still being myself too.

But I don't say any of that to Anubis. Instead, I feel his chest beneath my fingers, the smooth skin still somehow stained with ink. And then I pause, my mouth going dry.

'Your markings,' I say, stepping closer and peering at the skin below his collar bones. 'The vow is gone.'

'What?' He blinks and looks down at my fingertips. Sure enough, only the ink of his tattoo spreads over his pectorals. The cruelly carved words in cuneiform have disappeared, as if washed away by the waters of the river.

I shake my head, glancing at Ramsey. 'How is this possible? You know Damian and the Order. How can a vow as unbreakable as the one he marked Anubis with disappear?'

'How can the convergence break its banks and wash away the compound?' he shrugs. 'Whatever magic is in those waters is more than I can understand.'

Anubis' fingers wrap around my own and I turn to him. His eyes are soft and unafraid as he looks at me. Like he's at peace, finally.

'Damian has the power of multiple gods at his disposal,' Anubis says. 'You might have the blood of one, but you and your magic, and that of your sister, are still bound by mortality.' He steps back, his fingers slowly separating from mine in a way that feels painful. Deliberate. 'But I have an idea – a way that you can fulfill the prophecy and face Damian. A way to fulfill my vow to Jae.'

The smell of the Underworld touches me, buries its hands in my hair and brushes lovingly along my skin. My throat aches with words I can't speak, with questions I can't voice. I breathe hard as Anubis' skin seems to glow, awash with power.

'What are you saying?'

'You trust me, don't you, Andromeda? Even though I was once as wicked as any god?'

'Of course,' I say, the words almost a sob as his eyes turn a bright amber, the golden blood on his skin drying as his magic boils forth, familiar and all-consuming.

'We said no more deals,' he murmurs. 'So, I have something to give you. No exchanges. No strings. I'm yours, Andromeda. I'm yours, including my magic.'

Understanding dawns on me even as that same expression of peace and contentment crosses Anubis' features. Jae's features. I sense the god that lives beneath the skin, the power that lies just beyond the surface. He's giving me his godly magic – the powers he holds as a psychopomp. Damian sensed it, even when we first stepped into Eidolon. He planned to use it to strengthen himself for his grand plan. My pulse flutters as I consider. Anubis' idea could work. With this, I could be strong enough to take on Damian Valerius. Maybe Violet always knew Anubis would offer me this.

I reach out and grasp his fingers in mine as Anubis, the god of death, reaches out his hand to make an offering that no god has ever made.

33

Ramsey, Anubis and I creep along the newly carved banks of the convergence. The water is low and dark, as inky as the river in the depths of the Underworld. The spires and lines of the rest of the university are intact, its inhabitants blissfully unaware of the horrors of the night as they slept. I wonder how long that will last once everyone awakens to the destruction in the Oculus Sanctum.

My spine tingles with awareness, with latent magic beneath my skin. We cross the once pristine meadow and forest that separated the Oculus Sanctum from the rest of the school. Now the earth is buckled, damp soil torn and thrown about as if from some giant's hand. Trees lie on their sides, roots dangling like bodies from nooses.

Silently, the three of us move deeper into the territory of the Order, following the line of the unearthed convergence like a path. The ruins of the grand building and parkland look like something from a war zone.

'There,' Ramsey murmurs, bringing us to a stop behind a toppled statue of one of the Seven Sages. The head has snapped off from the rest of the body, staring disapprovingly at us from where it rests, half buried in soil. 'Dark magic is coming from the courtyard there. Damian must be trying to use the powers of Hecate he managed to take from Violet's blood.'

Amidst piles of rubble and broken bodies a few hundred yards away, behind a copse of mutilated trees, is a courtyard that has survived the earthquakes and destruction somewhat intact. The ornamental gardens that once surrounded it are in disarray, muddy footprints staining once pristine white flagstones. But there is a group of Order members huddled together, their torn robes like a bloodstain against the night.

'There must still be over twenty of them,' Anubis says, his eyes picking out the details where mine cannot. 'And I'm certain the alumni members all over the world have heard about what happened. Dozens more could come by morning.'

Ramsey nods thoughtfully. 'Damian will make sure that every member knows what he's accomplished. We need to act now, if we want to stand a chance against a smaller number.'

'Let's go,' I tell the others, moving to skirt the ruins of the forest that protected the Oculus Sanctum from prying eyes.

Ramsey and Anubis move behind me, creeping silently as we approach the courtyard. When we reach the copse of trees that acts as a small windbreak for the courtyard, I pause. Damian kneels before the waters of the convergence, his eyes completely white as he holds his hands over the body of a dead Order member.

Ramsey makes a sound in the back of his throat, his powers rising to life within his chest. The jagged, frantic energy swirls from his skin, making the hairs on the back of my neck stand on end.

'He's trying to reverse death,' Ramsey hisses, a hard look crossing his features. 'Look! He's having Rohan help gather the dead. I thought we'd taken care of that bastard.'

Sure enough, when I tear aside a creeping vine, I spy Rohan, his chest still bearing the dried stripes of blood. He moves frantically as Damian murmurs in multiple languages, his voice echoing off the statues and flagstones.

Rohan finishes moving another broken body next to Damian.

Damian begins another string of words, some in English and others in ancient Greek. The broken and bloodied hand of the dead Order member twitches.

'The blades,' I say, pointing to a flower bed behind Damian.

An Order member crouches in the dirt and lifts the lid of a battered chest that must have been salvaged from the compound. Inside is a glimmer of bronze and the wicked teeth of the familiar daggers. They glow with life and heat, as if the Apkallu that once blessed them have inhabited the bodies of the weapons. The member drops the lid again and moves to watch Damian, bent over the twitching body.

I let the vines fall back into place, facing Ramsey and Anubis. 'We can't let Damian touch them. If he gets hold of the knives, he'll be much harder to kill.'

'I'll take care of Rohan,' Ramsey says, his eyes narrowed to slits. 'Anubis, you take the chest with the daggers and get it far enough away to start the spell to destroy the blades.'

They look at me, waiting for my part to take effect. I shiver in the cold air, frost sticking to the tree limbs that brush my shoulders. Despite the cold, I dig my hands into the damp earth, ignoring the sting against my knuckles. Though my eyes are shut, I stare into the depths of the earth, seeing past the layer of grass and weeds, the pile of loam and rotting leaves, to the roots and soil. The feel of the Underworld thrumming far, far below that, and then the bones of the dead in between.

Though the flesh that once clothed them has long rotted away, I can still feel their stories. Their lives and loves and hungers. I dig into the soil, sifting through the dead, through jaw bones and ribcages and teeth until I find what I'm looking for.

Blood that cries out for justice.

A surge of power radiates up through my body, filling it with heat and light. I smell a hint of burned hair and singed clothes as I open my eyes. Though nothing has changed in the world above, I can feel the Underworld beneath my feet. The connection that the convergence shares with the river of the dead.

Anubis shudders, his eyes dark and fathomless as he tilts his head and listens. 'They're coming. All of them.' His voice is tinged with a hint of awe as he gazes at me, pride clear on his features.

The magic he gave me has done its work. I'm strong enough now to control the dead themselves, as if I were a god.

I swallow hard, nervousness and an ache for my sister battling in my stomach. But I have work to do. I straighten, letting clods of soil fall from my fingers as I withdraw my hands from the earth. Ramsey crouches, his eyes trained on Rohan, waiting for permission to strike.

Anubis focuses on the chest, on the seven blessed blades of the Apkallu that allow Damian to host the power of the gods he has killed, without burning to ash. I reach out and brush his fingers with my own. They are warm and alive against my skin, and I relish the feeling.

And then, with the power of death rumbling at my feet, I step out into the courtyard.

Green mist curls around my throat, tightening until I can hardly breathe without tasting sulfur from the belly of the earth. The remains of the Order seem to bathe in the fog, eyes watering and reddening from the strength of it. But Damian kneels in the middle of the chaos, unaware of the fear the members of his society feel as they scurry around, doing his bidding like frightened rats.

Small fissures snake out from the ruins of the compound,

each leaking their own stream of the green mist of Hecate's magic. They swirl around Damian like angry vipers, hissing into his ears as his white eyes scour the surface of the new convergence, searching through the threads of fate that dictate every mortal's life. He is so engrossed in his work, attempting to reanimate the dead Order member, lost in rapture, I'm surprised that his is the first head to snap in my direction as I step into the open courtyard.

'Hello, daughter of Hecate,' he murmurs, the milky whiteness of his eyes disconcerting as they track my movements. 'I see you've come for revenge. A pity, because I can see every outcome of your desire. And each one ends in your death.'

More fumes rise from the fissures surrounding Damian. His nostrils flare as he greedily drinks them in, tasting power, sweet as any wine. I say nothing as I come to a stop a few yards away, the curve of the convergence at my side. The waters seem to rumble uneasily, as if wishing to sink back below the earth and hide from the polluted magic spinning in the air.

Order members pause in their frantic work, contacting alumni far and wide, and tallying the dead. All watch with a sort of horrified trepidation as Damian gets to his feet.

He sweeps his robes aside like a king and steps toward me. I don't back away, only let him approach. His clothes whisper along the pebbles and rubble covering the ground, creating a cacophony in the still night.

'Don't you have questions for me, Andromeda?' he murmurs, pacing slowly closer, his scarred chest bared.

Despite the burst of rage that tears through my chest at his honeyed tone, I merely shrug. 'Why should I? The magic you have is the same I was born with.'

Damian laughs, the sound entirely without mirth as he

stops his pacing and stands before me, curiosity and interest written across his face. 'How you survived the collapse of the sanctum is beyond me. It seems your mistress only wants one sister to dwell with her in the Underworld.'

'Don't mention Violet,' I snap, a cold rush tingling through my fingertips. I force down the urge to attack Damian right here and now. Patience. I can't risk him turning and fleeing with the blades.

'She died honorably, giving her rare blood to a cause greater than any society has dreamed of. Look around you, Andromeda.' He spreads his arms, showing the few remaining members and the bodies littering the surrounding ground. 'This is only the start of what I can accomplish with the powers of Hecate at my beck and call. I was destined to bear this burden. To live my life in an eternity of service to the Order.'

'Your Order is dead,' I spit. 'Buried beneath the rubble of the sanctum because of what you've done here.'

He shakes his head, white eyes gleaming like bone. 'We are everywhere. Centuries of spreading out across all nations and governments. The ones who died here tonight, the ones not worthy of my gift of new life, are martyrs. And we will rebuild with the promise of more magic than anyone can imagine. Stronger. Eternal. The Age of the Gods is over. Now it is my turn.'

'This isn't power, Damian. This will kill you, and everyone who defends you.'

An uneasy murmur ripples through the few remaining members, tired and bruised and shivering in the cold. They dart furtive glances at their leader, drunk on power and glowing with a crazed sense of grandeur.

'Kill me?' His face hardens, losing the cruel benevolence of a leader guiding wayward souls to certain doom. 'I am immortal. No one can touch me, not with Hecate's powers in my blood, strengthening me to hold the magic of all the gods I have killed. And not with the convergence blessing me with the most ancient branch of the river.'

Even as he says the words, his eyes dart nervously to the side, as if the small part of him not consumed by power realizes something is wrong.

The earth rumbles below our feet, the vibration sending dust up from the rubble of the sanctum nearby. Some members let out high-pitched yelps, ducking and cringing as if expecting another chasm to rip apart the ground beneath them. No doubt they believe Damian has called on his supernatural powers, threatening them and me with death.

'You forgot you never completed your ceremony,' I say, feeling the roll of soft soil beneath the paving stones. The earth pushing them apart, bleeding rich brown dirt over the white marble. The river grows rougher at my side, as if agitated. Damian's face falls as he looks around the court-yard at the strange boiling soil spreading out around me. 'Your blade never absorbed Hecate's magic. Violet gave it up before you killed her. And without it, the powers of the gods will burn you up and drive you mad.'

Damian jerks his chin back as if struck. He glances at the tattoos on his skin, sickly and wrong. Circular burns, the edges a terrible black, mark his hands and dot his chest. But these aren't wounds sustained from the fire Ramsey hurled during the ceremony. It's as if he is burning away from within. Even his lips look parched and dry.

'I already have Hecate's curse tablet. I forged it years ago, just waiting for the day I could summon and kill her. Despite what your sister has done, I can capture the goddess at any time,' he says, loudly enough for his nervous members threatening to break ranks to hear him. 'But I think it is time I put to rest your interruption of my plans. It's too late for you, Andromeda. You don't belong here, among other magic-wielders. You're not worthy of the power in your veins, and your blood is certainly not worthy of my last blade.' He curls his lip at me in disgust as he takes a single step forward. 'Look at you. Weak and pathetic, never strong enough to stand on your own. First you let Anubis die for you, and then Ramsey and your sister. You are incapable of doing what it takes to accomplish *anything*. An average girl with futile dreams of being so much more.' Damian's lips contort in a cruel smile. 'I think the convergence will enjoy tasting your blood as it carries your body down to the Underworld to be with your sister.'

He raises his hands and the tattoos along his skin burn a sickly silver. The air turns ice cold, sucking away any trace or hint of warmth. But just as his power rises, threatening to overwhelm me, the earth explodes beneath our feet. Order members jump aside, falling over themselves, as bones crawl from deep within the ground.

Skeletons and corpses in all states of decay claw their way from their graves, surging from beneath the courtyard like a swarm of ants as they answer my earlier call. Screams echo off the stone. Rohan jumps to his feet, murderous gaze trained on me. Just as he moves to launch himself in my direction, palms burning with burgeoning power, Ramsey darts from the trees, colliding with Rohan in a painful tangle of limbs.

Damian's shouts and commands are swallowed by the sound of dozens of the dead rising from the earth, their open jaws and reaching fingers tangling around the limbs of fleeing Order members. A dark streak to one side tells me that Anubis is racing for the knives, ready to destroy them.

Damian notices him at the same time as I do, wheeling around in a flurry of outrage as he stretches out his hand and murmurs a spell. Anubis goes flying, his body collapsing in a heap against a twisted tree. I cry out, reaching in his direction wordlessly. All around the trunk of the tree rises bleached white bone. A rattling sound echoes as the skeletons assemble themselves, hoisting their rotten bodies out of the soil.

They circle Anubis like soldiers, guarding him as he comes to his senses, shaking his head. Damian screams a curse as he launches a volley of pure magic at the undead sentinels. Some shatter into dust the moment the light touches their bones, but more rise from the ground to take their place, forming ranks around Anubis as he reaches into the chest to draw out the first knife.

A burst of golden light flashes through the clearing. Anubis lifts a rock and strikes a bronze blade. It shatters into pieces, unleashing a torrent of scattered magic. Damian screams, the sound torn from his chest as the first blade splinters into nothing. Blood stands out stark on his palms.

His eyes are red as he staggers, clutching his chest, already weaker with one blade destroyed. With hate in his gaze, he points a palm at me, magic swirling and ready to strike. Suddenly, a flare of white-hot pain spreads from my chest. I gasp, staggering and falling to my knees as warmth spills across my front. My fingers scrabble at my clothes as I choke on something hot and coppery in my mouth. My hands come away red with blood.

Damian murmurs another spell, Anubis and the army of skeletons forgotten. More blood pours from my mouth as Damian stalks toward me, eyes blazing with images of death. His skin, once pale, is now as red as flames, bubbling with blisters.

'Andy!' Ramsey shouts from behind me, clawing his way to his feet as he pushes Rohan's limp body off him.

'What did you do?' Damian demands, spittle flying from

his lips as he grasps my shirt, yanking me against him. 'You and your sister. What curse did you put upon me?'

A wild laugh rips from my chest, the sound swallowed by rising blood. I spit and gasp as he lets out an outranged sound and drags me toward the convergence and its dark, boiling surface. Ramsey shouts my name again, closer this time. The water is cool as flecks of it dot my face, and I feel no fear as Damian hauls me to the edge and pushes my head below the surface.

The dark waters are familiar, whispering spells and stories that feel like second nature. But the river senses a sickness within it, a desire to purge the evil it feels. I breathe deeply, letting the water bathe my lungs and fill my throat. It tastes sweet to me now, without a hint of bitterness. The feel of a heavy obsidian key in my hand grows stronger, even as water fills my lungs instead of air. Death kept at bay by Hecate's blessing. My skin grows cold, my heartbeat stilling. I see flashes of keys behind my closed lids as I listen to the hum of the convergence. To what it wants me to do if I am to heal the hurt Damian has caused it.

Suddenly, the grip of Damian's hand leaves my neck and hair. I pull away from the water, wiping it from my eyes without a single cough. Ramsey grapples with Damian on the broken marble tiles nearby.

'Enough of you, Remus!' Damian screams. A frantic burst of energy collides with Ramsey, sending him flying until he lands next to a pile of shattered bone.

Damian gets to his feet, whirling to face me. His blank white eyes widen as he stares at me, dripping with water but with the warmth of life coloring my skin. I take a step forward, a jolt of pleasure running through me as he staggers back a single step. One hint of the fear that must be rushing through him.

The river grows still, the magic in the air freezing in place. Damian looks around at the skeletons dragging his Order members down into the earth. Rohan lies curiously still, a familiar golden dagger pulled from his chest by a blood-splattered Ramsey who is already back on his feet. Damian sees Anubis hunched over the other blades, his hands spread as he murmurs ancient words to tear them apart, atom by atom.

Outrage overtakes any hint of surprise. With pained forcefulness, Damian shouts a spell. The skeletons and corpses stop moving, their joints cracking as he tears them apart. The smell of burning flesh grows stronger as bones fly around the courtyard, disintegrating into pieces. The screams of Order members fade as they crawl away from the gaping holes in the earth, lest more undead reach for them.

Damian breathes hard, his voice jagged as he shouts, 'Enough of your games! With your death, Hecate will have no other protectors.'

Despite the burns growing along his skin, he still raises his hands in my direction. I can feel his strength building, the power he's gained through years of discipline and torment.

'You killed my sister for nothing,' I say, voice clear even as water streams down my clothes. 'And now you will die too.'

For a moment, Damian falters, hesitating as he prepares to wipe me from existence. He looks at the convergence, at the way the water has quieted and lowered. The way it's lost its strength and become less a river and more of a stream. 'That is impossible. I can see every death and life before me like a patchwork. I *am* Death.'

A torrent of magic washes over me, singeing the grass and trees into blackened curls of charcoal. Other Order members, those not half buried in the ground, rally, struggling to gather around Damian as he glows with power so intense it threatens to overwhelm me.

My skin seems to melt away under the heat of Damian's gaze, his immeasurable power. But just as quickly, I heal, protected by Hecate's keys and the magic she blessed me with. I take a step forward, the convergence slowly sinking back into the ground, retreating to the Underworld where it belongs. And I let my magic rise, colliding with Damian's as the cracks in the earth grow larger, like the delta of the River Nile. They branch around us, swirling in an impossible pattern.

Damian grits his teeth and sends another swell of magic in my direction. This time I don't buckle. I don't feel a hint of heat as I let the fissures widen, let the magic that connects the Underworld with the mortal world fade away. Something else lifts from the openings in the ground. Instead of the pale green mist, there is a delicate white vapor, soft and ethereal.

Even as Damian struggles to burn me away, the white mist takes shape. Shoulders and heads. Hands and arms. Eyes that speak of revenge.

Spirits, hundreds of them, rise from the ground, using the magic of the convergence to pull themselves up from both banks of the river. My spell grows stronger as women from centuries of sacrifices take shape, their blood crying out for justice. Damian's magic falters as the convergence fades away, leaving nothing but a damp impression on the earth.

His eyes flash back and forth as the spirits gather around me, their silent voices flitting through my head as they advance on the Order members still standing. All at once, magic flies, spells and desperate curses, as Damian's few remaining allies struggle to protect themselves. But nothing seems to stop the growing number of ghosts.

Damian gasps as the spirits press into the small clearing. They reach out their hands, smothering the power of anyone who tries to stop them. Some gather around Anubis, letting their power mix with his as he struggles to destroy blade after blade. Flashes of gold spark each time one shatters. And each time Damian cries out, his body growing pale and weak. Soon, the soft white glow of the spirits of the women drowns out the poisonous green.

'No!' Damian shouts through gritted teeth. He reaches for me, fingers curled into claws, and unleashes another burst of power.

It washes over me like lava, burning with a sense of wrongness. Some spirits momentarily lose their shape, slipping back into the ground as wave after wave of Damian's desperate magic beats against them. But undefeated, another girl reaches down and pulls her companion back up, letting their magic grow, building and building, until I feel like my chest will burst from the pressure.

All light fades from the courtyard as Damian drops to his knees, gasping for breath, sweat slipping down his bubbling skin. I stand before him, the ring of spirits closing tighter around us like a fist. Slowly, Damian reaches for me, as if torn between begging for mercy and wishing to rip my throat out.

My powers cringe away from the evil emanating from Damian as he gasps and struggles, crawling on the ground, desperate to reach a convergence that is no longer there. His magic flickers like a flame starved of oxygen, and I crouch down before him, my hands itching as I hold them over his body, sensing the wrongness that lurks there.

'You'll never stop the Order,' he hisses, even as he struggles to touch the impression left by the river, his fingers digging into the damp earth. 'We are everywhere. Even without me, without the powers of the gods, you can never get rid of us.'

The obsidian dagger of Hecate melts into my hand. The symbol of her control over life and death. Damian's eyes widen as I press the blade to his wrist.

But it doesn't sink into the flesh. Instead, it snaps almost invisible threads of power, severing them from Damian's body. He howls in pain, worse than even the cries he made as Anubis crushed the bronze daggers. Slowly, the green light separates from Damian's body, slipping away. His eyes follow it as he tries to lunge for the magic of the six murdered gods he and his family struggled for centuries to obtain.

A sense of peace settles over me as the magic slips into the earth, retreating from Damian and his greedy hands. Perhaps that is what Hecate was trying to teach me with her keys. Magic is not inherently good or evil. It is the one who wields it who decides that fate. Each of us faces choices. Violet, and Tooth and Talon chose a dark path, one full of dire consequences and pain. But people like Anubis have used their magic to help others. A balance between all things, like life and death.

'There,' I murmur, standing and joining the army of ghostly women waiting for me, 'now you're nothing but a man.'

Horror grips Damian's face as he looks at his hands, at the blisters and tattoos that are misshapen and torn. 'No.' He spreads his fingers, murmurs a spell in Sumerian, one meant to tear enemies asunder. But the clearing is as quiet as death, and not a single breath of wind whispers in response to his spell. He scrambles to his knees. 'What have you done?'

He lunges for me, his fingers closing around my shoulders. We tumble to the earth in a tangle of arms and legs.

His eyes are wild and frantic, webbed with cataracts and shattered by visions of a death he cannot escape. He closes his fists around my neck, desperate to squeeze the life out of me.

'Why won't you die?' he screams, baring his teeth like a wolf.

A choked wheeze slips from my lips as the ghosts murmur, hundreds of them whispering their own spells, their own desires for peace and revenge. And then, over Damian's shoulder, I see a familiar head of silky black hair, dark blue eyes and pale, perfect skin. A cunning, precocious smile on her lips. My heart leaps into my throat and I stop fighting Damian, my chest tearing open.

'Violet?' I try to whisper, the word swallowed by a sudden breeze that smells of incense, ash and the Underworld.

She says nothing as she looks at me, a wealth of emotions on her face. But it's her, skin gossamer and silvery as any ghost. I want to throw Damian aside and run to her, to grab her hand and force her to stay with me. I grasp Damian's arms, struggling to heave him off me. But then Violet disappears. Hot blood spatters on my skin. A shard of bronze appears from the center of Damian's chest. He looks down in surprise, blood welling around the wound as it pierces straight through the talons of the eagle tattoo.

Shock and outrage spill over his features. The bleached white of his eyes fades, a glimmer of silver returning as blood stains the corners of his mouth. Damian clutches at his chest and tears away his robes, fingers smearing the blood spilling down his stomach. His weight lifts off me and I take in a sharp breath as he falls onto his side, a terrible gurgling sound coming from his throat.

Ramsey joins Violet's spirit and they both stand over me, a sliver of one of the seven blades in their joined hands.

Violet smiles at him and lets go as Ramsey heaves for breath. He drops the bloody bit of metal, his face hard, even as moisture wells in his eyes. Relief, maybe. From the terror of the Order. From the endless torment of the Valerius clan.

He drops to his knees next to me and we watch as Damian writhes on the ground, struggling to form words as he chokes on his own blood.

Violet looks down at Damian once, before she joins the other spirits, lost in a shapeless mass of softly glowing white. The ghosts watch Damian struggle, their eyes sharp with emotion. Anubis approaches, the echo of his limping foot-steps absorbed by the endless procession of dead girls. He joins Ramsey and me on the ground, kneeling beside me as his fingers wind through mine.

'I'll . . .' Damian pauses, coughing up more dark red blood, 'come back.'

A threat. Perhaps once it would have frightened me. I've seen what people with magic can do. How it can warp them, make them bend the laws of nature. But the ghostly weight of Hecate's keys tickles my palms. And I think of Violet, my sister, who got her own revenge.

'No, you won't,' I promise.

His eyes scream with hatred even as he chokes again. No one moves forward or speaks. After what feels like an eon of watching Damian struggle to die, it is not a spirit who steps forward, but a goddess.

Hecate melts from the depths of the earth, her eyes boring into Damian's. 'Your family spent centuries search-ing for a way to avoid death. To control it. And now you are just like them, soon to be nothing but bones and dust. A shade damned to wander the east bank for eternity.'

Goosebumps ripple over my arms at her words.

Damian's reddened face pales. He clutches at the wound

in his chest, the steady stream of blood pooling around him. 'No,' he murmurs, his voice fading even as his limbs grow still and cold.

When he stops moving completely, Hecate steps back from his body, her face serene and calm. 'There. The last thread of the gods' magic has returned to the Underworld. Where it belongs.'

Anubis' fingers tighten on mine as he watches her. 'What will happen to the convergence here?'

The goddess smiles, her form shimmering. 'It will return to the Underworld, resting in the soil there. The Order is at an end. It will wither like a flower plucked from the vine. But it will need a guiding hand.' Her eyes move to Ramsey, exhausted and blood-spattered at my side. 'An Arskell helped found the last age of the Order. Perhaps another will end the atrocities.'

Ramsey's mouth is open, and he looks at me, and then Anubis, as if for confirmation. 'I . . . I don't want anyone else to suffer like I did.'

Hecate nods and steps back from Damian's body. 'My work is finished, and my promises soon to be fulfilled. We can now find rest on the west bank. All of us.' The ghosts of the other women stir, their eyes fixed on a point behind me.

'What about me?' Anubis asks, his fingers laced so tightly with mine that the bones ache. 'Will I be drawn back to the Underworld too?'

'The spell my daughter weaved over you was powerful.' The goddess cocks her head, and I'm choked by the wealth of emotion in her eyes. 'It culminated on the winter solstice and your time in the river. When your vow to the Order was broken, and you gave up your godly magic for Andromeda to use, you changed irrevocably. This will be your last life, Anubis. A mortal one.'

Anubis inhales, the sound catching in his throat. He looks at me, wonder crossing his features. 'And when I die?'

'Which bank of the river you end up on depends on you, just as it does for any human.'

My chest feels tight with emotion as I look at him. A mortal. I won't lose him to the Underworld, to a place where I can't ever truly belong until I'm dead. This is everything I have wanted, what I have dreamed about for a year. An ache takes over the elation bubbling in my chest. Once more, I've lost someone so I could keep another. This time, it's Violet's death that has allowed me to keep Anubis. I search the sea of ghostly women in vain for my sister's face.

'Goodbye, daughter,' Hecate murmurs, her eyes full of peace as she turns to the spirits of the women all around.

My throat closes on any protests as Hecate disappears. A soft glow touches my skin, and I turn to see what has the ghosts so entranced. The sun is rising over the horizon, a golden dawn burning over the two peaks that rise over Eidolon. This dawn feels different to any other. It is Hecate showing the spirits the way to their rest.

I watch as hundreds of spirits, their forms soft and delicate, move together, away from the horrors of the night. From the blood and carnage and rubble that led to their deaths.

My skin prickles as the spirits move, gliding through the air toward the hills. They fade away as they cross into the faint sunlight, one by one. Tears burn my eyes as I watch them go, still searching for my sister. But I never see her face. Slowly, the stream of ghosts fades to a trickle, until at last, the unearthly silvery glow they brought with them dwindles.

Violet is gone.

The sun finally breaks over the horizon, warm light

streaming over the valley, staining the rubble of the sanctum gold. I blink, my eyes stinging as I get shakily to my feet. The earth has been torn to shreds, flagstones scattered, and the courtyard rent to pieces. And with the fissures marking the ground, and the empty bed of the convergence, the entire area of the Oculus Sanctum is ruined.

Ramsey turns to me, exhausted, but with a lightness to the set of his shoulders I've never seen before. 'The Order isn't obliterated yet. There are dozens more members scattered all over the world. More will arrive today. I'll need help to make sure no one else tries to take Damian's place. That everything ends here. Tonight.'

I look at Anubis. For once, I don't have a plan. A goal. For so long, it has been to find my sister. Then to save her. Now, she's gone, and the world is yawning beneath my feet, waiting to swallow me whole. What am I meant to do without her? Who can I be when she's gone? When I watched her die to save me?

'I don't know what to do,' I finally whisper, my throat raw and stinging.

Anubis squeezes my fingers. 'I'll go wherever you do, Andromeda. And we'll figure it out together.'

I turn from the wreckage around us and look in the distance to the quiet expanse of Eidolon. The dark stone buildings and the gothic arches. It's a beautiful place. A place that has even felt like home at times. The warmth from Anubis' skin at my side chases away some of the bone-deep chill, and I let myself wonder what tomorrow might be like. What our life could look like a week from now. A month. A year.

I don't have any answers. But maybe . . . maybe it could be something as beautiful as it has been heartbreaking.

I face Ramsey again, his scars prominent in the pale

morning light. His missing fingers and the burdens he's carried alone. The Order won't be easy to snuff out. Maybe I could find some peace, some purpose even, in helping him create a new world. One where no one suffers like we have. Maybe magic could be good and simple with us.

'What do you want us to do?' I ask Ramsey, and Anubis smiles, his face warm with life.

Ramsey purses his lips, but his eyes are full of emotion. 'I think destroying the sanctums is a good place to start. And after that, I'll sever any connections between Eidolon and Order alumni. Destroy all of Lector's libraries and artifacts. I'm the last living direct descendant of the founding families. I can work with the board to help remake Eidolon into something better. Get rid of any loyalties to the Order from within.'

Together, the three of us turn from what was once the most powerful sanctum of the oldest magical society in the world. With the sun at our backs and the peaceful expanse of Eidolon ahead, I could almost have faith that things will get better.

Anubis and Ramsey pull ahead, crossing toward the twisted gates. But I pause, turning back to the rubble and facing the sun where the spirits Hecate helped in the Underworld disappeared. Everything feels different here now, like some of the bruises and blood that mark the ground have been erased and washed clean.

Just before I can turn again, a glimmer catches my eye. A familiar emerald green burning low against the smoldering remains of the compound. One of Hecate's torches. A marker at the beginning of her road. I squint, wishing my glasses hadn't been lost in the river.

The green light fades a little as the sun rises higher. Something familiar washes over me. The scent of vanilla and patchouli and memories of laughter. I squint into the sunlight until the outline of a gossamer spirit becomes clear.

Violet stands next to a wavering Hekation. And behind her is a woman wearing an obsidian crown, her arms adorned with writhing snakes. Hecate puts her hand on Violet's shoulder, as lovingly as any parent. The goddess of death, of magic and crossroads is free to do her duty to those who still worship her. She's come back to guide the dead to their rest. To bless those with magic. Including my sister.

Violet nods at me, her eyes brimming with silvery tears she can't seem to shed. I swallow hard as I desperately drink in her appearance. She doesn't move from her spot next to the Hekation, and I don't run toward her. We're separated now, by something other than death.

As the Hekation fades, and as the goddess offers her hand to guide my sister to her realm in the Underworld, the sweet breeze carries gentle words to my ears.

You will live an amazing life, Andy. Don't waste it missing me or feeling guilty for having dreams.

Violet looks at me one last time before she faces the road to the Underworld, Hecate at her side.

I'll be waiting for you when it's over.

The familiar smell of the Land of the Dead washes over me as the tunnel to the Underworld closes, carrying my sister away.

Epilogue

Six Months Later

I sit on a bench just inside the gates of Eidolon, overlooking Appian Way. The sun is warm, blanketing the university and its buildings in bright light. Students bustle through the streets and buildings, juggling books and laptops as they race around, taking their last few examinations before the summer begins.

I'm lost in the last few chapters of my textbook on the works of Plato when someone sits next to me on the bench, long legs stretched out in front of them.

'You'll have to hurry if you want to make it to your exam,' Anubis says, a smile in his voice as he presses his lips to my temple.

I shut the textbook, my eyes swimming with dates and names, and glance at my phone. 'I still have an hour,' I say, leaning against him as he kisses my lips softly, delicately. 'Besides,' I say, a little breathless, 'Ramsey wanted to meet us before we head back to my parents' place for the summer. There are some Order members he wants us to look up in the States, make sure they're falling into line.'

I stand, tucking my books into my bag. Anubis takes it from me before I can sling it over my shoulder. We walk together, his arm around me, and head for the offices that Ramsey has commandeered for himself.

'Have you decided, then?' Anubis asks as we cross Appian Way and reach the steps leading up to the offices. 'It's been months since the funeral. Since we talked about what we would do at the end of term.'

I'm quiet for a few steps, letting the muggy air inside the building settle over my shoulders. Anubis has been patient, waiting on my decision if I want to stay on at Eidolon and pursue my degree in classics next year.

I still remember the funeral Anubis and I flew back for after Damian was killed. The way Anubis used his magic, now that of a normal mortal magic-wielder, to create the illusion of my sister's body. To smooth away questions and make everything seem normal. It hurt too much to be home, where reminders of Violet were everywhere. So we returned to Eidolon. Since the events of December, we've been busy helping Ramsey organize what's left of the Order, and disassembling the institution itself. It's taken most of my time and energy and kept me from worrying about my parents. Witnessing their grief over losing Violet to what they think is cancer.

But now, summer is approaching. There's no good excuse to linger around Eidolon. To stay away from home and all its painful memories. Anubis has already made it clear he will follow me, no matter what I choose.

I pause outside Ramsey's office, the brass plaque bearing his name gleaming in the fluorescent light. Despite everything – all the late nights and endless work, ensuring no Order member tries to seize power again – I've enjoyed my studies. Like when I first settled into classes in the autumn, I've almost relished being buried beneath heavy tomes that smell of dust and stories. I hardly miss a lecture, and spend as much time as possible crafting perfect essays and studying the past. It comforts me, somehow. To understand the past and its mistakes. To learn from them.

Is it wrong to enjoy the place that cost my sister everything?

That's what makes me pause. What has made this conversation between the two of us drag on for months on end.

Finally, I wrap my fingers around the handle and push the door open. 'I don't know,' I admit. 'Maybe after my last exam. When I have time to think.'

Anubis nods, but his eyes are knowing. He sees right through me, just as he always has. But he doesn't press the issue as we cross the waiting room to Ramsey's small office and let ourselves inside.

Ramsey sits amongst a pile of papers and files. His dark auburn hair is messy, like he raked his fingers through it one too many times. As he looks up, a steady stream of emails lights up the monitor of his computer. He's exhausted from his time with the board, as well as from dismantling the Order from within. But he smiles as we sit down across from him, and he looks lighter and happier than I've ever seen him.

'Heading back to the States tomorrow night?' he asks, turning off his computer and rubbing his eyes.

'We take the train back to London tomorrow morning,' Anubis confirms.

As they discuss the journey, I look out the window that faces the large open quad near the gates to the university. Ever since classes began winding down for the end of the term, I've had too much time to think. To worry and agonize over this place and whether I belong in it, now that Ramsey is more settled. He's a good man. I know he can root out the last of the Order on his own. He and Anubis have even become friends. And I sometimes wonder what it would be like if Violet were here. If her broken pieces might fit together with Ramsey's.

'Andy?' Ramsey asks, his tone indicating this isn't the first time he's called my name.

I look away from the window and force a smile onto my face. 'Sorry, I was a bit lost. Just thinking about my exam.'

His dark eyes are full of empathy as he sits forward in his chair and pushes a paper across the desk to us with a list of names, addresses, and the dangers associated with the Order members we are to look into this summer. I scan it absently and pass it to Anubis to peruse.

'I hope you'll come back next year, Andy.'

I give him a coy smile. 'You don't need us, Ramsey. Eidolon is doing just fine in your hands.'

'Still,' he shrugs, 'I think you could be happy here with me. That is – I'd like to see you happy. I think you've found a home at Eidolon.'

Home. I always thought my sister was my home. My smile fades and I have to look out the window again. Six months now without Violet, and I can't go more than an hour without thinking about her. Worrying about her in the Underworld. I don't trust myself to speak, so I stay silent as Anubis puts his hand on my knee.

'No word from Violet?' Ramsey asks gently, but I see a spark of interest in his eyes. 'She hasn't responded to your attempts to summon her? To communicate?'

'Nothing,' Anubis answers, giving me a moment to collect myself. 'I can't travel to the Underworld at will anymore, not since I gave up my godly powers – I have to use the complicated spell with *Subitae mortem* petals. But we have had no luck contacting her or any spirit that has heard from her. The Underworld has changed since Hecate returned. Gods we thought were long gone are shaking off their dust and trying to find new purpose without worshippers.'

Ramsey sits back, crossing his arms. 'Maybe she's gone to the west bank. She could even be with Min-Jun and Jae.'

'Maybe,' I agree, but it falls flat. I thought that if anyone could make themselves heard beyond the grave, it would be Violet. But since I saw her spirit disappear with Hecate in December, I haven't seen her or received so much as a sign that she's alright. And Hecate has been just as mysterious. I can't help but feel abandoned by her after all she asked of me.

Ramsey watches me warily before he says, 'You know what Hecate said. She gave you her keys. Perhaps the only mortal who has ever had control over life and death. Maybe she trusted you with them for another reason.'

I glance up at him. 'I can send people to the Underworld or pull them back if I have to. But I can't forcibly summon them from their rest. A spirit can cross the river to the west bank if they want. Violet doesn't want to see me. I can't reach her.'

'You and Violet have a connection that transcends death,' Anubis says softly. 'The two of you have both traveled the Underworld and returned as something more. Nothing can keep you apart. Violet has the same powers you do. I'm sure there is something she is doing in the Underworld, something for Hecate.'

I try to feel encouraged by the confidence of his words, but, like always, I feel numb. Like I'm missing a part of myself I can never get back. Ramsey and Anubis speak for a few more moments before we stand. I only have a few minutes to get across the campus and to my exam, so I say goodbye to Ramsey.

'You'll think about coming back? You know I'll always hold a spot for you,' he says as he gives me a quick hug.

I smile at him, the familiar warmth in his eyes comforting, even if I can't return it in the way he wants. I glance at Anubis and struggle to push down the old feelings of guilt as I consider another year at Eidolon. Maybe building a career with history. Something that can distract me from Violet, while also honoring everything she once loved. My heart thuds against my ribs, but I've made my mind up.

'I'll see you in the autumn,' I finally say, though my voice is tight.

Ramsey grins as I slip out of the door. Anubis follows me as the late afternoon sun slips further down the horizon, casting long shadows over the cobblestone roads. We pause outside the building where my exam is, and I face him, fingers tight around the strap of my bag.

'It's the right thing, coming back next year,' he murmurs, caressing my jaw as he tips my head back.

I let out a shuddering breath. 'I hope you're right.'

'I am,' he says stubbornly, lifting an eyebrow as he leans down and brushes his lips against mine. 'I'll meet you at your room when your exam is over.'

He kisses me again, and the taste of incense, of deep earth, still clings to his skin. He pulls back, brushing his thumb over my cheek before he steps back. 'I love you, Andromeda.'

The ache in my heart fades a little at that, and I brush my fingers over his as I step back, fingers wrapped around the door handle. 'I love you too.'

He grins as I turn and enter the building. The tattoo on my thigh tingles as I wind my way through the labyrinth of hallways, searching for the examination room.

The low murmur of voices reaches my ears and I pause, digging through my bag for everything I need for the long test. The hum gets a little louder, and I look through the open doorway to see what the commotion is.

The exam room is completely still. Students are bent over their desks, preparing for the test. My blood runs cold and I listen hard for familiar signs. The whisper of another language, the smell of magic in the air. The way my blood heats in response.

My leg tingles again and I wince, rubbing my thigh hard even as I peer into the long shadows of the narrow hallway. I expect to smell death. Rot and loam. But instead, the faint sweetness of the convergence reaches my nose. But that's impossible – we destroyed any connection to the rivers at Eidolon. I straighten, peering hard into the shadows that seem to move once more.

Another cacophony of whispered voices. They murmur something in ancient Greek. Something I can barely hear. And then my thigh burns and itches again, and I reach down to rub it once more through my jeans. I pause as my fingers come into contact with the fabric.

My tattoo. Soft green light marks the edges of the tattoo, the curves of the antlers and the wings of the moth. I straighten, my breath puffing in front of my face as everything goes eerily quiet. Something moves in the shadows. But this time, I'm not afraid. Long dark hair and bright blue eyes appear, as the flurry of voices fades. The scent of the convergence is overwhelming, but beneath it is the familiarity of vanilla and patchouli.

Violet.

'You're where you belong, little star. Welcome home.'

Acknowledgments

Writing a sophomore novel, especially a sequel, is painfully hard. There aren't endless stretches of time to beta read, edit and revise. Instead there are deadlines, people waiting and readers to think about! But in the end (and with lots of help) we're standing at the end of Andy and Anubis' story. I hope it resonated with those like her: people afraid to stand on their own, willing to give all of themselves away just so those they love can be happy. I hope they learned that what they want matters too, and find the strength to reach for it. I also hope some people understand Violet, and forgive her for her failings, and see her for who she is: a fiercely loving sister terrified of losing the one person who truly understands her.

I wouldn't have made it to the finish line without the help of my number one critique partners: Kaitlin and Camille. Thanks for listening to me whine and wail about how 'I've never written a book worse than this one before' (I most certainly have), and the endless refrains of 'I know what's going to happen but can't figure out how to write it!' (spoiler: I was just spiralling). I quite literally cannot function without both of you reading my work in batches and calming me down, reassuring me I actually do know how to write. Get ready for the next book guys, because I'm sure I'll need plenty of pats on the head and lots of sweet treats.

Thank you of course to Susan, my agent, who seems to live in my head and *always* has the most perfect suggestions to tighten up a manuscript. Of course, a thousand thanks to

Rebecca, my editor, for somehow understanding what I'm going for even when it's as clear as pea soup. Jorgie, thank you for your kind words about Andy and this story (and helping come up with the beautiful series name). It means the world to me! Another huge thank you to Shan, my copy editor who miraculously fixed my timeline that was as balled up as that lump of cords in the back of your junk drawer, and Riana, for making proofs a breeze. To the whole team at Micheal Joseph: thank you for loving Andy and believing in this story so passionately from the beginning!

I must of course thank my sisters again. Being a trip-let is weird. You don't think in singulars, but in multiples. Everything is always 'we' and 'our', not 'me' or 'mine'. This book is not just mine, and Andy's story isn't either. It's theirs. It's ours. And I hope you see the love I have for both of you in every word, drop of ink and overuse of en dashes. Both of you exist in every story, but this one more than most. Camille, the next book is for your history loving ass. Courtney, yours is coming after the fourth. Sorry, your mus-cles are just too big to encapsulate into a heroine just yet.

To my husband Taylor, who has encouraged me, followed me across the Atlantic to attend events and been my number one cheerleader: thank you for building me an entire library to write in. There is nothing hotter than that. I'll always laugh (and be embarrassed) when you force fellow construc-tion dudes to read my book. I love you more than anything.